MILL VALLEY

MILL VALLEY
Copyright © 2021 by Patrick J. Hagan

Additional copies may be ordered from the publisher for educational,
business, promotional or premium use.
For information, contact ALIVE Book Publishing at:
alivebookpublishing.com, or call (925) 837-7303.

ISBN 13
978-1-63132-155-9

Library of Congress Control Number: 2021923171

Library of Congress Cataloging-in-Publication Data
is available upon request.

First Edition

Published in the United States of America by ALIVE Book Publishing
and ALIVE Publishing Group, imprints of Advanced Publishing LLC
3200 A Danville Blvd., Suite 204, Alamo, California 94507
alivebookpublishing.com

PRINTED IN THE UNITED STATES OF AMERICA

10 9 8 7 6 5 4 3 2 1

MILL VALLEY

PATRICK J. HAGAN

ABOOKS

Alive Book Publishing

DEDICATION

MILL VALLEY, my second novel, as was my first, *SAUSALITO*, is dedicated to my family: Marge, Jennifer, Kristin, Katherine, Patrick, Phillip and Michael (who is keeping me company as I write this). It is also dedicated to the members, past and present, of the United States Coast Guard, and all of the other Armed Services of our country, especially Phillip Sprincin, MAJ, USMC.

The legal system of the United States is often criticized, and sometimes held up to scorn and ridicule, but along with that of the United Kingdom and a few others, it is the underpinning that holds our Western Civilization in place. Most of my adult life has been dedicated to the practice of civil litigation, most often for the defense. This is possibly the least appreciated, and quite often most abused practice area in American fictional legal literature. This novel is dedicated to those attorneys who practice in this area in the real world as well as to their worthy adversaries, the Plaintiffs' Bar, who are far better treated in legal fiction.

This story is legal fiction told in an historical setting: there are real characters who are interwoven, but the trials and other legal maneuvers all have been essentially fictionalized. Any actual resemblance or behavior attributable to any real person is wholly unintended.

ACKNOWLEDGMENTS

As was the case with my first novel, *SAUSALITO*, I owe an enormous debt of gratitude to Bruce McDonald, my 1967 U.S. Coast Guard OCS classmate, an inspiration to my becoming a litigator, and with whom I worked while on active duty, then from time-to-time between 1982 and now. His contributions to *MILL VALLEY* have been too many to mention individually, but his persistence and presence have been an enormous boost to my completing this project.

Also, I should like to thank my son-in-law, Phillip Sprincin, and his wife/my daughter, Kristin, for their technical assistance; and, Jane Wells, my former partner, for her comments.

ABOUT THE COVER

The town of Mill Valley is depicted on this cover as lying between the western edge of Richardson Bay, at the bottom, and Mount Tamalpais, which is shown much more graphically on The Great Seal of the State of California. The artwork for the cover is from a photograph of a painting by Thomas Stanley Painter that hangs in a medical office in Greenbrae, California.

THE *MILL VALLEY* BACK STORY

To fully appreciate *Mill VALLEY*, the reader should be aware that many of its characters first emerged in Patrick Hagan's earlier novel, *SAUSALITO*, which features a younger Ronan O'Neill, his family, and a number of others, largely the women in his life.

SAUSALITO began with its storyteller, Ronan, arriving in that Northern California bayside town in 1971 as a junior Coast Guard officer assigned to a major oil spill investigation. He had recently returned from the Viet Nam War, highly decorated but still suffering the traumatic effects of combat. On arriving, he first met Carolyn Tyne, an aspiring young model with whom he immediately became involved, and eventually ended up sharing a Sausalito apartment. Ronan's reaction to the oil spill investigation and his Sausalito friend Joel Tinker's being in law school led to Ronan's decision to leave USCG active duty and to become a lawyer. While attending Hastings Law School in San Francisco, he fell in love with a school mate, Sandra Allen, and they became engaged. Her father was the managing partner in a large san Francisco firm where Ronan clerked and was expected to start his law career. However, the engagement ended abruptly when Sandra reacted violently to Ronan's decision not to join her father's firm. Shortly thereafter, Ronan experienced a serious emotional crisis, which might have been far worse, but for the very timely appearance of his old college girlfriend, Mollie Phelan. With the help of his psychiatrist, Margo Arnaud, MD, his mother, Kate, and Mollie, Ronan confronted his fears and moved forward with his life.

Following law school, Ronan joined Klein Kelly, a small Oakland law firm, and quickly began to thrive as a defense litigator hired mostly by insurance companies. He married Mollie, who was fast becoming a much sought-after computer applications developer. Ronan achieved initial prominence in the California defense bar at a time when asbestos was fast becoming a medical and legal pandemic. Almost fifteen years after his initial arrival in Sausalito, Ronan is becoming immersed in nationwide high-stakes litigation, often collaborating with his friend Tinker who has relocated his practice to Washington, D.C. As *SAUSALITO* ends, Ronan and Mollie and their four young children have relocated to Mill Valley, from which this novel draws its name.

PROLOGUE

O'Neill's Eco-Strife Begins

*H*otel *Le Meurice* is located most discretely on the *Rue de Rivoli* almost across that boulevard from the *Louvre*. Its Salon, so much more than a bar, is located just off the Lobby on the ground floor with a few windows having a view of foot traffic on the arch covered walkway just outside. The great bulk of tourists who ply this sidewalk looking for the chic or famous have no idea that some of them may be but a few feet away in that very salon. So it was that I was there, seated in a chair, a very splendid wooden chair with a not too comfortable seat cushion and facing the couple with whom I was sharing cocktails. We had met on the plane, on this my first trip to Paris, from D.C. to Charles de Gaulle and at that baggage carousel our small talk led to the discovery that we were staying in the same hotel. In sharing the taxi to the hotel, I came to learn that they were a couple only by virtue of business. He was the head of the landing gear division of Colt Industries, while she was the chief information officer for that division. They were in Paris for meetings with the power to sell to, and purchase from, Airbus, an upcoming Euro economic consortium powerhouse.

While sipping my vermouth-free Vodka Martini and sitting at a right angle to the couple, I could swivel a bit to see out one of the windows or look at the "Bar" and see the backs of its several glamorous patrons. (Please understand that the "Bar" in *Le Meurice* should not be confused with the American concept. This one was made of a white-ish material with a finish that had a level of sparkle, a two inch top of shiny marble, and was backed by a mirror seemingly 15 feet wide that rose from a surface matching the bar to the ceiling. Glass shelves at appropriate heights for displaying expensive alcoholic substances rose up the first three levels or so blocking actual observation of the bar patrons themselves.) The three bar stools nearest the door from the lobby and several tables between where we sat, gave me a view of three backs – all women, all stylishly dressed in outfits that showed tan skin but no jewelry. The three seemed engrossed in each other as I listened to Melissa describe the superiority of the strut arrangement in the landing gear of choice for a certain model Airbus. Two of those patrons were brunettes, one with blonde streaks and highlights, while the third had a golden blonde hair with touches of brown.

When the three women rose and turned to leave, I noticed they were all quite tall. They glanced in my direction. I felt my eyes widen and my mouth drop an ever so small amount. The blonde streaks was Carolyn! At least, I thought it was. Her eyes passed over me with no sign of recognition. In that split second, I stood. That movement brought her eyes back to me. She said something brief to the other two, then crossed the few steps separating us in no time. "Ronan! It's you. Whatever are you doing here in Paris? In this salon? At this moment?"

I introduced Carolyn to the Colt Industries couple as a friend. Carolyn grabbed my elbow and propelled me over to the door to the lobby where her equally finely dressed friends were waiting. "Ronan, this is Monique, a friend, with whom we have been on a shoot." I shook her proffered hand; no cheek was presented. "And this is Lisette! You may remember that my roommate in Sausalito was Lisa who moved to Paris?"

"Yes," I finally got to say something, but then Carolyn continued, "When Lisa got here that name was somewhat a trademark of a very successful model then working. To avoid confusion, Lisa's manager suggested the diminutive as a name change. So can you join Lisette and me for a small dinner?" I returned to my two companions, made my excuse and returned to the three ladies, saying, "I'm all yours for the rest of the evening."

Monique departed. We walked a few blocks crossing a bridge onto the *Isle de Cite* where we were seated just inside a very pleasant bistro. Dinner was a delight: wonderful flavors, chicken like none I had ever tasted, and as light as was the conversation. Carolyn and I had quite a history and Lisette seemed to know some of it, at the least. The banter between the two women was fascinating, especially as much of it was in high spirited French. (I can read some French, speak less than I can read, and understand almost nothing when spoken by a native, as at that moment.) Lisette signed the tab when it arrived. Carolyn then said, "Why don't you join us for a nightcap or two? We are staying at Lisette's place which is right around the corner. You can walk back to the hotel. I'll even take you as far as that if you need to find your way."

What could I do but agree. In a few hundred yards, we were walking through buildings that all seemed to be hundreds of years old, yet pouring bright lights through most windows. We entered a modest lobby using a code to open the front door. A lift took us up to floor five. We walked down a hallway with three other doors to finally enter a magnificently furnished apartment. They both took off their light coats. I took off my raincoat and my suit coat. Carolyn took all of the coats, while Lisette asked what I would have as a night cap as she opened a refrigerator just behind a small bar and pulled out a bottle of champagne. I asked for a scotch on ice. We briefly played pick a brand and I was rewarded with a hearty pour in a cut glass tumbler, including some ice cubes. Carolyn returned to this sitting room and she looked great in a somewhat light appearing robe over top of her dress. No shoes. She took her glass from Lisette, had a sip, moved toward a small sofa, sat and patted the place next to her. Carolyn's eyes met mine. Her lips parted in a bit of a smile, and she spoke lowly, "Do you remember the day when you went into the lease on the *Cote d'Azur* with me?" I nodded. "Do you remember I told you that Lisa had taught me so much?"

"Yes."

Carolyn, "You taught me all the rest."

1

Introducing Evelyn Mullen

E arly in the spring of 1984, CAL Products was served with a class action complaint filed in Contra Costa County Superior Court in Martinez. The first named plaintiff, Evelyn Mullen, sought relief on behalf of herself and all persons similarly situated in California as owners of their own homes which were joined with another home by one wall or were free standing, built before 1975, and utilizing one or more construction products that contained asbestos as a component, including but not limited to ceiling coatings, paint or spray, floor tile, sheetrock wallboard, joint compound used between wallboard and other joints, all different types of insulations and spray coverings, seeking as damages the costs of inspection, removal, and replacement of any of these identified types of products, and living expenses associated with her family's removal from the premises during that entire process. This was a potentially monstrous lawsuit that threatened prodigious liability.

CAL Board General Counsel, Austin Smith, sent a copy of both the Summons and Complaint to Manny Garcia, Manager of Major Claims at Desert Mutual Insurance Company (DMIC) in Scottsdale and to me, as set forth in their written Protocol for receipt of new suits. I immediately sent a copy by overnight mail to my long-time colleague, Joel Tinker (always known as just Tinker) in Washington, D.C. I asked my assistant, Harriett, to make me a copy and set up a file. Also, I asked her to pass a copy to Mary Smith, one of my 4 associates and arguably the brightest.

Heading home with my copy, I stuck my head in Mary's

office as I was heading to the door, saying, "Mary, Harriett's sending a copy of that new *Mullen* class suit to Tinker overnight for 8:00 a.m. delivery, please let Tinker know that I would like to have a call with him tomorrow at noon his time to get his first impressions. I'll be here at 8:30 tomorrow to get yours, my office, and please plan to be on that call. Have a good night!"

With the *Wallboard* matter pending and needing a rapid resolution to protect DMIC from defense costs and further tenders, together with the recent service of the SCHOOLS Class Actions in the federal District Court for the Eastern District of Pennsylvania in Philadelphia as well as The *Los Angeles Unified School District (LAUSD)* matter venued in the Central District of Los Angeles Superior Court, our firm and my team were being seriously taxed to defend these high end cases as well as the various bodily injury claims being brought against CAL Board in Northern California (NorCAL).

Just a week ago, I had asked our firm's managing partners, Klein and Kelly, to approve hiring two more associates. They only agreed to one. My associates were billing more time at a higher rate than any other lawyers in the office. I was having growing concerns that the profits from this work were finding their way into the pockets of my three more senior partners and that we needed more firepower locally, especially to make up for the recent departure of Tinker to D.C. I thought more about that when driving home that night.

I talked to my wife, Mollie, about these staffing issues. Rather than respond to my concerns, she expressed her concerns that I was drinking more, working longer hours and still had my commitment to the USCG Reserve program where I was once again the lead on Legal Assistance for the Eleventh District Coast Guard Regulars and also in charge of Call-up Legal Preparation for all of the District's Reservists. Mollie loved her new job, her newly refurbished Mill Valley home, our four wonderful children and me (not necessarily in that order). She appeared to have an ever-expanding capability to take on new responsibilities. My work stress was building. I spent a few minutes with the older children, Maeve and Robert, then some time with Mollie as she nursed our almost one year old twins, first Meaghan, then Patrick, telling her more about my staffing concerns. I got up to briefly greet my mother, Kate, now living near-by, who doted for hours daily on our children.

When Kate left, I turned back to Mollie who was burping Patrick, and said, "What you need is someone like that nanny you said I had to have when those first two came along. You were so right! Maeve and Robert are quite used to Yolanda because she was already here when the Twins came along and hopefully will be here after Kate leaves. You need someone like that. Someone who can run local litigation so that you can run the overall litigation and focus more on the bigger cases. What do you think?"

I headed down to my study, turned on some sports, poured a Johnny Walker Black over some ice, then settled into my chair to see what Evelyn Mullen's lawyers had come up with. While trying to concentrate, Mollie's idea kept popping back into my head. Three Scotches and a ham sandwich later, I decided to turn in. Mollie was still awake reading, "Thought I'd wait up for you.

Want to make love? It's been more than 2 months and I'm sure ready."

We did. It was a long-awaited treat!

— — —

The next morning the *Mullen* class matter and my team's staffing needs were dueling for my attention as I drove across the Richmond-San Rafael Bridge, through Richmond surface streets to I-80, on my way to Jack London Square. Arriving at 8:20, I grabbed coffee and found Mary Smith waiting for me with a one page neatly typed agenda for the call with D.C. to follow our meeting. When we talked, I started giving her a list of things we would need, like what firms would be representing what co-defendants, when the responsive pleadings would be due and what should we consider as starting issues: especially, whether to attack the complaint itself or attack the class on its size, insurmountable difficulty in ascertainment of its members and the like. Mary asked why not just file an Answer to the Complaint? I spent about five minutes explaining my concerns. At the end of my explanations, she agreed with me.

We got on the phone with D.C. Tinker had brought along a couple of younger partners from his firm and one more senior who had successfully defended several class actions, including one alleging price fixing among cement suppliers, before joining Tinker's new firm. That call lasted almost two hours. Our outline changed. We faxed it to Manny at DMIC and asked for a call at 1:00. He responded affirmatively. DMIC brought its senior claims staff to the call: including Dudley Chisolm, VP-Claims, down through Larry Decker, his number two, Manny Garcia, Major Claims, and Angela Lenovo, Manager, Casualty Claims, who had replaced Gerry Dwyer and reported to Manny, and whom I had yet to meet or address. Tinker was on from D.C., along with Mary in Oakland and Austin Smith, CAL Board's General Counsel, in Sacramento.

They all listened to our defense team's thoughts on how to proceed. Then the questions started, primary among them, how to get the cooperation of our co-defendants. Our only suggestion was to ask for it. Once we began to get counsel appearances from the Contra Costa County Clerk's office, we could try to set up a meeting. Meanwhile, I pressed to take a bit of a leap ahead to talk to Plaintiff's lead attorney to see if we could obtain a 60-day extension to respond to the Complaint in return for a more organized response rather than twenty or thirty different defendants filing separate, and likely discordant, pleadings. Finally, I suggested most strongly that we, and whichever defendants would join us, should start CAL Board's defense by attacking the Complaint itself. Tinker and I both felt most strongly that failure to do that first would be taken by the Court as essentially an admission that this case had some level of merit: something we should simply never admit, if we were ever to win the case.

As soon as that client call ended, I called the lawyer who appeared to be Evelyn Mullen's lead counsel, the first lawyer's name on the Complaint, Marvin Jones of Walnut Creek. After some actual pleasantries, I got down to my limited business and within 20 minutes, we agreed on a date certain for all defendants to file their initial pleading and that I would urge as many defense counsel as possible to join in a single responsive pleading to minimize time, cost and judicial resource. Mr. Jones asked if I would acquiesce in his advising the Contra Costa County Presiding Judge (PJ) of this tentative agreement. I agreed and he was back to me late that afternoon with the PJ's preliminary agreement to that proposed tentative plan.

I asked Mary Smith to put together a notice to all defendant law firms for when they appeared, and to send it to all those firms whom we knew regularly tended to represent most of the named defendant parties. It was out by 10:00 the next morning.

Shortly before noon that same day, I got a call from Ken Allen, senior partner at Allen Talbot, National Counsel for Wallboard, and Sandy, my former fiancé's, father, "Ronan, you are making quite a name for yourself. I may have been wrong about you. Anyway, we have a big conference room. How about if we cancel a day of depositions in the *Wallboard Coordinated Coverage* (*Wallboard*) matter and set a meeting here, next week? I know a number of firms in the East who will also want someone senior to attend. I'll write something, run that draft with a list of addressees by you, and attach your agreement with Marvin Jones. Once you approve, it will be an invitation jointly from our firms and any others which may wish to be included early on.

What do you say?"

I paused for a perceptible amount of time, "Sure. When can I expect to see something?"

— — —

Evelyn Mullen was a Viet Nam War widow and mother of four. She owned a four-bedroom duplex which had asbestos in its wallboard, joint compound, various acoustical ceiling sprays, and floor coverings.

Marvin Jones and his firm had twice successfully concluded smaller property-type class actions, but neither involved asbestos nor included any issues approaching the financial magnitude or potential complexity of this *Mullen* matter.

2

The *Wallboard* Decision

T his was the beginning of when the stress I have mentioned from
time to time began to mount. I tried explaining it to Dr. Arnaud, my psychiatrist, as I did to Mollie. Neither of them had
a real solution in light of all the demands on my time. Mollie said, "Do
less and delegate more." While Dr. Arnaud said something like, "Learn
to create time for yourself. Drink less. And, you really must learn to
say, 'NO!'." AND, there was also some on-going contact with Carolyn,
including pictures of a growing Patrick who really was beginning to
look a lot more than a little bit like me.

This chapter, as was the last, and the many to follow, is a product
of multiple therapy sessions, some of which the good doctor recorded,
which accounts for many of the quotations, others of which are drawn
from my best recollection.

While the *Mullen* case awaited its first defense counsel meeting, the *Wallboard* case had hit a critical juncture for DMIC: first,
DMIC's coverage turned out to be for two years, neither year a
full twelve months, but effectively doubling our client's exposure for attorney's fees, due to the insured's slow replacement
of the original primary carrier, SF Mutual; and second, we had
completed the deposition of Millard Granger, former Risk Manager of Wallboard, so we had to decide what to do next, and
when. Phil Hassard, a very bright fifth year associate, was as-
sisting me on that case. He had quickly developed the needed
skill set to perform in the insurance coverage world. In seeking
a decision from Manny Garcia, Phil suggested I fly to Phoenix
the next day to meet directly with Manny, his bosses and their

new claims manager, Angela Lenovo, to talk through that decision process in person. I asked Manny if I could bring Phil as he was most on top of the applicable California law. I was surprised when Manny agreed. Phil was delighted when I asked him. Then I told him the flight was at 6:00 a.m.

On our flight, Phil and I talked about options. I was fairly certain that the client would insist on a motion for summary judgment now, without any further waiting. Phil, who had been privy to a few of my calls with excess carrier counsel, knew that the excess carriers were unanimous in favoring delays. But when pushed, none of them offered anything approaching a persuasive reason for delay. My thoughts centered on whether these carriers had other related entities that might have a relationship that could prove disadvantageous to DMIC and its posture in this setting. Little did we then realize the breadth of their indiscretion!

We caught a taxi at Sky Harbor Terminal Two to Scottsdale and were seated in the Desert Mutual executive conference room with Dudley Chisholm, Larry Decker, Manny Garcia and Angela Lenovo, in less than an hour from wheels down. They began with the impact of Gerry's leaving, Manny's responsibilities for major cases would be increased. They pointed out that others of their insureds were now getting sued for asbestos bodily injury (BI) claims and Manny would be in overall charge with Richie Goldberg (not present) handling all other non-environmental casualty matters and Angela, who was a lateral hire a year ago, would handle all environmental matters which largely consisted of CAL Board matters, the other asbestos BI cases and the *Wallboard* coverage case.

Then, we got down to the major reason for this meeting: Dudley, who rarely spoke even when he attended one of these fly-in meetings, lead off, "Desert Mutual is in a very difficult position on this case. On one hand, we are getting some tenders of defense from Wallboard and we cannot refuse to defend them at risk of being in bad faith to our insured. While at the same time, the other active primary, San Francisco Casualty (SFC), is tendering the defense of those cases which they are defending to us by asking that we pay a share of those defense costs, going forward. That number of Wallboard BI cases is staggering and seeming to grow with each passing day as more plaintiff law firms across the country see this as a highly lucrative field. Then, our current reinsurer syndicates in London are refusing to reimburse us because we assured them that the Granger drafted exclusion was valid to prevent these types of claims. Further, it's only a matter of time until Wallboard will demand that we pay indemnity to settle a case. Put bluntly, we simply cannot afford to wait."

I explained about the excess carriers. Phil explained much of our rationale for filing that summary judgment motion sooner rather than later. I echoed the need to move urgently lest Wallboard come up with something or someone to counter Millard Granger's testimony, or conjure a means to create a factual question to undermine the basic summary judgment rule that the motion judge was barred from deciding any significant (or potentially controlling) factual issue in what was, at its essence, a motion based solely on the law. We asked for their questions. In light of Dudley's opening remarks, their few were like soft balls. Then, Angela asked a key question, "If the excess carrier attorneys have no good reason to wait except to run up their fees, what other motivation could they possibly have?"

I waited, no one else spoke, so I asked, "Do any of you know about the actual ownership of each excess entity? Could they have conflicting reinsurer issues? In other words, for example, could one or more of these excess carriers be related to either primary carriers or reinsurers at some level that might stand to take a hit if DMIC gets out of the litigation?" I paused.

Dudley and Larry looked at each other, then at Manny. Larry shrugged his shoulders, "Frankly, Ronan, I think you have stumbled onto a bigger problem than you realize. Some of the syndicates that offer reinsurance are being pressed for reimbursement payments by their insured primaries at this very moment. These syndicates generally have very little cash reserves readily available as they operate utilizing significant lead time lags while retroceding their own risks (*essentially, the reinsuring Lloyds syndicate reinsuring any of its losses that initial year, and repeated annually to cover as yet unreported losses occurring, but not reported, during that initial year of reinsurance coverage {these latter years are also referred to as "long tail coverage," here: asbestos BI claims}.*) at the end of each reinsurance period, generally a year. Those demands, we believe, are resulting in some syndicates having to make calls for contribution by their name members, a rarity which well may become commonplace. We cannot be certain what this means in the long run, but it could prove dire, especially if those names do not, or cannot, come up with their needed contributions."

"Why is that?" asked Phil.

"Many of the reinsuring syndicates, and almost none of the name member/investors, including those in retrocession syndicates have any stop loss provision (*most U.S. based casualty insurers have coverage for each occurrence, but a maximum of coverage for an insured period, usually one year; on rare occasions, some do not. Lloyds syndicates routinely did NOT have STOP LOSSES*) in their policies. Many of those investors could face ruin," said Larry, "I know. I'm a name in more than one syndicate, but I have not received a call for any funding, as yet."

My response was a rhetorical, "But isn't that all the more reason for DMIC to act promptly?"

Silence followed. Dudley said Larry and he needed to be excused for a few moments. Only Dudley returned. He shrugged, bowed his head, then looked up, saying, "Larry has to recuse himself further from all of these matters. We'll tell you more on a need to know basis later. Meanwhile, please proceed to get a

winning motion on file posthaste! You all do lunch on the company. Talk the motion through, get on the plane. If we need a
Declaration from the company, I will sign it. So, please have it
to me soon. Thank you all!"

— — —

This reinsurance issue may well be why Gerry left. We might
never be certain.

3

Our Launch into *LAUSD*

CAL Board Products, Inc. (CBPI) was added as a defendant to the Los Angeles Unified School District's suit more than a year after it was filed. We immediately got a copy of the *LAUSD* docket sheet filed in the Central District of Los Angeles (CDLA). Mary Smith brought it to me as it was over 60 pages long. She had gone through the first 10 pages and determined that there were at least 25 defendants. Not only that, but the plaintiff school district was represented by Charlie O'Reilly of Greene, O'Reilly, a huge LA plaintiff firm. O'Reilly had earned serious notoriety just a few short months before by winning a verdict in a ferociously contested matter against the Church of Scientology. This *LAUSD* case represented a serious potential threat to our client as it had operated a somewhat large plant which may have produced a variety of asbestos containing wall-board products (ACM) in the Long Beach area for about twenty years. That plant was now closed as part of a reorganization, but we still did not know at the time of this service whether or not any of its product actually contained asbestos or if any asbestos containing products had been shipped south from CBPI's much larger NorCAL operation.

We got Tinker on the phone. The three of us looked at the operative Complaint first, then the docket and found nothing specific concerning our client. The Amendment to the Complaint simply substituted CBPI for a fictitious defendant and no more. We began a list: halfway through the docket sheet it was more than 40 items! Who was going to do all of this work? On page 44 was the LAUSD response to Defendants' Request for a Statement of Damages. The amount, hedged with the usual "still under on-going investigation" language, stated at minimum, Special Damages to safely remove and replace the offending building materials as well as temporary facilities to continue its function as "the United States largest school district" of between $5 and $10 billion, with General Damages, "According to Proof." This represented a whole new ball game! (And we were still awaiting the docket sheets on the SCHOOLS Class Actions venued in federal court in Philadelphia. This BUILDINGS litigation was getting HUGE!)

I went to see my senior partners and told them about all of these developments. I made it clear that we needed at least one more senior associate or a new junior partner to help out, and perhaps to appoint someone, who would report to me, to run the day-to-day NorCAL CBPI Bodily Injury (BI) cases, and at least one more associate to work on these sizeable out-of-area cases. Moreover, if we did not add this staff fast, DMIC could tell us to associate another local California firm or two in So-CALwith the attendant loss of significant fee revenue to us. I believe to this day, that my last point finally swung them around. It certainly kept the firm together for another 15 years and made them both very rich. (They always paid themselves more than me. Heck, I bet Tinker made at least two times more than me.)

When I got home to Mill Valley that night, I told Mollie about what was evolving. Her facial expression changed, saying, "Can you seriously do all of this? It sounds like too much!"

Me, "Tinker will help out back East. He can add more counsel. Klein and Kelly told me to hire three more attorneys, two with experience. Only problem is this is all so new that few associates are going to know much about it. Still, once we get over this hump, we should be OK. But it'll be tough going for the next few months!"

Mollie, "You love this. Don't you?"

Me, "Makes me forget a lot of bad things from before you

saved me. Too busy to ponder them during the day and too tired to dream about them at night."

We made furious love that night.

— — —

Two of the three hires were great. The third, a bit of a disaster! Unfortunately, he was the new lead BI attorney for Nor CAL. But I am ahead of myself.

Phil gave me a first draft of the Points and Authorities for the Summary Judgment Motion in the *Wallboard* matter. It was only against Wallboard and SF Casualty. Without reading further I said, "I'm sorry. I should have been clear. We need to bring this motion against not just Wallboard and SFC, but also all of the other insurance carriers those two have named. Just deny that DMIC had any relationship to all of those in that latter group and put a paragraph on that lack of relationship in Dudley's Supporting Declaration. You have all you need to include those other carriers as responding parties and you've done great job so far. So, get something together fast, including that Declaration for Dudley and try to have all of this to Dudley and Manny in a few days!"

In one of my many daily calls with Manny and Angela during the week after our Scottsdale meeting, they got the drift that this whole bundle of asbestos litigation was going to get to be a whole lot bigger before it got any smaller. Moreover, it would not get smaller at all if we could not achieve some victories. In that week since Phil and I had been to Scottsdale, my whole world was seeming to change. My thought processes were becoming way more global. CBPI got served in the State of Washington (WA) and the State of New Jersey (NJ) in BI matters. DMIC had a very good counsel in WA, but no one in New Jersey. They asked me to look into it because of my East Coast background and my relationship with Tinker and his firm. At the end of the call, Manny asked, "Ronan, we think we need one outside counsel to run this litigation as it grows. Any ideas?"

"Gee, Manny, this comes as more than a small surprise!' A lengthy pause, I continued, "I can think of only one, …Me?"

"Great answer: you're the one everyone here wants! Consider the job yours! Dudley will be delighted."

I called Tinker and told him the news. He was less enthusiastic than I expected he would be. To me, this meant he would stay locked in with a major role in the bigger cases and help out with briefing on East Coast matters which was one of his firm's specialties. When I told him that, he seemed to perk up. When I told Mollie, she said, 'Just more for you to do. Did they give you a title? More money? Did you even think to ask?"

Just the same, Mollie grew warmer to the concept as the evening wore on. Thinking on Tinker's reaction, she suggested, "I wonder if the Scottsdale folks talked to Tinker first? Maybe he thought he should defer to you? Or, maybe they told him that he was the fall back if you turned down that job?"

I said nothing to all of that (but I remember those words to this day and still wonder about Mollie's speculation— to no conclusion). Instead, I responded "I'll ask about money in a few days, but first, a title, how do you like National Coordinating Counsel (NCC for short)?"

Mollie smiled and signaled that it was bedtime.

4

The Initial *MULLEN* Meeting

Seven days after our phone call, I arrived 30 minutes early for the 10:00 a.m. defense counsel meeting at Ken Allen's office. His conference room table was almost already fully occupied. As I made my way to a seat at the far end of the table, I noticed Ken's daughter, Sandy, sitting next to Ken. When our eyes met, she smiled. (A very different reaction than when I was taking the deposition of Wallboard's former Risk Manager, Millard Granger, in the *Wallboard* coverage matter which she attended in Oakland.) Many of the attorneys present I did not recognize. A woman with a distinctive East Coast accent was holding forth about class actions in general, and her beliefs about "these asbestos buildings classes" in particular. Her speech seemed somewhat logical and well thought-out. When she paused, not at all certain that she was finished, Ken Allen interrupted, saying, "I want you all to meet Ronan O'Neill, counsel for CAL Board Products in this *Mullen* case…" I nodded around the room, while Ken continued, "Ronan got Marvin Jones, lead plaintiff counsel in the East Bay to agree to a single firm date to Answer. Ronan is a rising star in this litigation." Ken then went through the names, firms and client affiliations in the room. No one at that moment was from Northern California (NorCAL) except Sandy and him.

Ken turned to Sandy and said something to her. She got up and took a chair behind him. Then, Ken gestured for me to sit next to him, Explaining, "Ronan and I called this meeting on the *Mullen* case…" and turning to me said, "All of these counsel are national representatives for their clients. We get together periodically to discuss these BUILDINGS cases and other matters of mutual interest to our clients, mostly monthly. Since they were mostly coming from places east, making most of them three hours earlier than us, we have been meeting since 8:00. Thus, you came into a very different meeting in progress, but mostly not about *Mullen*."

From a sitting position, I asked, "Is there a sign up sheet? I do not think I can remember all your names, firms and clients. Just so you know, a few days ago, CAL Board and their lead primary carrier appointed me to be CBPI's National Coordinating Counsel. Our office will be representing them in this matter and *LAUSD* where our client was recently added. Also, we will be securing local counsel in Philadelphia to appear in those consolidated SCHOOLS class cases and will seek admission so we can appear as *pro haec vice* (visiting) counsel."

Most of them looked nonplussed. Ken seemed stunned. Sandra leaned up from behind me and whispered with what sounded like restrained enthusiasm, "Congratulations, Ronan!"

As the clock moved toward the 10:00 meeting start time, the conference room became close to overflowing. The early arrivals, often two, even three, for a client clung to their seats at the table. One had an early arriving local counsel making four! I leaned into Ken who seemed to know almost everyone and made a suggestion, which he echoed to the others, "Mr. O'Neill suggests that each client should have counsel at the table. As I understand there are 26 defendants and only 30 seats, that should be enough, if we use all the seats along the walls"

Chairs scraped. Any number of lawyers moved and rearranged themselves. Still, one lawyer from Oakland did not have a seat at the table. Ken said to what was a threesome, "National Gypsum is a target defendant and we know each of you matter greatly, but can one of you give up your seat?" The woman from the East who was speaking when I entered, looked at a lawyer I vaguely knew from Piedmont and said, "Earl, please sit behind us for this. Len and I will be doing all the talking for the client."

Earl moved. Everyone settled in. An agenda was passed out as well as a sign-in sheet. The first order of business, before any *Mullen* discussion of "what to do first" was the attorney-client privilege. Clearly, no lawyer in that room wanted anything disclosed that was discussed. A lengthy discussion followed on establishing a joint privilege to effectuate cooperation and save on judicial resources, not to mention client fees. Although the efficacy of a joint privilege was unclear in California, joint agreements among parties were afforded protection, so it was agreed that three of the local firms would prepare a draft, vet it among themselves, and then circulate it for comments and signing. We all agreed that time was of the essence. Ken volunteered Sandy to be the lead drafter and asked me to participate as well as another senior attorney from San Francisco.

We then turned to the matter at heart. Noon approached. No break occurred. I got up and returned quickly, my past clerking experience at that firm allowed me to know the restroom location. Alicia Goines, the woman with the distinctive Eastern twang, kicked off the discussion on how to approach this matter in a joint fashion, " With all of these parties defendant, the only orderly way to attack this suit is to file a very basic, but all-encompassing Answer to the Complaint, and then go after the class as overbroad and ill-defined, damages as indefinite and not subject to class determination, and finally that the class representative as well as her counsel lack the capacity even to begin to adequately represent this potentially amorphous class. Any other course will certainly fail." Others, including Ken, chipped in supporting Alicia's plan.

When that ended, a San Francisco attorney asked, "Why not go after the Complaint at the outset? If we don't, we will never get another shot! This matter is in California state court and not federal court where the complaint is always amenable to attack for failure to state an actionable claim as a matter of law. We really need to think about whether we can make this Complaint not sustainable under California law. For example, Ms. Mullen does not say she is suffering any actual physical injury, only that these products being in her home present some future threat to her family's well-being, and, as a result, that she needs to remodel and will incur abatement costs. How does any of that rise to the level of any cognizable injury to support these potentially massive class damages?"

A pause, then I began to chip in with a slightly different line of complementary thought: How could a California state court be expected to rule when this is a master calendar matter? This led to a discussion of how Contra Costa County Superior Court was organized. The non-CA lawyers began to almost visibly cringe. Then, I came up with some suggestions for dealing with that issue: meet with the Presiding Judge after conferring with the lead plaintiff attorney and try to work out a single judge assignment for the whole case. Many of the California types were doubtful and negatively verbal about this, but the national counsel types seemed to like the idea. (At this point, I began to realize that the national types probably practiced more under the federal rules of procedure, while the local counsel spent most of their litigation time in state court.) Then, I pointed out that using this method would allow us to go outside the pleading page limits because there were so many defendants, so we really could make one concerted attack on the entire *Mullen* complaint. The Plaintiff pleaded five theories of recovery: one firm would write an Introduction and Statement of Facts, while five other different client firms could each write a section of an encompassing brief attacking the law on each separate theory of recovery. If all of that failed, we would still have preserved the full fallback of the attacks that Ms. Goines was advocating. I ended with, "Nothing ventured. No Advantage Waived!"

Discussion lasted another hour and a half. Slowly, more

attorneys warmed to my concepts. When a consensus was painstakingly reached, they decided that Ken and I should meet with the Presiding Judge (PJ) of Contra Costa County in Martinez after we first conferred with Marvin Jones.

— — —

When the meeting broke up, Sandy asked to walk me out of the office. She waited for a few minutes, and asked if I wanted to get a quick snack. I looked at the time and agreed. We had a nice talk. I showed her pictures of Mollie, the Twins at birth, and the two older children. I asked about her. She said her marriage had been a mistake from the start and had ended in less than a year. She hadn't found anyone else as yet, but she was looking in her little bit of spare time. I asked, "How about another lawyer?'

Sandy grinned, "I am pretty certain that will never happen again." We parted on good terms and agreed we might need to work more together in the future.

5

The City of Brotherly Love

Less than 24 hours after the *Mullen* meeting ended, I received a fax from Alicia Goines inviting me and a whole list of counsel with client names next to each to attend a meeting in Philadelphia on matters of mutual interest to the respective clients of each in about eight days. A draft agenda was attached. The meeting was at 17th and Market Streets. to begin at 9:30 a.m., doubtless timed to allow East Coast counsel to make it a one-day trip to Philadelphia. A quick perusal of the list of invitees revealed quite a few names which I had just learned from the *Mullen* meeting. The agenda listed several topics, including expert witnesses, and major cases, including *LAUSD*, *Mullen*, a post office class action (about which I knew nothing), and the SCHOOLS Class Actions consolidated at the moment before a judge located in Philadelphia's federal courthouse much closer to the Delaware River, further east down Market Street.

I asked Lily, my new assistant, to fax a copy of this invite to Tinker and to give a copy to Mary Smith (Harriet stayed on with my firm's two remaining named partners in a reshuffling at the top which left me as a higher percentage owner of the firm equity.), and to set up a call with DMIC at Noon PST to talk about the potential value of attending. The time, considering travel, and the expense would not be insignificant. The overall value was clearly uncertain, but since some of these lawyers had been engaged in this type of litigation from its seeming inception, this appeared to be, if nothing else, a learning opportunity. Tinker offered that instead of totally breaking up my week, it might make sense to fly to D.C. on Monday, train to Philly on Tuesday, return to D.C. that afternoon and to work there until flying home mid-day of Friday. It seemed like a good plan. But now I needed to run it past Manny at DMIC and probably Austin Smith at CAL Board. I made those calls myself and, to my surprise, Manny and Austin both agreed that I should go.

That night I explained to Mollie what was happening. To say she was less than overjoyed would be a gross understatement. She reminded me that I had to go to USCG AIRSTA Sacramento on Saturday and Station Rio Vista on Sunday, meaning I should spend the intervening night near Rio Vista. To avoid that additional absent night and spend more time with my young children and Mollie, I would forego that night away. Still, I would have to take a 6:00 a.m. flight to Dulles to meet Tinker for dinner that Monday night around 6:00 in the Lafayette Square area not far from his office and the Mayflower Hotel where he had booked me.

The days flew by and I found myself on the Marin Airporter headed to SFO at 4:00 a.m. Even before 9/11, the Mayor Moscone shootings and other Bay Area violence produced some serious security at the airports. As I checked into TWA Business Class, I heard the passenger next to me ask if there were any free upgrades to First Class. That ticketing agent answered, "Yes, maybe. Check back in about a half hour." So, I asked my ticketing agent what that was all about and she explained: different criteria could lead to an upgrade, including award travel status, ticket price and other considerations, such as active or prior military service. She gave me a form which I completed and then told me to come back in 20 minutes or so. Because my ticket was so last minute, I had paid dearly for it, and added to my USCG service, I got an upgrade to seat 1B –

I will never forget it - such comfort and the food! Only one problem: it was too early to drink. Still, the flight attendant gave me four miniatures of Chivas Regal which I carefully stowed.

(Boy!! Are those Good Old Days long gone!!)

A taxi ride, a quick check-in, splash my face and off to meet Tinker at a quaint downstairs place closer to his office by a block. He had two other lawyers with him, Mace Snow, that slightly older, experienced gentleman, and Tod Clifford, who had a pronounced Southern accent. Snow was the class action veteran lawyer. Clifford was a rising star trial lawyer at their firm. Tinker had shared the draft agenda. After ordering drinks and very little small talk, we set right to a discussion about the next day's meeting. Mace Snow knew any number of those who would be attending from past SEC and other big ticket antitrust litigation, including a huge building materials price fixing matter. He was free with his opinions and grew a bit louder around his second drink. Tod wanted to know what any of us knew about expert witnesses in asbestos litigation, and especially for cases like these where it was unclear if anyone was actually injured. Two-plus hours flew by and at the end, we all agreed to meet for dinner again the next night to analyze the goings-on at the NCC Meeting while it was all still fresh in my mind.

— — —

The 7:10 a.m. AMTRAK Metroliner was scheduled to get me into Thirtieth Street Station in Philadelphia, shortly before 9:00. An expensive, bland coffee, tasteless pastry and a short taxi ride later, I stepped off the elevator on the 22d floor of Liberty Place ONE at Abbott and Tweed LLC. I asked for the meeting site and was directed to a huge windowless room behind the reception area. Any number of attendees were already present. I signed in and pasted on a name tag. That firm's Danish and coffee were superb. Alicia swept into her conference room with another lawyer who turned out to be Leonard Tweed himself. They took two seats at one head of an extended egg-shaped table of apparent mahogany. Two or three others who were part of their party took seats behind them. I sat about halfway down one side. Ken Allen came in and sat almost directly across from me. Sandy was right behind him and took a calculated seat behind her father. The room began to fill quickly.

Promptly at 10:00, Alicia called the meeting to order. Her first order of business was to introduce all first time attendees to those who were veterans of this process. She called on me first and I gave a 20 second thumbnail of myself. Before calling on the next first-timer, Alicia said, "A number of us attended a meeting on the new *Mullen* class matter at Ken Allen's office in San Francisco last week. It was co-hosted by Mr. O'Neill who, in turn, was extremely persuasive in his relatively novel approach to a California state court action. We shall hope to hear more from him this morning."

Ms. Goines continued through her agenda: the first hour seemed to be all introductions and housekeeping. Apparently three of the Philadelphia firms, all of them being very large appeared to have cornered the market on hosting these meetings, but one of them wanted to start an assessment program for all attendees. We broke and Alicia sought me out, "Ronan, hope you don't mind my using your first name. Also, hope you do not mind being an anchor on the *Mullen* case. Ken has a lot on his plate with coverage right now. *Wallboard* has some fierce primary carriers! Anyway, don't pay any attention to this assessment nonsense. I'll make short work of Brian when we get back in there." All I did was nod. Alicia was impressive: a veritable lioness at home protecting her den.

Later, "Brian, we all understand there is expense associated with hosting these meetings, but…small expense to be able to bring your own people with no travel time or other expense. I move we table Brian's motion." Seconds resounded. Next was Experts which turned out to be a dire topic. Apparently, the Mt. Sinai crew headed by plaintiffs' chief expert, Dr. Irving Selikoff, was having a major impact in undermining all of the experts the defense proffered. The BI litigation was a disaster and the growing number of Mesothelioma claims presented a nightmare for that defense as there was no other known cause but asbestos. One type of asbestos fibre, crocidolite, was particularly virulent in causing this largely fatal disease, especially in Africa where it was mined and especially to its miners. An increasing problem was that putative defense experts with little experience or no real expertise were not faring well with potential defenses, which in and of itself could not only undermine an expert and the client proffering him, but also was confirming in the minds of the asbestos defense litigation system that the only potential Mesothelioma defense was becoming that the plaintiff's exposure was to non-crocidolite fibres. New experts were sought, but none who were offered had any scientific concepts of real utility, or any good ideas for this type of bodily injury litigation. (Steve McQueen, the movie star, who was a race car fanatic, cleaned his own brakes which were manufactured with high percentage of asbestos component to prevent burning and squeaking in usage. He ultimately died from Mesothelioma, accounting for serious publicity for that specific ACM related disease.)

After a lunch break, with great Philly Italian hoagies, we started on the BUILDINGS cases. *LAUSD* had been active for more than a year, but that plaintiff was adding more defendants. I indicated that CAL Board was one of them and we would be representing them. Our investigation was just starting and one of the reasons I came to this event was to get brought up to speed on that case. So, I listened. The *LAUSD* single-assignment judge was proving very unpopular with the defense as he often and openly sided with that newsworthy plaintiff's counsel, Charlie O'Reilly. Seems there is a four year statute of limitations in California (CA) to commence property damage cases (with certain exceptions), and that the then CA Superintendent of Schools, Dr. Wilson Riles, had sent a letter to every school district in CA well over four years before LAUSD made its initial filing warning the

state's districts not to let their students, teachers, or other employees be exposed to any form of asbestos dust. Some defendants filed a motion to dismiss based on this letter, but the judge
refused to rule on the motion, stating that the letter on its face
was vague and uncertain, and lacked any evidentiary scientific
foundation.

My turn came on *Mullen*, I repeated the high points of last
week's meeting and the extant plan. Then, I added that I had
spoken with Plaintiff's lead counsel, Marvin Jones, last Friday,
"He liked the idea of a single-assignment judge, so we came up
with a plan to pick one or two judges on whom we might agree.
We each wrote down five judges, all with at least two years on
the Contra Costa ("CoCo") County Superior Court bench while
ranking them 1-5 in order of preference. One judge was second
on my list and third on his, the Honorable Andrew Kendall. That
was the only judge on both lists (Sandy's father did not participate in that choice, deferring to me as an "East Bay Lawyer.").
We agreed to take this choice to our groups and get back tomorrow. Most of the Bay Area/Sacramento firms are on board, but
a number have deferred to all of you. Can I answer questions?"

None of the East Coast people spoke up at first. I pointed out
that Judge Kendall had been on the bench for about four years
and that I had been a lawyer for the defense in his very first trial.
His background was all public service. He had clerked in the
CoCo County District Attorney (DA)'s office, but went to work
as a lawyer in that county's Public Defender's Office. He spent
his last couple of years there mostly doing appeals. He was very
adroit at following the law to the letter where it served his
client's interests and he was transparent as well as fair. Others
in the area felt the same, as did Marvin Jones for the Plaintiff.
Then, Ken Allen kicked in that a number of his attorneys thought
this relatively moderate judge an excellent choice for the defense, especially considering the vast number of Democratic lib-
erals appointed by Jerry Brown during his past (first) eight years

as Governor. He then turned to Sandy, who stood and said, "I have appeared before Judge Kendall recently while he was sitting Law and Motion. He was a very straight shooter as described. If we are going to try to get this case thrown out on a Demurrer (the name for California's Motion to Dismiss equivalent to Federal Rule 12(b)(6).), Judge Kendall is perhaps the only judge in Contra Costa County whom I believe would have the courage to rule against this class plaintiff. Any questions?"

Finally, Alicia broke the silence, "Thank you Ms. Allen (I noted she had signed in using her maiden name (left me wondering if she had gone back to it for good.). If no one has any comments, does anyone have anything else on *Mullen*?" She then called a voice vote. No one objected, so we were off and running on Judge Kendall for the Defense. During the break, I asked Alicia and one of the other Philadelphia lawyers if they knew any smaller defense firms in New Jersey that were not currently involved in the asbestos BI litigation, but might want to be. Alicia ducked out for a minute, came back and told me she might be able to come up with one or two firms. The other lawyer seemed less willing to be helpful. Then I heard Sandy telling two or three of the East Coast counsel, "Oh, I have known Ronan since law school when he moved to California. He grew up mostly in the D.C. area and his parents were from like Chestnut Hill and Germantown, somewhere near Philadelphia."

One responded, "Is his mother Kate O'Neill by any chance?"

When Sandy responded affirmatively, her group broke up and they all began to talk among themselves. (I do not believe that Sandy ever realized how famous my mother was in Philadelphia for the selfless political role she played while the men in her life were away fighting World War II.) Alicia only smiled. She must have done the research.

When we got back, the discussion turned to the SCHOOLS Class matters. All three consolidated matters were before Judge James McGirr Kelly, who was described as slow moving, but very pro-Class. The expert issue was briefly revisited, but the primary focus was on getting the named plaintiff's documents for the Lancaster School District in PA; Spartanburg School District in SC; and Napa School District in CA. A committee had been formed to do the work and reported on its preparedness to go forward. These documents were sought to aid the Defense in resisting the Class Certification Motion pending before the Judge.

(CAL Board had a plant which it bought from a defunct competitor about 20 years ago in Bergen County, NJ. They closed it about five years ago before the initial filing of the *Lancaster* suit. Many of its products, even some wallboard, contained asbestos for most of the years of ownership. However, CAL Board had kept that plant and one other in a separate corporate entity, CAL PRODUCTS, Inc. [CPI], which only Spartanburg had sued. *Lancaster* had sued CAL Board itself. Napa had sued neither!)

The group approved the document productions protocol and the teams were decided. Sandy volunteered to be involved locally with Napa. When heads looked at me, I told them that my clients had not been sued by Napa, so we would have no role and I trusted them not to bring that to the attention of the Napa Class Counsel.

As we broke up, Alicia gave me a piece of paper with three firms written on it, and said, "They are ranked by best to less, all are good. Your mother is famous here in Philadelphia for holding down Senator Burke's seat while he was a congressman and absent during the Second War."

Sandy came up next and said, "You never mentioned that about your mother. Can we grab a cocktail before you leave? I am on the 4:00 to New York. You?"

Me, "Sure, I'm going the other way, to D.C." With that Sandy said an adieu to her father, I waived and we left. I could swear I saw Ken Allen sigh as I was turning to go. During our drink which went quickly, Sandy wanted to know more about my mother. We talked briefly. She was going to see Stanford classmates in NYC. She said she might stay in D.C. some time as she had a number of Stanford friends there as well. We also talked about our law school friends, Tinker and his wife, Elaine, briefly.

Two hours later, the four of us from the night before reassembled in the same restaurant. Dinner and discussion lasted almost 3 hours. We discussed a number of proposals. I agreed to be at Tinker's office about 10:00 next a.m.

On Wednesday, we agreed that Tinker and his people would do the lead briefing on the SCHOOLS Class action while consulting with Philadelphia local counsel on the Local Court Rules, and running drafts past them and me. I told them I planned to use Mary on SCHOOLS as well as *Mullen*, and Phil on *LAUSD*. By the time I got home that Thursday night, I was barely able to talk to Mollie I was so tired (and I had gotten upgraded again to first class—free drinks. NOT so good an idea after a hard week's work)!

— — —

The next morning, Mollie said, and I remember her few words to this day. "If you keep this up for a while, you are going to kill yourself. THINK about what you really need to do. AND think about your family and about ME." Mollie was not at all pleased with me. Neither was Dr. Arnaud when I saw her the next afternoon!

6

The Tasks At Hand

As the mid-1980s rolled by, the number of tasks needing to be undertaken in defending all of these asbestos cases became such that both Tinker and I were feeling overwhelmed as were Mary and Phil in my office and Mace and Ted in Tinker's.

Thomas Jones, the lead hire for the Nor CAL BI cases, turned out to be not at all satisfactory. Although he told me he had experience trying cases, his first result was a qualified disaster. Granted he went up against a relatively top flight attorney in Andy Bigelow in a Mesothelioma case, but in our prep for the trial, he seemed more than up to speed on the key issues of plaintiff's actual exposure to any of our client's asbestos containing products (ACM, "m" for "materials"), that plaintiff's overwhelming exposure to other manufacturers' ACM, and the absence of any definitive diagnosis that the plaintiff actually had Mesothelioma and was not, instead, suffering from lung cancer as he was a two pack/day smoker for 40+ years (greater than 80 pack-years!). During the trial itself, Thomas went into a complete shell. He would not return my calls, so finally I went over to the Alameda County Courthouse in Oakland to observe. Much to my shock, Thomas came down the inside steps as I was about to enter. I nodded. He stopped, saying, "$750,000 for the plaintiff."

He went back to our office, cleaned out his desk and was gone by the time I got there. I continued into the court building finding Andy Bigelow inside. He looked at me and smiled, saying, "We won, but I made a big mistake." I looked at him quizzically, and he continued, "I only asked the jury for $750,000; should have asked for two or three million. Your man read his questions, but never followed-up. You need to assess that young man very carefully."

My answer, "Can we talk tomorrow?"

Thomas's wife would not put him on the phone. I was left to tell Desert Mutual the result with no preparation other than what Andy had told me. Needless to say, Manny and Angela were not pleased, but we had discussed the risks of a loss going in, and thought we had a reasonably good chance. So, I tried to make it a group decision. Then we talked about what we could do to try to ameliorate this loss. I suggested trying to save some money, but not being terribly greedy in the process lest we have to pay the winner's trial costs or buy transcripts for an "iffy" appeal and the like. They agreed. One small problem: they had agreed that Austin Smith could have input on settlements as he was concerned about running through his company's coverages. After a couple of tense calls with Austin, I was finally able to call Andy Bigelow, and offered him $500,000 for a waiver of our client's right to appeal and in return for getting the cash right now, not in 2 or 3 years (if that plaintiff really did have Mesothelioma, he would probably be dead in 6 – 12 months and if he settled, he would know his family was far better off), and with both sides to bear their own costs.

After 2 days going back and forth with Andy, we settled for $600,000, the amount which I took away from Scottsdale after my trial report. I replaced Thomas Jones with Reggie Foxx, a U.S. Navy 20 year retiree, UC Berkeley and Boalt Hall grad, and Oakland native, an African-American, whom I had met at several JAG conferences at The Presidio doing CLE (Continuing Legal Education for members of all service's Judge Advocate General Corps). He suggested and I agreed that we needed to have at least three trial ready counsel on our team for CA. (Southern California had yet to take-off as no plaintiff firm down there had seriously gravitated into the Asbestos BI practice area.) Beginning in 1985-86, our Asbestos BI practice volume started to increase markedly. The firm was making big money and some of it drifted my way. Klein and Kelly continued to make more. Our third named partner took ill and retired. They did not offer to put my name on the firm (another warning which I unwisely ignored!).

— — —

The *LAUSD* case had bogged down a bit with picayune discovery and motion practice. Phil spent a fair amount of time in Los Angeles on depositions, many of which seemed not to advance the ball much for either side, but did drive up the expense. Moreover, with all the defendants, each deposition took at least 4 or 5 days! Tinker was writing a motion for summary judgment on the statute of limitation issue with a view of leading toward some type of "appellate practice" to end the case. Pressing this issue among the defendants, I finally got them to the critical point of seeking an order from their not so favorite judge to break the case up into three parts: first, a trial on the statute of limitations issue; then, liability of any defendants left; and as a third phase, if need be, damages. I was one of three defense lawyers asked by the group to meet with plaintiff's counsel to try to negotiate a stipulation to proceed along this path. Reasons to do so included: chance to end inexpensively, fewer experts, and if plaintiff prevails on the first two phases, much more likely to achieve an early settlement. So, with relatively minimal arm twisting, *LAUSD*'s attorneys indicated they thought this course was a good idea, but they needed to run it past their client. With some tinkering, we got a stipulation to proceed on the Statute of Limitations issue first with further bifurcation to be deferred until needed, if at all.

With Phil so tied up, we were having trouble finalizing our

motion for DMIC in the *Wallboard* coverage matter. Despite all of the work, we managed to keep the major balls in the air, filed the DMIC Motion for Summary Judgment with several declarations, including hundreds of pages of exhibits, such as insurance policies and drafts of the "Asbestosis Exclusion," the actual Motion itself, and a hefty set of legal Points and Authorities. I was "ready" to argue the motion, but the parties against whom the motion was filed sought additional time to respond, all made more difficult because both the other primary carrier, SF Casualty, and Wallboard itself, continued to tender new filings to DMIC. Another 120 days minimum until a hearing and then we had to await a decision by Judge Goldberg.

— — —

Then, there was the *Mullen* case. Ken Allen (though more often than not Sandy) and I had the task of being coordinating counsel for the Defendants' Joint Demurrer (motion to dismiss). Five other firms were working on arguments: one for each different theory supporting a different legal path to claim class relief, including negligent manufacture, negligent failure to warn, breach of warranties, strict product liability, and intentional conduct, with fraud and fraudulent concealment imbedded in some claims to give rise to exemplary damages. Each assignment turned out to be a law review article unto itself. After the first draft, and with an abbreviated statement of facts, we still had more than 100 pages, and the styles were different throughout. Three of us did rewrites: two each rewriting the Statement of Facts section of the brief. There was an agreed upon 50 page maximum using a certain font for text and a smaller font for footnotes. Sandra and my writing styles were sufficiently similar that we produced 53 pages for the five arguments and sent them back asking each firm to try to stay in the same style and to try to save two more pages/ section. Plus, time to file was becoming a problem, and I had a USCG Reserve weekend coming up. Three of us met on a Friday with the brief needing to be filed the following Tuesday. Tinker, Mace, Mary and I had come up with a series of small concepts that we felt could be implemented by footnotes to the Fact section and a Request for The Court to Take Judicial Notice of a number of demographic facts which our CAL Board team had created. The gravamen of this research on demographics was that the huge number of inspections based on the amount of houses putatively in the case, coupled with the costs of repair and replacement of 50% of those properties inspected, with relocation costs for 2-3,000,000 households would be more insurance money and corporate equity than was remotely available among these 26 defendants: and, so would mean the probable inability of those actually injured by asbestos (the BI Plaintiffs) to collect anything if this class received anything remotely approaching the monetary relief which it sought in this suit.

Ken and Sandy were not enthusiastic about those footnotes, but they finally admitted that the overall concept created an *in terrorem* closing argument of great power when combined with the failure of the plaintiff to plead any actual physical injuries or damages, only the possibility of some future physical harm, throughout her complaint. So, those other drafters reluctantly agreed. The other non-drafting defendants fought those footnotes as well with some threatening to make their own filings with a joinder in part and a disavowal of this "all the money in the world argument" as the most vituperative opponents deemed it.

When we could not get unanimity, I suggested they take it to their clients and let us know by 0600 on Tuesday who was not to be "fully on the brief."

A few filed their exception to full joinder documents, more relented: 23 of 26 defendants were on the entire brief. When *Mullen's* lead lawyer, Marvin Jones, got the moving papers served on him at 4:45 that afternoon, he called me by 5:30, "Ronan, this is one brilliant piece of lawyering, just to get this filed. I ran through it quickly. You seem to have addressed all of our major concerns. But, there sure were a lot of footnotes, not to mention supporting papers, for an attack based solely on a matter of law (a not so oblique reference to California law on its Demurrer which many think has an inelastic rule that "you cannot go outside the four corners of the complaint in your legal attack.") Hence, I explained in that call, we used Judicial Notice, the one obscure exception to that rule!

At that point, I was confident he had not read that Request at all in his limited analysis.

Nothing to do until we got their response, not due for 60 days. The Defense had 30 days thereafter to draft and file a joint Reply brief. Then, the judge would set oral argument. It could be six months or more by the time we got a decision from Judge Kendall.

— — —

The SCHOOLS Class Actions took on some changes and we got motions to dismiss on file for CBPI and CPI in the 2 cases in which they were named. The statute of limitations had run on all of the plaintiffs by now, so Napa USD posed little threat going forward. That soon proved to be even more true than I thought possible. When Sandy and one of the East Coast defense counsel sought a telephonic "meet and confer" with the Napa USD Class counsel on that school district's production of documents, they kept getting put off. The other two class rep districts were moving forward and producing their documents (turns out SC counsel decided to add Charleston as a name plaintiff along with Spartanberg and recaptioned their complaint as Charleston USD and certain other SCUSDs).

Sandy wrote a demand letter to Napa's counsel. He responded to her alone with a phone call: turns out that in the course of dealing with that school district's vast backlog of paper, someone unfamiliar with this lawsuit ordered most of the responsive files destroyed. No amount of attempted tracing could turn them up, as yet. Napa asked for, and its named defendants agreed to, a dismissal of its complaint without prejudice (thus, it could be a class member, somewhat hobbled without documents to give rise to any proof of loss) and for a mutual waiver of costs.

I made several more trips East. On one, I briefly saw Sandy who once again was visiting her good friend in NYC. The last trip back for the year was to be the second week of November. I asked Mollie if she wanted to go to see all the decorations in Philadelphia and New York. With so much on her plate for the holiday season and four children, she looked wistful as she turned me down. The next day I got a call from Sandy about that upcoming meeting, she had questions about staying in D.C., including dinner with Tinker and Elaine. When I told her Mollie would not make it, she asked if I wanted "to make it a foursome for old time's sake." The meeting was on Wednesday in Philly, so she said Monday night and I agreed, thinking no more about it. As she was ending the call, she asked me, "What flight are you taking?'

I told her. She said so was she and maybe we could ride into the city together.

Turns out Sandy was staying at the Mayflower as well. After a spicy Indian dinner on Lafayette Square, three hours of sparkling companionship and perhaps just a bit too much to drink, Tinker and Elaine had to get home. That left Sandy and me to walk the three blocks or so back to the Mayflower. It had gotten considerably colder and neither of us were dressed quite warmly enough, so Sandy put her arm through mine and pressed a bit close for warmth. I felt her snuggle a bit. As we got close to the hotel, she gave me a big snuggle whereupon I felt perhaps less comfortable than I should have and dropped her arm from mine, to open the inner door to the relative warmth of the lobby. It was a bit past nine, but only six at home. Mollie would be in the midst of the dinner, bathing the kids, and reading a story, our bedtime ritual that sometimes spread out for 2 – 4 hours. I looked at the bar and asked Sandy, "How about a nightcap?"

She looked up at me, smiled a small smile and said, "How about my room, I really need to get out of these shoes after 15 hours! I have a small suite and a room bar?"

After Gerry, I should have known better, but I just seem to have a judgment vaccuum sometimes. Still, when we started to kiss, a light went off and I pulled away before anything really untoward happened. After all, we were on opposite sides of the Wallboard Coverage case. Dinner and drinks were OK, but nothing more serious. Sandra said she agreed, but the spirits had made inroads into her judgment.

When I called Mollie, just after midnight, I sounded fine. Gave her greetings from Elaine and Tinker, told her Sandy was also there. (By then they had met a couple of times and were seemingly cordial when their relative backgrounds were considered {Sandy did not know about that Bridge episode shortly after she dumped me and where Mollie had been there to call out my name. Very few people did.}.) And then we spent the rest of the call as usual talking about her work, mine and mostly about the children. As I got ready for bed, I realized that I had almost experienced what Sandy had withheld during all of our time together. In retrospect, I wondered ironically if it was ever worth it?

7

Coordination:
Growing The Cal Board Network

With all of the work associated with the *Wallboard* Coverage case and the various huge PD cases, becoming referred to as BUILDINGS Cases by the defense parties, I still had to continue to be certain that we had a viable defense network in place for the BI cases and that it was appropriately staffed with lawyers who knew their way around a courtroom. We started in Washington state, then New Jersey, and we used Philadelphia local counsel for the SCHOOLS classes as well as all of the Pennsylvania BI cases (this would change when CAL Board got sued a few years later in western PA, even in Harrisburg. Turns out that Philadelphia lawyers were not very welcome moving west, or north for that matter). Scott Kelly did know a lot of BI defense people in Philly, but not many of the Buildings Defense Co-Defendant counsel, but he made it his business to find out about them and keep the rest of us apprised. When Arizona got its first BI, case, Angela called me and told me they wanted Bob Hoover to be local counsel for that state. Next was NYC: DMIC had counsel there and wanted to use Reggie Black, the first non-Oakland based African-American we were able to retain and a nephew of Joe Black, a former celebrated Dodgers' pitcher from before they relocated to the LA area.

As the numbers of CAL Board local counsel grew, so did our BI workload in NorCAL. We were once again getting stretched pretty thin. Again, I went to Klein and Kelly asking for three more lawyers, two paralegals, and more space to store documents with DMIC willing to pay the rent on the added space. First, they agreed to the space, but wanted a paralegal and a clerk to organize and access the growing shelves of documents. Finally, they agreed on two attorneys, one experienced and one a rookie. I turned to Mary Smith to be in charge of that leasing and the hiring of support staff. Also, I put her in overall charge of coordinating all CAL Board responsive discovery for all states so that it would be, and remain, consistent. I also got her a healthy raise. Meanwhile, the discovery of documents (and soon it would be witnesses), the science about asbestos, as well as U.S. experts was becoming more convoluted, making them areas requiring my attention to go forward before delegating. With briefing in a gap on *Wallboard*, I asked Phil Hassard to work with Ted Clifford at Tinker's firm and the local counsel to pull as much together as we could to understand what was out there that might help if we needed somebody to talk about the science of actual causation, fiber entrainment, and mode of inflicting injury (or potentially so, for cancers). My preferences were to locate the types who were not conflicted by early incongruous, or just wrong, prior testimony.

As the tasks became more complex, the scope of the overall litigation began a gradual drift. The Johns Manville (JM) coverage case, along with two other major defendants had been joined in one Coordinated Proceeding by the California Judicial Council before Judge Greenberg; and while we awaited our responding parties to file their briefs, we continued to stay abreast of developments. JM was locked in seeming mortal combat with the judge over its failure to get many of its documents produced at its HQ outside of Denver. Then, in unrelated CA BI cases, a plaintiff attorney in Oakland with help from some SC counsel sought to amend all of its Nor-CAL cases against JM to add a claim for punitive damages for knowingly concealing the fact of its own conspiracy with other companies and one or more unnamed insurers to cover up secret testing showing that asbestos actually did cause diseases, undertaken more than 30 years ago in upstate New York at a place called Saranac Lake. This also included pleading JM's knowing removal of all of these documents from its home office to a facility in San Francisco where they were sequestered. JM's role in the world of asbestos use in construction and insulation products cannot be underappreciated. (Harry Johns, one of its co-founders, was seemingly related to a pre-eminent School of Medicine, Hospital and University in Baltimore. Manville was both a person and the name of the Canadian town in Quebec Province where its first mine was located. These two individuals gave this megalithic company its name. JM mined, milled, classified, created uses for, and marketed asbestos to more than half of the other major defendants. It was fully vertically integrated and by far the largest company in the industry.) In other words, this was potentially the beginning of the end for Johns Manville since if these allegations were proven, that entity would be wiped out by all of the millions of dollars of punitive verdicts, which in many states (including CA) were uninsurable!

A rumor began to circulate that one of JM's San Francisco lawyers had committed suicide. No substance ever appeared to give truth to that rumor, but these factors did nothing to enhance JM's counsel's standing in front of Judge Greenberg where his motion practice, already vituperative between the carriers and the manufacturer plaintiffs, began to degenerate down to an outright warlike footing. Meanwhile, Phil and I eventually got all of the Oppositions to the DMIC Motion for Summary Judgment; and in the space of two weeks, we put together a relatively short Reply Brief (against more than 100 pages of briefing by our opponents and boxes of spurious exhibits asserting facts that had no real world bearing on the gist of our motion which was: That to get its needed primary coverage in place, Wallboard, through its Risk Manager, Millard Granger, agreed that Desert Mutual would not provide coverage FOR ANY TYPE OF ASBESTOS

BODILY INJURY claims.).

In late October of 1985, Judge Greenberg held oral argument on his preliminary ruling favoring DMIC to grant summary judgment against all of the Responding Parties, and, notably, with costs assessed against only Respondents Wallboard and SF Casualty. Oral argument lasted more than an hour and was the last matter that morning on Judge Greenberg's heavy Law and Motion Calendar (His only other main task at that time for the City and County of San Francisco's Superior Court). He did not reverse his ruling, told his clerk to so enter it, and signed his Order then and there in front of all counsel. Clearly Judge Greenberg, brilliant jurist that he was, saw this as a teaching moment for all those assembled before him that morning. He said, "Court is dismissed. Mr. O'Neill, please approach the Bench."

As I walked up there, conscious of all of the eyes on me, the judge whispered something to his clerk, who, turned and began marking and stamping documents. The judge beckoned me around to the side of his bench, took a piece of paper from his clerk and handed it to me, saying words I will remember to my dying day, "Mr. O'Neill, brilliant lawyering on your part. This litigation is rank with intrigue! My reputation is on the line with this decision as it may well be read by many as extending California law in such a way that our legislators may not have intended. But enough: Make certain that **you** get this reduced to a Judgement forthwith and that **WE** are upheld on Appeal!"

My response, in a stage whisper, "Thank you, Your Honor." His eyes met mine and I knew he was dead serious.

When I turned, there were Ken Allen and Sandy. Both put their hands out to be shaken, Ken saying, "We congratulate you. A brilliant *coupe* so far, but we will see you down the street in the appellate courts in a matter of months, we hope."

Sandy said, "I will be going to D.C. in two weeks. You?" Her eyes met mine as I nodded affirmatively while putting papers in my briefcase.

— — —

When Scottsdale got the news on the ruling, they were ecstatic. Dudley Chisholm got on the phone and praised me for
several minutes. Mercifully, I don't think anyone else could hear
him. He asked about my upcoming schedule, then asked me to
come down the next Monday to have a celebratory dinner,
spend the night and have a planning meeting the next morning.
When I got home, I told Mollie all about my day. She was delighted. Moreover, she had been pleased with my decisions to
begin more delegation to my most trusted associates as well as
to Tinker's office and local counsel, which now numbered nine.
Then she changed topics suddenly and with a wry smile said,
"I have hired a new *au pair* for the children. We talked about it
once or twice and now seems like the time, especially since the
company wants me to be more involved in application creation
process from the ground up. The money is well more than double what I make now, with possibly even bigger bonuses. But
this also means I will have a higher level of client interaction,
more office time, and much more travel. What do you think?"

All of that came out before I could tell her about Scottsdale
on Monday night. When I asked if she wanted to spend a night
or two at the Biltmore, she explained that she could not leave
the children with the new *au pair* quite so soon, but otherwise
would have loved the opportunity for some alone time with me.
I told her the same and expressed my love and congratulations!

That weekend was great and the new addition arrived on
Sunday. Regina Nordstrom, who was half English and half
Swedish, spoke with a tiny bit of an English accent and spoke
both languages as well as Spanish, which Mollie and I had both
expressed interest in learning as well as having the children be
fluent (they had started Spanish with Yolanda). Regina was
pleased with her small suite. The weather cooperated, so we had

a Mill Valley cook-out on the back patio and good time was had by all with the introductory process going well through, and after, bedtime. Mollie and I cuddled that night after a period of fondness. We whispered nice things, then drifted off. (*Later, when I told Dr. Arnaud about that night picking it out as a signal change, I had no premonition things would become so complicated for us in the years not far ahead.*)

— — —

Dinner at the Biltmore in a private area just off the main dining salon was nothing short of spectacular and my first thought was that I only wished Mollie could be with me. Dudley Chisholm had issued the invitation but his boss Chet Moeller, the VP of Finance, and his wife, Irene, attended, as did Dudley's wife, also an Irene! Manny was in attendance with Esmeralda, whom I had met before, while Angela Lenovo attended alone. I was seated in such a manner that I had access to everyone, but looked directly at Angela. Cocktails and congratulations lasted a good hour, so it was well past 7:00 when we ordered our main courses, and the first course of *hors d'oervers* for the table arrived with white wine all around. At that juncture, Dudley and Chet switched seats and suggested that Manny and I do the same. Only the glass of white wine needed to move. After the main course, we were back to our original seats for dessert and Port.

By then, I was delighted that I was spending the night at the Biltmore. Turns out, so were all the others. As we broke up, we set out to our rooms. Angela and I walked toward the rear of the property, up a steady grade. Soon, we passed the main fountain, and I asked her where she was staying. Turned out to be in the same building and on the same floor as me. So, I asked, "Who made the room reservations?"

Angela looked up at me, saying calmly, "I did. Gerry told me what a dear you are, and I hope to find out. Would you please join me for a nightcap?"

It happened again!

— — —

That next morning, we assembled in a meeting room just off the casual cantina area: no spouses, clearly a working start to the day. Chet stayed only long enough to eat, then announced he needed to get back to the office to discuss the ramifications of the *Wallboard* matter on a Board conference call at 10:00. Dudley started with that case; I explained our immediate need to move the Court's Order to the status of an actual Judgment, a *pro forma* function. At least I believed so. Upon service of that Judgement on all parties, this would allow an appeal filing by any losing parties within 30 days of that service, if they desired.

We then discussed whether or not to stop accepting all tenders of cases from Wallboard and SF Casualty. Of course, there were risks if our Judgement was reversed on appeal. However, a failure to do so might be taken as negative signal in the extreme by DMIC's own reinsurers if the company failed to start rejecting. In fact, that lead to my suggestion that perhaps a letter to Wallboard and SF Casualty offering not to seek reimbursement from them for their tenders of BI defense fees and costs to date as well as a waiver of the motion costs would be forthcoming if they would agree not to appeal. We all agreed that there was nothing to lose and we could use that letter to show the reinsurers as a demonstration of DMIC trying to minimize their expense as well as to point out that DMIC had a 20% retention on all those legal and potential indemnity dollars as part of its contribution. One matter down.

Next, we discussed the growing volume of BI cases against Cal Board and two added BUILDINGS cases in L.A. Superior. We would have to decide what to do about SoCAL soon. I explained how I was delegating more responsibility to the senior associates and Tinker's firm, but would retain oversight. I stressed two themes: first, Cal Board's defense should speak with a single voice, not just in discovery, but in every courtroom and with every plaintiff attorney. But since I could not be everywhere or do everything, we needed to assure coordination. Second, in the same vein, all of our defense attorneys needed to be certain that all discovery and briefing positions be thoroughly vetted by Mary (discovery), Tinker (briefing), and me as NCC to assure absolute consistency. They were all nodding in agreement when I stopped. Dudley said, "The three of us have been using some of the same phrases about how this will need to be controlled going forward. We think there should be a meeting of all of our attorneys soon, before year's end. What do you think?"

When I agreed, Manny stepped up explaining that with the Savings and Loan Scandal, which hit big here in Greater Phoenix, where Charles Keating, who was a kingpin in that scandal, was in the midst of erecting a huge resort property called the Phoenician. The feds had seized it, and together with some of Keating's lender banks, they were going about finishing off various sections, and had even opened one restaurant. Manny knew someone, had called and we could get a meeting room, all the rooms we would need, food at or from the restaurant AND do so at way below costs at the seasonal rates available elsewhere which started soon. We all agreed. They would run this by all their people to be sure. I would run it by Austin Smith who would need to attend and would do a quick sample of the lawyers.

Then we talked about the BUILDINGS cases and I went home. Mollie and Regina were busy with the kids. I ate dinner alone, leftovers from Sunday's cookout!

8

On The Road Again

Flying around the country was becoming a way of life, not just for me, but Mollie as well with her new level of responsibilities which seemed to have no geographic limitations. Late 1986 found me once again at the Mayflower on a Monday night. Sandy had sat next to me on the flight, we rode to the hotel together and her room was down the hall from mine. Even so, neither of us had broached the topic of what had almost happened those months before on that very different Monday night. Was I looking forward to something? Anything? As we rode up to the 8th floor, Sandy turned to me, and said, "We are too early for dinner with Tinker and Elaine. Do you want to stop in my room?"

There it was. If I said NO, that would probably end the whole thing; but if I said YES, I was quite unsure of what would follow (even at dinner). Using that latter thought, I responded, "I would really like to, but I think I had better call the newish *au pair* to make sure she's OK since Mollie is in New York this week. How about we take 30 minutes, then we can meet, walk to the restaurant and have a drink at the bar while we wait for our friends? I think we need to see what happens on *Wallboard*, just to be safe!"

Sandy stopped at her door, put down her bag and let herself in, saying on the way, "Too bad! I had a surprise for you!!"

Four old friends having dinner works really well maybe once a year, especially when it's almost impossible to talk about work. Most of what Tinker and I worked on was with each other. Sandy and I were allies in some matters, but enemies on *Wallboard*.

Elaine worked in a different growing field—Intellectual Property. Since hers was different, she spent a lot of her dinner telling us about the nuances of copyright law. Instead of three hours, dinner was closer to two. Tinker and Elaine were anxious to relieve their *au pair*, so the meal ended by 8:00. (This was still the era right before the cell phone. So, messages had to be picked up either from the office or at home. Mollie had multiple extensions at home which made getting through to Regina less problematic. We had not connected when I called earlier. I did leave a message.)

On the walk back to the Mayflower, I told Sandy all of this. She smiled ever so slightly, then said, "How about if I come to your room for a drink while you check for messages?"

"Not a problem, but some of these calls can get boring. And we are approaching dinner time in Mill Valley."

Her smile got brighter, "That's OK," was her only response. We rode up and went to my room. By then I had stayed at the Mayflower so often, they gave me a complimentary suite, whenever one was available. Sandy and I made drinks, then she sat on the couch in the living area while I checked the phone in the bedroom for messages. Only one: from Mollie saying she arrived in NYC, staying at the Waldorf, had dinner at eight and would call if it finished early (OK to put a DND on my phone if I was going to sleep, that way the phone would go straight to voicemail without ringing to wake me.)

Sandy was being crystal clear that she wanted sex. I had thought about it – hard! Finally, somewhat muddled from alcohol, but not too much, I just told her not until *Wallboard* ended -- For Good!

Later, I checked messages again, only one from Regina asking me to call and say a Good Night to Robert and Maeve. I did, but felt better in the process, with no pangs of guilt. Then I realized, Mollie had not left me her room number at the Waldorf. I called and asked for her room by name. Three rings and a breathless woman answered. I asked for Mollie, but the woman said, "Wrong room!" How strange? When I called back, Mollie picked right up.

The next morning, I mulled the strange answer on my first call to Mollie's room. When the woman hung up, I had called right back and told the hotel operator about the error. She said simply. "I put your call through to the correct room." Then connected me again. This time, Mollie answered. I quickly decided not to mention the mix up of moments ago. (After all, I did live in a glass house when it came to these kinds of things!)

A week later I was seeing Dr. Arnaud and I happened to mention that call as I was going through my week with Sandy at the Mayflower. She looked at me knowingly. Started to say something, but seemed to think better of it. I thought that was the end of that crazy call business. But not until it happened again in December when Mollie was once again in NYC and staying at the Waldorf Astoria. This time the breathlessness lasted longer, and there were no words, only the phone being hung up on the other end. Oh, MY!!

That Thursday afternoon, Sandy and I met at the plane to SFO. I offered to drop her at her apartment on my way home, It was only a few blocks off of one of many routes to Mill Valley. We talked about yesterday's meeting in Alicia's offices, particularly LAUSD and the SCHOOLS Class which was moving forward at a glacial pace, but held out a promise of some action after the first of the year. Sandy told me that her father wanted her to be a lead trial attorney in LAUSD. The first phase on the Statute of Limitations was set to begin in this next April and promised to be exciting. Sandy asked what hotel I would stay in. I told her that DMIC was renting a two bedroom apartment just two blocks from the LA Superior Main Courthouse building for me. Sandy smiled at that. She smiled at me a great deal lately and I hoped others were not noticing that so readily. As the plane landed while I watched the lights of San Mateo County homes, I thought to myself, I may be seeing more of Sandy these days then Mollie.

9

Arizona Biltmore

Little did I realize the impact having so many people central to my life in one place at the same time would have on me. With less than 25 people, our Cal Board Group was small enough to have a conference room in the original Biltmore Building, a Frank Lloyd Wright structure located not far from his home for the latter part of the great architect's life. Much of the discussion preceding the opening session actually focused on that historical factor and gave a gravitas to this meeting which I had not anticipated. For many of the counsel, this was their first moments of meeting many of their colleagues in this coordinated defense effort. For the insurers and their client, Austin Smith, CAL Board's General Counsel (GC), this assembly gave a visceral reality to the scope of this enterprise in which they were all engaged: this gathering accounted for substantial expense both in terms of bringing all of these counsel together with some supporting staff for this meeting, but also for the long-term potential outcome for Desert Mutual as well as the continuing livelihood of CAL Board.

As for myself, I still had not met Reggie Black of New York City, Lucy Baines of Portland, Oregon, David Sims of Fort Worth, Texas, or Joyce James of Las Vegas. Many others I had met but once. Few of them knew any of my office team except possibly Phil or Mary. We also brought Deirdre, our lead paralegal, and Lily, our legal assistant. Tinker, Mace and Tod were present from D.C. Arizona (little cost), Washington state and New Jersey asked to bring second counsel and Manny had agreed.

These three states had proven the busiest, beside California, for BI cases so far. Finally, we also had Reggie Fox and his first new hire, Martha Walsh, a somewhat older woman (perhaps mid-30's) whom he had told me was a third year associate having had plenty of court time while working for Alameda County Welfare Department for 6 years while going to law school at night. She had then gone to work briefly for a family law firm. When Reggie interviewed her, she confided that the entire family law system had quickly taken its toll on her and she was looking for a litigation job with less personal/emotional impact on her every day. He came to my office, told me about her for 3 or 4 minutes. I told him to hire her on the spot. He did. She was extremely pleasant and looked a good five years younger than a few weeks ago when I first saw her (so the change to concern about monetary outcome instead of the troubled lives of distraught people must have proved beneficial to her). Reggie saw Martha as potentially one of his three trial lawyers!

The meeting came to order at about 9:30 with introductions and opening remarks by Dudley, Austin and Manny, all of whom took quite a bit of time and then they answered questions. We had a short break before lunch and then worked while we were interacting. The afternoon started with a panel of Tinker, Mary, Deirdre and me to talk about discovery with an emphasis on the client's documents. This was supposed to have been a general briefing, but as we went on, this format turned into being much more about the nuts and bolts of interacting on the client's documents and coordination of written discovery than originally intended. When time began to expire, I signaled to Manny and whispered that I thought it was important to finish this discussion and to end with a recap. He agreed. Austin Smith, who was not on the panel itself, probably was more engaged than any one of the panelists. I was pleasantly surprised to see how well Mary Smith interacted with everyone. She had gained enormous confidence and skill in our years together. She fielded questions, giving patient explanations to detailed questions, while sometimes deferring to Deirdre to be certain that our lead paralegal, despite her relatively tender years, would be accorded the respect her key job required.

Tinker and Mace, from his seat, spent time explaining their document reviews on the history of the client's product line. I spent a few intervals talking about consistency and attention to detail. Also, I explained the entity relationships between CAL Board and its subsidiary CPI which was the entity with plants in New Jersey and Texas, which I dubbed "the Entity Defense." In closing this session, I went back to the concept of "ONE VOICE." This needed to be the major take-away for all of these lawyers. We had three hours left for the next morning before everyone would break up and go home. Manny, Tinker, Mary, Phil, Reggie and I shuffled the agenda for the next day which was largely focused on the Buildings cases. We cut that to ninety minutes. The rest we set aside to deal with potential Bodily Injury (BI) trials outside of CA.

After the Agenda adjustments, I went right to the bar to take the opportunity to get to know more of the lawyers whom I was meeting in person for the first time. Before I could get to our bartender, Reggie Black, who was talking with Barry Brown of Newark, asked me what I would have to drink, and within seconds a glass of good vodka with a lemon twist had appeared in my hand. Both of these handsome African-American men were of about my age, and they quickly engaged me. When they found out that I had grown up in the East, they began to pepper me with questions, and in no time, found out that I had played varsity 'hoops" at Georgetown. They were avid fans of East Coast "round ball" and we were soon immersed in that topic. As much as I was enjoying myself, I tore away, paused to greet Austin Smith who was talking with Phil and Mary, and found Lucy Baines of Oregon and Joyce James from Nevada talking with each other. They both seemed delighted to meet me as I was them. Joyce did not look me in the eye, but we both somewhat towered over Lucy. They wanted to talk business, so I accommodated them, exchanging stories of a few past cases. Another cocktail, some chatting with the DMIC people and it was time for dinner. (I had made my own reservation in the main building {smaller rooms, but close to the meeting site} and I badly wanted to avoid any entanglements during this meeting!)

When everyone was seated at 4 tables, and all had something to drink (I ordered the wines ahead of time to control the costs), I rose, said a few words of welcome, followed by words of thanks to those paying us and for the event, commented briefly on the day's meeting and tomorrow's revised agenda and sat down. Dudley briefly, then Manny, spoke, followed by Austin. I had placed Tinker, Mace and Tod at different tables as I had also done with Reggie Fox, Mary Smith and Phil Hassard. That way the people with more background would be spread among the 9 local counsel and the client types. Limited choices were allowed for the three courses. Dinner proceeded at a comfortable pace which was not too fast, but promised to have the evening over with by 8:30 or so (Arizona is an early start state). At my table, I met David Sims of Fort Worth, a big man who looked every inch the image of what one would imagine a Texan would look like, and he sounded the part as well. Angela sat next to him, appearing enthralled by his banter with everyone.

Deirdre, the paralegal, was at the same table as Mace and Mary, both with whom she worked a great deal, but this was her first chance to meet Mace face-to-face. They seemed to hit it off nicely and I could foresee a continuance of their good working relationship in the future. By 8:45, dessert was finished and the wait staff could be seen hovering to collect all the empties and be on their way. I had declined having after dinner drinks again as a cost measure; but, with the reluctant agreement of Klein and Kelly who were getting rich off this litigation, I announced as a departure suggestion that anyone wishing a final drink could join me at the Main Bar as those drinks would be on our firm. More than half joined. Dudley and Manny went home. Austin went to his room as did Lily and Deirdre of our team. All of the lawyers stayed as did Angela who was standing with Mary and Martha as well as Tod. We stayed in knots of 3 or 4 and I agreed to a second round, but the crowd began to thin. Angela came over to thank me, but said she was taking a taxi home (some relief on my part there!).

Tinker, who said they would buy the next round, and Mace were going round and round with Reggie Black, Scott Kelly form Philly, and Barry Brown once again about East Coast Conference basketball. I saw Lucy leave and then Joyce looked around for a second seeming undecided on whether to stay. I caught her eye and she came toward me. At the same time, so did Martha Walsh, Reggie Fox's new associate (and a last minute addition), who was taller than I had realized. We began to talk while the basketball conversation was getting louder from the Northeast Corridor group. Martha turned to Joyce saying, "I played at Cal for two years, but not much court time, How about you?"

Joyce answered, "Colorado, four years, started my last three."

Soon basketball was a major topic with the three of us and the night seemed almost destined to get away from us when I said, "I had better go call and check in with Mollie. She keeps some mean hours with her new job and our four little ones. Excuse me."

— — —

The next day's program went on without complications, although the group seemed a bit subdued for the first hour or so. Quite a few of the local counsel as well as Reggie and Martha from our firm were not much involved in the Buildings cases, however, some of the issues, especially the science involving the different fibers, potential means of causation and the different actual medical conditions had potential cross-over with the BI case involvement. The fact that there were no physical injuries actually being alleged in any of the Buildings cases filed to date made the science potentially more significant. As we wound down, I tried to keep everyone focused on the key messages from the day before. We ended at noon.

It was a Friday. So, I said if anyone wanted to have lunch we could try to do something. Martha asked if she could come as she was staying on for a few days with friends who were still at work. Joyce asked as well; she wanted a couple of days off and our room rate was great for a place this nice. Almost everyone else left except Manny and Angela. We went out toward the patio where I had done my first lunch with the Desert Mutual folks years before, a familiar venue to me now. Martha and Joyce were talking, and I heard Martha say, "That's really ever so nice of you."

To which Joyce responded, "My pleasure."

We five had a convivial, simple lunch. No alcohol. I left at 1:25 and had no problem catching the 3:00 flight. The meeting had seemed successful. Why was I feeling so apprehensive?

10

A Coast Guard Weekend

*F*rom my many mentions to Dr. Arnaud and from memory at times, I hope to impart to the reader how I came to feel so very invested in the USCG, and its people, over the years. Not all of the members, active or reserve, are or were perfect: however, they all, to the last man or woman, really cared about their USCG job, their duty, their honor and their country.

During my three and a half years of active duty, I saw this on a first hand basis, and on repeated occasions. I came to appreciate these Coast Guard people, and to this day I consider it a privilege to have served with them, even when I was not paid. It was, for me, my way of paying back to those blessed with less than me, and especially those who died with me. SEMPER PARATUS: Always Ready!!

My last 8 years in the Reserves involved not being paid, which was just fine, and I did get my reasonable expenses compensated for all of my travel. Somewhere in that time, the Twelfth Coast Guard District, headquartered on Coast Guard Island in the Oakland Estuary between Alameda Island and the City of Oakland on the mainland, ceased to exist and the whole of California and Nevada became the Eleventh Coast Guard District. However, Commander, Pacific Area (a 3-Star Admiral) remained on Coast Guard Island, at the time presided over by VADM Clyde Robbins, with whom I had served at USCG HQ those many years ago. It was VADM Robbins who asked me to take on the Readiness assignment of having all of the western states (CA, NV, OR, WA, AZ and UT) properly educated and documented to be ready for a major call-up, should one occur. I, of course, undertook that assignment working with the Legal Office in Long Beach for a day to get my curriculum straight and to coordinate the appropriate level of follow-up *to see that this was all carried out. In order to make certain that this would occur, it was necessary that I visit every reserve unit in those six states on at least two occasions to carry out the needed indoctrinations. In some instances because of the unit locations, I would also continue to provide legal assistance to the Regulars who were too far away to get help or counseling from the district legal offices in Long Beach and Seattle.*

— — —

Mollie was not due back until tomorrow from her latest trip to New York City. This time, she answered my call fairly promptly when I called her around 11:00 p.m. EDT. I was still mystified by those two strange "answers" I got on her last trips, but I put it down to inadequacies of the Waldorf's switchboard.

I left home at 3:00 a.m. and pulled into USCG STA Morro Bay, on the coast, having driven south about 175 miles on US 101 and hung a right at San Luis Obispo. 0800-1130 was set aside for Readiness Training for the Reserve members of the Central CA coast units (Santa Barbara and Morro Bay). We met in the dining hall of the Mess Deck. Everyone snapped to attention as I walked in, now a Commander, I outranked them all. I began rather quickly following a very brief introduction by the CO of the Santa Barbara unit, "Fellow Coasties, please be seated. If you speak, please give me your rank and name. My name is Ronan O'Neill. I am a lawyer. I do not believe any of you have ever heard me speak, but if you have, please do not share your opinions until we are done. If you have questions, please wait until I pause and call on you to ask them. Now, how do you tell if a lawyer's lying?"

There was a pause, some of the audience looked quizzically at each other. When no one volunteered, I filled the soundless void with, "Watch his lips and see if they are moving!"

A moment of silence, then a couple of the older members,

whom I was certain actually had heard me tell that joke before, began to laugh; and almost instantly, they were all laughing and the ice was broken.

As I had over the years, I liked to build on the less than usual dry legal type of lecture by trying to turn our time into a useful series of life lessons. The first one was what not to do when the police stopped you and you had been drinking. Some were just warnings, but one was quite a trick. *(But alas, not here.)* Next came, the car: what was the first thing a young man who came into money would buy? What did he look at, the price! Anything else? NO! So, what about gas, tires, upkeep, insurance? And so on. (I would change gender at times, and even cover when a married couple were both Reservists and subject to the same call-up.)

This became a series of real-life stepping-stones starting with how car insurance actually worked. From that, we would move into each member's living arrangement. If with the parents, little to worry about in the event of a call-up (BUT wait until I finish!). If you are single and rent? If you are married, and only the member works? (AND so on.) Now, you would need fire/property/liability insurance on your dwelling: one kind if you owned, but a different kind if you rented. AND now, depending on your living status, you needed to have someone who could act for you when your call-up lasted more than a month or two. That led to explaining the need for a Power of Attorney. All of this took time and there were all kinds of questions.

Finally, we came to the hard one: what happens if you get called up and do not make it back? (Later variants could include capture and serious injury, but I avoided these if I could as unlikely and not really within the framework of what I needed to accomplish.) This brought us to the need for a will, and an explanation of the California laws of intestate succession (a law professor's favorite topic which I tried to make simple by having your siblings get an unfair share of what you leave behind, maybe even that car from an hour before). I tried to end with, "What do you call a bus load of lawyers going over a cliff?"

The senior members present, this time chorused, "An excellent beginning!"

Questions sometimes followed into lunch, then I would take Legal Assistance matters from whichever Regulars signed up until they were done, on their way out, I heard one of the newer Reservists ask one of the Chiefs, "What's that ribbon the Commander has first? I've never seen that one before."

The Chief put his arm around the recruit and said *sotto voce*, "That's the Silver Star. The Commander was a war hero during Viet Nam. They say he saved his cutter and some of the crew after his CO was killed."

After more than two hours of counseling Regulars, including a great deal of domestic relations issues, alcohol issues, debt difficulties and agreeing to get some wills done. I shoved off up the Pacific Coast Highway for the three plus hour drive to Spanish Bay in Pebble Beach, which gave me a room for the night and any of four dinners for $90. A huge discount! They treated the Coast Guard very well!

The next day I was at the USCG Base Monterey located just above Cannery Row in the City of Monterey, the heart of John Steinbeck Country. This time there were no Reserves, just Legal Assistance, but I had been doing Monterey twice a year for a decade or more. I had a large group to see. Missed lunch, stopped at McDonald's on my way out of town and was home in Mill Valley by 5:30. That first Stoli on the Rocks tasted great!

11

Big Ticket Litigation

That Monday after my Coast Guard weekend in Central California, my mail from late Friday was waiting in my office In-basket. On top was an Order from Judge James McGirr Kelly of the United States District Court of the Eastern District of Pennsylvania (USDC ED PA) in the *Lancaster* schools class matter (The Pennsylvania and South Carolina SCHOOLS class actions were now consolidated as a single vehicle before that judge with plaintiffs' counsel for each case now being co-counsel for the entire class) setting a Status Conference Hearing in his court room for a Thursday at 10:30 in the upcoming mid-January. Next was an Order from Judge Kendall of the Contra Costa Superior Court setting oral argument on the *Mullen* matter for the week following that Pennsylvania hearing. My imagination turned to the *LAUSD* case and what should I find, an Order setting a Trial Management Conference in Los Angeles Superior Court for the first week of February. The upcoming year would prove to be the beginning of the busiest 5 years of my life!

I asked Lily to make copies of these documents for Mary, Phil and me, then to fax them to Tinker in D.C. Phil had been spending vast amounts of his time in L.A. in depositions on *LAUSD*, so I was a bit surprised that he was in the office that Monday. The three of us talked about these three big cases. Phil thought both of us should be at the Trial Setting for *LAUSD*. He would draft a brief implementing the Bifurcation Agreement for Statute of Limitations as the first phase for trial to be ruled upon in early January. I agreed and said I would take care of discussing it with Manny. I asked him where we were on the *Wallboard* briefing.

Phil told me that the Appellate briefs were due next week, meaning probably working over the Christmas Holidays (no reason to procrastinate with all of these major matters upcoming in January).

Then I turned to Mary, who had quickly become a rock on our team: hugely dependable, always ready to do more. On *Mullen*, she thought I should lead the entire argument for the Defense team (seemed to me that Ken Allen would want that for himself); we needed a defense meeting for that level of planning. I said I would call Ken Allen to use his conference room. I asked Mary to put together an outline of the key points to be made by each section of the defense brief.

Then we got Tinker on the line. He said he wanted to go to the *Lancaster* hearing and to bring Mace. I said I thought it was high time Mary got to Philadelphia. Then, Tinker kicked in that the W.R. Grace counsel in New York were hosting the NCC Meeting in January in Downtown New York during the week before the *Mullen* hearing, but at least the day before the *Lancaster* hearing in that same week. I thought for a minute. Then said, I better call Manny about all of this: a scheduling nightmare. I suggested that Tinker might have Mace work with Mary on a detailed Status Conference brief in the SCHOOLS Class to try to get our Motions to Dismiss on calendar for a hearing.

Finally, I asked everyone to get back together at 4:00 EST to finish this call and to ask Deirdre to attend as well. As they were leaving, Mary stopped, turned and said, "Martha Walsh and I were talking. She said she would really like to do some work with you. She does have a good background in medicine as she was pre-med for a while in undergrad. Can she sit in?" (I thought I had better talk with Reggie Fox before I involved Martha much, but having someone who knew more "science" could be extremely helpful).

So, I called Manny and we talked along with Angela for almost an hour planning everything. I kept warning them that all of this was going to become ever more expensive as we were coming up against some crucial junctures in all of our major cases. They agreed that more help was needed and liked having someone involved who knew more science. Then, I took Reggie out for a quick sandwich and beer to talk. He told me about key developments in the NorCAL BI cases. Then I asked him about Martha. His reply was not what I expected, "Martha is really smart, so I've been thinking that if all I can give her is a steady diet of BI cases, she'll be gone in a year or so. The firms in the City will find out about her and offer to pay her more than we can afford. But, if you use her, and challenge her, she might be worth more and just stick around for a longer run. So, it's fine with me. Just know, we'll need more people soon."

When we got back to the office, I went over to Mary's office and asked her to bring Martha to the meeting if she was in the office. We assembled in the conference room at 1:00 PST, Tinker was on the line with Mace and Tod. I told them what Manny and Angela thought. Planning ensued. Martha would go to the WR Grace Meeting with me, so would Tinker. (Mary was fine with that!) Austin Smith would join us. Austin would also attend the *Mullen* Status Conference. Mary would be there with us for that. We still needed to call Ken Allen to set up that meeting. For the *Lancaster* Status Conference, Tinker, you and one other from D.C. can come. I will be there along with Martha and Mary (Glancing at her, Mary blushed. Martha smiled ever so slightly.). Afterward, we'd all stay to meet at Scott Kelly's office to decide on the next course of action in that matter. Finally, in *LAUSD*, Tinker, and either Mace or Tod could come out for that. The hearing was at 9:30, so Phil and I would fly down the night before and we could discuss any developments over dinner. Of course, there was a great deal of talk, but this day was the start of sorting out the cast of my main helpers as we would move forward into this land of highly complex, and heretofore unimagined, high stakes litigation.

As we left, Martha came over to me, she wore heals and seemed even taller than Mollie, "Mr. O'Neill, thank you for giving me this opportunity. I'll do my best to see that you don't regret it. On the flight, if it's alright, I would want to spend that time doing background reading on the pulmonology associated with asbestos. I'll assemble the articles in the office with Deirdre and see if I can supplement those. If that's OK?"

"Sounds good. You really can call me Ronan. I do not believe I could be that much older than you, I will look forward to working with you…." was about what I said. I just hoped Reggie Fox was right about her. Science and Medicine could turn out to be a major battlefield in this property litigation and we would need to be on top of it.

— — —

The Appellants' briefs for the *Wallboard* Appeal arrived on time. After reviewing them, meeting with Phil, then phone calls with Dudley Chisholm and Manny, Phil and I decided that we had anticipated virtually every argument that Wallboard and SF Casualty had made in their briefs and covered those points in our motion briefing. Accordingly, Judge Greenberg had adopted our version of the law and applied it leading to our trial court victory. Much of that was covered in our *Wallboard* Reply Brief from that motion practice. I asked Phil to draft an initial single Opposition brief to all of the Appellants' briefs. We spent less time than I would have thought possible during the Holidays.

Mollie, Kate, Mollie's Dad, and our 4 children had a fantastic Christmas. The last for Mollie's Dad, who did all he could to make it the best ever for everyone. When they left after New Year's, Mollie went to our room and broke down weeping. I had never seen her so upset! I tried to console her, but she just needed time more than anything else. In 48 hours or so, Mollie was pretty much back to her extraordinarily energetic self.

— — —

This year had proven more than transitory as I explained it to Dr. Arnaud: not just Mollie's Dad's cancer, or our concomitant concern for Mary Catherine losing another husband, but a premonition that things in our lives were somehow slowly beginning to ebb toward a more troubled future. I tried to express this sense of foreboding to Dr. Arnaud, but somehow seemed mostly to fail. She put my dawning anxiety down to an overarching worry as my work responsibilities continued to increase. The good doctor did warn me that at some point in time I must stop undertaking more responsibility at work and that I should become much more mindful of my extracurricular sexual behavior.

Turns out most of her warnings essentially fell on deaf ears at that time.

12

My First New York NCC Meeting

The week of January 17 was complicated. The National Co-ordinating Counsel Meeting in New York City was on a Tuesday at 10 a.m. in the Wall St. area of Manhattan (definitely not Mid-Town), which would not have been a problem if Judge Kelly had not set his Status Conference for that Thursday, the 20th at 1:30 in the Federal Courthouse at 4th and Market Streets. in Philadelphia. I wanted to meet with Tinker and his people before that NCC meeting as usual. That meant flying to D.C. on Sunday, meeting Monday, flying to New York later that day and taking the subway Downtown on Tuesday to be sure to be timely. Flying directly into any NYC airport and then taxiing was just too risky to undertake with the Big Apple's chronic traffic congestion going into Manhattan in the a.m. That meant 3 different hotels over 4 nights and plenty of connections. I asked Martha, as the planning went on if she was up for all of this. Of course, she agreed. Lily and she worked everything out with Tinker's assistant. Mary would be there for just Philadelphia. Scott Kelly would attend the Judge Kelly matter and we would use his office afterward. (Scott had a great relationship with one of the BIG Philadelphia firms and got all of us rooms at the Four Seasons at their client rate – a huge discount and conveniently close in to Center City.)

Came Sunday, January 16, and I met Martha at SFO about 7:00 a.m. at the TWA Ambassador Lounge. I had put in both of our names to upgrade to First Class having paid coach and used my miles to upgrade us to Business. As it was a Sunday with few business travelers, we got the full upgrade: Seats 1A and 1B!

Martha was very impressed when I explained the whole process (Funny how that worked the first time with everyone. After that, people were always disappointed when we did not get First Class, or worse, only I did!). We settled in with coffee before take-off and had a small snack soon after wheels up. Martha got right to reading and note making on the stack of medical articles and papers she had brought with her. (Reggie Fox kept her busy, billing 45 – 50 hours each week on the BI matters with depositions, brief writing, hearings and meetings.) At 12:30 EST, I asked our flight attendant if I might have a cocktail and ordered a double Stoli with a twist. Martha looked at me, California woman that she was, smiled after a few seconds, then asked me, "Can I have one of those too?"

When I nodded YES, she stopped reading and said, "I hope you understand that a great deal of what I am covering today and during our travels is quite duplicative. There are very few truly original articles on asbestos causation, almost all of them focus on Asbestosis and its effects on the lungs and their machinations. Asbestosis is essentially a single cause disease. Seems to me that the greater issues are those cases that we get all the time, where the radiological proof for demonstrable Asbestosis is weak and so the plaintiff will try to build up his condition with a variety of subjective complaints."

At that point, I decided Martha would do just fine on Science and Medicine.

As we sipped our first cocktails of the day, Martha expanded a bit on the other conditions with which we were being confronted with asbestos as the alleged cause. Mesothelioma seemed to be another single cause disease, although the peer reviewed articles to date seemed to focus on only one type of asbestos, Crocidolite, and especially in those who mined it. Then, "I have not read anything particularly convincing on the issue of asbestos as a cause of cancer. Irving Selikoff and his team at Mt. Sinai make a case for it, but their treatment of confounding factors in their studies, especially for so many smokers, is hardly anything approaching a dispositive replicable process so far. I am surprised they got such an obvious pass on this point in their peer reviews. This issue seems to beg more scrutiny. If we are looking for an expert or two, we might need to try to get ahold of some of those peer reviewers. What do you think?"

So, I told her one of the main problems is that so many of the research types did not want to challenge the Labor-connected Mt. Sinai juggernaut, which was well-funded by the plaintiffs' bar through expert fees, speeches and programs. Martha could not believe that. Moreover, the complement to that was that any number of the peer reviewer types having testified for the defense early in the BI litigation were not well-prepared, then made errors on the record which the plaintiffs' bar would, and in a few instances did, call up with devastating effect when those same people tried to testify again for the defense. Nonetheless, I asked her to keep looking and see what she could find, especially making a list of the potential peer review scientists who might become potential defense witnesses.

After a light lunch, Martha went back to reading and so did I, catching up on some fiction about a Catholic priest who was having an affair with His Brother's Wife.

The rest of the flight was uneventful as was our taxi ride to the Mayflower in the light late afternoon Sunday traffic in the gathering darkness of the dead of winter. At least there was no dirty snow accumulation and none forecast for our time on the East Coast. But it was bitterly cold and our California outerwear seemed a trifle fragile, especially while we waited for our taxi. Carlton, the Mayflower's younger doorman, was on duty for our arrival. He was great with names, "Good evening! Mr. O'Neill! How have you been?"

A few moments later, Carlton had whisked us inside while handing us off to Eddie, the bellman, who saw to it that we got expedited check-in, and then guided us up to our rooms. On the way, saying, "Mr. O'Neill, as always, we have upgraded you. Ms. Walsh, you are right next door."

Eddie took care of Martha first and she returned with a tip for Eddie as he was opening the door to my complimentary suite. As Eddie took my bag to the bedroom, Martha asked, "Would you mind if I look around for a few seconds? This is kind of fabulous."

Eddie smiled when I gave him a $5 bill, turned and left. I said, "OK, go ahead, look around." Martha opened the cabinet housing the color TV, pulled back the curtains and fastened them open, then turned on the table lamps for more light in the living room. She even went over to the wet bar and checked it out right down to the icemaker. Then, "How about the bedroom?

"Go ahead." And, she did! "Oh my God! A four-poster!! That is so great."

So, I decided it was time to get this over with and get some dinner before it became too late. Most of the restaurants in downtown D.C. were closed on Sundays, so I suggested we freshen up, then meet in the lobby. Martha said she would make reservation in the hotel dining room so we could meet there in 15 – 20 minutes.

— — —

When Martha walked toward our table, she had done more than freshen up. She wore a dress of vibrant blue, had pulled her hair back on the sides, and actually appeared to have applied make-up (something I had not realized until that moment that she must routinely skip as a matter of course).

We started talking: this time, mostly about her. She told me about her life in greater Los Angeles growing up: how it was largely taken up with sports and school, not much of anything on her teen age social life. Then onto her time at Cal-Berkeley, where she played basketball for the Women's team for a few years, and got immersed in Pre-Med only to lose her enthusiasm for it in the lab sciences leading to an inability to find the level of satisfaction which she somehow had thought was going to be there as she progressed toward her Pre-Med degree.

So, she shifted to Pre-Law and liked that. She tried to get into Cal-Berkeley's Boalt Hall, but had to "settle for Hastings." At which point, I intervened. I guess I was funny enough because she laughed at my mention of Hastings as my law *alma mater*.

We split an appetizer and did the same with one main course followed by a cordial in lieu of dessert. I suggested we retire to our rooms to work on adjusting to the East Coast time frame with its three hour earlier time difference, adding I would need to call my family before retiring for the night.

Martha was silent as we rode up to the 8th floor in the elevator. At her door which we came to first, I paused for her to get her key from her purse. Instead, she turned and faced me, her eyes gazing a bit downward and said, "I was hoping you would invite me in for a nightcap from that wet bar in your sitting room?' and with that last word, her eyes came up meeting mine.

I was not at all ready for what Martha had in store for me, but she was a woman of her word. We only had that one drink, but it took a couple of hours to finish!

— — —

We were at Tinker's office in the conference room on the seventh floor overlooking K Street by 9:00. We would need to run back to the Mayflower to grab our bags on the way to the airport. Over the next three-plus hours, we had a light lunch delivered and covered what we saw as potentially important that might happen in NYC, especially on the issue of expert witnesses for the Buildings Litigation, an emerging sore point among the defense group. We also discussed *LAUSD* and spent serious time on the upcoming trial, which we expected to be set at the Los Angeles hearing in a few weeks. Tod was volunteered to be my second chair, which I had cleared generally with Manny. Phil was busy getting subpoenas issued and served on all of our potential witnesses. We had a meeting set with Dr. Wilson Riles, our star witness who, as former California Superintendent of Schools, had sent a letter telling all California school districts about the dangers of asbestos more than 5 years before *LAUSD* filed its case (the statute of limitations for property claims in California is 4 years). Tinker said his motion to avoid the need for a trial was set to be filed on Thursday of that week and he was working with Phil and Deirdre to make certain that happened.

Finally, we spent time on *Mullen*. The briefing was done. I asked Martha to explain the tentative ruling system on motion practice in use in Contra Costa and many other Bay Area Counties. When she finished, Mace asked if we really thought that Judge Kendall would use that device in such a major case, especially as a single assignment judge? Tinker started to respond, but stopped, and with a nod, deferred to me. "My gut feeling is that if he is going to deny the motion, he will want all the lawyers there to talk about what comes next. But if he is going to grant the motion, in whole or in part, he will want to give the plaintiff's counsel as much incentive to prepare for, and argue against, that tentative decision. So, I guess I do see a chance he will do it. Anything else?"

We said our good-byes, hopped in a waiting taxi, grabbed our bags from Carlton and headed to D.C. National Airport (now Reagan Airport) in ample time for the 2:10 Eastern Shuttle to La Guardia. Martha was non-stop about our D.C. meeting. She just loved it, saying things like, "That's why I wanted to become a lawyer. Watching and listening to you all use your brains demonstrates real collegiality and shows me what it takes to succeed in this law business."

Our bags were waiting for us in the LaGuardia Shuttle claim

area and we got a taxi before the big commuter rush hit. Tinker would come up in the morning because of an Elaine commitment that night, but Austin Smith would meet us for dinner. When we got to the Waldorf Astoria, I found a message from Austin saying his flight would be delayed and would we mind waiting until 7:30 for dinner, he should be there by then. Martha looked over at me and with a quick glance gave me to know that she would see to dinner. In five minutes, she was back from a quick visit to the concierge. Dinner at 7:30 in the Bull and Bear Restaurant on the street floor of the Lexington Avenue corner entrance of the hotel. We picked it for its convenience for Austin and their great cocktails. (I was first there as a lawyer in late 1980, soon after Ronald Reagan had won the Presidency. My first night, I wore faded jeans, a blue button down and a camel hair blazer. It was the bar tender Justin's first night as well. A well-tailored man standing next to me leaned over and said, "Love your outfit. Where you from?" When I told him, "California," he told me he was a vice-chair on President-Elect Reagan's Transition Team. Within five minutes, I met the Governor of New York, and then, a young golfer named Mark O'Meara. Lots more happened. Very memorable! Justin never forgot me, and always poured me a very mean drink!)

Martha had us rooming next to each other again. We even had a connecting door. I said something to the effect of calling the office. We did, but by 5:15, she called my room and asked if we could talk. I allowed we could do that. She knocked on the adjoining door. When she came in, she was wearing a robe. However, she did proceed to sit in one of the chairs while I sat in the other. We did talk about work, then a bit about dinner. She stood, I thought to leave, the robe fell away, and there was nothing but Martha underneath.

— — —

We were sitting at our table in the Bull and Bear Restaurant when Austin Smith arrived a bit breathlessly, apologizing for his delays (closer to 8:00). It was a relaxing evening as we went over the developments of the last few days with Austin. A post-dinner drink and we were all off to bed. Austin went to a different elevator tower as he was in the newer high-rise wing. My bed was turned down. I brushed my teeth. Finally came the knock. There was Martha. She stood in the doorway for a few seconds looked at my eyes, reached up and pulled on a ribbon. Her hair cascaded down as I watched her cross those few steps, she seemed to melt in my arms. This might be a very real problem, a little voice said in my head!

— — —

The next morning was a rushed affair. We all met with our suitcases at checkout, left our bags with the bell stand, grabbed a quick breakfast at the buffet restaurant next to the Bull and Bear (closed that early in the day), then back to the lobby, and out to the taxi stand at 8:30. Almost 9:00 by the time we actually left the hotel itself. Lexington Avenue was a madhouse down as far as 33d where much of the traffic thankfully turned east for the Midtown Tunnel to Brooklyn and Queens. Despite not having moved all that fast, we arrived for the NCC meeting at close to 9:45. What a morning! NOT Philadelphia for getting around, especially with luggage.

The Black, Weiss and Muench meeting room was huge. The table was slightly oval and not even half full as yet. Unlike Philly, the meeting did not come close to starting on time. I thought about our 2:30 train to the Quaker City. Austin sat next to me. Tinker arrived a few minutes after the three of us and sat next to Martha behind us. The table eventually filled with Alan Maycroft calling the meeting to order at almost 10:30.

Discussion on the *Lancaster* SCHOOLS Status Conference that coming Thursday was surprisingly straightforward until we got to the issue of opening discovery. (CAL Board was a later addition to these cases and as such had missed all of the class certification briefing which had followed close on the heels of all of the initially served defendants answering complaints and with virtually no discovery of either the lead plaintiff's suitability to represent the class or of its counsel to do so as well.) Now, any number of defendants wanted to reopen those issues to take more meaningful discovery as a prelude to seeking a decertification. (Our research of Judge Kelly showed that this process would be a waste of time and money as his history of rulings in class actions as well as in this case were such that even if he allowed that discovery, it was so highly unlikely to be successful as to waste any resources pursuing that avenue.) We tried to talk about proof of actual injury by each class member as well as the derivatives of that point to no avail! The great divide seemed to be about whether to focus on the suitability of the class representation as opposed to determining which school districts would actually stay in the class. (That brought us to LAUSD, NYCSD, Philadelphia and other huge school districts that were filing their own suits in their home state courts.)

Not surprisingly, the outcome was no agreed upon plan, but the glaring hole in the entire discussion was an overall lack of anything approximating a scientific approach to the defense: a crying need for expert witnesses, or at least one of them! Essentially, there was no plan at all, not even a pretext of creating one!

We ate lunch as we talked. Any number of the attendees had trains or planes to catch. *LAUSD* was discussed as were others in which CAL Board was not a party. The same themes tended to recur with aberrational differences here and there brought about by the differences in the geopolitical make-up of the various judicial jurisdictions. At 1:45, we asked to be excused. Downstairs, a car was waiting to take us to Penn Station for the Philly train. We all met up at the Four Seasons, on Logan Circle, bisecting the magnificent Ben Franklin Parkway between City Hall, with William Penn atop its spire, and the Philadelphia Art Museum whose steps were so recently adorned with the "Rocky" statue.

Mace from D.C., Mary from our office and Scott Kelly were waiting in the bar when we finished our check-in and began to gather. On our ride up to our rooms, I noticed Martha got off at a different floor from my room (at least she showed some discretion). On the way to the bar, Martha got on the same elevator as me. We were alone. I said, "Different floor?"

She turned her head, and smiled saying, "I told Mary I would stay next to her. Hope that's OK?"

"Great!" was all I could come up with! We spent drinks and dinner rehashing New York. Some of us for a second time (our train ride had been my first). Later that night, I had a nice long talk with Mollie, who was home for two weeks in a row (and thereby absent from the Waldorf during our stay). She allowed that travel itself had become more exhausting and her job more intense as the competition continued to improve its products and its sales techniques. We talked about the kids, and right before I was ready to hang up, Mollie in a tired voice, said, "Ronan, I am really looking forward to a long love-making session with you when you get home. Sweet dreams!"

13

A Judge Kelly Experience

Judge Kelly's court room was immense. The counsel table for Plaintiffs was almost full with only two actual clients but a coterie of lawyers, more than a few with notable Southern accents. The defense spilled over from its counsel table to include an entire row of chairs inside the bar and the first row behind; those scheduled to only observe filled much of the remaining court room. Two other matters were on docket before ours, but both had been resolved before this hearing.

The court reporter was in place. Several U.S. Marshalls stood around the room scanning the assembled lawyers and perhaps a few clients. The bailiff came out of a chamber's door, strode to the forefront of an enormous bench and in a stentorian voice, cried, "ALL RISE! The United States District Court for the Eastern District of Pennsylvania is now in session, the Honorable James McGirr Kelly presiding!"

In flowing robes, with white hair and looking every inch a federal judge, His Honor climbed quickly to his seat, and as he sat, said, "You all may be seated."

"In the Matter of a SCHOOLS Class Action, counsel, please state your appearances for the record if you intend to speak when you are recognized by the Court. Mr. Berger, you may begin."

Attorney David Berger, a senior Philadelphia lawyer who portrayed himself as a master class action plaintiff litigator, strode a few steps to the podium, and as is the case with many lawyers, seemed to be intensely pleased with the sound of his own voice as he meandered for the Court about how this matter was moving forward not only expeditiously, but prudently. He was followed by several South Carolina plaintiff attorneys, most notably Ron Motley whose firm had broken away from a staid old Charleston firm when that firm's senior partner took an appointment to sit as Judge Blatt on the U.S. District Court bench in Charleston. He said many of the same things as David Berger but with a far more engaging accent. After seemingly an hour, Judge Kelly finally turned to the defense. Ms. Goines rose, addressed the Judge and suggested that there were motions to be argued first and then the matter of Case Management.

After a Motion to Amend an Answer was granted, I rose to address the Motion to Dismiss CAL Board for Lack of Venue now eight months pending in this Court, based on Austin Smith's Affidavit denying that CAL Board undertook any business whatsoever in Pennsylvania. That evidence was still unrefuted by Plaintiff *Lancaster*, but resolution of CAL Board's motion was delayed to allow that school district to conduct discovery which had garnered it nothing to date. So, I stated in words to that effect. One of Mr. Berger's associates rose, and without any show of temerity, went on about CAL Board's failure to adequately respond to discovery which was being negotiated with our local Philadelphia office. Our attorney Scott Kelly rose in rebuttal and flatly denied any such negotiations had taken place whereupon the Berger lawyer produced a copy of a letter that no one on our team had ever received. Judge Kelly shook his head and said, in effect, I am not here for a "He said, she said argument." Turning to the Berger lawyer, he said 90 more days to complete your discovery and that would be his final deadline. My first experience with Judge Kelly and I, foolishly, believed him to be a man of his word. (I asked Scott Kelly if we got any written opposition to our motion.) I continued standing and asked the Judge to order the Plaintiff's counsel to file and serve a written opposition to any motion following the Federal and Local Rules. He said, "But, of course, Why?"

"Because there was no written Opposition today and we feel sandbagged by this charade," as I sat, Mr. Berger jumped to his feet in defense of his associate decrying my crass comments as a Californian. Ron Motley was smiling. I rose, turned toward David Berger and said very slowly, "My mother is Mary Catherine O'Neill who served two terms in Congress during World War II representing Chestnut Hill, Mt Airey and other sections of Philadelphia. My Pennsylvania roots are deep and quite genuine. Your firm failed to serve an Opposition. In the future, we will seek sanctions from you for that kind of conduct."

Motley was almost laughing. Berger was aghast! Judge Kelly's face formed a slight smile. I sat again, as the Judge spoke: "My Order is unnecessary; but, because you are so concerned, I shall enter it. That Order will cover all parties and all counsel. Please give your mother my regards, counsel." *(Strange how I remember that part of that hearing so vividly even until I typed it today. When I first told Dr. Arnaud, it may have been one of the first humorous things I told her about my mother. I remember my psychiatrist saying, "You must be very proud of your mother.")*

— — —

The largest part of the Status Conference was a fight over the scope of the case, would it be bifurcated on liability? Any issues of statutes of limitations? Who would produce what documents and when? Much of this was unseemly at best. Some parties had tendered briefs, but most counsel sounded like they were shooting from the hip with their ideas.

Finally, Judge Kelly and many of us lawyers had had more than enough. The Judge said words to the effect that the parties had one year from that day to take whatever discovery in whatever form they believed useful. He also warned that failure to cooperate on documents or witnesses would not be tolerated. He set another Status Conference for six months to test compliance on discovery and to hear any motions. He would also accept briefs from each side on further Case Management and on Trial Structure (Class actions are very rarely fully tried. Most, but not at all, settle!)

— — —

Back at Scott Kelly's office, we gathered for a short rehash of the hearing. His office was on the way to the hotel. Dinner that night was at the Philadelphia Racquet Club where Scott was a member. It was cold and clear walking to that club. I spoke with Austin for a few blocks. Then Martha came up next to me. She reached something into my hand – her room key in an envelope. Without much thought, I put it in my pants pocket.

We drank for several rounds before dinner and the wine flowed freely; mostly white with the appetizers served family style, mostly red with the steak and roast beef which everyone but Mary, a vegetarian, enjoyed. After dinner, we waited for taxis a few minutes. Martha asked if we could talk about how to find an expert witness or two on the flight home. I allowed we could if we sat together.

Instead, the next day, when we met in the a.m. at Scott's office, the expert need came up as a topic. Several of the lawyers at Scott's firm did medical malpractice defense. Two of them had been to Harvard at different times. One had taken a course at Harvard Law in Public Health Basic Concepts from an M.D./Ph.D. who knew a great many leaders in that field, not just in the United States, but elsewhere. For example, that class had covered how an English epidemiologist was able to put together and track a study for over 12 years which essentially proved conclusively the causal link between cigarette smoking and lung cancer. When asked if we wanted to hear more, we all agreed it sounded worthwhile. We checked our calendars and set up a conference call for right before I had to leave for the *LAUSD* hearing in early February.

— — —

On the flight home, only I could get upgraded to First Class, but Martha was in Business from my earlier upgrade. Mary was in coach. After lunch, I went back to visit them both. When I got to Martha, the seat next to her was empty on the aisle. I slid my extra long frame into it. She leaned over and *sotto voce* said. "You never came to my room last night."

Only then did I remember her handing me her room key envelope. She could tell I had not remembered, but smiled, "Guess you didn't miss me that much?"

I responded that I was so exhausted that I would have been useless anyway, or words to that effect. She came back, "That's OK, Mary had a great time two nights in a row, thanks to you!"

— — —

When I came in the front door of our home, I was greeted by four beautiful children and a wife who looked downright glamorous. Mollie said, "You are going to sit through an early dinner for the children. Then they are going to have a movie night watching a new a Disney animation release, while we have a lovely dinner at the Buckeye and then come home to our cozy bed." And so all of that came to pass, but not until I unpacked my suits, finding that hotel room key in my pants, and discarding it that night in the Men's room trash at the Buckeye. We had a marvelous dinner, each starting with the "House Specialty of Oysters Bingo!" Later that night, while slightly tipsy, Mollie and I made passionate love: seemingly with more enthusiasm than we had assembled since the Twins were born some years before.

No feelings of foreboding, either, for a change!

14

Mullen Oral Argument

The afternoon before oral argument in *Mullen*, Judge Kendall did issue his Preliminary Ruling on the Defense Consolidated Demurrer Motion to dismiss the Mullen lawsuit. Mary brought a copy into my office, walked around my desk so she was alongside me as I began reading that paper on my credenza, and without a word, placed the order in front of my eyes with yellow highlighter on the following words;

> The Consolidated Demurrer of the Defendants in *Mullen vs. United States Gypsum et al* is SUSTAINED as to all Causes of Action WITHOUT Leave to Amend.

By the time I had read that twice, but before the impact of the decision had settled in, Lily buzzed me to say that Ken Allen was on the line to talk. I gestured for Mary to take a seat across from my desk, and put Ken on the speaker phone. He had Sandra with him. I still remember his words, "You were so right about how to proceed. This may go down as one of the great defense results in the history of California class action law!"

Sandra chimed in with her congratulations. Mary's face was wreathed in a huge smile. Then I said something like, "This is all well and good, but I cannot believe that the plaintiffs will take any of this lying down. And, there is a second paragraph to the order: any interested party can call a phone number and get a copy of the Court's entire Preliminary Ruling which sounds as if it might be like an actual opinion like you might get from a federal trial court.

Moments later, Lily entered while we talked holding several documents. She handed one to Mary and the other to me saying, "I only paused long enough to fax a copy to Mr. Tinker." It was eight pages. We agreed to read the document and talk again in a few minutes. I asked Lily to send it to about 10 different counsel around the state and Back East, especially Alicia Goines for National Gypsum, Fred Talcott for US Gypsum and Alan Maycroft for W R Grace.

The decision turned on key points that we stressed throughout our briefing: unifying themes that converged to defeat each different theory of recovery pleaded in the Complaint as different Causes of Action. First, the Plaintiff herself, Evelyn Mullen, had suffered no actual injury based on the facts alleged; and second, based on the Motion to Take Judicial Notice, which was GRANTED, the number of structures potentially covered by the suit was so large that the Court thought any recovery would fail at the appellate level (adding a lengthy footnote which almost directly quoted the footnote that Tinker and I caused to be incorporated in the final Motion as supported by the facts set forth in the statistics on California housing of which we had sought, and herein had ultimately been granted, Judicial Notice).

We got Ken back on the phone. He had put together a conference call for 5:30 with almost all of the lead defense attorneys. We had Tinker already on the line after we undertook our own quick discussion. Ken got to his point first, "I think you should be the one to argue this motion tomorrow. After all, you helped to write the final version, along with Sandy. (A pause.) But my feeling is that the great bulk of counsel will want me. If that is the case, please know, I would want you to sit second seat. What say you?"

I paused not to think, but to adjust my breathing (kind of like I would do on the free throw line in a game in college), "Ken, I respect you and have found working on this matter with you personally not at all onerous as I feared it might be. But, I do not believe that we should say anything in the first instance other than to thank Judge Kendall for the time and effort he put into coming up with this most difficult decision. As you doubtless know, if he does not change his mind on NOT AMENDING the Complaint, his ruling will most certainly be appealed. So, I would ask that you graciously step aside and let me be first chair with Sandra as our second, since we are the ones that did the bulk of the heavy lifting during the writing AND are best positioned to support the Judge in the face of any argument raised by the Plaintiff counsel. Your call now?"

"Let me think on it. We'll talk again at 5:30."

I did not make him happy when I ended the call with, "Ken, please no early meetings to which we are not invited." I hung up on the very last word, mindful of his meetings with national counsel preceding more fully attended meetings.

— — —

At 5:28, we called into the conference call. The host, Ken Allen, joined promptly at 5:30. The business discussion began two minutes into the call. Ken asked me to speak first. I told the group what I had told Ken little more than an hour ago. When I finished, Alicia Goines jumped in, "I was completely against that crazy idea on how to proceed in this case when first raised by Mr. O'Neill minutes into the very first time I met him. However, he was steadfast, and in the end, most logical. He won me over that day. I do not see that what he says really requires any discussion. Ken, I cannot imagine that Ronan would object at all to you being part of the lead defense team at the hearing as is your usual spot. I can see his point about Sandra as second chair and to me, that also makes sense. She has not proved to be any kind of shrinking violet. Ken?"

Alicia's strategy placed Ken Allen in a tough position: clearly he wanted to be recognized as, at the very least, a co-architect of this outcome, but at the same time, he had been in Alicia's camp at the outset in that pivotal first meeting. Plus, he was slow to come around and only did so after Alicia announced she was persuaded to go for a Demurrer instead of filing an Answer and then attacking the class as the defense's main strategy. Now, he would be at the table next to his daughter, but two seats down from the lead counsel on oral argument (I then wondered how many, if any of them, knew Sandra and I were once engaged and if that would impact Ken Allen's decision process).

No one else spoke and the silence had just begun to breed tension when Ken finally spoke, "Mr. O'Neill is a force. We are on opposite sides in other litigation as some of you may know. (He paused: WHAT NEXT?!) But he is a far better lawyer than I could have ever imagined he would turn out to be. It seems that he makes legal sense much of the time. Sandra has worked hard on this case and deserves credit, more than most of you will ever know. She should sit second chair and I will proudly sit by her side."

Alicia followed-up, "Let us hope that this final bit of strategy from Mr. O'Neill pays off tomorrow. Anyone else?"

Someone said, "So Moved." Another seconded and the call largely ended. I asked Sandra if she would drive to Martinez with me in the morning. We met at Hilltop in Richmond, where she parked and hopped in my Volvo. She leaned over toward me and gave me a kiss on the lips, saying, "You are more gracious than I ever think I could be. My father wants you back in the firm in the worst way when *Wallboard* is over."

— — —

Then we talked about Judge Kendall, his Opinion and what we actually thought Plaintiff's counsel would try. The hearing was set for 10:30. Parking near the Court in Martinez was brutal. Yet, we still had time for coffee in the courthouse basement before adjourning to Judge Kendall's court.

Arriving outside the courtroom, we encountered a throng of defense counsel. Ken Allen was among them, holding personal court. But when they saw Sandra and me, most of them broke off and came over to crowd around incoherently. The five drafting firms that had researched and written the different demurring arguments to each cause of action were among the first to offer congratulations. One even admitted he was more than a little upset with the changes that Sandra and I had made to his section to meet the Court's page limitation as well as to make the brief seem more cohesive than the original five diffuse arguments.

With about 5 minutes until the judge would call the matter, Plaintiff's lead counsel, Marvin Jones, came over, grabbed my elbow lightly and asked if we could talk. I agreed but there was little time. Instead, all he wanted was to thank me for having to address only one set of briefs and for making the record to date so clean. With that, I figuratively grabbed Sandra. And the three of us walked to the counsels' tables together, with Marvin splitting off to sit at the table nearer the jury box in the seat closest across the aisle from me at the opposing counsel table.

Judge Kendall's Bailiff called the room to order and the Judge took his seat looking down at counsel, "Good morning, Gentlemen and Ms. Allen. Does my Clerk have your appearances?"

A chorus of affirmatives rose from all those assembled for this one hearing. Then, "Mr. Jones, since my Preliminary Ruling is adverse to your client, I trust you would wish to be heard first?"

Marvin Jones rose to his full height, not a small man, and began in an elegant voice; talking about California civil procedure, about California substantive construction law, about California product liability law and how the nation looked to our state for guidance in that area, and lastly about asbestos, seeking to demonize it one more time as if this case was a personal injury case. He talked about Ms. Mullen and her deceased husband's house and how it contained a wide variety of building materials such as wallboard, the joint compound applied wet, dried, and sanded to create the smooth surface appearance of those boards, floor tiles and ceiling tiles, creating vast dust clouds when cut by power saws, as well as surface sprays, all of which had utilized asbestos as a component, and in powdered form, created dust clouds when mixed with water. After what seemed hours, but was actually less than one, he allowed, "Your honor, we have had the Mullen's house tested since the Consolidated Demurrer was filed. It has asbestos particles in the air in five of its eight rooms. We would request this Court change its ruling on amendment and allow Ms. Mullen to amend her complaint to reflect these new facts? We rest for now."

Judge Kendall looked down from his bench, then at the clock and said, "I have another matter at 2:00 today that needs to be heard. I will put it off for 30 minutes, but that's all I am going to allow on this matter. Let's take a real five minute break,"

We rushed to the restrooms. Sandra said only, "We talked about something like this. Do you have it?"

I nodded as I went in the Men's Room door.

Back in the Court Room, I went directly to the lectern as Sandra whispered to her father. "May it please this Court. The assembled Defense Counsel as well as many others who cannot be with us today, thank you for the time and energy you devoted to all of the briefing in this most novel lawsuit. Asbestos usage in construction has spawned what my team refers to as a series of 'Mass Torts.' This potential litigation would, if certified, lead to ever more tenuous causation pleadings and a concomitant exhaustion of resources, especially where no actual injury to the Plaintiff, or her property, is pleaded.

"Now, Mr. Jones comes here today and allows that testing has somehow detected an injury to Ms. Mullen's house. But even if you assume what he says does present some arguable form of injury, which the Defense does not concede for a moment, how is this putative class action going to come into being? Would every putative member have to undergo similar testing? Would that in itself be claimed as compensable? What if the testing showed nothing in many, or even most, cases? What if the ambient air outside the residence had asbestos particles? Where did those measured fiber particles come from? How did they get there?

"None of this is addressed by a mere assertion that some form of air testing revealed some uncertain amount of asbestos particles in some rooms of Ms. Mullen's house. This is far short of establishing a basis to plead any actual injury, or even beginning to do so.

"No, Your Honor, this is just the kind of slippery slope that your Order addresses by not allowing an Amendment. You possibly foresaw these, or many other, types of possible tactics to try to come up with some attenuated theory to support pleading a phantom basis of recovery where there is simply no actual, compensable injury to the Plaintiff who seeks to represent a gigantic, amorphous class with these types of ephemeral assertions as its linchpin. Thank you, Your Honor."

And so, Marvin Jones came back arguing that they had showed enough on a factual basis for one more try at the Gold Ring!

Sandra went up to the lectern to administer the *coup d' grace*: "Your Honor, imagine you somehow became convinced to certify this matter as a class, how would you go about ascertaining who would be class members suitable to have Ms. Mullen as their class representative. Admittedly, that issue is not before the Court here and now, but Counsel Jones invites you to open that door which would lead to an overwhelmingly enormous waste of resources with no actual explanation of how this last minute testing has shown any science-based actual injury giving rise to legal damages. We ask that you enter your Order as stated in your Preliminary Ruling."

Marvin Jones had one more thought to convey, "If this Court is inclined not to change its ruling, on behalf of the Plaintiff, we ask that you enter a Final Judgment immediately so that we may begin the appellate process expeditiously. Thank you, Your Honor!"

— — —

The Court did not change its ruling, but did enter the requested judgment. We still won! At the car, Sandra asked if we could stop for a celebratory drink. I shrugged not knowing any place to go on the way to Hilltop in Richmond, but she suggested a circuitous route past the Lafayette Park Hotel with its magnificent bar. She told me she could even take a room with a magnificent view.

I was learning at last: I took her up on the drink, even a second, but declined on the room at the outset. When I later dropped her at her car, we kissed warmly, more than amicably. But when I was driving home alone, I asked myself: Should I draw a brighter line for those with whom I would in the future transgress my vows to Mollie? And if so, on what side of that line would I find Sandra?

15

New Expert Source

In the days before going to Los Angeles for the *LAUSD* hearing, we had that conference call involving Tinker's office, our office and Scott Kelly's firm. One of Scott's younger partners, Ted Darrow, joined our call as the guest of honor. Scott gave more background than he had at our meeting little more than the week before, and he had circulated Ted's Firm Resume.

Ted explained that while an undergraduate at Harvard, he was taking a liberal arts type major to prepare himself for law school, including majors in French and Physical Sciences. For the latter, he had enrolled in a course which was sometimes taught by a then Teaching Assistant named Jeremy Nobel. This man, now about 12 years older than when Ted first knew him, continued to be associated with Harvard in the field of Public Health, which was the survey course Ted had taken. Turns out that Dr. Nobel had an M.D. and a Ph.D. in Public Health. Moreover, he was a direct lineal descendant of Albert Nobel. Ted had enrolled for a newsletter from Dr. Nobel and kept in touch loosely. How could he help?

My first reaction was to try to meet Dr. Nobel in order to see if he was what we were looking for. Ted, rather emphatically, did not seem to think that was a terribly good idea. He felt Dr. Nobel would not want to lend his name to any defense litigation position in such a vexatious public health area as asbestos. However, he might be willing to facilitate something, if a position with serious merit was brought to his attention. Toward that end, I asked if he thought we could get our meeting. Ted said he would make an inquiry; but in doing so, he would have to tell

Dr. Nobel something about the topic of the meeting.

I asked if we could have 5 -10 minutes to confer without Scott's office on the line. Mace said, "Seems we need to come up with a scenario that does not seem like we are trying to undermine public health, and possibly to help with it." Most of the others agreed.

Then, I said, "How about if we try to use one theme from the *Mullen* Demurrer footnote to the effect that this type of property litigation is so potentially expensive and wasteful that it potentially will swallow the funds available for BI litigation claimants and thereby do more harm than good for the real victims of asbestos use?"

Tinker added, "I like that. What if we tell him that the abatements being triggered under the current EPA rules and this litigation are actually unnecessary because the products are rendered safe when they are sealed in place, yielding the ultimate result that this whole grand abatement scheme would be needlessly exposing potential new cadres of workers as well as innocent by-standers to the asbestos fibers that are the by-product of abatement."

Ted and Scott were back in a minute. We rolled these ideas out for them, embellishing as we went along. Ted liked it. I asked Martha who had been keeping careful notes to put together a draft for us to review and have to Ted in the next few days. I also covered the need to advise the client and the people at Desert Mutual of this potential breakthrough. Lastly, I asked Ted if he felt we should try to go, hoping he would say "yes." He did.

— — —

Jeremy, as he ultimately asked me to call him, was at the beginning of teaching a second semester at Harvard. So, in response to Scott's request, allowed he felt he could not travel at that time, but did add that a meeting could take place if in

Greater Boston. The Good News: at least he did not say, "NO!"

Turned out that everyone on that initiating call wanted to go to Boston to meet with Dr. Nobel. No big surprise, I guess. He did seem brilliant as Ted presented him, and then again, there were his degrees and his relationship with Harvard, not to mention his lineage. First, I called Desert Mutual and spoke to Manny and Angela. They were still basking in our winning the Summary Judgment in *Wallboard* and the Demurrer in *Mullen*. At this moment, we were all heroes. We had sent them a fax with Martha's memo as sent to Dr. Nobel, via Ted. Otherwise, this call was something unusual. I blamed it on *LAUSD*, starting by saying I would have a report on that trip in a day or two, but that we were moving ahead on this one as well. (I pause to make clear that insurance carriers like Desert Mutual in the latter 1980's had almost an absolute right to totally control litigation. After all, they paid the attorneys, the experts, all of the associated expenses, and any settlement or judgment. Thus, winning cases, short of full trial with tens of millions dollars potentially on the line could save untold dollar amounts. Still, in this novel litigation, with teams of attorneys billing and an ever-mounting BI case load, the ever-mounting legal costs could become quite daunting for any carrier.)

I talked about Dr. Nobel and Ted in more detail, explaining that I thought we should have Ted along on the first meeting as he provided the underlying nexus for this relationship. They asked, and I agreed, if this might mean Ted's further involvement, and I allowed we might not want to rule that out. This became especially true when I broached bringing Martha. Fortunately, several months ago, they had bought into her as an excellent option to get up to speed on experts for both these Buildings cases and to try to find suitable experts for the BI cases. With me, that made three. So, I tried for Tinker. They balked, seeming reluctant. The bills were getting bigger. I allowed that if we had one Science and Medicine expert on each coast, and if we had to try cases, that would help immeasurably with savings on travel and expenses for pre-trial or depositions.

They relented! (After all, we were heroes in those days!)

I brought Martha into my office to tell her the general plan for the meeting. Ted had given us three dates and the only constraint on the site was Greater Boston. I asked Martha to talk with Ted to try to hone things. She allowed that she had been to Boston multiple times (Me: once on a trip with Mollie before the Coast Guard, and again on USCG duty with ultralow travel pay! Neither worth mentioning.) We had one BI lawyer there, Ramona Kinsley, who had recently broken away from a Boston insurance defense firm, and set up her practice to specialize in defending environmental litigation. I suggested that Martha see if we could use her office after the meeting. She was located in a third floor walk-up in a not especially fashionable block of Newberry St. according to Martha.

We ended up staying at the Copley Plaza Hotel on Copley Square, about a five block walk to Ms. Kingsley's office. We arranged a conference room at our hotel for the meeting. Martha booked us on a 7:00 a.m. flight to Boston so we could have a nice dinner at Loch'Ober on arriving. She made certain Ted would be there for dinner so we could discuss the meeting the next day, including any further planning with him. Only a week or so away: Winter in Boston: California clothes!

Tinker called. He had thought about Boston. He really did not care for travelling all that much. Neither did Mace, whose wife was not 100% healthy. So, he said he thought that in the long run, Tod would be the better attorney to acquire the necessary skills to work with Martha and me. I said, "Me?"

I remember Tinker saying, "Sometimes, I think you underrate just how smart you are. Since I've known you, nothing seems to be all that hard for you to grasp. Certainly, none of this science or medicine to date has caused you a problem. Your only real problem is spreading yourself too thin. Me, I just cannot commit to a whole lot more. Remember, I do have other clients, too!"

So, we ended up with Ted from Philly and Tod from D.C. Martha thought the proximity of those two names was pretty funny. So did Mollie when I first told her what Tinker had said. But after she thought about it for a few minutes, she came back with something like, "Maybe you should listen to Tinker about spreading yourself too thin."

I retorted, "Look who's talking!! You are travelling as much as me and working harder on your flights."

"By the way, a new *au pair* starts tomorrow, "Ingrid. She's Norwegian. Very nice. Been in D.C. two years. We'll be her second family. The last one had 5 children. Glowing recommendations. They're moving to Minneapolis. Too many Scandinavians there for Ingrid! She wants to see the West Coast." Mollie said laughing at her juxtaposed humor.

— — —

The flight to Boston went off without a hitch with both of us ending up in First Class. Martha worked most of the way putting together an outline for the meeting. (She had a new laptop computer, an overnight sensation with the ever-swelling digital crowd.) It was just a two-night trip, so baggage was easy as was the taxi ride to the Copley Plaza Hotel, a grand old dowager of a place on an immense public square with an Episcopal Cathedral, a sizeable park and a huge paved area big enough for thousands to assemble, as they did on Summer weekends. The wind howled as we made our way inside for check-in and then off to our rooms. Why was I not surprised when we had adjoining rooms? Mine was a corner, hence larger and had a pleasant view of the expansive plaza below.

Dinner was at 6:00 at Loch'Ober in a hidden little street across a somewhat bigger side street holding the main entrance to the once famous Filene's department store, with its gigantic discount basement and its always chaotic annual bridal gown sale. We found Ted in the bar waiting for us. Tod was to fly up from D.C. on an early commuter for the meeting tomorrow. Our table was in the old main dining room on the first floor with two sides bordered by the giant serving bar holding giant shining silver serving dishes, by then, little more than century-old museum pieces in what had become a rather high turnover lunch spot having once been Ober's main fare before the two merged and became an incredibly swank restaurant after World War II.

We had cocktails and shared a big shrimp cocktail to save space for Lobster Savannah, the house specialty that each of us ordered. Interestingly, Ted who had wanted to come to this 200 hundred year old restaurant picked up the tab after regaling us with a story about a movie called *The Verdict*, starring Paul Newman and James Mason, about a medical malpractice trial in Boston wherein the James Mason character, head of a huge defense trial team, says to a down trodden associate, "Mr. Smith, you stay here and get that research straight. The rest of you can join me for dinner at Loch'Ober!"

The three of us taxied together back to the Copley Plaza. We decided to have a one drink night cap in the hotel's famous bar with its huge roaring fireplace and oversized stuffed brown leather furniture not to be seen again in the decades to follow. Ted said he could only spend a few minutes because he wanted to talk to his three-year old daughter before she went to bed for the night. She missed her Daddy who hardly ever travelled on his job.

Martha and I talked about our conversation with Ted at dinner. He seemed terribly bright to be working in a defense firm like Scott Kelly's place. Then Martha said, "You seem terribly bright to be working in a defense firm like Klein Kelly. May I ask how you ended up there?"

I responded, "Only if you tell me how you ended up at our

firm as well." said with a smile, and went on, "Seems I had cold feet at the last minute about taking the job at the firm where I had been clerking my last year of law school. So, I looked around, called my friend Tinker who was at Klein, Kelly and Weinberg as it was known then. Next thing I knew, I interviewed and was hired on the spot."

Martha seemed to look ever so slightly downward so her eyes came up to me from under her brows, and holding my eyes for a second, said, "Any truth to the rumor that you were engaged to Sandra Allen and that was the firm you decided not to join?"

I did not know that our engagement was really a secret. I never talked about it, even with Mollie. So, "That's never been a secret. I decided not to take the job. Things went rather poorly, rather immediately and the engagement ended abruptly. Now, Sandra and I are OK. We can work together as in *Mullen*, and we are cordial on opposite sides in *Wallboard*. Plus, now I have Mollie and four kids! How about you?"

"I'll tell you upstairs," Martha said as she signed the drink tab and we rose to retire for the evening.

Later, with our heads facing each other, Martha said, "I saw this great looking guy when I was interviewing with Reggie Fox. I got two offers, essentially the same terms. So, I took the one where the handsome guy worked. Now we have sex on occasion. That was all I was after anyway. Plus, I like the work. The pay is good. As are the fringes, especially that guy."

— — —

Jeremy Nobel was about my age, perhaps a few years younger. He was tall, in shape, and dressed like a professor in those days (after I came to know him better, I concluded that if he lived in California, he would be more of a Hippy-type). Tod arrived early. Ted made introductions all-around. Jeremy was direct, asking, "You all obviously think I can do something for you. Please explain. I hope you do not mind if I ask questions when they occur to me?"

We all had the outline created by Martha, except for Jeremy. I began with that, "We would like to retain you as a consulting expert to help us perhaps meet people like yourself who might prove willing to testify in certain types of asbestos-related litigation, the type involving asbestos abatement from buildings where the products do not produce airborne fibers and those potential friable fibers are encapsulated in the product or surrounded by other product." I explained that we would provide him with our full outline at some point, but we hoped he would first focus on our message, including how we perceived this overall litigation could best be resolved on the basis of differing types of plaintiffs, exposures and injuries as well as our client and its insurer's willingness to settle the "right BI cases with a fair contribution."

Jeremy had questions, but he quickly grasped the differentiation we were drawing between the BUILDINGS class actions and mega-cases, like *LAUSD*, with their potentially disproportionately gigantic cash payments if those cases were to begin to settle, resulting in the inability to pay out smaller sums to deserving BI claimants in future decades.

After almost 2 hours, as we broke for lunch, Dr. Nobel's casual conversation seemed to indicate he was buying in. He began to ask about U.S. experts. At that point, I let Martha take over as she had a dossier of sorts on virtually all of those who had tried and been damaged in cross-examination, many to the point where they were essentially rendered unusable at all. We stayed talking in a sequestered section of the Hotel restaurant, adjacent to last night's bar, until about 2:30. Jeremy departed on an optimistic note saying he would get back to Ted and Martha within the next week or so after he had taken enough time to try to assess a potential role for himself in all of this.

We adjourned to Ms. Kingsley's firm, a charming 3d floor walk-up in a building like many we had passed by so far on this trip. After almost 3 hours on the phone while postulating or hypothesizing what might happen with Mace and Tinker, we decided to break up. Ted and Tod both wanted to get home that night, so they headed to Logan Airport. Tod had the best of it because he could catch a shuttle to D.C. Ted needed to do a scheduled flight. We invited Ramona to dinner and she asked if we would mind going to the Bar in the Copley Plaza for a light meal. After the lunch and last night's Lobster Savannah, that sounded great. By 8:15, Martha and I were headed upstairs. She waited until the elevator door closed and we were alone, "I hope you won't mind, but I would like to try something a bit different tonight. Would you come to my room when I give you a ring? It's a surprise."

It was, and our relationship began to evolve quite differently from the way it started.

16

LAUSD Case Management

I was getting exhausted from the non-stop legal activity, not to mention the extracurricular activity in which I engaged from time to time. On the eve of my flying to Los Angeles for the CMC on *LAUSD*, Phil came into my office and asked to talk. He explained how his role was proving pivotal in some of our biggest cases, while I moved from case to case, he was doing a lot of the heavy lifting with discovery and motion writing. Moreover, now he would be doing the briefing on *Mullen* with Mary Smith in addition to the *Wallboard* appellate briefing and he had just put our CAL Board *LAUSD* brief on Case Management to bed, causing it to be filed yesterday. He asked if he could get two things: a raise of $750/month; and second, some time to work on BI cases to round out his skills (which meant his giving up one of our big cases). I thought for a minute. Mary was maxed out on her workload and there really was no one else. Martha was doing Science and Medicine (I refused to call it, or write, "S & M"), but spent the actual bulk of her time on BI matters where Reggie considered her a whiz. She was a natural at it and had good rapport with the plaintiff lawyers as well. I told him I would see what I could do and get back as soon as I could. (Something about our conversation, including the way he left my office, gave me the sense that he had been approached with another job offer!)

I went in to see Klein and he asked Kelly to step in. I explained what had happened, and what I thought we needed to do. Reggie, Phil, Mary and Martha were all associates. Reggie should make partner very soon. He was an African-American and we were an Oakland firm—making him a great fit, and rel-atively unique for a defense firm in those days. Still, I sensed them balking. The other three were also invaluable. My team's five other associates, one paralegal and two clerks, besides Deirdre, were all good, but not exceptional. They didn't say much of anything. So, I went on asking for $600/month for Phil and Mary, $750 for Reggie, and $400 for Martha, the newest of the key group. I explained that we needed to maintain credibility with Desert Mutual if we wanted to continue to get all of this work FOR THE WHOLE STATE OF CALIFORNIA for the fore-seeable future. When I said the whole state, I think a light went off.

Klein said, "Do we have any BI cases in LA County?"

The answer was not for now, but that will change, and it won't take long. CAL Board had a plant in Long Beach for Heaven's sake. Then I mentioned the profitability of my team. That was a trump card, but a potential sore point as well, so I just slid it past them at the end. After they had huddled while I went to the restroom and checked my messages, I was called back in. Kelly said, "What about you? Do you want more?"

"Only if you think more is fair, but what I need is to hang onto my key people." They both got up, came around the desk and shook my hand.

Kelly said, "Spoken like a true gentleman! You can have what you want for them, and $2,000/month more for yourself. More than anyone, we do not want to lose you, Ronan!"

I went straight to my office and called Phil in. When I gave him the news on the money, he beamed from ear to ear. But I had not covered his second request, so I asked him to see if he could find Reggie and to send him in. "Reggie, I have three things with which to deal; first, starting this pay period, you are getting a $750/month raise; second, you are to become a partner as of right now, Congratulations; and third, Phil wants to take on BI case responsibility and work more in the field with you.

As you know, Phil is a really good lawyer and we do not want to lose him. So, I would like to do that, but it means I have to take him off one of my big cases. I'm thinking *LAUSD* as it's just really getting started. So, who could help?"

Reggie, wincing said, "Martha is my best and brightest, by far! I simply cannot give her up entirely, especially with Phil just getting started on BI cases. How do we do it?"

"What if we fully tier the associates under you with Phil, Mary and Martha in between? They would be able to delegate with your approval. It would help the new people as well as keeping you from getting stretched beyond your control; and maybe get the newer, younger attorneys more involved, faster."

Reggie took a deep breath, "Do you think that will really work? All of the BI associates already have me on top? Would these be mini-teams?"

"Yes and no, when you become a partner next week, this tiering will be more appropriate, mindful that Martha is newer, but a bit older than any of the others. By the way, she got a smaller raise than Phil or Mary. Yours was the biggest. I trust you do want to be a partner?"

On his way out, I asked if Martha was in the office. She was not.

As I got ready to go home, I saw Martha come in. I asked her to step into my office. She looked exhausted. I said, "Are you OK?"

When she settled into her chair, she nodded her head affirmatively. I looked at her, but not right in those eyes, "Klein, Kelly and I had a discussion today after I had a meeting with Phil earlier today. Then I met with Reggie, Phil again, now you and I will see Mary tomorrow. There are going to be some changes. Phil wants to work more in BI to get more hands-on litigation experience as well as to work in the BI area. To do that, he will have to not work on one of my big cases. I decided it would be *LAUSD*. We are making Reggie a partner next week.

Phil, Mary and you will work directly under Reggie on the BI cases with delegation ability to the more junior associates to help control all of our workloads. You will assist me, along with Mary, on the *LAUSD* matter. Also, you have a raise of $400/month starting next week."

Martha's chin sagged ever so slightly as I was going on. When I stopped, she closed her mouth visibly/no sound. She shook her head slightly: all of her dirty blonde hair seemed to move, "What can I say? My two favorite people in the office and even more opportunity and responsibility with more money AND me a relatively new associate, but no longer junior. Thank you!" (And *sotte vocce*: "I cannot give you a hug here, but hopefully soon.")

"So, are you good with all of this?"

"Absolutely" was her response. So, I asked her to change her schedule to go to Los Angeles the next afternoon for the hearing at 9:30 on Thursday and then on to Phoenix the following day to meet with the carrier types and Austin Smith in Scottsdale on Friday. I would stay over for a USCG day on Saturday in Phoenix. She asked if she could stay Saturday night at her own expense and I agreed.

— — —

Mary was delighted the next day with her news as was Phil with the rest of his. Martha and I caught a 2:00 Pacific Southwest Air (PSA) flight to LAX. We stayed at the Sheraton on Sepulveda at the foot of Bunker Hill. The Los Angeles County Court House, Central District, was on the top of that hill. A tiring walk, but a relatively short distance, making it a $5 taxi ride with a big added tip.

We went to dinner at the Club Car, just west of Downtown. The atmosphere was different, the food was great, the drinks big and the bill more than I expected for a one course meal, but I was full. Martha was somewhat subdued during dinner and I asked her about that when we were taxiing back to the hotel. She said the last few days had been a bit overwhelming and she was behind on her sleep. I did not give voice to my next thought. In the lobby I asked Martha if she wanted a night cap. She thought for a second, smiled and said, "How about in your room."

She had two sips, pulled off her shoes, and laid on my bed. She was asleep in seconds. I got ready for bed. When I went to wake her, she rolled toward me, pulled me down and then things started happening. She seemed very well rested after such a brief nap!

— — —

Department 31, the Courtroom of the Honorable Bernard Weitzman: Charlie O'Reilly for the Plaintiff with two other lawyers. Guessed correctly that one was from LAUSD itself. The defense seemed to fill the rest of the Court. Avery Schein of Glass, Schmidt and Schein was the self-appointed spokesman for most of the LA defense types in the room. His client was U.S. Gypsum (USG). I made my appearance and for Martha as well. So did the others.

Judge Weitzman allowed that he had read all of the Case Management Conference briefs and had preliminary comments: there would be a bifurcation; the Statute of Limitations would be the first trial issue, since it was an affirmative defense to the Complaint, the Defense would go first and have the burden of proof (and of going forward, although not voiced); each side should plan to minimize the number of counsel actually trying the case, if at all possible. Trial would start the Monday following Memorial Day; no motions, except pretrial matters could be filed after 15 February; and Discovery would close 15 April.

O'Reilly rose and made four requests, all simple, all granted without opposition. Mr. Schein strode to the lectern, "May it please this Court, US Gypsum was the party requesting the number of defense counsel actually trying this case be reduced as the issue of Statute of Limitations is essentially straight-forward. Of the 33 defendants present through counsel today, 29 have agreed that my firm shall act as the lead defense firm. The other four have not been heard from. May I have the Court's permission to poll those firms now?" Judge Weitzman agreed and Mr. Schein proceeded. The first 2, for minor client players in the case, agreed. The third allowed that he and his client had not yet been able to confer, but thought their answer might well be "NO."

I was last, "CAL Board does not have a sense that any trial involving Mr. O'Reilly would ever be straight forward and sees no reason to waive its own constitutionally guaranteed right to a jury trial, Your Honor. I look forward to the honor of representing my client before a famous jurist and a renowned adversary."

"Thank you, Mr. O'Neill, we shall look forward to working with you," from Mr. Schein.

"Thank you, Mr. Schein. Oh, by the way, what lawyer from your firm will be your lead trial counsel?"

He looked at me a bit askance, "Rodman Gorman will have that task."

The hearing continued another 30-40 minutes, but the real business was done. Charlie O'Reilly came over to me on the way out, saying, "Should be fun to go up against a youngish Irishman for a change. Don't suppose you know the history of the O'Neills and the O'Reillys in Ulster centuries back?"

I smiled, introduced Martha Walsh, and then said, "Ah, sure but you might be referring to when the O'Neills were the Kings of Ulster and the O'Reillys from time-to-time coveted that throne openly, but never successfully!"

He smiled, a wide smile and this time with a wicked grin,

replied, "This game is on, Lad, and there'll be no prisoners."

I smiled back saying, "No quarter given, and none asked!"

AND the game truly was on from that point forward: AND there were NO PRISONERS!

One of Alicia Goines' partners came over to us following that exchange and whispered, something to the effect: Alicia told me to tell you that her money's on you, especially if the Defense uses Rod Gorman.

— — —

We taxied from the L.A. Court House to LAX and caught a PSA flight to Sky Harbor in Phoenix. We got a sedan at Hertz, right next to Terminal Two, drove up 44th Street to Camelback, then made a right going a mile or so. The Phoenician still functioned as "Club Fed," Charles Keating's biggest project before his indictments and the biggest federal takeover resulting from its payout by the Federal Home Loan Bank Board of hundreds of millions of dollars to Keating's depositors who trusted their funds to his defunct Savings and Loans. (For its first annual CAL Board defense meeting, the Biltmore had given a huge discount to DMIC to get the business. Manny believed they saw the Phoenician as their biggest rival in the entire Phoenix area in the years to come.) The rooms were still an excellent price. We checked in, rolled our bags to our rooms (adjoining as always), unpacked and called the Claims folks at Desert Mutual. They had made a reservation at our hotel's Terrace Restaurant. We had enough time to make some calls, change and get up to the Terrace. Dudley, Manny and Angela were all going to join us for dinner (Must be a bigger deal if Dudley was showing up.)

We met at our table overlooking the green swathe of Hohokam Park below while also affording an astonishingly close view of the final flight path for westbound landing approaches to Sky Harbor. When everyone was seated, I was between Dudley and Angela, with Martha between Manny and Dudley (no conspiring by the two women), we first ordered cocktails. When they arrived, so did our menus; but beforehand, Dudley raised his glass and said, "We seem to spend a great deal of time these days talking about our environmental cases here at Desert Mutual. It's no longer just asbestos, now groundwater contamination is becoming a big issue and there are all sorts of toxins out there that underwriting never foresaw as risks. This area of claims is becoming our biggest headache, and cash drain. And CAL Board is still our biggest risk. We have years of coverage with relatively low deductibles for each case, and they are getting named with increasing frequency. The bright spot, so far, is the work that you and your people are doing, Ronan. Despite the massive exposure, we feel confident in you and your network. So, here's to your continued success. Young Lady (looking at Martha), Mr. O'Neill is a treasure. He actually tries to end cases in short order and he is clever at finding solutions that seem to escape so many others. You can learn a great deal from him. We all have. Look at Gerry Dwyer, she got a promotion to go to the Hartford and has already been promoted there for instituting many of the same claims strategies that we have come upon here in no small part based on recommendations by you, Ronan."

They all gave a "Hear! Hear!"

Martha looked nonplussed, "He has been marvelous to work with in the brief opportunities I've had."

I felt like I was turning red. Angie said, "The one problem we have is we do not see enough of you, Ronan. You always seem to have something new for us. How about tonight?"

I looked at Manny who nodded for me to talk next, "I have a couple of major initiatives I would like to talk about: One for tonight is Dr. Nobel. For tomorrow, an idea to try in order to reduce the increasing volume of BI cases. But first, maybe we should order something? Martha and I did not have lunch in getting here."

When the waiter took our dinner order, we had another round of drinks. Dudley knew the least about Dr. Nobel, while Martha probably knew the most. So, I asked her to explain the background of why and how we found him. When she was done, I explained that as we had left Boston, there were issues that Jeremy Nobel wanted to consider carefully.

One was what, if anything, could he do that might help redirect the Plaintiff Bar away from the BUILDINGS cases. He had called and left a message which I got an hour or so ago after checking into my room. Dr. Nobel wants to have another meeting with just Martha and me as he has to fly to San Francisco for a quick conference in two weekends. He asked if we could have dinner, "Do one of you want to meet him? If so, I think we should invite Austin Smith as well?"

I waited. Dudley looked at Manny and Angela. He seemed to look inwardly for a few seconds. Finally, he said, "Since this could be something novel, I hate to pull rank, but I think I shall be the one to go to San Francisco. Please provide the details of where and when. And, yes, I think Austin should most definitely be there. He has proven to be a staunch ally in all of this."

We settled into more discussions, sometimes in two small groups. Manny was talking with Martha when Dudley excused himself, and Angela leaned a little closer, saying, "Any chance to get together one night while you're here this time?"

I explained that Martha was staying over and our rooms were so close that she might be seen which would make any assignation a bad idea. She seemed to understand that. Then I told her that I would try to come back sooner and alone. That caused her to smile. Clearly, Angela might be a potential problem waiting to manifest itself at some point down the road.

— — —

Before Martha arrived that night, I tried Mollie at the Waldorf, her last night in NYC. Her receiver seemed to get picked up, but then as happened several months before, instead of a voice, all I heard were what seemed to be deep breathing sounds. Strange! So, I hung up, tried again, and the same sounds were repeated!!

— — —

The next day, Martha and I got to Desert Mutual by the appointed 10:00. We reconvened from dinner with the addition of Richard Goldberg who was in charge of Casualty Claims and reported to Manny as did Angela.

I reported leaving a message for Dr. Nobel, hoping that four of us would not scare him off, suggesting some restaurants, and asking for details on his weekend in San Francisco. Next, I began to explain my thoughts on trying to change the dynamic in the BI litigation where the volume of cases threatened to overwhelm some carriers, many clients and even smaller defense firms. My strategy was about money, so I began by explaining that every case had incremental costs that drove the overall price of litigation upward for all of the participants in all of those suits, especially with too many defendants actually having no potential for liability payments in a great many of the cases. This was true for Plaintiff counsel as well. (Some of them wanted volume to encourage mass settlements to save on a defendant's overall cost of defense [A/K/A "Block Settlements:" Fool's Gold as we all had agreed long ago!].)

At this time, and over several years now, our office had been, and was currently, involved in over 700 cases. We also had resolved almost 400. Of that second number, only 31 had settled, with just that one having been tried, then settled. Putting aside that more than a few of these cases had plaintiffs who were not actually injured, we estimated that between 10 and 15% of the cases actually involved CAL Board as a viable defendant. What I proposed was that Desert Mutual Claims consider, and if they agreed, that I begin by going to Austin Smith and suggest that we settle the "REAL" cases against CAL Board sooner and at a slightly higher dollar number than had been forthcoming in the past; coupled with explaining to each lead plaintiff counsel that we wanted to stop wasting so much asset on the defense of useless cases with no real chance of a Plaintiff recovery against our client, and that going forward, each of them would make a very real effort to forebear from meaninglessly naming CAL Board in all of their construction product cases (and it would save those plaintiff counsel money as well by reducing their processing/litigation costs.).

When I paused, Dudley was the first to speak, "How would you convince Austin Smith that this is a good idea? And how about Plaintiff counsel?"

My rejoinder, "As to Austin, we will get him to see that the money you all save on defense costs will allow you to defend all of these cases for a much longer time. In other words, wasting your insurer's assets is never a very good idea in the long term. Austin, as I'm sure you all know, is a long view thinker, able to grasp multiple time frame scenarios and how they will all fit together. He was truly quick in rejecting any type of Block Settlements because he could see that going down that road only encouraged the less scrupulous attorneys to name his company in every suit without cause or investigation. This convincing may prove hard, but we need to try.

While, at the same time, I will try to appeal to the self-interest of the individual Plaintiff's counsel by explaining that by naming CAL Board in cases where they have no real chance for a recovery not only wastes our client/insurer's assets, but it also wastes their own assets in having to pay all those fees to serve process, then deal with our tactics in all those cases in which they virtually always ultimately dismiss CAL Board without payment since we will not pay tribute solely to avoid a trial. In other words, with a little sweetener of a bit more money on their revenue side for meritorious cases, and much less expense, particularly if they do this with added select defendants who agree to change their tactics like us, then their operation can become far more profitable."

After further discussion, they all agreed. We went to the Biltmore for a late lunch. Had a few drinks and the four claims people left. Martha said, "What now?"

We both had ideas we wanted to indulge, and we did so. But one thing stood out: that afternoon, I heard Martha make a sound much like the one I heard on my call to the Waldorf the night before!

17

The Calm Before The Storms

Two events had to occur before I could make my way to Los Angeles and the *LAUSD* trial, Phase 1, Statute of Limitations Trial: Our meeting with Jeremy Nobel in San Francisco and a trip to Philadelphia for an NCC meeting. Of course, there was my getting ready for the trial itself and preparation for my own downtime on other matters while in trial.

Dr. Nobel's professional meeting was at the Hyatt Embarcadero. Austin was planning to spend the night because Dudley would be doing so. Since our other three attendees were going to be staying there, and dinner was not to start until 7:00 to account for Dr. Nobel's Meeting Agenda that Friday night, Dudley suggested that Martha and I spend the night as well. Mollie was not thrilled as she was spending so many week nights alone on the road. With no wives invited, I could not bring her. At least my USCG Reserve duty the next day was at Coast Guard Island, Alameda. So, I would be home by 4:30 that Saturday afternoon. I asked Mollie if she wanted to go out that night, but she graced me with a resounding, "NO!"

Mary, Martha and I were getting ready for the *LAUSD* trial in small increments. Tinker had finished his Motion for Summary Judgment on the entire limitations matter and we filed it several days before the Motion Cut-off Date. (I remained concerned only that it gave all the other litigators and the Court a road map of most of our case. Still, it should not be factually refutable, the key to winning the motion and avoiding trial.) Mary and Deirdre created sub-files for each of the witnesses we would call or were likely to be called by the other sides.

Each such file contained the entire deposition, if deposed; that deposition indexed by page and line numbers to key testimony; a summary of their potential testimony, their employment history, and any critical documents for their testimony as well as their contact information. Martha and Deirdre would be in charge of insuring the timely attendance of all witnesses. (The parties had waived the need for subpoenaing persons under a party's control. However, all others, including retired personnel, needed to be served.) In this process of assuring attendance of witnesses, we came to learn for the first time that Frank Smith, the LAUSD Health Officer, who was the recipient addressee for the Wilson Riles warning letter, which created the trigger date to start the statute running, had died suddenly very recently. He was not deposed because we were told he was ill, and unavailable. (We found his replacement's ID information and added him to the LAUSD witness list with notice to Mr. O'Reilly. We also asked that we be allowed to depose him although the Discovery Cut-off Date had occurred a few days before. Our request was ignored by all.)

On this note, I arrived at the Hyatt Embarcadero with Martha. We checked into our rooms, adjoining as always, and went to freshen up. Alone in the elevator, I told Martha that I had USCG on SAT a.m. at 0800 on Coast Guard Island, so I would have to be up by 0600 and on my way by 0715. I was ordering breakfast in my room if she wanted to join me. She said she would let me know later.

We were all to meet in the main Hyatt restaurant in the lobby with its vaulted 20-something story ceiling and all of the room walkways looking down at the sprawling lobby floor layout below. Not my favorite hotel by a long shot, but quite popular for meetings and with tourists. I was 15 minutes early, but I found Dudley and Austin already imbibing at the huge Lobby Bar just inside the Restaurant's entrance. I joined them and ordered a double Stoli on the rocks with a twist. While waiting, and listening to my clients, I spotted Dr. Nobel across the Lobby. At that same moment, his attention seemed diverted to the Restaurant's entrance. There, arriving with a flourish of sorts, in the same blue dress I had seen some months before in the Mayflower Dining Room, was Martha. She saw Jeremy looking at her, waived and started toward him. (I started toward where they would intersect, then stopped abruptly. Jeremy had asked for Martha by name. Could there be an ulterior reason? Was I jealous?) Having waited, I watched Martha start to shake his hand, but he drew her to him, and kissed both of her cheeks, ever so European. A few words exchanged and they both turned to see me now approaching them.

At dinner, Dr. Nobel sat between Martha and me. Austin was on my other side and Dudley was across. We made introductions, talked about his "conference," said to be highly interactive with the other attendees and quite meaningful in the expanding field of Public Health, ordered dinner, and while enjoying our second round of drinks, began to get down to the business of the evening. I asked Jeremy if he was comfortable in talking as we all shared the attorney-client privilege (He too as a potential conferring consultant). When he said, YES, I asked him to tell us his thoughts since our first meeting. He did, "When I first heard about your initiative from Ted Darrow, Ronan, I thought that it represented something different, but did not have an intuitive sense of its potential monetary enormity or any evolved concept of how I might fit in. Yet at our meeting when you recited your version of what Ted had told you about Dr. Doll's epidemiological study on the relationship between smoking and lung cancer, I must have subconsciously begun to formulate how I might be able to assist. This was reinforced by the thoughtful way you described some of the vices of this essentially needless litigation moving forward and potentially consuming vast financial resources, while diverting much of the money from more utilitarian social uses, not the least of which being the protection and treatment of the very real extant cadre of workers, and perhaps average citizens, like spouses, who have been, or might be, harmed by this very real, and continuing, exposure to asbestos fibers over decades caused by the potentially needless renovations resulting from this litigation.

"After our meeting, I came to realize that the very people who could do the most to help you in stopping this wasteful litigation here in the U.S. are the very same experts who are acting as the Plaintiffs' champions, like Dr. Selikoff. That got me to wondering who would do this, and my thoughts went back to your story, Ronan.

"How about if we try to involve Sir Richard Doll himself? Of course, he works out of the Ratcliffe Infirmary in Oxford, and he does not like to fly. But still, what say you"

To say this little speech was jaw-dropping for the four of us would be a gross understatement. Several of us talked at once and the discussion continued on through most of the meal, with a few breaks here and there. In the end, we settled on Dr. Nobel alone making an initial approach to Sir Richard, preferably in person. (They had met when Sir Richard had won the Nobel Prize in Medicine some years before, and again when Dr. Doll was elevated to the peerage by the Queen, herself being pleased to meet Dr. Nobel.) Dudley was almost dumbstruck by Jeremy. Dudley and I could see the power of a knighted expert on an American witness stand. This might prove a course to winning some of these cases, perhaps even putting an end to all of this *faux* abatement type of litigation.

Jeremy, as he now insisted on being called by all of us, allowed at 10:00 p.m. that he needed to be off to bed as it was 1:00 a.m. in Boston. Once he left, after again bestowing the dual French buss on Martha whom he had not ignored all night, we had a night cap and retreated as a group to our various rooms. Mercifully, neither Dudley nor Austin got off at our floor. Martha did not stop at her door, but went directly to mine.

She went to the adjoining room door, opened it, then turned around. Reaching behind her back the dress zipper was down in a flash and her dress fell to the floor instantly. She kicked off her shoes, laid back and asked if I would like to do the Honors? I did. Once again I heard that breathing sound and now I knew its source for certain!

— — —

That Saturday night, I listened when Mollie and I made love, did I hear that same sound? Just imagining things?

— — —

Weeks flew by! So much to do, so little time!

Time for Philadelphia: fly to Dulles, taxi to the Mayflower, meeting at Tinker's firm the next day. At SFO, who should I encounter but Sandra Allen. She said, "I am going to spend the day tomorrow with Elaine and her son. Do you mind if I join you on the flight and taxi ride?"

"Delighted," was my response as it seemed we were allies again. Our Appellate Opposition Brief to their client's appeal would be filed next week. So, for the present, we were both fellow NCCs. After dinner that night, while lying in my bed, I pondered that same sound heard on the Waldorf room phone, brought on by the same techniques I had used on Martha, but without the seemingly same significant affect on Mollie. How interesting?

— — —

The meeting in Philadelphia at Alicia's office began timely, but bogged down quickly on the *LAUSD* trial. Any number of those in attendance were not very happy with USG's choice for trial counsel. It appeared that Rod Gorman had alienated more than one or two of the lawyers at the table. These sought to have him replaced, among them, Alicia. As the bantering continued, I stayed tuned since I had never met Mr. Gorman. Words like self-important and rigid were used.

However, because he was a Naval Academy grad and a fighter pilot, many thought of him as a team player (I thought of the Tom Cruise character in TOP GUN – anything but a team player!). Finally, 3 or 4 of the lawyers for other entities asked Fred Talcott, USG's NCC, if they could participate in work-ups during the pre-trial. He only offered to check with Mr. Schein. (Left me wondering how much real power the USG NCC team actually wielded?)

Then came the issue of expert witnesses for the SCHOOLS Class Action and the other potential BUILDINGS class and mega-trials. Names and CVs were floated, but none seemed to catch the sense of the group as being any kind of match for Dr. Selikoff and his crew. No real ground was gained on that issue (and it was far too premature to raise Dr. Nobel's role, if I were ever to do that).

The *Mullen* appeal went smoothly as I let Sandra do almost all the talking on that despite my office carrying a heavier share of the actual brief writing. Several of those present hinted that more class actions would be filed later in the year or early next year. Alicia opined that the plaintiff's bar in these BUILDINGS cases was small, and they might wait to see how the *LAUSD* Statute of Limitations trial played out before investing serious resources in working up more classes.

As we left, Sandra asked if I minded her riding to the train with me. Turns out her Stanford friend in NYC had to cancel their time together at the last minute and she could not get a flight out of Philly, so she was going back to D.C. to fly home tomorrow. I told her I was having dinner with Tinker and two of his partners to talk about the meeting (After thinking for a minute or two, I told her, once we were in the taxi, that I would call and see if she could join us since most of our discussions would be topics just covered, but I might need to ask her to excuse herself for a few minutes after we arrived). She was OK with that.

Tinker was not happy with the subject of my call, but I pointed out that Sandra was Elaine's great friend (and former roommate), his friend and she might just spill a few beans about the *Wallboard* defense in *LAUSD*. I also told him I would delay her arrival so we could have 15 minutes on Dr. Nobel without her present. (He agreed to get the others to mind what they might say on that topic.)

— — —

Arriving at Georgia's, an African-American Southern food Bistro, located fashionably on a corner of Farragut Park, a few blocks from the White House, I left Sandra in the bar having ordered her a side-car (which I later was to learn she had converted to a "Between the Sheets!") and put it on our bill. I joined Tinker, Mace and Tod. My double Stoli preceded me by only a few minutes as the ice had not yet started to melt. We got right to Dr. Nobel. It took 20 minutes to leave them satisfied for the moment. I also explained that although Dr. Nobel was in Boston, I still was planning to use D.C. as my base of operations as both CAL Board and Desert Mutual were most pleased with our current working relationship. Then I got Sandra.

Interestingly, Tinker made the introductions having known Sandra longer than I. She sat between Tinker and me. I asked her to start off our discussions about the NCC meeting. She did so. And we all found out what she was drinking when we ordered our second round. In the *LAUSD* segment, I asked her outright why Wallboard had decided to join in that Group defense with Schein's team? Sandra said it was more a client thing which she could not discuss. Of course, several of us took that to be it was about saving money and they all thought the issue was simple and the proof straightforward. Then I asked, "Do you know about Frank Smith?"

Sandra said, "Who's he?"

That response told me that she was not active on that matter even though her firm was NCC for Wallboard. I told her who he was. She asked why it mattered? I told her he had died AND not been deposed. (I could see lights go off, but dimly.) Then, I moved away from that target. We let Sandra talk at length on the Defense BUILDINGS Expert issue and added virtually nothing. Then she got into the rumors, but never finished that topic when the main courses arrived and we wound-up the night.

— — —

Back at the Mayflower, Sandra asked for a room. They were full. Oh my, I said, I have a suite as you know. So, we went upstairs together. With Sandra in the living room, I called Mollie and told her about my day with certain exceptions, gave her greetings from Tinker, went through the kids, their school, Ingrid, the new *au pair*, and she told me she was going to be in NYC for 2 straight weeks, and, "Would I be home most of that time?" (Oh, WOW!! A successful wife has its drawbacks!)

When I went out to check on Sandra, she was sound asleep. When I woke the next morning, she was gone, leaving a note that she had gotten the earliest flight back to San Francisco.

18

LAUSD Limitations Trial

*A*s I write this for unknown readers of unknowable backgrounds, I write it in a style not unlike the way I have sent
emails, text messages and memos to myself and others to
whom I am/was close for years. Also, I am often given to writing as if
I am talking to my long-time confidant, Dr. Arnaud. That said, I will
point out that although it may be exciting in small bits and spurts, unlike on TV or in the movies, most trials are deathly dull affairs. But for
Charlie O'Reilly, and me at times, this trial which lasted 37 trial days
and 7 days of jury deliberation was right up there on "The DULL
Scale."

Finally, the civil law in California is nothing if not exceedingly pro-
lix (For those of you who have not read Catch-22, that means exces-
sively wordy.). California Statutes actually refer to this state's Statutes
of Limitations in a whole chapter called LIMITATIONS of ACTIONS.
Since this is not a law course, nor would I want to teach this chapter if
it was, I shall try to supply some legal background:

The LIMITATIONS actually in play in this Phase 1 Trail ran four
years from when the party seeking to bring the action was placed on
notice about the factual basis for the Property Damage lawsuit. (This
is what most people, if they ever confront the issue, think of as a statute
of limitations in a civil suit.)

— — —

So, on a warm day in early June, Tod Clifford, Tinker's young
partner, and I made our way to the courthouse about two city
blocks from Bunker Hill Towers in which Desert Mutual had

rented a two bedroom/two bath apartment for one year, commencing 1 May. (We used the living room/dining area as our working space with two chairs and a TV for brief relaxation intervals. The second bedroom was largely document storage and the dining area credenza served to house our fax machine, an early version with a roll of slick paper, and our photocopier. Services, including take- out food, were in the basement. Tod was staying at the Sheraton on Sepulveda about six blocks away at the base of Bunker Hill.) The Los Angeles County Main Court House, Bunker Hill Towers and a few other public or Utility-owned buildings occupied the top of that hill. Parking was at a premium. Taxi service was actually pretty good at the court building itself. The real problem was finding taxis elsewhere in Los Angeles to bring you there. Tod and I had walked the short distance from where I was staying and our defense spaces were located.

When we arrived at our court room in Department 23, one floor down from the main entrance, with our six boxes of documents in tow, there was a crowd buzzing about near our court room door. Charlie O'Reilly was standing there in the midst of the news media holding forth! Suddenly, in swept an entourage which contained a famous actress, Joan Collins, from the *Dynasty* TV show. She was appearing for the start of her divorce trial in Department 24, the court next to ours. The press abandoned Charlie in a flash. Left alone, he looked at Tod and me. I introduced Tod after his saying, "Good Morning, Counselor!" in a good-natured voice, and then Charlie held the door open for us so we could wheel our boxes into the oversized court room.

We went to the Defense table (farthest from the jury box) and to its far end. There, we took two chairs and created some separation before Rod Gorman, Avery Schein and their team showed up. (After all, as the firm located closest to the Courts, it was so very *Los Angeles* that they would be the last to arrive.) We took the opportunity to get our files in order for the first day. Charlie introduced us to Abel Stoneman, one of his young partners who was his second chair for the trial.

Moments before 10:00, the rest of the "Defense Team" as they saw themselves arrived. Avery Schein took a seat on the aisle immediately behind the bar and right behind Rod Gorman's chair. (Someone else had been sent very early by their firm to occupy that seat so it would be available for Mr. Schein that day. That same process was followed every trial day. The person might be different, but someone was always in place before we ever arrived!) Rod's team had six people inside the bar (some formed a second row behind defense counsel's table). Others sat further back in the Court Room. Tod and I could only wonder how many people Glass, Schmidt and Schein had working on this one case. The only face I recognized behind the bar belonged to one of Alicia Goines' partners. The bailiff, with an expression of growing irritation, watched the Gorman team get settled. As soon as they were all seated, that bailiff pressed a button on the side of the Judge's bench. An invisible door, until you saw it open, swung out and the clerk was followed by Judge Bernard Weitzman in his flowing robes, looking every inch the highly re-garded sage jurist, who went up the steps of his dais to sit at his oversized desk with its very high-backed chair.

The Court Room was called to order by the clerk: the case was called, the only item on the docket. The judge asked for ap-pearances and they were completed quickly. At the Pre-Trial Hearing about ten court days before, the rules for Jury *Voir Dire* and Challenges were reviewed and all pre-trial motions were ruled upon. In addition to Challenges for Cause, which were un-limited in number, and each was ruled upon by the Judge, there were 12 Preemptory Challenges per side (a bone of contention as the Gorman Team felt they should exercise all of them since they represented all but two defendants). The judge felt that the two lead Defense Counsel should agree on the exercise of any defense pre-emptory challenges. (That ruling held the promise of being an issue for appeal!)

Judge Weitzman went back over his ground rules for this trial phase in grinding detail and then had the bailiffs bring in a pool of 160 potential jurors. The judge described the trial for that pool and said it might go as long as 4 weeks. About one third of those potential jurors had a problem with that length of time. The judge cajoled them a bit about their civic duty, with about half of those relenting. In a little more than an hour, we lost about 25 jurors for hardship. The Judge called a lunch break and we came back at 2:00. During that break, each juror had to complete a survey (called a Potential Juror Questionnaire) and submit it to the bailiff before the start of the afternoon session.

The bailiff reached into what looked like a bingo machine and began to pull out balls with juror ID numbers on them. The first one selected became juror #1, and onward until we had a jury of 12, plus six alternates who would sit through the entire trial and become jurors if one of the 12 originals had to be excused (O'Reilly had wanted 12 alternates, but Gorman only 4. We wanted 8. The Judge sided with us and ordered a compromise of 6.). When the 18 were seated, the Judge did his own *Voir Dire* first, asking each potential juror questions about prior jury service, knowing anyone associated with the trial or related to a party, and on the basic issues of fairness. He addressed all at once, but paused frequently to get their answers and to deal with any affirmative response. By the time Judge Weitzman finished, 4 potentials had been replaced and 4 more added to the end of the alternate juror line. It was 3:45, so we adjourned for the day. The Judge told us the rules on what might happen to any items we decided to leave behind. We left 4 boxes which were the documents pre-marked as Exhibits for the trial. We were given two small boxes which contained the completed surveys. On the way out, I said to Tod, "It's going to be a very long trial if we get no more than 4 hours of court time each day."

We went back to Bunker Hill Towers where each of us read each survey, then wrote a grade on a preprinted sheet with potential juror numbers on it. We compared. They were very similar. Rod Gorman's lead paralegal, Marigold, called and asked if we wanted some burgers as she invited us to come to their office to talk about challenges. We agreed. By nine o'clock-ish, we had a consensus that the potential jury was not good for the Defense (The ratings A – D, F were pre-agreed.) There were NO-A's; 2- B's; 4-F's; and the bulk of the remaining prospects were C's and D's, with the D's about 2:1 over the C's. Very SCARY!) Almost half were governmental employees of some type (None worked for LAUSD and the Judge had excused several who had some type of relationship to that plaintiff entity.). Not terribly satisfactory from the Defense perspective. (Several of Mr. Gorman's people wanted to talk about race as a disqualifier. We actively discouraged that. Our firm practiced in Oakland as a matter of choice: Race was in no way a viable disqualifying topic with me.)

The next day, Mary was in town for a deposition in the case, so she stopped by the courtroom for an hour or so. (As the parties with the Burden of Proof on the Phase 1 issue, the Defense should have had the right to begin *Voir Dire*, but neither Mr. O'Reilly nor Judge Weitzman saw it that way.)

Abel Stoneman began the questioning of the individual jurors. He did it in a very clever fashion: with no notes: he would call a juror by name, ask him or her a very specific question always created to seek a negative answer, and when that juror responded, he would then ask the other prospects if they agreed with the first juror's answer. (Within minutes, Mr. Stoneman had earned the prospective jurors' respect because he knew their names without notes and he was saving their time by moving through his questions in this fashion. We also deduced that he had an excellent, probably, very expensive, jury consultant who put together a book with pictures of the prospects after they were picked the day before. The court room was so full, we could not come up with a suspect for that person.)

Mr. Gorman did the Defense examination of prospective juror # 1. It was excruciatingly detailed, and disturbingly repetitive. The impaneled prospects looked very nervous. Plaintiff Counsel Stoneman was even quicker with Juror #2. Gorman's second chair carried what appeared to be either the same notebook which Gorman had used, or a copy, to the lectern whereupon he began to question in a style almost duplicative of his lead counsel.

Juror # 3 was markedly different, a somewhat elderly lady of uncertain temperament. She responded affirmatively to several of Mr. Stoneman's questions about her tax dollars and the like. She was the first prospect who owned her own home, and therefore, paid property taxes that went to help pay for LAUSD schools. Nonetheless, she claimed she could be fair and would not prejudge the case. Five others also owned their own homes: four said they could be fair, but the fifth, # 14, said she felt the schools needed that money wherever it came from. Mr. Stoneman paused for a moment, seemed to glance at his counsel table and began to move on. But before he could formulate his next question, Mr. Gorman was on his feet, saying that prospect #14 was clearly prejudiced despite what she told the judge in responding to his opening questions and, therefore, she should be excused for cause.

Judge Weitzman paused, then asked that prospect, "Juror number 14 are you telling us that you will not listen to the evidence and not decide this case on the facts as they are shown to be, and not follow the law on which I shall instruct you?"

"Oh NO, Your Honor! I would never do that. I will do just as you instruct," was her response (And I remember it to this day as we used that very quote later in this continuing judicial saga. I told Tod to make a note of that.) I rose, and during a pregnant pause, said, "CAL Board and my other clients do not join in seeking to have this Prospective Juror discharged for cause based on these responses." We watched a number of jurors react to my remarks.

Shortly after the lunch break, the *Voir Dire* would end and the preemptory challenges would start. The defense asked for, and got, a caucus room. Rod got sandwiches, soft drinks and water delivered. (Rod always paid.) We huddled. One of Rod's many minions had the Defense rating of each juror ready at the beginning: the average of the first 12 was a high C. One of the two B's was on the 12 person panel. Rod wanted to knock off a couple of the C's who both just happened to be African-Americans.

The gist of my presentation on juror challenges was that Charlie O'Reilly would almost certainly pass the first challenge. That way he would get control of the selection process since the challenges alternated between the two sides (Two passes in a row and the jury was set.). "The jury as presently constituted was more favorable to the Defense than it very likely would be if we started knocking off these perceived weaker prospects. Look at the potential replacements: weaker people, more easily led. This is going to get tricky! If we go ahead, then my money says O'Reilly will knock off the only B on the panel. What do you think are the odds of drawing that other B, and even if we do, of keeping him? What if the replacement is an F (Gorman's team had more F's than Tod and me.)? What if F's start to pile up? I think if the Plaintiff passes, we should pass. Are we guaranteed a win? No, but we have to play the percentages, and this panel, as constituted, is stronger than what is left in the remainder of the pool."

Gorman started to refute my argument, but before he could complete his first thought, Avery Schein intervened, "Mr. O'Neill is correct. This process, in this courthouse was never going to be perfect. I agree. Let's save your enthusiasm for another argument, like what happens next if O'Reilly does challenge Juror # 2 (the B)?"

— — —

And so, the trial went about getting started, over the next several days: the jury remained unchallenged, motions blocking evidence in Opening Statements were argued, and those statements given. My Opening included the Wilson Riles letter to LAUSD advising them of the dangers arguably posed by asbestos-containing products installed in the schools, including suggested inspections, testing and abatement. (But under the rules, I could not argue the date on which the Limitations started to run because the Judge had ruled in the Pre-Trial that the finding of that date was a fact question determination solely within the province of the jury as the sole finder of fact in a California jury trial. That would not be true in Closing Argument. More later on that.)

Plaintiff Attorney O'Reilly went last making a relatively short statement in which he tried to begin to undermine the State Superintendent of Education's letter as the evidence triggering the statute. He also indicated that they would read for the record a series of authenticated documents to show how some of the key Defendants had deliberately suppressed the grave dangers of exposure to invisible asbestos fibers over enough years to amount to a period of decades, as to those, amounting to fraudulent concealment. But his key point was that the Riles' letter, as it came to be known in the trial, was ultimately initially delivered to Frank Smith, not a doctor, but the Los Angeles Unified School District's Chief Health Officer and to NO OTHER EXECUTIVE OF LAUSD. This became the ultimate strategic course the Plaintiff would follow, "Blame it all on the dead guy who is not around to be questioned." (My words by the fourth day in Mr. Gorman's ever tedious presentation of evidence.)

— — —

It took six court days for Mr. Gorman to put on his case. He tried to do it without admitting that asbestos fibers represented any danger and without calling any significant LAUSD witness.

Then it was our turn. I started with Dr. Wilson Riles by asking him if he wrote his letter (he did); and, what was the letter's purpose (to warn every school district in the state and to inspire them to get rid of their asbestos dangers). I spent less than 40 minutes with Dr. Riles, who, in my opinion, bore a sttriking physical resemblance to Dr. Martin Luther King and was himself an extremely accomplished gentleman.

Mr. O'Reilly went after Dr. Riles tangentially being careful not to offend any of the seven African-Americans on the twelve-person jury panel. He asked if Dr. Riles had any medical training. Dr. Riles repeated that he had a Ph.D. in Education, not an M.D., but that he understood some science and had his staff investigate the perceived dangers of asbestos containing products as well as consulting with California's chief health officer who was an M.D. Still, O'Reilly kept pecking away: Did any agency of the California State government actually undertake a study about these supposed dangers? Was there any follow-up to his letter by him? By any other California agency? Why only one letter? Did he ever discuss his letter with any senior official of LAUSD, California's biggest school district by far? Why did he not do more when there was so little action and so very little feedback?

Dr. Riles responded to each of these different themes, explaining that because the California Superintendent had no actual direct jurisdiction over any of California's school boards, that "state official" was not empowered to compel action or provide funding; that role was essentially limited to acting as an advisor. Dr. Riles got some of this into evidence in responding to

Mr. O'Reilly and the rest on my re-direct. However, Mr. Gorman may have done more harm than Mr. O'Reilly when he challenged Dr. Riles about his actual knowledge of the dangers of asbestos (that came up in Plaintiff's Closing Argument.).

— — —

LAUSD's defense was a seeming unending string of senior district executives and school board members, all of whom had a single function in the trial: to show that they knew nothing about either the Riles letter nor the very real dangers of asbestos until shortly before LAUSD filed its lawsuit. They were good and the school district had produced only one copy of the Riles letter from the Frank Smith chronological file from among thousands of other documents received and filed about 6 years before the suit was filed. Frank Smith's secretary of many years had done the document search, carefully recording her efforts, and also searching all the other files where communications with other LAUSD staff referencing that letter should have been, if they existed at all. She did all of Mr. Smith's filing so she would know where to look. Mrs. Huddleston, gray haired as she was, was the Plaintiff's star witness. Rod Gorman went after her for about 6 hours. I spent little more than an hour. Despite some other references to testing and abatement in some other context which did not refer to Mr. Smith, there was little to refute about this woman's testimony.

— — —

Some of the key, incriminating "Conspiracy Documents," involving Johns Manville, a number of other companies by then little known with most having filed bankruptcy, and perhaps U.S. Gypsum as well as a major U.S. insurer, were read into the Trial's record as uncontested evidence. After eleven court days,

Mr. O'Reilly rested. It was a Thursday afternoon. Mr. Gorman said he had one rebuttal witness, but could he wait until Monday morning to call him as he was not in California, rather New York City.

I thought LAUSD would object, but they let it go. We had three, perhaps four, days to put something together to refute Ms. Huddleston. Tom and Mace had shuttled over the past five weeks. Both had commitments. I decided to stay in L.A. rather than waste time flying twice. I called Lily and asked her to check with Martha and Mary to see if either or both could fly down and help me. I got them both on the line and we started our final drive to save this case! I called Tinker to get his other people busy on the needed research. If the defense failed to prove actual knowledge, our clients would try to prove Constructive Knowledge!

— — —

We had a good case by virtue of Dr. Riles' letter to the correct recipient. LAUSD was functionally on notice. If Mr. Smith decided to bury the letter in his chronological file, or even if Ms. Huddleston filed it improperly, the existence of the letter in one of Mr. Smith's files was enough notice to satisfy the applicable limitations statute for property damage.

Our team's six lawyers working on this trial (five were part-time), which included Mary and Martha, had come up with hundreds of potential Jury Instructions, but I felt that to get the needed California (CA) Basic Approved Jury Instruction (BAJI) on Constructive Knowledge (CK), we would need a brief to support that specific request. I did not have all of the prospective jury instructions with me, but I did have a volume of California Approved Civil BAJI, annotated with supporting law from the drafters of those jury instructions. I saw the weekend tasks as firming up the BAJI and the Special Instructions, seeing what else needed to be briefed and writing authorities to support the CK BAJI. That was largely Mary and Martha with some input on the law provided by Tinker and his lawyers.

— — —

Mollie was NOT AT ALL pleased when I told her I would not be home. She said she understood, but I doubted it. I did know she understood the very real importance of this trial to my, and the firm's, continuing role in the defense of these cases. I had explained to her that we were now the smallest defense firm on the national scene. Mollie finally did say that when this trial was over, we needed to get away for a long weekend — with no USCG duty! I agreed.

— — —

Martha and Mary stayed at the Sheraton on Sepulveda. We worked until 10:00 on Friday night with a delivery from downstairs as dinner. We had some wine when we wrapped up and the ladies taxied back to their hotel about 11:00. The next day we went at it until 5:30. I thought we could get done on Sunday by 2:00, so they could get a nice flight home (they made reservations right away on the 3:30 PSA flight. On Saturday, when we broke, they went back to their rooms to freshen-up. I showered, picked them up in my taxi and we went to Smith and Wollensky in Beverly Hills for a nice dinner, partly on Desert Mutual and partly on our firm.

We had a great meal and an equally great time. Martha brought out more humor in Mary than I ever thought she possessed. It was the first time I became aware that Mary, smart as she was, just might make a business getter as well as be a potential partner (I had already put Martha down for that, extracurricular activities notwithstanding!). I dropped them at their hotel and was in my room no more than 10 minutes when my phone rang: Martha! She wanted to come over. I told her to give me a half hour so I could call Mollie. That's just what she did. I hung up with Mollie and in less than 60 seconds, there was a subtle knock on my door. Martha took three steps inside and pirouetted for me to take off her coat. I did. Surprise! Nothing underneath but panties. She led me over to the couch where she sat comfortably, removing her last garment. Later we went to bed.

— — —

The Defense rebuttal was over by Wednesday afternoon. Nothing terribly telling, but we laid a bit more foundation for Constructive Knowledge (CK). We argued Jury Instructions on Thursday morning and the Judge told us to come back at 3:00 on the contested ones, including the CA BAJI on CK.

That afternoon, Judge Weitzman ruled and we got the CA BAJI on CK as requested. All of the losers preserved their rights of appeal. Then, the Judge told us he wanted Closing Arguments the next day. All of the Trial Defense counsel met after court. Tod was there from D.C. Mr. Schein hosted us at the Jonathan Club where we had a business meeting to be followed by dinner. They proposed that Rod Gorman argue the entire Opening Argument for the Defense Close for all of the Defendants, and knowing how crafty Charlie O'Reilly could be, that I should do the entire Rebuttal Closing Argument for the Defense. (Gorman did not look at all pleased. I was guessing that his boss had come up with this plan.)

I said I would run it by the clients after dinner and let them know our decision. Of course, I knew this plan might be "a best possible world." I would get the last word, could try to repair any damage O'Reilly might inflict, and could flesh out the Constructive Knowledge argument after Charlie put in all of his negative evidence on Actual Knowledge.

That night I spent 10 minutes on the phone and 75 minutes

redoing my Close into a Rebuttal Outline. I went to sleep thinking "I could see the Light at the End of the Tunnel."

(I had to wait until Monday to realize that "Light" belonged to an on-rushing locomotive!)

On Friday at 10:00, Attorney O'Reilly asked to address the Court outside the presence of the jury. Judge Weitzman told the bailiff to hold the Jury in abeyance. O'Reilly had two points: first, he sought to change the Judge's mind on Constructive Knowledge; and second, he felt he should have two hours for his argument since the Defense had 2 hours for their two arguments taken together. Judge Weitzman ruled that the BAJI on CK would be given and LAUSD would have full appellate rights to challenge that; however, the Judge ruled in favor of LAUSD getting two hours.

O'Reilly seemed satisfied. I was not and asked the Judge if he would keep the jury late on a Friday afternoon to instruct them? He said he would not and that he never intended to instruct until Monday a.m. because he did not want to have them isolated from their families for the upcoming weekend. (Innocent enough, or so it seemed.) So, about twenty minutes later, Mr. Gorman began his OPENING which lasted 65 minutes. The Judge decided we should break early for lunch and come back to hear Plaintiff's OPPOSITION, take another break, leaving me with 55 minutes to give my Rebuttal.

Everything went about as well as could be expected. O'Reilly was outstanding. My argument consisted mostly of summing up the facts creating LAUSD's constructive knowledge with constant reference to the BAJI on CK. It was as good as I had ever done. At the end of the afternoon once the jury left, all counsel shook hands all around and wished each other good fortune in the future.

— — —

I flew home, went to Yerba Buena Island for a two day USCGR administrative weekend. Had a marvelous night with the family on Saturday, with a great later evening with Mollie. That Sunday, I changed at the Coast Guard base, then flew back to LAX on a 6:00 p.m. PSA flight. When I got to Bunker Hill Towers, I was tired. A good tired. I got a sandwich with one beer from downstairs, watched a bit of TV and went to bed by 9:30 to read.

The next morning, I went over to the Court alone. All we had was the Judge instructing the jury and then to begin the wait for them to bring back a verdict. O'Reilly and all of his people were there. Gorman and Schein, with all of their people, were there. Alicia's partner was there, and almost no one else. The Clerk popped through the invisible door and in moments Judge Weitzman emerged. He sat, cleared his throat and told his Bailiff, "We'll hold the Jury in abeyance for a few minutes. I need to talk with Counsel." Looking down at the various tables, starting with O'Reilly, he scanned slowly across until his eyes rested on me and his head stopped moving.

Then, with a stern look in his eyes, Judge Weitzman began, "Mr. O'Neill, you did an admirable job advancing your Constructive Knowledge argument and in getting me to allow that BAJI. But over the weekend, I thought on it more, changed my mind, and have decided to reconsider my ruling on Mr. O'Reilly's motion of Friday morning. This Court will not be giving that instruction to this jury. Moreover, to the extent that the jury might find it confusing if I do not give that instruction in light of your oral argument, I am going to instruct them to disregard your entire argument on that point of law. Thank you, Counsel."

I rose, having now realized that Judge Weitzman was that "oncoming locomotive" and not a benevolent "...light at the end of the Tunnel," and said, with a smattering of heat in my voice, "Your Honor, if you move ahead as you say you intend to do, you will have ever so effectively committed an error so great that this entire trial will prove a nullity. I request that you forebear from any further action so that my clients may seek an emergency Writ of Mandamus forthwith. Or, in the alternative, that you declare a mistrial and recuse yourself from any further connection with these proceedings. If it pleases this Court, we ask for an immediate ruling on these alternate motions."

O'Reilly was smiling. Gorman and Schein were livid, albeit speechless. Judge Weitzman, obviously anticipating an unhappy response from me, glowered for 30 seconds or so, then, "I paused lest I find you in contempt, Mr. O'Neill. Do not address this Court further until I address you and give you permission to speak. Your tirade is no motion. I must do what I must do. All of you, be seated."

Me, "I have every right to defend my clients. I respectfully ask for a thirty minute recess before you bring in the jury?"

"NO! NOW SIT DOWN and do not speak again until after I finish my Instructions. Mr. Clerk, pass out copies of those Instructions I intend to give to the jury as soon as they are seated."

— — —

Late on Tuesday of the following week, the jury returned with a unanimous verdict in favor of LAUSD. (If it was unanimous, why did it take them so long? I always thought they liked getting away from their families, or the hotel beds, or maybe even the food. But the point is they took six full days.) On that following Friday morning at 9:00 a.m., in the Clerk's Office of the California Court of Appeals for the Second Division (for Greater L.A.), CAL Board, by and through its counsel, joined by two other Defendants filed their Petition for a Writ of Mandamus to Judge Weitzman's Order of that fateful Monday asking that Second Appellate District to order that the trial judge vacate his decision not to allow a jury instruction on constructive knowledge after jury argument and before he instructed the jury. We served it on all other trial counsel that same day right before the close of business. We served it first on Judge Weitzman that Friday at the end of his morning session.

Mr. O'Reilly called me at about 3:00 that same afternoon asking why he had not yet received his copy of our Petition. Since no one on our side would have told him about our filing, and since no other defense party would have been aware of it by that early in the day, he must have learned about it somewhere else. Ah, well!! That left only the Court system. It was fair warning to know his probable source.

19

As Time Goes By

*T*he weeks and months that followed the LAUSD trial became a blur in my mind.

I had missed several appointments with Dr. Arnaud, but when I did see her, she was not happy with me. She never really got on me about Carolyn whom I had not seen for about a year, but I did get some photos of Patrick: very scary how much he was beginning to look like me.

But when I finally broke down and told Dr. Arnaud about Martha, she was livid. She could not stop talking about the devastation that Sandra had heaped on me to bring about what had almost proved to be my end. She accused me of rationalizing about my relationships. Then, in our first visit post-LAUSD trial, Dr. Arnaud asked about Martha, "You never really think about how a relationship like this will play out in the long run. Do You?"

When I told her that she was seemingly correct, she went off on me again. Not a great visit, but maybe I had that one coming!

The source of her newest irritation with me being Martha persisted. (Somehow, she correctly sensed that the Angela-thing had no future.). Dr. Arnaud kept emphasizing that having an affair with an associate was very bad idea for the firm, my career, and my family, not necessarily in that order. Dr. Arnaud had other things to say about Martha as well. From what I had told the doctor, she somehow inferred that Martha was bisexual. I started to deny that, but thought for a few moments and instead came back with, "What if she is?"

There might have been no right answer but that was a really bad answer, maybe the worst. Another lecture ensued. (What is truly interesting is that Dr. Arnaud was not very big on giving lectures as she felt it was too parental. On the other hand, when it came to what she referred to as my "rampant womanizing," that topic seemed fair game for lectures. Maybe it had something to do with her. While writing this, I went back and read her final note to me. Perhaps more truth was disclosed there than I had, at first, ever given her credit for.)

Another point on Martha: Dr. Arnaud implied that I was using her as a substitute for Carolyn. I did not like that observation much at all either. But also, I feared in my heart that on that point, the good doctor might be somewhat accurate. There was a light-handed sweetness about Carolyn that I did not find in Mollie, great fun that she could be and love her as much as I do to this day! And that same sweetness, albeit to a lesser degree, seemed to be present in Martha (In the months to come, I began to dwell on this issue, but then another unexpected locomotive pulled into my emotional station.)

Then there was Mollie: spending way too much time working and much of it on the road, especially in New York City. When we talked about this, Mollie said she hated the travel, but not so much New York because of the Waldorf, especially the Bull and Bear, and her company really tried to take great care of her. She had become an Applications (APP) genius.

She had ideas that seemed to catch on with the masses: games, home support APPs, and especially business.

Mollie loved her work, but one thing preyed on her: she felt there were more powerful ways to mass communicate than the APPs which she was creating. She was always looking at the newest specialized systems, processors, memories, access devices, modems and changes to operating systems. Mollie felt the future was close to being found by Microsoft, but she was uncertain about that, yet very certain that her APPs to date were not the ANSWER for that unverbalized mystery which she sought to solve.

Whenever we got together in bed, she was just great, and sometimes even seemed to be getting better! But it was happening less and less. Somehow, I could not bring myself to ask Mollie why that was, nor could I ask Dr. Arnaud about what seemed altogether too personal! So, Mollie and I slowly drifted apart, then back together, but then slightly further apart. Each time the distance apart seemed to get just a small amount greater, just like our separations.

I could not bring myself to ask either Mollie or Dr. Arnaud about the occasional sounds on Mollie's Waldorf room phone. Perhaps that was becoming a tiny bit of an obsession with me?

— — —

Less than two weeks had gone by and we got a postcard from the Los Angeles office of its California Court of Appeals summarily denying CAL Board's Writ Petition. No reason was given (not unexpected as this was the usual treatment for a writ denial). I spoke with Manny in Scottsdale and Austin Smith in Sacramento and both agreed that having spent the money to do the first petition, a second petition seeking the same relief to the next highest Court with a few needed amendments was more or less a bargain (and, if the gossip about Charlie had any truth, we might find that out). So, we filed another Petition for Writ of Mandamus to the California Supreme Court. Within a week, we got a postcard which gave no disposition, but two justices had recused themselves (Austin knew about one of them who was a member of his Country Club. No one else knew anything about the other recusal, but we were free to speculate).

— — —

Meanwhile, the *Wallboard* Appeal was fully briefed and pending before the First California Appellate District Court of Appeals in San Francisco. That court scheduled oral arguments. I was the designated representative for Desert Mutual. Sandra was designated for Wallboard. We had to wait five weeks to argue the case. (Mollie had a week in New York City. Sandra called to invite me to see her new condominium on the north side of Knob Hill. She had been a partner for quite a few years at that point: her address said she was doing better than just OK!)

Martha lived in an East Bay town called Kensington, located just east of, and up the hill from, Berkeley. (We had agreed that getting together in the Bay Area might be a very bad idea. Her roommate was in the data processing world with an expanding software company called Oracle which was trying to become more full service.) The same week that Sandra invited me to see her place and we agreed on a late afternoon that Wednesday, Martha had invited me to see her place on that preceding Monday. (She was so anxious about it, I found I could not say NO.)

Those weeks had the makings for a comedy of errors. Neither assignation had the usual light- heartedness that accompanied our get togethers when we were travelling. Both Sandra and Martha wanted to make me feel at home. But my home was on that other peninsula on the Bay in Marin County. All the more reason not to do anything possibly, even arguably, romantic in your home area other than with your spouse. Neither fixed a dinner, but we did have snacks and drinks, and I saw where they lived, even their bedrooms.

It was all kind of wonderful in the end (Was it like playing house for either of them? I would surely never say that!). And with Martha, there came a time in our love making where I became lost in the moments of passion, sometimes in pain and often extended periods of ecstasy. Yet, my conscience never bothered me when I was away; but on that occasion, near home, it was problematic (but why not when I was with Carolyn?).

One other matter of serious import was awaiting completion; Jeremy Nobel had been in written contact with Sir Richard Doll, but their schedules could not seem to fit. Finally, Jeremy asked me if I would be willing to meet with Dr. Doll. After consulting all of the client types, we decided that such a meeting, particularly with the groundwork now laid by Dr. Nobel, could actually be the best of all worlds. So, we set it in motion for the early Spring of 1988. I went about getting a passport (and in the face of my going to the UK, shockingly, Mollie agreed to go with me.)

Also, Scott Kelly, our Philadelphia local counsel, asked if I would be interested in being invited to join an invitation-only defense civil litigation society called The Society of Insurance/Civil Defense Counsel (SIDC). As he explained it more fully, the idea began to make sense. I took it to Jerry Klein and Sean Kelly and they both agreed based on the possibilities of new business doors being opened. So, I went through their vetting process, was accepted and my first meeting was set in Bermuda in April of 1988. I asked Jeremy to write to Sir Richard Doll, tell him about my honor, and to ask if we could fit my visit with him in a week or two after Bermuda. Amazingly, he agreed if I would drive up to Oxford for our meeting. (Sir Richard even told Jeremy to have me write him directly, and if I were spending the night in Oxford, to let him know and he would reserve a nice room at the Randolph Hotel.) Mollie was "on board" in a flash! So was Kate who planned to move in for as long as we were gone to help to run our home and spend quality day-to-day time with her four California grandchildren.

— — —

Sandra and I, along with other involved counsel had a brief, but spirited, oral argument before the *Wallboard* Appellate Court's three judge panel. It seemed the questions to me were more difficult, but many relied on established negative presumptions about insurance policies, especially very limited construction of its EXCLUSIONS terminology which were exculpatory and patently in favor of the carrier which was supplying the "take it or leave it policy" drafted with its own carefully crafted language.

My argument kept coming back to the point that in the end, at least in its most meaningful terminology, the DMIC/Wallboard manuscript was not a "take it or leave it" policy, and as such, was a negotiated contract and that the California general rules of contract construction should be used whenever disputed terminology was potentially ambiguous; thus, if the Exclusion drafted by Wallboard's Risk Manager was somehow ambiguous, it should be construed in light of the expectation of the parties, or against the actual drafter – here: Wallboard through its Risk Manager and as approved by its then General Counsel!

After the close of argument, some of us repaired for cocktails. Sandra and I behaved sportingly toward each other in the presence of all the other local lawyers. But in a moment of our solitude, she said she would be going to Philadelphia for the last 1987 National Coordinating Counsel meeting next week, and where would I be staying? Thankfully I had invited Mary, not Martha; so, I quickly gave Sandra my itinerary. (I knew I would miss at least one of those meetings while in Bermuda and the UK.)

Almost eight weeks after filing the second *LAUSD* writ petition in the California Supreme Court, we got a post card – no writ would be granted! This was a definite disappointment and it pained me to call both the client and the carrier to give them the news. Since CAL Board had a plant that manufactured asbestos containing products (ACP) of the type that could be used in schools in Long Beach, that fact alone would increase its potential for liability. But it also enhanced the need to generate a serious threat of a defense expert witness: so, now seemed the time for a meeting in Scottsdale with Desert Mutual's people and Austin Smith, but with no other defense counsel present. I asked Lily to set it up. I would fly down the next Tuesday later in the day and would spend the whole day on Wednesday in client planning meetings, and then that second night taking whomsoever wished to go to dinner. (I got one final booking in a suite at Club FED which was about to be renamed The Phoenician.) I called Angela to let her know I would be there, and available, on that second night.

The meeting in Scottsdale had everyone there from Desert Mutual as well as Austin Smith. It started with an assessment, yet again, of what went wrong in the *LAUSD* Limitations trial, followed by an outline of the ramifications for needed future action, including an assessment of potential liability, how to establish whether or not CAL Board's ACP was actually in any given building (a theory which I postulated the Plaintiff counsel would move to circumvent); the actual dangers that each location of ACP actually presented, if any (an actual assessment done scientifically); and, the actual real life risks associated with an abatement project for each site (requiring general and specific expert scientific testimony) as opposed to encapsulation of the offending ACP. All of this foretold that my meeting with Dr. Doll was now becoming ever more critical!

On we plowed that day with lunch brought in, calls to different defense team people to get their thoughts and assessing how to involve them. Then, about 3:30, I got a call, it was Phil from my office. In the mail that day was an envelope from the San Francisco branch of the California Appeal Court. It contained an Order and an Opinion. Lily was faxing them as we spoke. Desert Mutual had prevailed on the *Wallboard* Appeal: 3 – 0. I held the phone up and put on its speaker and asked Phil to repeat the news. The mood in the room erupted into jubilance (even Austin Smith smiled: He knew about the *Wallboard* case, and that his company was getting a first-rate defense from DMIC!).

We had a great dinner with it starting earlier than planned, proving festive (I called Mollie beforehand to tell her), and in the end, it was only Angela and me in my suite. She had a great time, but at the end of the evening, as we walked to her car, I told her that I had come to the unwanted conclusion that our business relationship was far too important for both of us to continue this affair. She smiled, saying, "I was going to tell you almost those exact words when we got to my car. It has been great! I will always have a special place in my heart for you."

With that another one of my affairs ended!

— — —

On my trip to D.C. and Philadelphia for the NCC meetings, meetings with Tinker's group as well as Scott Kelly's group, I ended up spending some time with Sandra in D.C. Those various meetings themselves added little to what was already in the works for our CAL Board defense team. The NCC meeting did yield a certain sense of desperation among some of the counsel in their efforts to get some viable expert witnesses to slow down the Dr. Selikoff/Mt. Zion juggernaut for the plaintiffs. (Over the last 18 months or so, Sir Richard had published several papers about the dangers of asbestos inhalation and how that might be an added cause of lung cancer, especially in chronic smokers. This weighed on me from the BI perspective.)

But from the standpoint of Sandra, I was beginning to sense that she was getting more serious about me. I dwelled on that on my flight home (Sandra did not get upgraded, I did). I concluded that an actual affair with her was simply untenable (Dr. Arnaud had been correct). Another USCG Reserve weekend intervened, but on that next Monday, I visited Dr. Arnaud on my way home. We spent the entire hour on Sandra. Of course, the good doctor was not a Sandra-fan. Still, she did realize that I would always harbor positive feelings for Sandra, especially since she was a primary reason that I moved west and by now, we had achieved a relatively positive level of reconciliation. She was adamant that I should take that relationship no further. What if Mollie were ever to find out? (Also, it made me think, but not articulate anything, about Carolyn and our son, Patrick. I always believed that Mollie would forgive that affair because it started in the interim of our having gone our separate ways. No such logic, however, was available to apply to Sandra.)

So, another of our therapeutic hours ended with my firm decision that I would not have an affair with Sandra!

20

Welcome To The West End

Mollie and I had a marvelous time during our 5 days in Bermuda for my inaugural meeting of the SIDC. So many new faces, speeches, meals, programs, and seemingly endless networking. (Thank God for name tags!) The Princess Hotel overlooked downtown Hamilton from a hilltop across the harbor. Our room gave us an entrancing harbor view from the balcony. The convention was chock-a-block full of events for members, spouses, and even children. We quickly came to realize that this group was very family-oriented as many of the members had brought their children (more than a few grandchildren!) in addition to their spouses. The beaches, the pool (more convenient than the long walk down, not to mention the uphill climb coming back, from the ocean's beach to the hill-top hotel), food, service and entertainment were all first rate. (At one point, I almost said to Mollie: if we had married instead of my going into the Coast Guard, we could well have honey-mooned here. Later, she said something almost identical to that, but added that had we done so, our lives would surely have turned out so very differently from where they are now. Better said by Mollie!)

I signed up to be active in two practice groups: Toxic Torts and Trial Tactics. Mollie agreed to help with the children's events at the next Summer Meeting at the Homestead in the Virginia Blue Ridge Mountains (they also had this Winter Meeting, more with spouses and fewer children, generally older, but that could vary depending on the meeting venue. Bermuda proved very attractive to those of all ages.) From Bermuda, we took our first class flight to London in the late morning, and still arrived at the Marriott on Grosvenor Square in time to unpack and get down to their dining room for a late dinner. We were checked-in for 3 days, then up to Oxford for two nights at the Randolph and back to the Marriott. (The Marriott food was good, but not great, especially in light of the prices they were charging. Moreover, there was the unfavorable conversion rate from Pounds Sterling to Dollars.) We had a fairly light dinner and thought we would sleep well, but the elevator, not far down the hall from our room was loud as it moved up and down, and especially so when its doors opened and closed on our, or an adjacent, floor. In the end we slept; but by 6:30, the early risers were about their business, doors slamming, and we were up and about somewhat unwillingly.

We started our first full day in London and the UK with a proper English breakfast (for Mollie, it was her last of those!), followed by time spent with one of the Concierge staff. We did not feel that bad as Bermuda had been more than a half-way point from California, but better sleep would have helped. We decided that a walk-about was in order. The Concierge suggested that if we went in one direction, we would encounter 221B Baker St., the fictional home of Sherlock Holmes, but a very real street address; and, that would include passing some of the City's finest department stores, including Selfridge's and Marks and Spencer as well as many shops and restaurants on Oxford Street, a main thoroughfare; and then, if we turned right, we could end up in Saville Row for Men's Shops. Another option was Hyde Park, one of the City's finest and but a few blocks away, which promised to be a day in itself being so large and our gentleman spoke of its many gardens, esplanades and other sites, e.g., the World Famous Speaker's Corner (Yanks Welcome, most days!).

Eventually, we did a bit of a mish-mash: toured Grosvenor Square relishing the statuary celebrating the greatest heroes of

World War II, admiring the fantastic houses fronting on the
Square, walking some of the residential streets, with some blocks
on Oxford Street, dropping in and out of shops, all while observ-
ing changing neighborhoods. A British pub provided a respite
with light luncheon fare and warm draft beer, then more wan-
dering with the city map oft-times in hand. So it was that we
eventually meandered to Berkeley Square, a charming area,
found a section called Shepherd's Market nearby, and wandered
up a bending Curzon Street of 4 -5 story stately homes, passing
one that displayed a plaque saying, "Here resided Alfred Lord
Cornwallis, Hero of India, 1797-1815." (Strangely, no mention
was made of the place where I had first encountered that very
name: USCG Officer Candidate School was reached by traversing a Revolutionary War Battlefield in Yorktown, Virginia, the
very place where said Cornwallis, no lord then, had surrendered
his British Army to George Washington, marking the functional
end of the Revolutionary War and the actual onset of freedom
for the United States from British rule. But there was that bit of
nastiness a few years later called the War of 1812 featuring the
same combatants. Mollie smiled as I said this, adding that when
the children are somewhat older, we really must take them on a
driving trip of our EAST. So many of our early memories, almost
all of them turned out good in the end. (Of course, the British,
in their usual fashion, did not give up easily, while during their
bombardment of Fort McHenry in Baltimore Harbor at the outset of the War of 1812, an American observer aboard a British
Man-of-War, Francis Scott Key, gave us the *Star-Spangled Banner*
celebrating that fight.)

Following our walk about, we paused in the Marriott's Lobby
Bar for a cocktail. But, beforehand, we asked one of the
Concierge staff to recommend a restaurant, preferably special-
izing in fish. He told us about a place not very far from the Cornwallis House with which he was familiar. He said it was casual
for London, some tourists, but a favorite of the locals as well.

When we asked for a 7:00 reservation, he looked somewhat askance at us. When I queried him for the reason, he readily explained that London was a relatively late dining city, not as late as the Spanish, but in line with the French, especially Paris. So, we settled for 7:30 as we were both quite hungry after our small Pub lunch.

We had time to kill when we got back to our room. Being not quite 5:30, and with an eight hour time difference, the children would be in school and the people working on the West Coast would just be settling in. I said we could call when we got back from dinner and Mollie agreed. I had only one short fax and she had nothing. We looked at each other, and as I started to undo my shirt, Mollie asked, "You're not going to shower again, are you? It wasn't very warm at all out there today."

To which I replied, "No, I thought if you take some clothes off too, we could make love in the afternoon, something we haven't done in more years than I care to count." A huge smile spread across her face, and she joined in the undressing task.

Mollie, "After Bermuda, where they kept us so busy, I was literally at a loss of what to do with myself. What a fine idea!" And with that began a very pleasant hour.

— — —

The restaurant, called Wheeler's, also on Curzon (and just off Park Lane as it would turn out), prided itself on being a first-rate English sea-food house. We were given a nice table not close to the entry, the kitchen or the restrooms and big enough to accommodate me. Of course, we were among the earliest arrivals, albeit a few minutes late ourselves. When we asked the waiter for cocktails, he immediately understood we were Americans and not Canadians or from anywhere else in the Empire, or as it was then being renamed: The Commonwealth. So, he brought a glass with extra ice with our cocktails as well as menus (London had that part right: they never let you sit and wait on drinks. The drinks come first, then you order at your own pace with no hurry at all if you are early! We asked our waiter, Albert, about the house specialty. Without a moment's hesitation, he told us Dover Sole, …actually from Dover, grilled. They served it whole, on the bone: he would filet it at the table, or you could filet it yourself. I asked Mollie, who said, "You fish. I'm sure you can filet it." Albert took a slight step back, and with some enthusiasm, said, "Oh, Ma'am! I do not believe you understand, only small children share our Dover Sole. Some of our clientele, including Americans, have been known to order seconds! PLEASE I insist you each have one. If there is a great deal of waste, I shall adjust the price accordingly."

Even after we explained that we wanted an appetizer and a side of asparagus (which got a negative shake of the head with a change to creamed spinach), Albert was steadfast. In capitulation, Mollie said, "Albert, you certainly are a man of fixed opinions. So, I will relish seeing you filet mine at the table. (Pause as Albert began to turn away.) Then, she continued, "How long have you been doing this, Albert?"

He turned back, saying, "My Dad was a waiter here when he was called to action in 1940. My 16 year old brother took up for him until 1942 when he joined up as well. I was just about to be eleven when I began to wait many of these very tables after Teddy. He never made it back, but Dad did. The place stood up the whole war. We served as much food as we could acquire. Neither a soldier nor sailor who wandered in ever left hungry or thirsty during those years. And, by the way, I do love you Americans!"

When he brought the next round (Doubles now! They were grand with the ice, but still a bit skimpy with their pours.), I allowed that I was still in the U.S. Coast Guard and my Dad had been in the U.S. Navy on convoy duty; and that later in the War, was stationed here in London on Eisenhower's staff preparing for D-Day. When the tab came, our first round of drinks were not shown. My tip was lavish.

Dinner was a masterpiece: that first authentic Dover Sole only improves over time in my memory. Mollie's too! Watching Albert debone that piece of sole, reducing it to four delicate strips of succulent white fish, was like watching an artist at his work: his movements were deft and Mollie's fish was ready for her consumption in well under one minute. Mine took so much longer, but Albert nodded in approval when I finished. All too soon the evening ended. We were back in our room, had the next day planned out generally, and were talking to our offices and the children, then Kate and Ingrid. My head hit the pillow and I was instantly asleep with the thought that tomorrow night was our last in this Marriott and I would ask Dr. Doll if he had another less noisy hotel he would recommend.

— — —

On our second full day in London, we decided to tour Hyde Park which looked formidably large on the map of London's West End. (Regent's Park, not that far to the north, was also quite huge and included the London Zoo.) We crossed into the park by taking an underground tunnel system beneath the junction of two major city thoroughfares, Park Lane and Oxford Street, emerging at Speaker's Corner where a man stood on a soap box of sorts holding forth about how the City of London was being overrun by Arabs and Asians, an obvious xenophobe and not given to the best English. Some in the smallish audience (not enough people to call a crowd) were jeering him and he had but a single female defender. We watched for five minutes and decided to move down the Park Lane side of that park toward the giant lake called The Serpentine, the formal gardens (no name that I can recall) in the general direction of Kensington Palace and Harrod's. After walking 4 or 5 blocks, we saw what looked like fleets of double-decker touring buses lined up on the far side of Park Lane (4 or 5 lanes of one-way traffic heading away from Oxford Circle). Eight to twelve story buildings lined the opposite side of Park Lane. We knew we were in Westminster, but I do not think, until that moment, either of us appreciated how well-to-do this area of London truly turned out to be.

There was so much to see in the Spring bloom of Hyde Park: a group of young men, British by their words and the oaths they cried, were playing American football on an open field; sun-bathers and picnickers were spread out everywhere by 11-11:30. There was a bridle path of sorts next to the paved walkway, and a bicycle path close by it. Ancient shade trees towered in rows over the first 50 -100 yards inside the park (bordered by a wide six foot stone wall with gates and tunnels for ingress and egress) between the far side of Park Lane and the more wide open park grounds. After touring some blooming sections of the splendid formal gardens, we came to The Serpentine, dotted with paddle boats and canoes as the weather was excellent. We saw people sunning on a deck which turned out to be an extension of a restaurant adjacent to a giant tourist shop, at the Park Lane end of the lake. (We could not see the far end, for as its name implied, The Serpentine curved as it moved away to the west.) We stopped there, had a snack in a shady section of the deck, talked with complete strangers for a few minutes (tourists like us, but hardly any English), then continued on our way.

At the south end of the park after crossing a much wider active bridle path, we came to a gate which took us behind a massive structure which turned out to be the Hyde Park Hotel, but it did not appear to be on Park Lane. We encountered a Bobby who was quite helpful: explaining if we crossed the main street (needed a tunnel or to go a few blocks to the right), we would be in Knightsbridge, going right from that crossing point would take us into a major high-end shopping district which included Harvey Nichols, known for glamorous women's clothes, and the world famous Harrod's, or if we went left, we would be headed toward the more historical district including the Duke of Wellington's House, St. James Park with its Palace, the Pall Mall or Buckingham Palace behind its vast enclosure of walls and fences.

We opted to go left. Our tourist map began to come into focus for us as did the West End itself, quickly, and forever afterward, becoming the real heart of London for us as tourists! By 4:30, I was ready for a cocktail. We hailed our first black taxi (having taken a car to our hotel from Heathrow) and were whisked, by a mysteriously convoluted route, back to the hotel. But we did see a few sights from our previous day's walk as the driver made his way through that maze of one-way streets! (LONDON: What a walkable city!)

We went to the hotel bar for cocktails, had one each, then re-treated up to our room where we had an encore of the day before, but only after asking the concierge on duty to make us a 7:30 reservation again at Wheeler's (and to ask if we could have Albert as our waiter). We had a marvelous time lasting more than an hour. The concierge had left a discrete message for us as we put up the Do Not Disturb sign. I called down. Albert was off, but his son would take care of us. Would I like a different route? So, he provided one, some of which was Park Lane where the buses had been parked earlier. Some of the buildings were huge, maybe some were hotels?

— — —

The next day, we packed after exercising in the health club of sorts, followed by a modified English breakfast, then getting driving directions to Oxford (and the Randolph Hotel—you cannot miss it—ask anyone: it's famous!). The final arrangements for the rental car were made with the concierge, who spent a great deal of time on driving on the left, English traffic signals and especially round-abouts.

By 1:30 we were on our way and within 15 minutes, we felt lost. Still, we stuck to the script provided by Hertz as modified with more detail by the concierge, and finally after about 30 minutes, we spotted our route sign number. (Route sign sightings proved infrequent in Britain, but were only matched by the directional arrows which were often within the round-abouts themselves giving the visiting driver a chance to go around a second time, if possible, to be in the correct lane to exit the round-about on the second or third try! ADVENTURES IN DRIVING, courtesy of the English!). Despite several missed turns, we found our way to Oxford and pulled up in front of the Randolph which looked far older, and not nearly as nice on first blush, as what we expected. A man of indeterminate age came out to help us, asked our names and for the car keys, indicated the steps leading up to the entrance, and told us that all of our things would make their way to "our rooms."

The Front Desk Lady looked to be at least eighty. Her expression appeared imperious, but she had a most pleasant, almost melodic, voice which I shall never forget, welcoming us with, "Ah! Mr. and Mrs. O'Neill, Welcome to the Randolph. Sir Richard called personally to see that you were well cared for. We understand that you are also a friend of Dr. Nobel from the American Cambridge. He has also stayed with us several times. Your rooms are on the corner of the fourth floor overlooking our main street and our park. If you just sign here, we can transact all of our business upon your leaving."

I thanked her, seeing a name plate for "Mrs. Madigan." With that, a bell man (no uniform: something almost informal instead) appeared, was handed keys and with a nod, we followed him to an ancient "LIFT" of see-through wrought-iron which rose slowly, but stately, up five levels to our floor (the Ground floor in much of Europe does not count as a "Floor", but is a "level."). On the way, we both observed a magnificent staircase with plush wall-covering, along with decorative furnishings and paintings on each landing. First thing we said to each other when we got to our room was something like WE must walk down that STAIRCASE! Upon entering our quarters, the first room was like a sunroom with a big window looking over the street to a beautiful small park, next came the bedroom on the hotel's actual corner: commodious with two queen beds, two washrooms, his (shower) and hers (tub/shower), two giant armoires, our hang-ups already in each, our suitcases neatly arranged on racks leaving us to feel right at home as we ventured into the reading room to complete our tour. Mollie, smiling broadly said, "Can we stay here for the rest of our trip? If the food is good, no reason for me to ever leave!"

It was a great routine in London, so we used Mollie's bed, but only after I made a dinner reservation downstairs for 8:00.

— — —

The next morning, we rose well rested, eventually tumbling downstairs, having once again navigated that magnificent staircase ever so slowly. It was a museum quality adventure in decorating. My appointment with Sir Richard Doll was for 11:30 at the Ratcliffe Infirmary. Our waiter provided directions which amounted to one turn while going less than a mile. Mollie would explore for a while after I left and we would meet again at the Randolph to seek out a small repast that would carry us to another Randolph dinner which we could only hope would be as good as the night before.

I found the Infirmary without incident. It was an oldish looking nondescript single story building that seemed to sprawl about. The construction looked almost as if it was a World War II relic (turns out it was). Upon entering, I was greeted by a young woman in a white, possibly nursing, outfit. She looked me over, and before I could speak, said, "You must be Mr.

O'Neill, here to see Sir Richard?"

When I replied in the affirmative, she asked me to follow her as we set out on a labyrinthian tour of the facility: a few clinics here, a few laboratories there, with many offices and vast amounts of files and paper. I was ushered by this young woman through a doorway and into the presence of the great man himself. Sir Richard Doll looked old, but well cared-for and very English. He rose and came around his desk to shake my hand with a firm grip. He gestured for me to sit, and immediately asked, "How is my friend, Dr. Nobel? So many plans and tasks. I do not know how he keeps it all up."

When the doctor sat, only then, so did I. He noticed that, saying, "Prior military service?"

Having two questions to answer, I addressed the second one first, "Actually, I am still in the U.S. Coast Guard Reserve as a JAG officer. As for Dr. Nobel, he is so very busy. He had 'an invitation only' public health meeting in San Francisco a few months back which was the last time I saw him. He always appears quite hardy to me."

"Ah, I believe he told me about that. As you may have surmised, Dr. Nobel is quite taken with your reasoning about abatement of undamaged installed asbestos containing products. I admit that I am as well. You do know, I am certain, that I have written several papers critical of asbestos as a public health hazard, but I must admit that your contention that the U.S. Environmental Protection Agency's Guidelines to abate it before it becomes an actual hazard may be problematic by its overreaching commitment to do unnecessary tasks with substantial risks to the people undertaking those suggested abatements, not to mention the public as a whole, and not to focus at all keenly on the great expense involved. Believe me, we here, which include many members of Lloyds, are immensely wary of your American litigation process with your quite aggressive judges, as it may be causing a level of ruin in the British upper and middle classes among those who became Lloyds "Names." Fortunately, I do not count myself amongst that group.".

I responded at length, waiting until the end of my logic tree to assert the need for an expert witness of unquestionable character and scientific pedigree to serve as an expert witness in the very largest asbestos property cases.

When I stopped, Sir Richard looked like a man who very much would like to light up his pipe (but, of course, he had long ago given up all forms of smoking!). The silence was deafening. He squirmed an ever so little bit, then said, "I have envisioned myself as not becoming involved as an expert witness in an American court. But that said, this conundrum with which you present yourself here has great merit. Surely your court system cannot condone this type of waste?"

I took a few moments to explain the *Mullen* case, saying that it gave me some hope for our court systems, but then explained that both the fifty different state court systems and many of the federal circuits were generally not always in agreement on issues of science and medicine. He nodded. But his mind seemed to leave the room for moments. He looked up, then sighed, "I shall have to think on this. Your presentation has great merit. But understand, I am not a young man and my work is here. Yet, it would seem you deserve support and, from what you say, are not likely to get any of that in the United States. Give me a few weeks, maybe a month. I'll get back to you. Anything else?"

I thanked him for arranging our stay at the Randolph and told him about our desire not to revisit the Marriott. He chuckled saying something about it was another brand when those Mormons bought it and put their name on it to insert their own brand into the West End. Then, "You shall stay at the Grosvenor House. Its façade faces Park Lane, but you access it from Audley, the street behind it that runs counter parallel to Park Lane. I'll have a quick call to them. Are you enjoying the Randolph?" And we chatted amiably until it was 12:45.

The same young woman had appeared in the doorway be-hind me. Sir Richard rose and we shook hands across his desk. He gave me a wry smile and wished me well. Saying to the young woman before she left, "Mary, come straight back when you have seen Mr. O'Neill out. I need you to place some calls for me. Good-bye, Ronan!" were his parting words. Was that fa-miliarity a harbinger of success?

— — —

Mollie and I met up as planned and we spent the balance of the day exploring Oxford, its many colleges, some dating back to before Christopher Columbus made his voyages, not to men-tion a Norman tower from the first millennium. We stopped and snacked lightly in a quaint restaurant across from Christchurch College. After a few hours, we were ready for what was becom-ing our now late-afternoon tradition, and yet another splendid dinner to follow.

The next day, we headed down the road toward the West End once again, equipped with very specific directions on how to get to the Grosvenor House (the one-way streets and dead ends in the West End made driving for tourists an especially high-risk affair for getting lost, not to mention heading the wrong way on a one-way street (only magnified by driving on "the wrong side of the road!"). Still, with Mollie navigating and reading off the course changes, we arrived without incident and were greeted in the hotel's elliptical drive by a doorman in fine dark green livery. His luggage cart looked substantial. The door-man took the Hertz lease along with my keys, telling me not to worry and that he would see to all the details of its return.

We were whisked to the front desk where a very pleasant young woman took our names, turned, pulled out a plastic folder with papers. I signed, and again in moments, we were fol-lowing the bell man. The lobby was huge, sprawling, with corridors that ran off in numerous directions. I commented to Mollie that this hotel might occupy an entire city block. (Apparently overhearing, the bellman turned, saying, "actually it occupies two city blocks. A street dead ends a few yards down Audley from where the driveway gives out.")

We decided to stay at this old beautiful place for the balance of our visit. While Mollie was unpacking into our very large mini-suite, I talked to the concierge finding out that we could book dinner at other Trust House-Forte Hotels, but that would need a trip downstairs. We settled on a high-end dinner pub a few blocks down Audley with a marvelous garden court leading into it.

We found we were even closer to Wheeler's and that one of its sister hotels was Brown's, where President Roosevelt had liked to stay, as did Truman. The concierge said that their seafood was among the best in the West End. The Hyde Park, with its meat trolley served the best cuts of beef as well as an exquisite duck. Despite the English reputation for bland food, Mollie and I were surprised by our continuing culinary good fortune.

Another bonus for us: the tour buses, which we had seen from Hyde Park a few days before, left from the Park Lane foot entrance of the Grosvenor! So, the very next day, we checked the weather, mostly sunny, almost no chance of rain. We waited to be first in line to board a bus, made our way to the upper deck sitting in the very first row (my legs were a bit crowded, but Mollie was so excited. Our tour guide was fantastic! We covered so many of the famous sights and got a very exacting history of London as well. For example, the actual City of London, which came into existence in Roman times, is only one square mile with the main roads traversing it and marking its boundaries with stone lions. The Courts as well as many ancient establishments, like Lloyds, itself only a building, which even back in the late 1980s was not, nor had it ever been, an insurance company

(—but that gets into a story from a bit later in my life.). Turns out that no active royal palace resides any longer in the City itself. But the Tower of London, the Crown Jewels, the Barristers' Inns, Cleopatra's Obelisk and so many more sights do! A great day really, a survey of the place for tourists, but only scratching the surface of London's physical vastness.

— — —

After fine dining, walking about and having a marvelous time, work began to intrude on both of us. I found we were spending increasing time on the phones and dealing with ever-increasing faxes. Three days to go: at dinner (our tradition becoming interrupted by the increase in our workloads), I suggested maybe we needed to get away for one more day. How about we go to Canterbury?

So, we did—the very next day (with a side-track to Ascot – no races in season quite yet), and had a fine time walking the ancient stone streets and touring its great cathedral.

Only too soon, time to go home. Our last dinner was at Wheeler's with Albert in requested attendance: both of us having Dover sole, but he filleted both. It had been a magical two weeks. Never to be repeated with a growing family, but so much first discovery. I liked to think for years after that it rekindled our marriage – and I was mostly right on that last point!

Home at last!!

21

LAUSD Reignites

Mary and Martha spent time making trips to Los Angeles to cover many depositions, an expense that was unclear in its benefits as we were often unable ahead of time to tell if the witness would have anything to say that would somehow be relevant to that school district's relationship to wallboard products (mindful that our client had a plant in nearby Long Beach, it would be surprising if some of its product was not in the LAUSD buildings.). Months had gone by since we had any type of hearing before Judge Weitzman. Finally, he scheduled a Case Management Conference. I stayed in Bunker Hill Towers which had a few more months to run on its lease. Martha went too, but nominally stayed at the Sheraton on Sepulveda.

A main order of business was some disclosure, pre-deposition, to allow the parties to sort out which depositions they might wish to attend at all, and which lawyers they would assign to the depositions (most of these were by LAUSD to preserve the testimony of retired or elderly employees who might not make it to trial or were beginning to suffer from dementia — a great deal of this construction went back 30 to 40 years, or more). Toward that end, I brought Martha because I had attended no depositions since the Limitations Trial, while she had been to more than 50%. Plus, it gave us more credibility having someone present who could speak to this issue from first-hand experience. Other matters included what issues would be covered in the next trial phase (of course, O'Reilly would argue no need for further phasing, but some defendants would argue:

if none of their product was present, why should they even be in the case, much less have to sit through a lengthy damages trial?). Other topics included what discovery could be launched and when would it end; but, the pivotal issue was the one of sequencing and what defendants would be held-in for trial. (All of this was the result of the manner in which LAUSD had constructed its buildings over the years: they did no construction work themselves, instead they had people who prepared requests for bids (RFPs), and wrote some specifications (but as things became more complex, they left all of that to their third-party consultant architects, or "their people." Then, after the bids were awarded, there were contractors and sub-contractors as well as materials suppliers to those different levels of contractors – a logistical nightmare to go back and reconstruct.) Added to all of these process issues over the years was an overarching failure to maintain records, or be able to locate any that were retained by virtually any of these entities.

It fell to Abel Stoneman, Charlie O'Reilly's second in command, to confront these issues for the court (failure here would greatly undermine LAUSD's whole case!). Abel stood there at the lectern and told the Court, "We will test all of the offending products and based on the product formulas supplied by the producing defendants, our experts will be able to tell whose product is in what structure. It may take some time, but we are confident that we will be able to identify product from every defendant before this Court."

I rose, "May I ask how many of these tests have been successfully undertaken to date?"

Judge Weitzman did not look happy with me. However, since his antics in changing the jury instructions in Phase 1, I had lost respect for him, and did not feel threatened because any attempts to punish me with contempt would generate a Habeas Corpus Writ Petition bringing back to any appellate court that conduct we were certain this judge would like to keep permanently swept under his judicial carpet. The judge looked from me to Mr. Stoneman and said, "Perhaps you should explain where this testing process is at this point in time?"

Poor Stoneman! The look he shot me told me that he had been made the sacrificial lamb on this one. He hemmed and hawed, but it was fairly clear that the LAUSD lawyers had no idea what the depth of difficulty was going to be in proving up their case for identifying the manufacturer of every offending product in every building. The Judge interrupted after a few minutes when the obvious answer was not going to come out. He was clearly not happy, but was not nearly ready to throw the school district under the bus (could not help that one!), "Mr. Stoneman, what I am going to order is a temporary cessation to your deposition schedule. If there is someone who must be deposed to preserve testimony because of some potentially imminent outcome, give at least seven court days notice to defense counsel including the subject and scope of testimony of your putative witness. Meanwhile, I shall give you 40 days to move to establish a testing process supported by competent affidavits, the defense may have 40 days to respond and your client shall have 20 days for any reply. I will hear that motion and review papers on any other matter in the product identification phase of this litigation in 105 days from today. No continuances, even by stipulation. Court is dismissed!"

We caught the 2:30 flight to Scottsdale, staying at the Phoenician for two nights. We both got upgraded!

After check-in, we swam. Then we made love. Then a light dinner. Then we made love again. Martha said she had missed me for all of those many weeks apart. For my part, I had thought about her from time-to-time, but most often in a work context and rarely in a sexual one. (My response was something like "I missed you too!") This little dialog set me to wondering after she went back to her room for the night. But tomorrow promised to be a long day.

We met with Manny and Angela most of the day, breaking only for a light cafeteria lunch. First, we talked about what had happened at the *LAUSD* hearing. The remaining major subjects were client document discovery and the meeting with Sir Richard Doll. Most of the time was spent on discovery, specifically the problem of accessing CAL Board's vast collection of sales documents which would disclose to whom they had sold product dating back almost thirty years. Apparently, they never thought to implement an actual document destruction policy, or even to just discard their documents! Moreover, they had no computer system to facilitate access, just what was written on the front of each box and there were thousands of boxes. We knew the documents could not be destroyed now that litigation was afoot, but we also knew they were too voluminous to produce. I knew that creating a box content index was risky because if some judge, somewhere, someday ordered us to produce that index over our claim of work product privilege, then the plaintiffs' counsel would have a road map of what documents to request from CAL Board. Finally, the three of them persisted, convincing me of the need to go down that "Box Content Index road" on the grounds that such an index would be useless to a plaintiff attorney without its having all of the sales documents (my big fear was that the index would create road maps of how to ask for that too!). Oh well, I would leave it to Mary, Deirdre and their crew of helpers to come up with a sample index first. We could judge better once we saw what they felt they needed in order to retrieve documents readily. (We really had to try to see if it was even doable.)

Then Dr. Doll: I gave them a blow-by-blow description of our meeting, which yielded a "What's next?" response. More than three weeks had passed and we had heard nothing. I expressed my concerns about his health and his antipathy for the American court system. We broke at 4:00 with plans to meet for dinner at a plush steak house in Fashion Plaza, not far from the Biltmore.

Phone calls took up much of our free time, so I put off any extracurricular activity. Dudley Chisholm and Richie Goldberg joined the four of us from the day's meeting for dinner. After pleasantries and the first cocktail order, the topic turned to Sir Richard Doll. There was a level of rehash of my concerns, but Dudley was optimistic, arguably without basis.

Finally, the topic shifted from the Cal Board litigation to the *Wallboard* appeal. When I began, it was right after the second round of drinks, and after we had ordered dinner, "I got a call from counsel for *Wallboard*, not Ken Allen, but his daughter, Sandra. She asked if we would waive the costs on appeal if they did not go forward with their appeal to the California Supreme Court. I told her I would recommend that we agree. Those costs are minimal, nothing really compared to writing another brief. You are my only client on this one. You don't have to answer now, if you want to think about it."

Dudley said, "I guess I'll be picking up the check for this dinner! It's the least I can do to make up for all of your lost fees. Another great job, Ronan! You and your team keep getting it right!"

Some "Hear, hears!!" followed and the mood lightened greatly. The wine flowed and a great time was had by all. Equally true for Martha and me later that night, but only after I had called Mollie and the children.

— — —

We were back in Oakland for less than a week, when I got a call from Mary, Sir Richard Doll's assistant, "Good morning there, Mr. O'Neill, this is Mary from the Ratcliffe Infirmary. Sir Richard asked me to ring you. He has been quite busy with his own work as well as a number of peer reviews, but he did not wish you to linger any longer. (I punctuated her remarks with occasional sounds meant to convey politely 'keep going' and 'please, get to the point.').

He told me to tell you that he has more to discuss with you than he is comfortable doing in a Transatlantic call. He requests that you fly here to meet with him, and if you have a helper, to bring that person along to assist. He would come down to London for a few days and would prefer to meet you at the Royal College of Physicians and Surgeons in Regents' Park for a full lunch on either next Thursday or Friday, if that would prove convenient for you?"

There was enough in what she said to make me think that the answer could be positive, so I said, "I have a few things on my calendar for next week, but I believe I can get them rearranged. So, can I tell you that I firmly believe I could be there for Friday lunch. If I cannot do that, I "will let you know by this time tomorrow. Do you have a telephone number I can use?" She gave me the number, then asked what nights I would stay at Grosvenor House.

I called Lily into my office to start making flight reservations. Next, after thinking, I called Manny and told him what had transpired. He said everyone will be ecstatic. I could tell he was. The only NCC Meeting left for that Fall was in New York. I told Manny and suggested Tinker go, or our Mary if Tinker could not make it. He asked if I was taking Martha, to which I replied I thought we had to. This is the very reason we have someone with her assignment. He agreed. I said I hoped we could get a bit more prep work done while we were there. His response was, "Come back with a viable expert!"

I called for Martha. Amazingly, she was in the office, not in Los Angeles or on a BI deposition. When she entered, she had a big smile on her face, "Lily could not keep the secret. We are all so happy for you. This could be the breakthrough of the entire litigation!"

"Yes," I said, paused, and continued, "but Lily did not know that Sir Richard himself suggested I bring my assistant so he would not have to repeat himself. Manny thought that should be you. I agreed. So, can you clear your calendar for next Wednesday through the following Thursday?

Manny agreed that we should get more work done while we are in the UK, if possible. Otherwise, we'll come home early, if we cannot."

Martha's smile just got bigger and bigger. *I thought that I hoped this would all turn out OK!*

Tinker, Mollie, Austin, and the Reggies were all excited. My partners were suddenly awestruck for the first time. Jerry Klein said, "This Sir Richard is a world-class Big Deal! And you think you are going to recruit him? WOW! Where did he invite you for lunch?" Jaws dropped when I told them.

Mollie said, "Oh my God! I wish I could go back there with you. I would love to meet him. Tell me your plans."

I did, including that I was taking that associate Martha who had worked so diligently on getting up to speed on all of the asbestos Science and Medical literature. But, Mollie was more interested in my going back to the Grosvenor House and the thought of it being just the two of us together again in London.

As for me, I started thinking about how to best use Sir Richard in the BUILDINGS litigation, starting with *LAUSD,* so we could gain maximum benefit while exposing him to minimum risk and inconvenience. We were almost there!

22

Oxford To London

Before departing to London, I received a package from Carolyn: large, brown and seemingly wrapped with care, marked PERSONAL and CONFIDENTIAL. It sat in the middle of my blotter on my desk, no doubt placed there by Lily. Before opening it, I went over and closed my door. There was no return address evident, rather a post office box in a town in Connecticut with which I was not familiar. As I began to lift the lid on the box, I realized it must have had an original use for high end stationery. Right under the lid was a letter in Carolyn's handwriting confirming that it had been her block printing on the brown wrapper. I opened it:

Dearest Ronan,

This box contains photographs and some memorabilia from Patrick's first almost 12 years. I know I have sent you some photos and have told you about some things and events, but you are his father and I want him to know you better, even though you will always be Uncle Ronan. I have arranged the photos chronologically (despite my profession, I am at best a mediocre photographer, very much into snap shots of real life). Also, there are notes on the backs of many. It took me more than an hour or two to put this all together. Your son's memorabilia require more detailed explanations; and, by the way, at 11 years, 9 months, Patrick measures 6 feet, 2 inches tall, and he is a lean-muscular like his Dad. (Hope you still are!).

So, the reason I am doing this is that I am taking this

coming Summer off from my modeling career to spend it with my son. I do not believe it will harm my career and I want to spend time with my son and his father. I plan to be at the Cote d'Azur for almost 2 months. I would like to start having visits. If we can come up with a background so I could meet Mollie and your children, that would be the best route. If not, perhaps we can come up with something else. I would love to get away with you and Patrick for a week up the Coast, any chance?

These are some of the reasons I am writing, not all. I do understand the need to be most careful, but I am hoping to open a door for you to have a real relationship with your son. As for me, I am more than willing to take what I can get. I have made my bed, and I am prepared to lie in it. I look forward to your considered response.

With my Love,
Carolyn

So, after all these years, the time to confront my past had arrived. I could hardly consult Mollie, or Kate, about what to do. That left Dr. Arnaud. I got an emergency appointment. She never really got on me concerning my continuing relationship of sorts with Carolyn. I had mentioned Patrick, but always as a passing issue. Now, he was very real. I took the package to my visit. The good doctor looked at the most recent photos of Carolyn's Patrick critically. Then, she said what I feared to hear, "You know there is some very real chance Mollie will see this Patrick as your son. Did you bring pictures of your boys?"

"No," I said.

"Is there a resemblance?" she asked.

I studied the same photographs on which Dr. Arnaud had fixated; and, "I suppose there is some resemblance, but I don't think enough to mark them as half-brothers. How about if Carolyn were to say that the father was a single serviceman of Irish lineage who was killed in Viet Nam and she only found out she was pregnant after he had departed.

What about something like that?"

"'Oh! What a tangled web we weave whence first we practice to deceive.' I forget who said that, but I have a tendency in my practice to believe that particular rhyme is mostly accurate. Still, I have supported 'white lies' in the past when the options are limited and the truth would be too painful or pointless to reveal. Do you think that to be the case here?"

I frowned. I could feel the lines in my forehead compressing as I turned over options. The doctor said, "What do you think happens if Mollie guesses the truth? Or, what if she believes you both now and learns the truth later? What about your four children? If you need more time, take it."

I told her about London and leaving in a few days. She seemed to understand that I really did need to reach a decision that would minimize potential damage to all of those involved. I responded, "Sometimes the first idea is the best idea; but not always. I still have to explain that Carolyn and I were roommates for almost four years, but I do have my relationship with Sandra to cover that. Plus, Carolyn is famous. She's on all those magazine covers. Neither Mollie nor I are big magazine people, so I would say it never came up. What do you think?"

"I think you need to think deeply about that web. Turn over this option and try to think of others. I can see you for 20 minutes, tomorrow at 5:10. Let's talk then?"

— — —

The next day we met ever so briefly following a night when I slept ever so poorly. I told Dr. Arnaud that I had considered at least five potentially viable options. All contained risks. The number two option was just tell Mollie the truth. That one might work for Mollie, but my children might be a very different story. So, I had come back to my first scenario.

Dr. Arnaud nodded, stood, and put out her hand saying, "Good luck. I hope you don't need it."

We shook. I left the room thinking that now the plan was up to Carolyn. The next morning, I was in the office early. I wrote a long letter to Carolyn explaining that I was off to London, would return in eight days, and what I had been doing, without mentioning Dr. Arnaud by name or profession, just as an extremely discrete friend. The letter was clear that I wanted to devise something, but the decision to proceed down this specific path might, and in all likelihood would, require much more effort by Carolyn than by me. I felt I owed that to her to explain. Asking for her response when I got back and how we might talk, I signed it, "With Love, Ronan!"

— — —

That afternoon, Martha and I boarded the TWA non-stop to London. We were both upgraded to First Class and with the help of the Purser ended up sitting next to each other. Sir Richard's assistant, the efficient Mary, had faxed that we would meet Sir Richard at the Royal College of Physicians and Surgeons on Friday at 12:30 for cocktails in the Bar with luncheon to follow. No business materials, e.g., briefcases or recording devices of any type were permitted on the premises. Attire was "dressy," but need not be formal. A "car" would call for us at the front door of the Grosvenor House at 12:10. Few people met cars during the day at that site, so the driver would recognize us.

We chatted about that message. I took it to mean a fancy suit with starched collared, French-cuffed white shirt and an elegant tie. I had packed accordingly. Martha seemed a bit disappointed. Turns out she wanted me to wear a tuxedo which would have been the perfect complement to the "dressy dress" that she planned to wear. When I told her my suit was black with an ever so light wide stripe of muted blue, I thought she was going to swoon. "My dress is blue. Hopefully, we won't clash."

"My tie is the greater risk. It's my custom-made U.S. Coast

Guard Navy and Yellow gold," was my rejoinder.

"I think we will be OK. After all, we really are not appearing as a couple. We only work together," was her rejoinder. With the onset of cocktails, the topic changed to how to begin the training and use of Sir Richard. Martha made copious notes. We had a relatively light dinner and tried to sleep for six hours before being wakened for breakfast.

Wheels down, cleared UK Immigration, collected baggage, passed Customs (not the types to be stopped), found a black taxi, and off to the Grosvenor House in rush hour traffic. Dead stopped, I asked the driver, "Any way you could get around some of this and take us to Eton to look at the town, the school and Windsor Castle?"

The driver turned in his seat, and said, "You may have been there before, but the castle does not open until 10:00, if at all. Not sure if the Queen is in residence. Still, I can tour you a bit whilst this sorts itself out some. Are you on?"

When I said yes, Martha grabbed my arm and squeezed it. She seemed to be quite beside herself, or something. The driver made an about-face of sorts and in less than15 minutes we were in Eton. We stopped for a bacon sandwich and coffee, including the driver, turned tour guide of our little group. The town was mostly open. We walked a few blocks. The boarding school was now full of students, so we could drive nearby to see the cream of British male youth and I would say to Martha, "From these very fields and a few others like it here in England came the Royal Air Force fighter pilots who single-handedly faced down the Luftwaffe in 1940-41 and effectively won the Battle of Britain, preventing the "imminent German invasion" planned by Hitler. Instead, he chose to turn on his Ally and to invade Russia. The rest is history. Oh, by the way, my father was torpedoed on the way to Russia, rescued, fought in the landings in North Africa, and ended up on Eisenhower's staff here in London to help plan D-Day. I never saw him. Only pictures until I was three, in late

1946. He was a Captain in the U.S. Navy."

We paused in front of Windsor Castle: an incredibly massive stone edifice. I said something like you really do need to take the tour some time. I did when last here a few months ago. It was time to go. Traffic had begun to lighten considerably and we made our way to the Grosvenor House, but I could never re-trace our driver's route. We were shown to our rooms. I got a slightly larger suite than my last stay, while Martha was in a very nice room next door (with an interior door). We went to our rooms to unpack and shower. No sleeping: if so, jet lag could ruin the trip and especially the next day. I dressed in comfortable clothes after my shower and started reviewing my notes. No one to call as it was the middle of the night all over the U.S.

As I concentrated, I felt myself drift. Just then, I heard a knock. It was the adjoining door. I opened it. There stood Martha in her bath robe, I knew what was about to happen, but could only stand there. She opened the front of the robe ever so slowly. And when open all the way, she just let it drop to the floor, and pirouetted, finishing where she had started, and saying, "You like what you see?"

When I nodded affirmatively, she said, "Why don't you do somethings with it?'

So, I did.

— — —

Then it was Friday. We had a light breakfast in my sitting room. (I had a conversation with the head concierge which led us to the point that this luncheon might be quite long and the food quite rich, and perhaps a bit heavy. Thus, go into the meet-ing hungry, but pace yourselves.) While eating and for an hour afterward, we went over all of our planning notes for a final time. Martha wanted two hours to get ready. While waiting for her, I got a call from the hotel operator, "Mr. O'Neill, I have a call from Paris. Can you take it from a Ms. Tyne?"

Shocked! How had she tracked me here? "Yes."

"Ronan, I hope I am not bothering you. I knew Lily's name, so I used that to find out where you were staying. Of course, you know I'm in Paris. Can you talk for a few minutes?"

"Yes. Of course. Great job tracking me. Go ahead. Is everything OK?"

"Ronan, I hope you are not upset at me. I did not want to wait. Of course, I will do exactly as you suggest. To contact me in the U.S., my home phone...." She gave me a list of numbers, including one in Paris; and she wanted to talk on a few occasions to flesh out her background story, and to meet at least once before meeting Mollie and the family, primarily to put Patrick at his ease. I agreed to it all, and she promised to write with more details and suggestions. The call lasted less than 20 minutes. We rarely talked that long as our encounters were infrequent and usually very physical. I realized I would have liked to have talked to her for longer, but had to get ready.

— — —

At 12:05, Martha and I stood outside the "Front Entrance" to the Grosvenor House in front of its ornate, highly-polished brass and glass double/double door facing Park Lane. At precisely 12:10, a stately limousine, pulled up at the curb. The grill looked like a Rolls-Royce, but the absence of that trademark ornament left me thinking it must be a Bentley. The driver, dressed in livery exited, came around the car, opened the rear door in a reverse direction, and while holding the car door handle, turning to us, and said, "Mr. O'Neill and Ms. Walsh?"

"Yes" from us both, being equally flabbergasted!

"Please enter the vehicle and I shall see you to the Royal College."

I caused Martha to enter first. Her magnificent blue dress of

Heaven-knows what material seemed to flow into the car. I followed. The car door was so large that neither of us, being well over six feet had any difficulty negotiating our way into the rear seat, which felt as plush as a fine leather couch.

Although the interior window between front and back was closed, I wanted to see if we had privacy. So, I asked, "Can you hear me?"

Nothing. So, I tried more loudly. On the third try, the driver pushed a button and said, "On the console in front of you is a blue button. Press it down and, hold it to talk. Release it to listen. Do you need something?"

"No. Thank you. You've answered my question." I let go the button.

He responded, "Very well, sir. We shall be there right on time. We are passing through Knotting Hill and coming up on Regents Park."

Martha looked at me, her eyes wicked and said, "During lunch, if you get bored, think about unwrapping me later."

Just what I needed.

— — —

As we entered the Bar of this fantastic, what appeared to be centuries old establishment, constructed of ornately carved, darkly stained wood and featuring black leather upholstery, Sir Richard Doll, dressed in a "Day Suit (formal wear of a sort, not worn in the States)" rose to meet us. "Welcome, Mr. O'Neill. A pleasure to see you again.'

With that, I intervened, saying, "Please allow me to introduce one of our firm's outstanding younger lawyers, Ms. Martha Walsh." Martha extended her hand to shake, but Sir Richard bent over that hand and kissed it instead.

"Welcome to the Royal Society of Physicians and Surgeons, Ms. Walsh. Your dress is quite exquisite. If only my dear wife was here to appreciate it more fully. I am certain that all of our members are appreciating it now. You are truly glamorous. Please, both of you, join me for a drink. There was a uniformed attendant behind each of us to make sure we were seated comfortably. Small talk about travel filled the first minutes. Then the menus arrived and we selected only our main course as our host had chosen the other four courses!

"I do not wish to do all of our business over these cocktails. By the way, I have ordered two rounds. Do not worry about memorizing things. Mary will send all you need to Grosvenor House. We were in rapt attention, as he continued, "I shall not be able to go to the United States to help you. I am sorry. The reasons I stated previously remain a factor. Moreover, within a week of your leaving, we were given the opportunity to lead a research project of substantial complexity potentially impacting world health in many African nations. I would be one of its several leaders. The request comes from someone highly placed whom I could never consider rejecting. I am afraid I cannot give you any more details at this point as no official announcements have been made."

I was shifting about uneasily as was Martha when the second round was placed in front of us. Sir Richard appeared not to notice our unease. He went on. "To the Queen. Long may she live! Now the good news. First, you need a brilliant epidemiologist with a reputation based strongly on his studies of asbestos and its mechanisms. The foremost such doctor in all of the UK, and perhaps the world, is J. Corbett McDonald, and as a bonus, you will have access to his wife, Alison, with whom he is a frequent co-author. She is a world class epidemiologist in her own right. I have spoken to them both. They would very much like to meet you both, if possible, while you are here on this trip. I suspect you planned your stay in order to work with me, so the opportunity to meet them can be arranged for early next week. Mary will be in touch with you whence you get back this afternoon to get your availability."

A deep inaudible breath and I had started to relax, saying, "Of course, we so looked forward to working with you, and we will greatly regret missing that opportunity. Still, Dr. McDonald is world renowned for his years of work and prolific writings on asbestos and its causation of diseases. We have Monday, Tuesday and Wednesday in which to meet them."

Dr. Doll smiled. "I may have saved the best for last and by no means is that a slight toward Corbett or Alison, whom I greatly admire. But a man somewhat younger than you, Mr. O'Neill, was my co-author on my relatively recent asbestos paper, peer reviewed and published in the *Lancet* about fifteen months ago. This would be Julian Peto, perhaps the best analytical mind in all of the UK. Utterly brilliant, and at times, perhaps somewhat difficult. If you are able to convince him of the vitality of your ideas, you shall have an asset of immeasurable value.

Also, I am working on one more, but that will not be possible for a few months at least."

The Dining Room Captain approached, "Sir Richard, if your guests and you find it timely, your meal is ready to commence." We spent the rest of that afternoon discussing the three new experts, learning more about Sir Richard, and his learning more about us. The Bentley took us back to the hotel. A fax from Mary laid out a schedule of available dates for next week. We paused in the lobby, formulated our response and a clerk sent off our reply: Monday for Mr. Peto and Wednesday for the McDonalds.

We went to our rooms; more precisely, my sitting room. Martha sat on the sofa with her feet upon a settee. I took my time unwrapping her. Quite the dessert!!

23

London: Julian Peto

After a dinner of Dover sole at Wheeler's, with my old friend, Albert the waiter missing, following some work, more touring and much other physical activity thrown-in, we stopped for a night cap at the Red Room Bar just off the Grosvenor's Lobby.

Martha seemed serious as she sat there just across from me, seemingly cogitating. I interrupted her reverie with a question, "Martha, I enjoy our physical relationship as well as our working together. But being together this long on this trip has led me to ask myself a question, and I want to ask you the same one: What do you expect to get out of our relationship in the long run?"

There it sat for at least five, if not ten seconds. Then Martha sat up straighter, took a sip of her drink and looking at me eyes over the rim of her glass and quite serious, saying, "Eventually, I know you will break my heart. I know you will never leave your wife. And, of course, I do not want to be seen as any kind of home wrecker! But I do love you, and I think you know it. Pointless for me to say, because you cannot reciprocate. And as I just said, I know you have feelings for me, but I know that your love for your wife and family come first and foremost, and always will. So, when it comes to the sex, I love all of it! I don't want it to stop." She paused. But before I could speak, Martha held up a hand, and went on, "As for work, I want to be your partner. I want to learn from you and continue to work with you. But I will want cases of my own, as well. And someday, maybe I'll leave, or maybe you will. But be certain of one thing: our sex life, about which I have told absolutely no one, will never be used by me as a *quid pro quo* for that partnership. I want to earn it, and I know you are in the very process of giving me that chance. So, I don't really want much more than what we have now. Just ever so much more of the same."

"Wow! You did not come up with all of that just now, did you?" I replied.

"No. In fact, I am glad you asked. I think I owed you that. I don't think you owe me anything. Also, one other thing: just so you know, as is the case with a great many more women than you might suspect, from time to time, I like to fool around with another woman."

"Like one from Oregon in Scottsdale a while back?" I asked.

"Oh! You picked up on that? Was I that obvious?" came her reply.

"No. But you are not the first woman I got to know in a carnal way who also liked sex with her same sex. She told me that it often starts innocently when girls are young and just fooling around. On the other hand, she was pretty committed to the lesbian side of her duality," I said.

Martha, sucked in some small amount of air, and asked, "What is it you expect to get out of our relationship since you said you were thinking about it?"

I gave her a small smile, took a sip of my drink and looked at her with my eyes over the rim of my glass, causing her to break into a smile no doubt caused by my mimicking her responsive technique, and I said, "Actually, everything you said was highly accurate. I know you are very, very smart, and not just book smart. Moreover, I think you are a natural litigator who is in the process of finding her way to the top. I would be personally pleased to have you as my partner. I enjoy being your mentor at a professional level. You are so very good at our craft. If it was up to me, I would move to do it at the end of this year. But that really is too soon and would doubtless ruffle a great many feathers, and might even raise some suspicions. Still, toward that end, what I am going to do is tout you as a top talent and start to try to get you in as a junior at the end of next year, God willing and all goes well!" I paused and Martha looked ready to jump in when I put my hand up, took a sip of water, and continued, "As to the sex. It is some of the very best I have ever had. You are gorgeous, talented, clever and inventive. I have been blessed in that regard by others as well. I will stop there except to say I hope it will continue into the future. I hope that tells you where I have been and would like to go?"

We had been careful to keep our voices down and our tone light throughout this banter. Martha finished her drink, put her glass on the table, and leaned across whispering, "All this talk about sex has made me horny. Would you please like to fix that for me right now?"

— — —

The next day, we took a black taxi to the University of London, a city institution with very little campus, not at all like Oxford, whose colleges sprawled and co-opted almost all of that city as a giant campus of sorts. Following Mary's detailed instructions, we located the building housing the Department of Mathematics (its name was longer than that, but I have forgotten the rest), and with a few questions were directed to the office of Julian Peto, its director. The sign outside his door read: JULIAN PETO—Department Chair. No secretary was evident, so I knocked. A youngish looking gentleman answered the door, looked me up and down, then held out his hand, "You must be Ronan O'Neill and this must be Martha Walsh. I am Julian Peto. Please do come in and make yourselves comfortable," he said while gesturing to a large oblong table with a number of chairs. His office was a corner with two windows, but in front of one was a huge portable blackboard on rollers. The other two walls were black boards from about two feet above the floor to the 8 or 9 foot ceiling. The written matter on the boards looked like hieroglyphics!

We took two chairs and he took a third, but before sitting said, "I forget myself. Would you like some form of beverage?" We asked for water. He disappeared out the door returning in moments with a pitcher of water, no ice, and three glasses. Clearly no frills here, I thought.

"So tell me about what it is that's going on in America that you believe I may be able to help out with?" And we were off and running!

It was almost 2:00 when we had finished our attempt to persuade Julianof our position. (He asked us to use his first name. He did not like titles.). He excused himself and was back in moments. He allowed that the building's cafeteria had stopped serving lunch. I asked if there was a pub nearby and he said there was, but he did not drink at lunch if that was OK. We allowed that would not be a problem. He looked in his calendar, smiled and said that he had no further appointments and since what we were doing constituted work, he would consider having an early supper in lieu of lunch. Also, that would allow all of us to imbibe, if we wished. We arrived at the nearby neighborhood pub a bit later. Julian asked if they were still serving food. The barman looked about and asked what we wanted. Julian asked for Shepherd's Pie. Martha joined him. I ordered a ham sandwich with English mustard, which elicited a smile from the barman and Julian.

We took our pints to a table and proceeded to chat. Martha and I each provided some of our backgrounds to Julian. When it was his turn, he was rather brief, "I grew up in Southampton as the second oldest son of very politicized parents. I suppose I was found to be exceedingly brilliant at math by the age of 11 or 12. I was sent to advanced classes, and by the time I was a few months shy of 15, I excelled on the math exams and was sent up to Oxford to study. Various professors found me and before long, I was working on projects and contributing to their research and studies. That was where I met Sir Richard. He was younger then and utterly brilliant at analysis. Working with him, a number of others, and once with my older brother gave me the chance to advance my skills to the forefront of that institution. So, when I was offered a position here, I took it. I really do not mind work, even the administrative drudgery, but I do like challenges. Which brings me to why are you actually here, talking to me?"

"In the U.S., you would be considered a consultant to our firm and our clients until we nominated you as an expert witness. Also, please understand that between the federal court system and each state having its own courts and laws, everything we tell you can be quite jurisdiction dependent. As an expert, with your huge background in published studies, including those with Dr. Doll, and your ability to evaluate other studies in more than a peer review sense, we would have you as one of hopefully three, perhaps four, experts to talk about why this concept of abating undamaged asbestos containing materials installed in buildings makes no sense from either a health perspective or as an economic proposition, by using up resources otherwise available to compensate those actually injured by asbestos."

I paused. He quickly filled the silence, "How would I do that?"

Martha, "We would work with you. Provide you the background on the other side. Explain the difficulties experienced by the defense experts-to-date who have testified, and help you to create and elucidate a position supporting the propositions which might allow our clients to escape this area of potentially overwhelming liability. For example, if you needed some kind of data research, our client would fund that. We would make suggestions and interact with you to be certain that you were prepared. We would vet your position with our other experts and use you to help vet them. Please also understand that our client and its insurer have a very real history of settling those injury cases where a plaintiff has been harmed by our client's products. As Ronan said back in your office, we would not seek in any manner to undermine your historical work or that of others of high competence on the very real dangers of airborne asbestos fibers."

"So, in its own way, this is just another project, but instead of my publishing a paper, I testify?"

Me, "That's essentially correct."

Julian, "Where would I testify? How soon? How much preparation will I need?"

I paused, thinking this sounds quite positive, go slowly and do not blow this, "Well, you are much younger than Sir Richard. In his case, we would have tried to have him deposed once, perhaps on the East Coast. In your case, we might have to produce you in different trials. At the moment, the *Los Angeles Unified School District* is probably the closest to a trial on liability; and there is a class action to abate ACM from all of the schools, grades kindergarten through twelve, in the United Sates, and that is pending in a federal court in Philadelphia. Both of those are critical as damages could well range into the multi- billions of dollars. If we are successful, we would try to produce you just once for deposition, but because the *LAUSD* case is in California in state court and the SCHOOLS class is in federal court in Pennsylvania, that might not prove possible. We will spell out the logistics when we know more. Is this at all helpful?"

Julian stroked his chin and I noticed that he had some whiskers, not many. He looked at Martha, then turned his focus to me, "You do realize I hope, that I am apt to consider all of this to be utter nonsense. I cannot believe that your American court systems can indulge in such tremendous foolishness. However, I feel duty bound on behalf of a lifetime of science to assist you.

Now, let's have real drink! Do you drink single malts?"

The waiter came over and we ordered, mine was Macallan's 24. Julian's was a whiskey from some island on the West coast of Scotland and began with an "L." Martha ordered Johnny Walker Red Label. I tried to get her to try Black, no luck. Turning to Julian, I asked, "May I ask: What will be your fee?"

He looked at me as if I had said something nonsensical, "Well, I cannot imagine charging money to testify! That would be like a form of economic blackmail or some kind of corruption: buying testimony! I cannot imagine that. No, no! I have my reputation of which to think. All I want is to have my expenses reimbursed. In fact, you can start with this supper." He finished by smiling at me.

When we offered to put Julian in a taxi after another round of scotches, he allowed that as an ardent Socialist, he always rode home on the bus!

— — —

We went back to our rooms. It was after lunchtime in D.C., so we called Tinker, who got Mace and Tod on the speaker phone, and Tinker was able to get Scott Kelly and Ted Darrow in Philadelphia. We talked for over an hour. Everyone was delighted. Next, we called Manny as the Desert Mutual people started early. He was able to add Dudley and Angela. They were so excited after we explained all that was happening. So, then we called Jeremy Nobel. He was mildly disappointed not to get Dr. Doll, but quite pleased with the overall arrangements as they were turning out. By then Lily was in the office and we told her.

We went downstairs to the main dining room, had a light dinner and a couple glasses of wine and retreated for the night. I called Mollie with the good news right before going to sleep. She sounded mildly happy, but was feeling cheated by missing out on London, the Grosvenor House, Wheeler's and me!

24

J. Corbett McDonald

On Tuesday, we went to see the Crown Jewels (Every woman's fascination, I thought of Mollie the whole time I was there. Men were there, but no more than 25% of the crowd. This trip, especially free time, was running overlong!). The rest of the day, we made outlines. Whereas Julian was a mathematician with epidemiological training, Dr. McDonald was a medical doctor who had come to specialize in epidemiology after World War II. He and his wife Alison were prolific in their publications, with their greatest concentration being the dangers caused by asbestos and the dose/response nature of its causing Asbestosis. Certainly, they had a massive understanding of Pulmonology and many other medical disciplines.

We took a black taxi to Brompton Hospital in the West End at far Chelsea. Dr. McDonald had vast facilities, shared with his wife and research teams, with easy access to meeting rooms and a huge lecture hall. Clearly, this was a man of true distinction, as was his celebrated wife.

Martha and I found our way to their outer office, a working facility, and were greeted by a number of his staff who also seemed to be expecting us. The door to his office was ajar and a gray-haired, stoop-shouldered gentleman of what appeared at least 70 years, smiled, straightened himself to a somewhat more erect posture and introduced himself as Corbett McDonald (losing years in this transformation). He stared up at me, saying, "Sir Richard forgot to mention how very tall you are, Mr. O'Neill." Turning to Martha, he had to look up as well, and added, "You are quite tall as well, Ms. Walsh."

"Please call us Ronan and Martha, Doctor," were my first words to him.

"You Yanks are so informal. I just love it. One of my sons who's a clinician lives in Burlington, Vermont, and he has become quite Americanized having married a Middlebury woman whom he met while they were together in medical school at Magill. Of course, you must call me Corbett and most of the people in this room are either M.D.s, Ph.D.s, or both, so we do not stand on titles. These four, gesturing and giving names and titles, will be joining Alison and me in our office. Please come in and take your seats."

So it was that we met Corbett, who became a friend of almost 30 years, Alison, his wife and senior by a few years, and his four senior staffers, each of whom was the lead on a different project. As mentioned, this couple was prolific in the scope of their epidemiological writings as well as collecting researchers at the very top of their respective professional disciplines, and bringing them into application of the strict standards of successful epidemiology.

After a short round of pleasantries, we got down to business. Corbett allowed that Sir Richard had spoken most highly of Martha and me as well as recommending Julian Peto. We affirmed that Julian had agreed to work with us. Corbett nodded sagely, "Julian does not suffer fools, gladly or otherwise. Did Sir Richard tell you that?"

"Well not in so few words," I said, Corbett smiled, and I went on, "In fact, we found him quite pleasant and hospitable. He certainly has a very quick mind and does appear brilliant. However, we see each of you as having somewhat differing roles, as you approach your tasks from a somewhat different, but perhaps overlapping at times, perspectives."

Alison added, "You are very well spoken for a Yank, Ronan. Such an Irish name. Are all of your relatives from Ireland?"

I found the question quaint, but interesting, "Yes, Alison. I am part of the third generation born in the United States. My paternal grandfather was a bricklayer for John B. Kelly in Philadelphia. My father fought in World War II for the U.S. Navy and was on Eisenhower's staff, here in London, for almost two years and went into insurance brokerage after the War. My mother, born Garrity, is a graduate of Dumbarton College in Washington, D.C. and served as the chief of staff for Congressman Burke of Philadelphia at the start of the War and when he joined the Navy, my mother took over his job and was re-elected three times, holding down that House seat while raising my older sister and me. They loved England and London, as does my wife. She's also Irish-American. I grew up in D.C., my wife in Philadelphia. I graduated from Georgetown and my wife from American University, both in D.C. The rest is a story too long to tell now."

Martha then provided her background, including years of her life about which I knew very little or nothing. Then, Martha got started talking about Corbett, then about Alison, then about two of the others present. The McDonalds and their lead staff became somewhat in awe of all that Martha had to say about them and our level of preparation for this meeting. Martha's looking at me served as a cue for me to change the subject by almost 180 degrees and to launch into our presentation on how they might help right the wrong being perpetrated in the United States court systems.

I finished by saying, "We understand that you are some of the world's leading authorities on asbestos fibers being the cause of so much generational suffering. We will not ask you to renounce anything you have written. Rather, it is the fact that you have written all that you have which makes you both the voices of risk and reality that we think could best convey the message that the removing of undamaged asbestos containing construction products from buildings poses risk for unnecessary potential future injury, as well as the huge resource wastage on that which does not now need to be fixed."

Corbett answered, "I thought you wanted only me?"

And I thought that it was good that Martha, Tinker and I had gamed this meeting several times, and that we had foreseen this circumstance as recently as yesterday, "We know that you function as a team in virtually all your work. We would retain both of you as consultants to our firm and our client. But when we have to declare an expert witness to testify either in deposition or in court, only then would just one of you go forward as that witness. The reason for this is not a reflection on either of you or your team, rather it is a reflection on the very nature of the adversarial system practiced in the American Courts where even the slightest hint of inconsistent testimony among experts can be used to try to impeach them. That is the sole reason that just one of you ultimately will be designated the expert for trial. We just have to ask you to trust us on that point until the time comes."

"We are honored that you ask this of us. Of course, you will cover our expenses associated with this endeavor?" And as I nodded affirmatively, he finished, "But of course, we cannot accept any fees as do so many American experts. Please tell us when we can begin on this project?"

We did just that for the next hour.

— — —

Our last night in London seemed a bit anti-climactic, yet we had accomplished all we had set out to do, but with a much different cast of characters. After packing, Martha came into my room, sat on my bed, and said, "I am going to miss going to bed with you every night so very badly. Please stop packing and hold me?"

I did. We made love. We fell asleep in each other's arms!

25

Planning, Carolyn and Clemson

Martha, Mary and I had a few days of planning when we got back from London. Some of the calls included Tod and Tinker as we began to look at the details of how we might utilize Julian Peto as well as Corbett and Alison McDonald. In addition, I spent a long day flying to Scottsdale to brief all of the Desert Mutual people on the London trip. (I wanted to take Martha, but with a rash of new BI cases in the Bay Area, we were getting swamped. In addition, two plaintiff firms in Los Angeles were beginning to file cases. Also, new filings in Long Beach and San Diego (including *SDUSD*, an imitation of *LAUSD*, but filed by a different law firm!). Since Martha was from deeper Southern California, after clearing it with Reggie, I asked her if she wanted to head up those cases for discovery purposes. Of course, she agreed.)

Mary's report on the last National Coordinating Counsel Meeting in New York was interesting. Several of the biggest firms for target defendants were going about creating new corporate entities while changing the functions of their historical manufacturing entities to try to protect the ultimate parent entities by utilizing intermediate layers of other entities and by acquiring other companies and appearing to merge functions, all in preparation for the potential event of having to file bankruptcy for a target entity.

The expert conundrum continued to remain outstanding, and any number of the defendants wanted to know the terms of our insurance client's escape from the *Wallboard* litigation. Sandra was present, but declined to discuss that topic as it was not on the agenda and I was not there. The next meeting was set for late January, a week after "the BIG *LAUSD* Hearing."

I had one more Coast Guard reserve weekend to earn my required points for the year. Only one more year to go and I could retire. I was planning to take a week at least at Christmas and New Year's. Two of my siblings were coming to town as was Mollie's brother. Kate was beside herself with planning. Then I got a call from Carolyn! She was going to be in town for a week just after the first of the year and could I get together with her at the old apartment on January 8th for lunch (She would have it catered!)? What could I say, but "Yes."

— — —

Before I responded to Carolyn, I got a phone call from Austin Smith at CAL Board. It had just been served with a class action in federal court in Charleston, South Carolina, similar to the SCHOOLS Class in Philadelphia, but for all of the colleges and universities in the United States, both public and private. That Complaint was terribly long. To whom should he overnight the papers in South Carolina? How about Tinker in D.C.?

I agreed to Tinker and told Austin we would have to find a firm in South Carolina. I looked in my Directory from The Society, my new honorary group. I began to make calls. Every firm already seemed to have one or more clients. Charleston counsel, then Columbia, fell by the wayside. Finally, I got the name of a lawyer in a firm in Greenville, South Carolina, all the way on the other side of the state from Charleston. I called Manny and told him what I was going through. He had no one as they did not write business in the Southeast states, as yet. He gave me the green light and I made the call. The Greeneville firm was heavily into Labor and Employment, but did have an environmental practice. I was put through to "Josh" Smoulders, whose accent was so thick I thought it could be cut. Turns out he was from

Alabama, went to Auburn, clerked for a federal judge in Columbia where he met his wife. His best job offer was "up here in Greeneville," so he took it, thereby making his wife happy by staying in South Carolina and setting himself on a Palmetto State career path. He said he would collect the case docket and send along all of the filings to date. We spent about an hour on the phone and seemed to hit it off really well.

Next thing I did was call Carolyn. A young voice answered the phone, "Hello?"

I responded, "Is Carolyn there?"

The voice, "Whom shall I tell her is calling?"

Me, "Please tell her it's Ronan from California."

The voice, "Oh my, you are my Uncle Ronan." And in that moment, I knew I was speaking with Patrick, my son, and I almost lost it!

Then I heard him calling to his mother, "Mom, it's your good friend, Uncle Ronan from California." With that, he was gone.

Then Carolyn came on the phone, I felt both relief and curiosity. We talked. I asked what Patrick would like for Christmas. I was surprised when she said she would let me know. Then I asked her about herself. She was fine, wanted nothing, but did want to talk about the January visit and the summer visit next year. (*I was shocked how much I enjoyed just talking with Carolyn, which got me to thinking how so much of our time together had been spent either making love or transacting business. We did need to talk more.*)

— — —

All of our "Buildings Team" took some time to read the Clemson Complaint, filed in U.S. District Court in Charleston, South Carolina. First Mary, Martha and I talked, then we added Tinker and his D.C. partners, and finally, we added Josh late in his afternoon. I said to Tinker, "Tinker, why don't you explain to Josh what we think about doing to respond to this complaint?"

Tinker took a deep breath and said, "Josh, we believe that Clemson University may somehow be part of the State Government of South Carolina. If that should prove to be so, then it could not be a citizen of that state, so the federal court would lose jurisdiction of the entire case. The problem is we do not have great access to the institutional background records of Clemson either in D.C., and certainly not in California. We do know that Courts will take Judicial Notice of governmental records, including legislation, charters, funding and the like. So, what do you think about some detailed fact research on your end and, if justified, putting together a Motion to Dismiss this suit for lack of subject matter jurisdiction?"

This was an early test for Josh: if we were right, he would not be around for very long since the lawsuit would die in federal court and it was legally inconceivable to have a nationwide class action filed in any state court because one state could not have jurisdiction over property located in another state. "Well, I must say that everything will turn on what gets dug up in that fact research, so we better get busy with that right away. By the way, some of those big Charleston firms want to have a meeting next week for all defense counsel. It will happen at the new Omni Hotel in Charleston. I am thinking that you all, or at least some of you may want to be there as you've been doing this kind of litigation for a while? Just let me know and I will make whatever plans you need."

We talked some more. I called Manny as soon as that call finished and filled him in quickly. I suggested that Tinker and I go to the first meeting along with Josh, so we could all get the lay of the land, meet the players and hear their thoughts first hand. Manny swallowed hard and said, "God, I hope this is not another huge class action like the SCHOOLS Class. You all go to that meeting. But do what you can to halt this thing in its tracks!"

When I told Mollie about this new case, she was not excited, saying that it meant more travel, more stress and less time together. At least I could hold out that the U.S. Coast Guard Reserve was winding to a close. We all had a nice dinner together. My children were wonderful. Their Mom and Ingrid, the *Au Pair,* were great. I began to wonder how to broach Carolyn's upcoming Summer visit. That would depend on our January meeting. A very busy year was coming up!

— — —

So it was that I first ventured to South Carolina. Charleston's airport was on a huge U.S. Air Force Base about 15 miles west of the city. Upon arriving in early December, it was dark. So when I took a taxi, all I saw were freeway lights, billboards, and exit signs. One sign I did recognize was for that famous Southern military college, The Citadel. A very famous graduate was General Westmoreland, Commander in Chief, U.S. ARMY – Viet Nam, while I was there.

The entrance to the Omni was up a dark, poorly marked street off of a main street in downtown Charleston, Meeting Street. However, the hotel's front entrance was well lit and exceedingly well-appointed. With Josh's preparations, I was checked in quickly, told that Josh and Tinker were awaiting me in the very modern bar, and escorted to my nicely furnished room. Its furnishings were a bit Spartan, but fine, and I put my hang-ups in the armoire and went back downstairs to the bar, easily locating my companions by virtue of seeing Tinker. They had another round while I had my fourth Vodka of the day, from a long flight and transfer in Chicago. We then went to dinner at a nearby restaurant on a second floor which must have been known only to locals. I can still remember my first taste of the "She Crab" soup – simply divine. The only thing that could make it better was a small shot of just the right sherry. Trusting the waiter about the choice of sherry was its own reward. The baked grouper was also outstanding!

While we dined, Josh filled us in on who would be the major players. When he went to start with the Clemson lawyers, we saved him time by explaining that we were aware of them from the SCHOOLS class action matter in Philadelphia where they represented class plaintiff Spartanburg. But we did not know any of the local defense attorneys except a couple whom I had met at my first Society meeting about five months before. Tinker knew none. So, we got educated on personalities in some cases and on law firms in others. Josh's firm was the only one from Greeneville. The rest were either based in Charleston, Columbia, or both for a few very big ones. It was these big firms that had seized control, essentially appointing themselves as Coordinating Defense Counsel to assist the Court, in this case, Judge Andersen of the U.S. District Court of South Carolina, Charleston Branch.

The next morning following a fine Southern breakfast, replete with cheese grits, we found ourselves in a massive conference room with one of the biggest conference tables I had ever seen. I recognized a face or two from the National Counsel meetings, but no one I perceived as a potential ally for our position (Josh's fact research was just getting underway). As was often the case, only two lawyers per firm could sit at the table. Tinker took a seat right behind Josh and me. There were sign-ins and introductions and speeches by some of the self-appointed leaders. There was a suggestion of a "Joint Defense Fund" to cover group expenses. The leaders did not explain the need for the fund, but suggested that each party start by contributing $1,000. There followed a discussion on naming the fund (and who would administer it). This proceeded to use up the bulk of the morning session: nothing accomplished!

Tinker and I were appalled. Even Josh, who had become a local after more than thirteen years of practice, was a bit taken aback. Tinker had a six o'clock flight while I was spending the night. Josh was planning to drive home, but decided to stay over to keep me company. We wondered when they would get around to discussing the case itself. The afternoon session started about where the morning had ended except that some compromises had been negotiated during lunch (brought in): the Fund would be called "The CAT Fund," short for 'Cocks [short for Gamecocks] and Tigers Fund' which were the college nicknames attended by most of the lawyers in the room, either undergraduate, law school, or both. (*Not kidding!*)

Finally, one of the co-chairs broached the topic of "what do we do next?" He (there was only one woman present and one person of color in a room full of at least 100 lawyers!) The majority and coordinators' suggestion was that the defendants answer and request a scheduling conference to set up a discovery schedule: not do anything like what was done in *Mullen* (No Class survived the attack on the Complaint in that case), but rather to follow the litigation model of the SCHOOLS Class, which was quickly certified following little discovery and was now an on-going nightmare for the defendant companies while their counsel, in many cases very big firms, were earning a small fortune defending that class case.

Josh was not yet sufficiently versed to advance an argument like the one I made in *Mullen*, so he sought to have me introduced to speak. Not well received! I had not yet been admitted to practice on a visiting basis in South Carolina (not really possible since CAL Board was only served last week), but I was given five minutes. I made a case to proceed as we did in *Mullen* and pointed out its success as opposed to the SCHOOLS "opening defense strategy" similar to the suggestion on the table here, suggesting by a relatively obvious inference that the leaders' pending suggestion was doomed to fail from the outset. No one seemed to care and they all agreed to proceed with an Answer to the Complaint with coordinating defense counsel getting a date certain to file and a hearing date for the scheduling conference. With that, they were done!

The paucity of discussion on the merits of how to proceed allowed us time for a drink before Tinker had to leave. We expressed mutual disappointment. I told Josh to be sure to tell the "Defense Leaders" to allow for a briefing schedule before the Scheduling Conference was set. He agreed to do that, as well as copying all counsel on that suggestion. I pointed out that if we were wrong on Clemson being a state entity, then we could advise the other defendants at the conclusion of Josh's fact research and they might shorten up the time lapse for the Scheduling Conference.

— — —

When I got home the next night, I was exhausted. Getting from Charleston, South Carolina to Mill Valley, by itself, was an arduous day's work. Mollie seemed so happy to see me as did the children who were simply growing up too quickly. It was great to be home for the Holidays!

The rest of the year was not so rugged. At our friends' New Year's Eve party, I had a premonition about the coming year and the ever-approaching change to another decade: some rocky events were going to occur, but I could not begin to sense what they might be.

26

Sausalito: Carolyn's Day

January 8th arrived. I left our office in Oakland, and driving through San Francisco, I noticed the chill, damp air made it necessary to turn on my window defogging system. I parked on the roof deck of the *Cote d'Azur*, popped open my umbrella as it was beginning to rain and made my way to Carolyn's apartment. No sooner had I knocked than the door was opened and there stood Carolyn, "Everyman's Dream." Somehow, she still had that "girl next door" beauty, but she also exuded something special (Was it sexiness?) and what a smile!

"Hello, Ronan, it's been way too long," as she looked me up and down. I was wearing a suit having just come from work. Carolyn was wearing burgundy wool slacks and a loosely cut white cashmere sweater. No jewelry at all. She ushered me inside whereupon we kissed and hugged. She felt warm in my arms and I did not release her immediately, savoring the moment as it were. My greeting was a big smile and a "Great to see you again!"

We looked at each other for what seemed like half a minute, then she said, "I never imagined a life *with you* until this very minute. Why did I not see what I should have felt that night you got out of your car in that uniform? In retrospect, every man I meet, I judge him against you. I keep thinking I should do it for Patrick, but I can never quite get started. Come over here," she beckoned to a chair in the living room looking out to the deck where the rain was now pelting down.

I went to sit where Carolyn indicated after she stopped me to help me off with my suit coat. I stopped right there. Carolyn asked about a drink and I asked for vodka. She poured from a bottle of Grey Goose, saying, "French. It's supposedly very good. (a pause) Me: I stick to white wine or Champagne." She came over and we touched glasses. Hers was wine.

I said, 'Do we talk now?"

Carolyn, "Yes."

"What do you think of my ideas on how to approach Mollie?"

Her, "I do believe you will need to tell her that you lived here, but not 'with me.' Did she ever ask where your things came from? Didn't she know you had lived in Sausalito all during law school?"

Ronan, "I'm really not sure. She never seemed at all curious about those years when we rarely saw each other, and always in Philadelphia. You see, she saw a fair amount of my mother who began to date her widower father. I explained Sandra right away when we got together after my event, including our 'sex life.' Maybe she thought I lived with Sandra. Then she just treated me as if that chapter of my life had closed and a new one was open, and that chapter became our story, our life together, and in that, it was all about her, us, and no one else. Somehow, you just never came up. Tinker and Elaine knew, but maybe to protect Mollie, or maybe even me, they never mentioned my roommate in Sausalito other than that I had one. Not even a mention of your gender, and certainly nothing about your fame. Frankly, I am not all that certain that either Elaine or Tinker suspected that you and I had any form of relationship. After all you were gone a great deal, and more so as time moved on."

Carolyn sat looking at me, not a sexy look, just an attempt at 'where do I take this from here' look, or something like that. At least that's what I was thinking. Finally, after some apparent reflection, and with a look straight into my eyes, she said, "You know I've told you before you are the only man I ever planned to be with. (She was looking, so I nodded affirmatively.) I have meant that every time I have ever said it and thought it ever since you signed that lease for me. As I sit here now, my feelings for you have changed just a little bit. I know I love you more because of Patrick, that I will always love you, and you will always be the only man I will ever love. (Another pause, and she held her hand up.) Yes, there are the women and I have differing relationships with three of them at the moment, although I intend to dial that back to two. Fidelity, sexual fidelity, is something I feel differently about by virtue of gender. How else can I say what I am trying to say?"

I wasn't certain I was meant to speak, but when she kept looking and her eyes widened just a tiny amount, I said, "You know, I never thought you wanted to take me seriously. You were always about the women in your life when we talked, and we often didn't talk that much. We both loved the sex, our sex. Nothing like it, with anyone. That was great and now I know we should have talked more, much more. Why…, as you sit here today…, can you explain, if you can…, why did you not tell me about Patrick when you were pregnant?"

Carolyn's head dropped, so she lost eye contact. Her hands came up, and much to my shock, her body shuddered. I went to her and pulled her up by her elbows until she was reluctantly in my arms. I could feel her sobs wrack her body. I squeezed her to me, but I could feel her resist. I pulled harder. Then, suddenly, she was fully in my arms. The weeping continued. Then, Carolyn took a huge gulp of air, and backed away pushing me ever so lightly until a space came between us. "You will never know how many times I have asked myself that question, or some version of it, over the years, starting even before Patrick was born. I thought I was sparing you. I thought I was being noble. I listened to one of my girlfriends, but in the end, I did not listen to my heart. Oh, Ronan, what would have happened if I had told you?"

My hands still held her arms and I pushed her backward just

far enough so that I could look in her eyes, and taking a deep breath, said words I shall never forget, "No sense worrying about that now. More than a decade has come and gone. Patrick and you have fashioned a life. Mollie, our four children and I have our lives. Neither of us is perfect, nor will we ever be. So, let's do what we have always done. Let's make the best of this going forward. I have told you before that I love you, and that I firmly believe that love cannot be limited to a single person. You must believe that too: look at your life!

'Now, let's work through this until we have a plan: a story, but not too much detail. We do not want to trip up either ourselves or each other."

So, we talked for almost two hours. We snacked as we talked, but then drank only water. We wrote no notes. We kept the story simple and the details were memorized. When we agreed to stop, we each had our second drink. Carolyn said, "That may be the longest we have been awake together without making love."

My response, "We cannot go back and fix that, but we can put an end to it, if you want to?"

Carolyn was in my arms by the time I said that last word.

Mollie was not home when I got there, so I grabbed a quick shower. Later, I put my shirt in the trash. Carolyn was going to be here for three more days. WOW!

27

LAUSD Phase Two

On Tuesday afternoon of the third week of January, I flew down to LAX. Martha picked me up outside the PSA Terminal in her Ford rental car. We drove to the Bunker Hill apartment building which Desert Mutual continued to rent for us for this trial, and which I got permission for others from our firm to use in lieu of a hotel if they were on Desert Mutual business and, if on other business, we reimbursed them $200/night which meant the more use we made of the DMIC apartment, the more of a "win/win" for everyone involved.

On the way up in the elevator, Martha said what a long time it had been since we had spent any time together other than in the office or on the phone. Of course, she was right: what with the Holiday season, business travel was often curtailed, and other commitments came into play. But my response was simple: the next five months were bound to be super-busy, and she would probably get tired of me. We had the NCC conferences starting next week, *LAUSD* tomorrow, expert meetings to set up in London, and the two federal court class actions in Philadelphia and Charleston. Martha was involved in all of that plus she had an increasing number of bodily injury cases in Southern California: now including San Diego, Orange and Riverside Counties in addition to Los Angeles. (Part of what I wanted to talk to her about was opening a sub-office, but only if she could split her time and handle it.)

When we got to the apartment, Martha poured us both a drink. We first talked about the *LAUSD* hearing the next day. She had made notes beforehand. We had received "nothing" from Charlie O'Reilly's team: NOT a surprise! The judge would be unhappy. Martha thought that with input from Corbett and a materials lab/expert, we could show that the suggested methodology advanced by the Plaintiff's counsel 100 days ago could not get off the ground.

At 5:15, Lily called Martha's mobile phone to tell her we had just received a fax from the Plaintiff's counsel about tomorrow. Martha asked her how many pages, and fifteen minutes later we were both reading *LAUSD*'s new position, which made our task all the more sensible. Plaintiff wanted the defense to produce all of its formulas, there would be split sampling and every defendant who made the type of product would have to prove that the sample was not from their product. (In other words, the Plaintiff sought to flip its burden of proof and to thrust it on the defendants, other problems were readily identified as well.)

We ordered from the deli in the basement and worked until about 9:30. I called home and spoke with Mollie and the two older children. When I finished I knocked on Martha's bedroom door, she having excused herself so I had privacy to speak with my family. She called, "Come In!"

When I entered the bedroom. Martha threw back her covers and there she was, all of her: an admirable sight! About an hour later, we went out to the living area, had a drink and then a later encore.

— — —

The next morning, we were among the first arrivals at Judge Weitzman's courtroom. Martha went up to the clerk and checked us in as attending, and that I would speak. Then she handed the clerk three copies of our Opposition to the Plaintiff's new discovery plan which we received after the close of business yesterday (Tinker and his people being three hours ahead of Pacific time had added legal citations and additions to what Martha and I had written the night before and faxed to them, so they could start on completing it while we slept.). I put a copy of the Opposition at the Plaintiff's counsel table for when they arrived.

Other defense counsel were milling about and one of them wandered over, asking, "I thought I saw your associate file something with the clerk. May I ask what?"

I replied, "It's an Opposition to the Scheduling Order filing we received at my office in Oakland last evening at 5:15 p.m. Have you seen it?"

When the attorney shook his head negatively, he called to several others who came over. None of them had been to their respective offices, so they knew nothing about the new Scheduling/Discovery Suggestion served on behalf of *LAUSD*. So, I explained what the plaintiff wanted and the bases of our opposition. About then, Avery Schein strode in. He went up to the clerk and asked to be heard first on behalf of the Defense. The grey-haired lady clerk looked up at him, smiled a sweet soft smile and said, "Mr. O'Neill was here before you and he has already made such a request. So, if you can change his mind, we can oblige you, otherwise he has the right to go first. By the way, do you have a brief to file?"

Avery strode over to me asking if I knew what the O'Reilly team had pulled. I allowed I did and we had arrived with a written Opposition, including objections in our brief which we filed about 20 minutes ago. Then Avery asked, "Am I to take it that you are prepared to argue the merits of *LAUSD*'s Submission?"

"No, not to begin with. Rather I plan to object to this hearing going forward as the Plaintiff is in violation of this court's express briefing schedule set 105 days ago, and seeks to undermine the opportunity for the defense to address any suggested discovery. Certainly, the one merits point I would make is the Plaintiff's counsel seeks to shift the burden of proof in this matter, and to do so, must show law and facts compelling a court to do so. None of which is present in the briefing served yesterday;

and as a consequence, the defendants would move that this untimely filing be stricken and counsel for *LAUSD* should pay monetary sanctions to all defendants in attendance."

Avery's chin drooped ever so slightly as he asked, "Is all of that in your brief?"

Martha reached over and handed Avery a stack of stapled paper, saying "A copy of our brief for you, Mr. Schein. Ronan said to save one for you." As at that very moment, Charlie, Abel and two members of the *LAUSD* School Board came in and sat, except Abel who went up to the clerk to check in.

Avery read two pages, turned to me and said words to the effect that I should go first and he would fully support what I had told him. Avery took his seat at Defense Counsel table next to me and then Martha. When Abel sat at Plaintiff's table, he immediately began to read and started passing the pages to Charlie. Before they finished, Judge Weitzman's bailiff began his wailing introduction of the Judge. We all stood.

The judge did not look happy. His face was not smiling and he scanned his courtroom which was full of lawyers, virtually all there for the many *LAUSD* Defendants. Finally, his gaze rested on Charlie O'Reilly and Abel Stoneman, saying, "Counsel for Plaintiff *LAUSD*, what is the reason for your failure to timely file your Suggestion for a Scheduling Order and Discovery in accordance with the briefing schedule which I gave you? That issue is NOT discussed in your papers received in my office a few hours before yesterday's close of business?"

I considered speaking, but decided to see how things played out for Plaintiff's counsel instead, thinking it might prove more beneficial if the Judge made our opening argument the day's deciding factor. Abel Stoneman rose, "Your honor, we were aware of your scheduling order and tried to meet the dates, but some of our consultants let us down, so we needed to evolve a newer version of what I was proposing more than three months ago. Perhaps we should have sought a continuance. For our failure to do so, we apologize. However, we came here today with a concept that the defense can analyze, even criticize, but that creates a workable methodology to bring this litigation to a rapid and accurate conclusion. Certainly, we did not expect your Honor to rule in our favor on a last minute filing, but we did hope to hear something from the many defendants, most of whom we were able to serve yesterday, albeit that most were served after their close of business. Certainly, that did not prevent CAL Board from filing its Opposition to *LAUSD*'s Suggestion."

I started to rise to address Mr. Stoneman's arguments, but Judge Weitzman put up his hand to stop me from speaking, "Mr. Stoneman, have you finished reading CAL Board's brief?"

"No, Your Honor," was the reply.

"I do not know how Mr. O'Neill was able to come up with twelve pages, replete with citations for all that is wrong with this *LAUSD* filing, but I do know this. I am striking *LAUSD*'s Suggestion. I am awarding sanctions of $5,000 to every party which sent counsel here today, plus the costs of travel. I shall hold those sanctions, except for the travel costs, in abeyance to assess the conduct of *LAUSD*'s counsel over the next months, but I reserve my right to enforce those sanctions. Now, your firm is to have a complete brief, supported by Declarations and citations filed with this Court in two weeks. No continuances will be granted. Every counsel is to be timely served with a full set of your briefing and supporting documents within 48 hours of your filing. The Defendants shall have 30 days to address that brief and to seek whatever relief they may deem appropriate, and *LAUSD* shall file and serve its Reply, if any, seven days after it is served with the Defendants' filings. I want to see everyone back here 70 days from today. And be warned, additional Sanctions are now on the table for abusing my Orders."

I rose before either Plaintiff attorney could respond, and said, "Thank you, Your Honor. May we request an expedited copy of this transcript?"

"So ordered," came the Judge's words.

Charlie O'Reilly rose, saying, "Our apologies to Defense Counsel, but your Honor, they are all paid by the hour, so they suffer no harm. Our client is a public entity, it should not have to pay sanctions in a case of this gravity."

Judge Weitzman held up his hand again to forestall anyone else from speaking, "Mr. O'Reilly, you have embarrassed this Court with your firm's behavior, I suggest you refrain from further comment at this time. I do not need to hear anything further on this docket item. Court is adjourned."

Abel Stoneman and O'Reilly conferred for a brief minute, and Abel came over to the Defense table, and said, "We know you have a firm in D.C. working with you, Ronan, but we were seriously impressed with what you put together so quickly. Can we talk in the weeks ahead? Please have a good day, Mr. Schein."

— — —

We went back to Bunker Hill Towers and called the office, then Tinker and his people, then CAL Board, and lastly, Desert Mutual. All were pleased with the result, although all of the client-types were unaware of the *LAUSD* last minute maneuverings. Our flight was at 5:00, so Martha and I changed outfits with a bit of activity in the process. Then we made our way to a Chinese restaurant for a nice lunch, during which I started to talk about how was Martha going to get everything done that was on her plate, which seemed overfull at the moment, and was likely to get worse if the rate of new filings continued.

When I stopped talking, Martha paused for a minute, then, "Ronan, you know that I want to be a partner, but I simply have not been with the firm long enough for that to happen, not to mention that I just might lack the requisite experience. It seems to me that if you are going to have a 'sub-office in SoCal,' then what you will need is a real partner to run it. That could be Reggie, but he has a family and he runs the BI for NorCal with mostly young lawyers. Still, you have Phil and Mary. Both are clearly more senior than me. Neither has a big connection down here, but neither do I really! So, why not pick one of them or worst case, hire a lateral. I can do some BI work down here, but I think you know you will need me on the Science and Medicine of this property litigation for the foreseeable future, and to do some BI trials where I will get the experience which I need to make partner. I will not feel passed over. Please think about it."

As that year unfolded, that Chinese lunch became a water shed moment for our firm, me, Martha, and my young partners. Martha proved wise beyond her years, and not greedy!

28

NCC Activity And Other Changes

It had been some time since I had seen Sandra what with my trips to London and missing the last NCC meeting followed by the Holidays. So, when I got a call from her on the Friday before the next National Coordinating Counsel (NCC) meeting in Philadelphia, I was not surprised. But the content of the call was not what I expected. Sandra called to tell me that she had started to see one of the Philadelphia defense lawyers, and was back there now. She wanted to introduce him to Elaine, still her great friend, and Tinker, a very small potential client conflict, which she was doing over this very weekend. She was calling me to alert me to all of this, so I was not taken off guard. His name was Adam Morris and he was with Bigstrom and Steel, counsel to US Gypsum. I asked if it was serious and she responded by saying she was staying at his place in Philadelphia. So, that seemed to put an easy end to my sometimes conflicting Sandra relationship.

Tinker, Manny, Angela, Justin, Marty, Martha and I, never all at the same time, had a series of conversations about what, if anything, to tell the NCC group about our evolving expert developments in the UK. We decided that we were not far enough along with those experts to identify them by name, but should alert the group lest one or more of them stumble into, or do, something that might otherwise upset our carefully constructed apple cart. So, it was to be Martha, not Mary, who accompanied me back to D.C., then Philadelphia, with Tinker coming up for the meeting day itself from D.C.

The meeting was on Wednesday. We flew into D.C. on

Monday and met all day Tuesday with Tinker and his people as well as Scott Kelly and Ted Dawson from our Philly defense firm. Most of the discussions had to do with constructing what we were going to advise our experts in preparing them to testify. The range of suggestions was incredibly broad, not so much as to our core presentation which was, at least to us, seemingly very straightforward; but rather on the topics in anticipation of cross-examination as well as potential objections from our co-defendants who might find themselves feeling undermined by our utilizing BI asbestos causation scientific advocates for the Property case defense strategy. I also asked Ted Dawson to call Jeremy Nobel to see if he had heard anything further from Dr. Doll about the other expert he was going to try to secure.

We broke at 3:30. The Philly lawyers went home. Martha typed up her outline of what she felt was decided with input from me. I made calls while she typed. One call was to Manny to suggest that Martha and I needed to head back to London to start the expert training program. He agreed. I mentioned that at some point, he or Dudley would need to come over and meet those witnesses, but suggested it would still seem premature for that step to happen on the upcoming trip. Ted Dawson called to say that Jeremy had not been in touch with Sir Richard for several months and had nothing new to report.

Martha and I fooled around a little before dinner, nothing serious. She seemed in a playful mood once London was mentioned. (I was wondering how Mollie would feel about my taking yet another trip to London without her; but I would suggest that the Spring would be a better time for her with much longer days and warmer weather.) As Martha and I walked to the Northern Indian restaurant where we were meeting Tinker and his partners, we talked about Sir Richard Doll and decided to see if a visit to him in Oxford might prove in order. (Martha mentioned maybe lunch at the Royal College of Physicians and Surgeons instead. I laughed making it a joke. She turned toward me and stuck out her tongue. I had a one word response, "Later!")

Dinner was about the next day, including *LAUSD*, the *Clemson* Colleges Class, and the SCHOOLS Class. CAL Board was also now a defendant in the *San Diego School District* and the *Riverside School District* cases. Six other commercial entities in California had also brought suit naming our client. We discussed these. Upon returning to the Mayflower, Lily called me to tell me that Orange County had just served CAL Board and Austin was sending the matter to her and faxing a copy to Tinker. I called Manny and told him. He was not at all happy to say the least.

Our discussion turned more to those California School District cases. The price of not being able to put an end to *LAUSD* was getting higher as the new filings mounted. Tinker volunteered that they could help with the briefing but they might need to add one more lawyer to their CAL Board team. (But I knew the big problem would be my firm's staffing for the California cases if we could not slow down the frequency of new filings.). So, I said, "How about if we try a version of the *Mullen* Demurrer focused on using the no actual damage tack?" As we talked, one thing was clear: we needed to buy time. A second thing would make sense: raise the *Mullen* defense tomorrow with our co-defendants and get them to join in. That sewed up the need to explain our expert program.

I decided we needed to get to Philly early, so Martha and I took the 6:30 Metroliner. On the way, I talked to her more about staffing SoCal, explaining that I thought making Phil a partner now would make sense and hopefully I could convince Klein and Kelly who still controlled the firm voting and its purse strings. I thought of mentioning Mary as well and lastly that you have huge potential. Martha was nodding, smiling and making notes. But we cannot do it all remotely, especially with the BI and commercial PD cases down there. So, I asked her what she thought about bringing in an experienced litigator with two or three years of experience, maybe even someone new to asbestos BI? Her response was that should be up to me. I told her that your place is locked in as far as I am concerned, especially as I see you continuing to function at an extremely high level.

The meeting was at Abbott and Tweed in Philadelphia. We went to their usual conference room, but on our way, I asked if I could see Alicia Goines as soon as possible. She was to chair today's meeting and the agenda included all of our discussion topics. I thought it prudent to give her a head's-up. Her secretary came in and asked if I would like to come to Alicia's office. I asked if I could bring Martha and the secretary shrugged her shoulders in a "why not" manner.

Alicia's office was a huge corner with a commanding view of Philadelphia, including City Hall with William Penn at its pinnacle, then all the way to the Delaware River, the Ben Franklin Bridge and New Jersey beyond. Alicia stood and gestured for us to sit while offering coffee and water. I began with the experts. She sat back in her chair and listened. Martha chipped in with just how "on-board" they were and world renowned. "People will start to guess. How can you not answer? Is one of them Sir Richard Doll?"

I looked over at Martha whose face was immobile. "We really cannot say until we are certain of all of them. We have one more to get," was my reply. Then I launched into the *Mullen* tactic for the new California SCHOOLS cases. Alicia smiled.

"Brilliant move to get here early. I remember meeting you for the first time at that first *Mullen* meeting in Sandra Allen's father's office. You were not happy about having been excluded. Seems you now see value in lining up the right votes. Let's get going. This is going to be the most fun I've had in a long time!" Alicia seemed to bound out of her chair, and we followed.

— — —

Tinker was there when we came back in. Martha moved her things to the chair behind us. Alicia looked over at her and said, "Martha, you have important things to say today. Take a seat at the table."

Sandra heard those words as she arrived. (I recognized the man with her from prior NCC meetings. They parted upon arriving. I noticed Martha watching them.) Martha moved back to the table. At 10:05, Alicia called the meeting to order. There were about 50 lawyers in the room. Alicia announced, "Ronan O'Neill and Martha Walsh came to see me about a half hour ago. They told me about their search for PD experts. As we all have seemingly failed to uncover anyone especially suitable, I would appreciate your indulging me by having them tell you what they have told me. Please listen very carefully. Also, please consider if we should appoint one lawyer to be in overall charge of experts going forward?"

So, we told them all about the trips outside the U.S. and to Europe. We told them the concepts, Martha threw in what she had said to Alicia. We told them our work was not complete, but we felt that the time was ripe now with all of the new filings coming out to begin to try new lines of defense. The experts would be our artillery, but our motion practice could be our cavalry. At which point I launched into my modified *Mullen* approach as extremely appropriate in California, having been upheld on appeal. At that point, Alicia jumped in supporting everything I was saying. When she stopped, Sandra rose and said that despite our past differences, she had worked on *Mullen* with me and felt this approach had the foundation to be successful in curtailing the new California SCHOOLS cases. (Please understand that any school district could opt out of the federal class action at any point in time under that Class Action

Affirming Order. The price was that those which opted out could not opt back in if their individual suit went poorly.)

Three firms were appointed to try to get briefing schedules in California for the newer filings to allow for demurrers. For some cases it might be too late as most Defendants had already answered. The meeting grew spirited. The discussion on *LAUSD* was sometimes vituperative, but the quality of arguments was often outstanding, as the various defendants present ultimately agreed to a united front in opposing the proffered Scheduling/Discovery Suggestion soon to be forthcoming from the O'Reilly firm. Sandra and I were two of the three person committee to do that opposition, with me as the lead.

— — —

We were staying at the old Sheraton on Rittenhouse Square, a few blocks from Alicia's offices. Tinker had time for a drink. We went into one of the restaurants lining the Square and, sitting at the bar, ordered our choices. We could not ignore Martha, as she was also there. Tinker said, "Sandra is having Adam Morris down to our place for dinner tonight so Elaine can meet him. She seems quite taken with him, even though we think he's two or three years younger. After all you've been through together, what do you think?"

Martha looked from Tinker to me and back. I said, "Sandra called me on Friday and told me about him. I guess you could say I'm happy for her. After that break-up and its aftermath, things went better for me with Mollie than they did for Sandra what with her failed rebound marriage. Besides, after our initial *Wallboard* experiences, things got even more than a bit ugly. Then with the *Mullen* matter, we were kind of forced to become allies of sorts. Then, when she began to come to some of these meetings, things became more cordial and we got along well the last few years. I think of us now as fairly friendly colleagues."

"Good to hear," was Tinker's response, "Elaine will be especially pleased to hear that. I better go. Stay in touch."

Martha watched Tinker go, then turned to me, and looking a bit quizzical, said, "Sandra and you had a relationship? I would not have guessed. You always seem so nice with her."

"Yes," I said, "We were engaged. I was in law school a year behind Tinker and his wife, Elaine. Sandra was Elaine's best friend and roommate before Tinker. She was one of the first California women I met when I was first in San Francisco on Coast Guard business. Heck, I guess I can tell you, Sandra was probably a main part of the reason I left the East Coast and moved out here and went to law school at Hastings. The rest of the story is pretty long and turns *tres* unpleasant toward the end. But the point is that Sandra and I seem to have put it all behind us. Or, at least I have, and the fact that she called me last Friday, probably indicates she has."

Martha looked at me and said, "Can I have another?"

"Of course," and with that she ordered a second round.

Then, half-turning in her seat, Martha said," I do not think she's over you at all. I watched you glance at her today when she first came in. But you never seemed to look at her again. Still, she must have looked over at you ten times if she did it once! Any chance you are still fooling around with her?"

When I failed to speak quickly enough, Martha inserted, "Oh MY! That was very rude of me. Please forgive me. None of my business, and more important, not my place to make that kind of inquiry! I am So SORRY!"

— — —

I called Manny when I got upstairs after our drinks and told him what happened, including Alicia's thinly veiled suggestion that the group appoint Martha and me to be the lead attorneys to develop the experts for all of the BUILDINGS cases. At that point I felt like the line went dead. After a pause, Manny said, somewhat ominously, I think you had better come down to Scottsdale next week — alone. Dudley and I have some things to tell you that do not need to be shared at this point. I asked if our work was OK? Manny said it was nothing like that. These were just some very confidential issues that were not to be made available to all of the attorneys on the CAL Board Defense Team, or Austin Smith.

So, when I called Austin next, he was excited about my news. But then, he asked how Desert Mutual felt about all of this and I told him they wanted to have a meeting with just me. Silence followed for several seconds, then Austin said, "I think that all of this asbestos litigation is putting a financial strain on their company, or at the very least, our friends in their Claims Department. No one has told me anything approaching as much, but I've been around the block a few times and I can sense when things are beginning to not go so well."

When Austin stopped, I was not sure what to say, and in those seconds, he went on, "Look, I know they appointed you to defend CAL Board and I was concerned about having a little firm in Oakland for our defense. But you have completely won me over and the whole board room here at CAL B (as he sometimes called it), so unless this turns out to be an ethical issue, I'm going to say, 'Go alone.'"

I thanked Austin and told him I would not do anything untoward about CAL Board without consulting him first. (The Tripartite relationship involving the Insurance carrier (Insurer), the policyholder being defended (Insured) and the defense counsel retained by the Insurer to defend the Insured is rife with potential for conflicts of interest. Thus, all three entities must be consistently mindful of their various obligations and duties, especially when involving brightly lit Big Ticket Litigation like that in which we all had become so fully embroiled. These concepts are far too complex to discuss in more detail here, but some will be revisited when more important, as time comes to pass.)

— — —

I asked Martha if she had ever had a Philly cheese steak. When she said "No," we took a taxi to Pat's in South Philadelphia. It was cold outside as we stood in line to order. The taxi idled nearby. I ordered three cheese steaks with fried onions and an Italian hoagie style sandwich. Then we jumped in the taxi and it zipped us back to the hotel. The taxi driver got half a cheese steak as his tip. We raided the mini-bar in my room for beverages and dug in. Pretty soon, we were both turning into greasy messes. After we finished, we showered—together—and had a splash party, of sorts.

After dressing, I called Lily and went over my schedule for next week and had her book me down to Phoenix/Sky Harbor on the first flight Tuesday morning. I asked her to let Manny know my tentative arrival time. I booked the 8:00 a.m. flight back to Oakland the next day. The Biltmore was booked full, so I stayed at the Phoenician and asked Lily to book an early dinner for three at its steakhouse.

Then I called home, talked to Mollie and then to my four children, one at a time. Between them, my calls lasted more than an hour. When I finished those calls, I buzzed over to Martha's room. She answered by coming into my living area. She said, "I feel contrite about what I said earlier about Sandra. You were very gracious about forgiving me. Can I make it up to you?"

With those last words, she opened her robe, and had her way with me.

— — —

The flight back was uneventful. We went right to the office having gained three hours with the time change. I spent the balance of the day with Phil, Mary and Reggie about all the matters on which I had been trying to keep up while flying around the country. Talking to each of them, I asked about SoCal and ended up with the certainty that Reggie would not go, but that Phil would, if pushed, and Mary would go willingly.

I saw Klein and Kelly separately and told them about Philadelphia and about the command visit to Scottsdale for next Tuesday. We set a meeting for 3:00 that next Wednesday for when I got back.

— — —

My Coast Guard that weekend was at Base Yerba Buena Island in the middle of the Bay Bridge between Oakland and San Francisco, easy duty that allowed me to spend some quality time with Mollie and the kids. They were growing up fast. I still remember that weekend as if it was yesterday. A fellow Coast Guard Commander who was in attendance for the annual administration and training weekend was a lifetime veteran of the IRS. When I asked how he was doing, he told me he very recently had been promoted to Chief of the Audit Section for the Western United States. After congratulating him, he invited three of us to join him for lunch and we had great fun listening to him talk about anonymous tax cheats and the new computer audits "the Service" had developed. A fun day and we learned quite a lot.

That night after dinner and the children going to bed, Mollie and I had a drink. I told her about my day and she told me about her upcoming travels. After making love and before turning out her light, Mollie said, "The children are growing up so fast. In another year or two at most, Maeve is going to be fully into boys. I've been thinking, we can take them during summers to your "Society" events at nice places, but we also need to expand their horizons. With all of your business trips to the UK, that would just be a natural as their first country to visit in Europe. What would you think?"

I rolled toward her and said, "Does not sound like it will be as romantic as our trip to London. Eh?"

Mollie poked me in the ribs, chuckled and added, "We can bring Ingrid or another *au pair*, if you think we'll need one."

"No, I think we can manage just fine. I have an old friend coming back to Sausalito in June for a month. I want you to meet her. She's very nice. Different, but nice. She has a son and wants him to see where she spent her early years after she was emancipated. They live in Connecticut. She's a model. How about if we look at the weeks in July after the 4th and I will see if I can arrange some business for while I'm there so I can get my flight paid for. Does that sound OK?"

"Terrific!" is all Mollie said, and with that, she rolled on top of me.

— — —

I arrived at Desert Mutual's offices at 10:15. Being winter, I had lost an hour. I was told to go directly to the Executive Board Room by the receptionist. By then, I knew my way around their offices pretty well.

Upon entering the room, I saw Dudley Chisholm and Manny, but there were two other men present whom I but vaguely recognized. All four of them stood, Dudley came around the table and shook my hand, pointing to a chair between the four of them at the head of the table, saying with a gesture to the man on my right, "Ronan, I want you to meet the President of Desert Mutual, Charles Ezra Sewell."

With that we shook hands and Mr. Sewell said, "Please call me, Charlie."

Dudley went on, gesturing to the other gentleman, saying, "This is John Patrick O'Sullivan, our Executive Vice President and Chief Actuary."

Again, a handshake and he said, "You can call me John. I have countless Irish friends and relatives, but have never met a 'Ronan' before this very moment. Please sit down and be comfortable. Can I get you some coffee?"

Charlie Sewell began the meeting, "What we are going to tell you today needs to stay in this room and any others can only be made aware of any of this if one of us clears their knowing. Do you understand?" As I nodded, he continued, "I trust you know the basics of casualty insurance, including its funding, reinsurance and all of that?" Again, I nodded affirmatively. "Now, we are presently faced with two issues: at least one of our reinsurance syndicate years for the Cal Board coverage is very possibly going to default because a great many of its names will not pay up; and for a number of the older years of our CAL Board coverage, our London broker went out of business, literally closed up shop, and we cannot come up with the necessary documentation to prove up those years of reinsurance coverage. In fact, for five of those eight years, we do not even know what syndicate was the lead. We need someone we can trust to interact with some people in London who come highly recommended to assist in handling this type of mess. Dudley and Manny recommended that person be you, especially since we are already funding your being over there quite a bit, and it sounds as if that will be continuing, if not expanding."

At that point, Dudley interjected, "We know how incredibly busy you are with the work you have in defending CAL Board, but you will be spending more time in London developing experts, so we are hoping that you can put all of this together and spend a little more time there serving as our "go between" with these recommended British legal types. We have to ask now, before we go into further detail, do you think this is something you can handle? And are you willing to undertake it?"

After pausing to take stock, I thought that if I succeeded, that was not a problem, but what if I failed. So, I raised that, "I feel I am willing to say 'yes' to what you have presented so far, But please realize, I know so little about the underlying facts or the applicable UK law and insurance practice, not to mention the personalities involved, that my major concern is what if somehow I fail?"

Charlie stepped in, "Ronan, any of us can fail as well. We are looking for our best option and right now, we feel that's you. If you fail, you fail. We'll pay your bills, and our lives may have to undertake a measure of change. Besides, we hear that the other major defendants may want you and Ms. Walsh to take the lead on the experts based on those you have unearthed. This would tie in with that and both courses of action may have a form of cross-pollination. John has spent a good deal of his time recently dealing with our current London brokers. He will be an able resource for you on this endeavor.'

Then I said "yes" and we got down to the work and analyzing the facts, the available documents, and a whole new cast of characters! They also agreed that Martha could know as could my senior partners, but only an outline of the facts, not anything about the risks facing the company, and that all of this knowledge was to remain exceedingly privileged.

I asked, "Should we have Non-Disclosure Agreements, in that case?" They promptly agreed.

I called Lily and had her change that night's dinner reservation to a half hour earlier and to make it for five. I asked about Tinker being in the loop and they said OK. My first call after dinner was to Mollie. She was proud, but ever more concerned for my well-being. Then I called Martha and told her. Tinker could wait until I got to Sky Harbor in the a.m.

— — —

We met in Jerry Klein's office at 3:00 promptly. We finished at close to six o'clock. Sean Kelly ended by saying, "Pretty soon, we'll all be working for you. Great job! And remember we are behind you 100%"

All of the senior associates and our junior partner, Reggie, were still in their offices when I came out. They all came together into the office core where the secretaries and paralegals usually sat. Reggie asked, "Do we all still have jobs?"

My response, "Let's all congratulate Phil and Mary who will be partners retroactive to January first!" From that point forward, things went really well!

29

Oxford And London

*A*fter *the meeting in Scottsdale and the changes at the Firm, my life seemed to change gears. Much of the time I was no longer devoted to practicing law so much as watching over and interacting with others in planning what they would do, e.g., instead of doing the research and writing, I was doing the conceiving, and then editing, of the work of those others.*

Mollie was immediately aware of the effects of that Scottsdale meeting and the resulting firm changes. She made her concerns very clear to me, including that for my health purposes maybe I should quit the Coast Guard Reserve as it was too much for me with all of my business travel and concerns (no chance with less than 12 months to retirement with vested medical for life!) and to cut way back on my drinking (I told her I would seriously try that).

I met with Martha first thing when I got to the office the next day. Behind closed doors I told her about the new assignment from Desert Mutual after swearing her to secrecy and getting her to adapt an Non-Disclosure Agreement (NDA) for our use. I also told her about the partners' meeting. Lily was told some of the background, enough for her to function. Klein, Kelly, Mollie, Lily and I all signed the NDA. I had Lily Fax it to Manny for DMIC's use and so they could see who was in the loop, and to supply to others as well.

— — —

With the new assignment, we made provisions to stay over in London for a few extra days. We set up to go straight to Oxford after we landed when Sir Richard gracefully agreed to meet us the following morning at his office. I figured that would be one day and night. The contact from John Patrick O'Sullivan at Desert Mutual (DMIC) was a barrister named Quincy Frandsen-Jones. He agreed to meet us for dinner that next night, our first in London, at the dining room in the Connaught Hotel (Mary at Ratcliffe Infirmary warned us that the Connaught was very expensive and did not accept credit cards; so I asked Martha to get an extra £1,000 (1,000 British pounds) in cash. Frandsen-Jones planned to bring his chief clerk, Wilfred Smythe, with him to dine. We also agreed to meet at his chambers in the Temple (one of the Four Inns of Court to which 16th century royalty assigned all of the barristers of that time!) on the next day at 11:00.

For planning, we thought we should have parts of two days for Julian Peto and three days for the McDonalds. By using part days, we could also meet with Frandsen-Jones further, as needed.

The next National Counsel meeting was in three weeks, again in Philadelphia. DMIC had agreed that I could lead the experts in the cases in which CAL Board was a defendant, but in other cases, those defendants would have to come up with a way to retain me and mine, because DMIC and CAL Board were not going to "share our experts" *gratis* after all of the time, expense, trouble and initiative to which we had gone. I felt we needed to meet with Alicia about that so she could help smooth that planning, or advise us if that position was a deal breaker.

A few weeks later would be *LAUSD*. Plus, we needed to get our SoCal staffing up and running. More work, less time!

Before flying to London, Mollie and I went out to dinner, just the two of us—a rarity. Again, she expressed her concerns. Again, I told her it would be OK. I explained just a bit about the new DMIC assignment, told her it would mean slightly more time in London, but I would try to have a timetable for my next trip so she could come along. I added that maybe we should plan something for the children on that next trip. Mollie seemed

OK with all of this and did not mention my two drinks plus wine with dinner. She did drive home. We had a great time at home afterward. I left early the next day, but was able to see all of the children off to school. I was missing them a great deal with all of my travelling. (As was Mollie who was also continuing to spend serious time away, now most frequently in New York City.)

— — —

We went straight from Heathrow, west of London to Oxford, where the same outside man that took our car when I was there with Mollie, saw to the car and took our bags. The same very nice lady, Mrs. Madrigan, was behind the desk and allowed "What a pleasure it is to see you again, Mr. O'Neill," followed by ,"And this must be Ms. Walsh." I could swear that the older woman had the faintest of smiles as she uttered those last words. She ended with, "I am sorry to hear that you will be staying only the one night, but perhaps we may have the pleasure of your company again? How is the delightful Mrs. O'Neill?"

I took the opportunity to tell her about our family and to see if perhaps we could arrange something come summer. She was delighted. Martha smiled the entire time. We were shown to our rooms which adjoined, but had no connecting door. That would be fine for one night, especially in what I guessed was a town where everyone made it a point to know everyone else's business. Dinner was excellent again that night and I had a good call with Mollie telling her about the Randolph. Of course, she had forgotten nothing and even asked if I was on the same floor and took the grand staircase down to dinner showing it to Martha (which made me think I should introduce her to Martha sometime). The breakfast was marvelous, some of the best poached eggs ever. Our bags awaited us in the car and again I carefully followed directions to Ratcliffe Infirmary.

Mary was there to greet us and lead us to Sir Richard's office. Martha said something to Mary which made her smile, blush a bit, and giggle. Sir Richard rose from behind his desk, shook my hand and gave Martha a buss on each cheek. Martha had a turn blushing!

Following our salutations, we all sat at Sir Richard's table. He told us he had heard from Julian who had greatly appreciated meeting us last year, but that he had not heard from the McDonalds. When we told him they were on board, he was delighted. He took a few moments to tell us about the amazing workload that this husband and wife team had performed over the last four decades, all while they raised seven children, all of whom became doctors, (more to talk about when we saw them in a few days).

Then, Dr. Doll got down to business by saying, "I do not know that much about the American legal systems other than you seem to have one, perhaps two, for each of your states. But from being recruited by your attorneys who wish to sue the tobacco companies, I do have a sense of the very adversarial nature of your American practice. In addition, I do know the medical providers who are the leaders of the experts who work for your victims' lawyers in the United States. Given that understanding I do not think that having all UK experts is the best solution for you. Toward that end, I have prevailed on a doctor in Paris for whom I have great respect. Jean Bignon is the head of INSERM. Do you know it?"

When we both shook our heads negatively, he nodded and said, "It is the French analog, or perhaps, the equivalent of your National Institutes of Health. But Jean is far more than just an administrator, he is a world class researcher and epidemiologist in his own right, even spending time early in his career as a clinician. We have been on several papers together, but nothing to do with asbestos. Plus, he can be quite charming. I am very close to convincing him. Please allow me one more occasion to chat with him in a few weeks when we will be at a meeting together and I think he will agree to meet you. Can you wait? To act precipitously might scare him off."

I agreed. We talked for another 30 or 40 minutes and then it was time to go. In the car, Martha said, "Sir Richard looks so much older here than he did when he had lunch with us at his club. I hope he does not work too hard. He's not at all young."

— — —

The Connaught Hotel was clearly one, maybe two, cuts above the Grosvenor House in terms of elegance and barely understated elitism. Martha and I were shown to the Dining Room where two splendidly dressed Englishmen stood as we approached their table. Both were about the same height, but the one who introduced himself first as Quincy Frandsen-Jones, call me "Q" as my friends do, was the more overfed of the pair. They had started imbibing without us, but a waiter was there in moments to see to our needs. (As the evening moved on, it became apparent that the entire staffing of this dining area had a pecking order with positions possibly passed on through generations. So, this first 'waiter' was actually a barman and his task was to assist on drinks from the bar, but not wine, etc.)

We engaged in introductions whilst standing. Martha was as tall as the two men, even possibly taller since she wore heals. Both of them fixed on her for a bit longer than appropriate, but Martha seemed unfazed. Once seated, Wilfred (Call me "Wil") said. "No one told us that you would both be so tall. Did you play basketball?"

When I answered affirmatively and at Georgetown, they both nodded. Seemingly, my *alma mater* was known on the far side of the Atlantic. So it was that our first level of conversation dealt with our educations. They were equally impressed that Martha had gone to UC Berkeley, only to point out that Berkeley

Square (pronounced Barkly by them) was a few hundred meters further down Mount Street. After our drinks arrived, we fell into a somewhat more comfortable, less inquiring, conversation about our tasks related to experts, a topic which had to have come from someone at Desert Mutual. At this point, Wil offered that if we should need meeting space, they had several conference rooms at their chambers which were most often available. This led to our asking about those "chambers" and they were off and running telling us the history of barristers in the UK, much like a multi-layered drama from Shakespeare!

As dinner progressed through two appetizer courses to a main course, we finally turned to the business that would be at hand for our joint effort. Q suggested that to more fully understand the London markets, including the many intricacies of Lloyds, a place, not a company *per se*, was a subject worthy of weeks of serious study, but in meeting over the next few days, we should be sufficiently up to speed (somehow, it appeared that Martha was being swept totally into this for the moment). Toward that end, we agreed that we would meet tomorrow afternoon for three hours at their chambers beginning at three because of Julian Peto.

When they suggested further drinks after dinner, Martha and I demurred on the basis of meeting with Professor Peto on the morrow at 10:00. On the way back, Martha broke the unspoken topic first, "Do you think they drink like that all the time? Three cocktails and six bottles of wine. And we barely drank any of the wine. Then Port with coffee! My goodness!"

I chuckled and responded, "Yes, I bet they do, at least when someone else is paying for it! I am certain they know we are on an expense account. Henceforth, we need to tone down dinner to a meal, not an event, unless there is a reason. Also, I am afraid that Desert Mutual does not really consider you as having a major role in this."

Martha jumped to answer, "I understand. They only need

you to act as liaison. But I am here and I need to do something to bill my time. Do you agree?"

Me, "You are right. So, first priority: are there tasks you can perform for, or with, our experts, where I do not have to be present? Say, for example, all of those areas of potential cross-examination that we generated in D.C. and Philadelphia need to be covered, explained and we need to gain their input on how they would respond to see if there are positions that we may need to restructure and the like. We could start some of that with Julian tomorrow and see how it plays out."

When Martha paused, I added, "Another reason not to drink like those two is how do you have any kind of sex after all of that alcohol?

Martha and I later tested that hypothesis. We had no problem from the alcohol.

— — —

The days in London began to go by rather quickly. Our time with our new experts seemed especially limited, mostly for me. Martha organized the potential plaintiff cross-examination topics into categories, which, in turn, generated more topics and more for us (and her) to cover with them. Corbett and Alison invited us to their London *pied a terre* for cocktails and appetizers. As we entered, Alison gestured to a park across the street from their condominium-sized residence and to what looked to be an older mass of stone buildings. She said, "That was Bedlam, home to the truly insane for generations. It was damaged badly in the Blitz and when the war ended, it was converted into the Royal British War Museum. If you have the time, it is extremely worthwhile. Plus, it commemorates many other British heroes besides just Winston Churchill."

Sitting in the parlor of their charming home, Alison and Corbett from time-to-time told us of their decade together pre-dating

World War II, their roles as clinicians treating the wounded as well as dealing with diseases, of their nine children, only seven of whom made it to adulthood and five of whom now lived and practiced in North America, three in Montreal and two in Burlington, Vermont. They spoke of Corbett's bicycling to work starting before the war and continuing until now. Alison now went to their work spaces only three days per week, always by public transit. All seven of their offspring had medical specialties and had practiced clinically. One, whom we had not met, was on their team here in London but, in all probability, he would not be involved with asbestos. He was engaged in reviewing the many studies and papers dealing with the potential health hazards of lead, particularly paints utilizing lead pigment. They confessed to dabbling in this area, but their son, the youngest, was serious about lead having developed a distaste for much of the work, especially from the U.S., which he reviewed as not sufficiently rigorous and lacking in controls, while failing to account for potentially confounding concepts and substances. In other words, that son thought the peer-reviews of lead science studies from the United States were not reliable.

Listening to the pair expound, I wondered if they were always like this, and found that despite their advancing ages, somewhere in their 70's, they spoke without pause or fault and were incredibly enthusiastic. Ninety minutes passed in a flash and it occurred to me that we had best leave them to their dinner and for us to get back to the West End and Grosvenor House. On our way by foot, Martha said, "They are the most charming couple. I love how Corbett lets Alison lead the conversation and slides in asides to add to the narrative of the moment."

We were moving at a brisk pace, after a few seconds, and I do not really know what lead me to this path, but I said, glancing sideways at Martha, "Martha, it is really time for you to meet Mollie, my wife, who, it turns out, is the love of my life. I say that for more reasons than I shall ever explain."

Martha stopped. So did I. She said, "Why are you telling me this? I thought we had an understanding?" Her shoulders seemed to slump ever so imperceptibly.

I tried looking at her full face, but she turned enough away that I could not see her eyes. "I am telling you this here and now, because I may not have been totally forthcoming with you. Look I believe with my whole being that people, many of them, can love more than one person at a time, and love them deeply, perhaps equally, perhaps not. But that's not important. What is? I will try to tell you: it's the sense of caring that you develop about someone. You hear the words, 'He seems very fond of her, or the reverse. Sometimes it can be about the same gender.' What I am trying to say is that I really care about you. I am more than a bit fond; but in the end, it will always be Mollie first. And I know that at some point, you will find someone. I do want you to be happy!"

We had started walking again as I was speaking, but Martha stopped again and turned toward me. I looked at her full face then. There were little tears running from the outside corner of each of her eyes. Her hands reached for mine. A strange expression came over her face as she tilted her head up to me and pulled me closer, saying words I will never forget (yet so like words I had heard from Carolyn but a few times over many years), "I have never said I love you. I never planned to say it. But I feel like you just said that to me, but not in those exact words. So, I will say it to you. I love you, Ronan. You are the only man I have ever loved. Moreover, you have not a thing to fear from me. I will never tell this to Mollie or anyone who we remotely have in common. I will be happy being your law partner for the rest of our lives and your friend until the end."

With that Martha put her hand behind my head, pulled my mouth down to hers and we kissed right there on the street: a truly public display of affection. Then it started to rain. I grabbed her hand, hailed a black taxi, told him Grosvenor House hotel entrance and went back to kissing Martha. It felt so very different from any time before and I knew that in addition to Carolyn, I now had Martha as a lifelong friend (and lover).

— — —

Quincey Frandsen-Jones was quite the character. It appeared over just a few days that he was not a morning person, and was not much for functioning until after his mid-day repast which always seemed to include one or two drinks and several pints of beer or some wine ("Never mix them at mid-day."). Everything was a teaching moment with him, and every lesson was taught with a story, a mesmerizing blend wherein background evolved over time into the state of functioning of the London Markets, their brokers, their syndicates, their leaders, the many and varied offices at Lloyds, and the hordes of followers (both clerks and especially investors, "Names!").

Other members of Q's chambers came into and out of his monologues. Wil, the Chief Clerk of Chambers, was often present as were any number of younger lawyers seeking to gain a mastery of the deep mystiques through which labyrinth Q knew his way with his inner being.

Each day or evening, I would spread all of what I had learned before Martha so that she could record it in the event we needed this guidance.

So it was that for our last afternoon together, Q and Wil suggested that I include Martha. Then, the four of us, based on what Desert Mutual had told me, told Q, and the documents they sent to Wil, we set about arriving at a consensus plan of action for the coming months to go about locating the needed people and documents to facilitate the recovery of those monies owed to date for reinsurance, but also to have a plan to accommodate future recoveries as they would come due. We agreed to exchange drafts of our thoughts as soon as we returned to San Francisco.

Q treated all of us to a gastropub dinner of startlingly tasty British fare that night.

A new working relationship was more fully formed!

30

Many Balls In The Air

In the weeks following London and Oxford, many events began to take place and I felt myself being spread ever thinner as I was pulled from one task to another.

Sir Richard allowed that Jean Bignon was agreeable to meet with me and had time in March. That was a bit soon to bring Mollie to London, and maybe Paris. The next day, Jeremy Nobel called to say he was also invited to meet with Dr. Bignon. More expense for Desert Mutual!

Q and Wil were a day late with their draft of a plan. They quickly acted on Martha's and my version. Within a week, we had the beginning of a consensus plan suitable for me to pass along to DMIC. I did with a note asking if they wanted to see me. They did.

We received the *LAUSD* Motion with many supporting papers. Tinker did the initial review and concluded that they had failed to meet their burden, rather completely, to shift the proof of the manufacturer's identity of installed products to the defendants as a group as well as to impose a "joint negligence" standard. (Two hunters in a duck blind fired their shotguns at a sound which they took for a duck taking off. Instead, it was another hunter whom they had failed to see before firing. The victim died. But the shotgun pellets could have come from either gun. The trial court required the decedent's heirs to prove which hunter was at fault. When they could not, the trial court directed verdict favoring the defendants. The appellate court made short shrift by concluding that both hunters were negligent and if neither could prove that the other was at fault, then they were both jointly liable!) As Tinker stressed, *LAUSD* missed the point by trying to claim that "a defendant's product being installed" was not an apt analogy for the "negligent gunshot," nor was being in the business of selling product generally. Unless *LAUSD* could overcome this point, all the rest of their brief and its supporting materials were just so much window dressing. Upon our agreeing, Tinker started on the opposition with help from Mary and his own people.

Martha had succeeded in getting ahold of Alicia Goines. We set up a meeting in Philadelphia, the night before the "Big Meeting." She asked if USG counsel should attend. I thought for a second and asked about Wallboard. That left WR Grace, a major player, uninvited, but I knew by now that Sandra or her father would back me to lead the expert portion of the defense. A bigger group and perhaps a needed consensus with USG (less than clear in its positions) might prove less than productive, but needing Alicia, meant we agreed. Alicia offered to host a private room at a very upscale Italian restaurant a few blocks from her office. We agreed to that as well.

— — —

The next day, I met with Desert Mutual's senior executives. They started right away with the problem that their London broker, Wellington Chase, was among the very first to go out of business in the face of the "Runaway Reinsurance Crisis" as Q phrased it. Although a trustee was brought in, their records were atrocious and being able to find anything seemed unlikely based on which Charlie, John O'Sullivan and Dudley agreed. This was consistent with what Quincy had learned, so the initial picture was bleak! However, that defunct "London placing broker" had a history of representing U.S. casualty insurers and placed most of its American casualty insurance client's business through a very large well-connected "London syndicate broker," which was akin to a gateway to many of the syndicate lead underwriters. As our memo stated, the strategy would be to formulate a position that would convince that London syndicate broker to search their own files to find out with whom DMIC's defunct broker had placed DMIC's reinsurance for all of the missing years, if possible. A big "IF!"

So, that was the goal, at least for now. Moreover, the UK law might need to be finessed, if possible, and a vehicle would need to be found, or even created, to open the door of that highly connected London syndicate broker, Cheshire and Booth, rumored to place even Royal business.

I asked those present at the meeting to search their histories of dealings to see whom they might know, or be related to, as someone who could provide that initial access which would be so critical. Meanwhile, Q had recommended that DMIC retain a solicitor firm in London which would smooth communication, thereby serving as a better pathway to provide access and have less expensive clerks and associates who could search documents. They could begin by undertaking a quick perusal of DMIC's defunct broker's Lloyd's Placement Office documents to assure that those impacting DMIC's reinsurance placement were, in fact, missing. Charlie came right out and asked the estimated cost. I could not give him any, but I could tell him that Quincy's rate was about four times higher than mine and he billed in units of no less than 30 minutes. Thus, a solicitor's firm would have many people, including the lead solicitor suggested by Q, who might be less expensive than Quincy and his more junior barrister mates. (The BAR is exactly that in an English courtroom and in the United States, and any number of English-speaking countries. In order to address a judge or the court as the case may be, one must be admitted "to the BAR." For example, all lawyers in the United States, but only Barristers in the UK, could address the Court directly. {This changed in the last decade or so, to include solicitors.} Solicitors then tended to interface with the client types and instruct the retained barristers from the other side of the bar. That's the very basic difference.)

Everyone at the meeting understood some of these basic concepts, but I was less certain about the scope of the potential expense. According to Quincy, even very big brokers like Cheshire and Boothe did not do much to maintain their documents for access after each Syndicate was finished with its run-off years of coverage. I was honest with them and said this seemed like a gamble of sorts and they might be writing a blank check with no assurance of success downstream, but it seemed to me that we should press ahead to see if the chances for success could be improved and to make decisions incrementally based on the evolution of what became known to possibly allow us to find those placement documents.

Discussions continued into drinks and dinner at the Biltmore. After two martinis, John O'Sullivan turned toward me, but talking across me, said to President Sewell, "Charlie, I think we should tell Ronan all that's involved here."

Charlie, working on his third vodka martini with his shrimp cocktail, said, "Go ahead."

John got up, motioned for me to follow him, and when we were out of ear shot of any audience said, "This could be a 'You bet the company' matter, or at least potentially so. We are about $20 million into defense and indemnity costs on CAL Board and our other insureds on all of this environmental litigation. Roughly 90% of that was subject to reinsurance AND we have no significant surplus premium revenue to offset these expenses. We can absorb this for just a few more years; but if the deficits get worse, time will get shorter. Other unattractive options are out there, but you have it right. Proceed incrementally and as expeditiously as you can. We have real faith in you. Questions?"

I shook my head and said, "No and Thank you," and we went on to finish dinner. Reinsurance was not mentioned again!

— — —

Because of the meeting scheduled for the night before the main meeting, Martha and I caught a 6:00 a.m. flight on Tuesday morning directly to Philadelphia. (TWA was beginning to have financial issues and was cutting back on its direct flights. This was now the only one; otherwise, we would have to connect through St. Louis!) We were at the Barclay on Rittenhouse Square by 5:15. A few calls and we were off to the meeting, a few blocks walk. The plane ride had allowed a nap and all the planning we needed.

Alicia was early. Sandra arrived two minutes after us. Fred Talcott and Adam Morris (no surprise there), for US Gypsum, arrived last. Alicia asked everyone to sit and to withhold drinking until the business portion of this meeting was complete (I was hoping that like a good politician, Alicia had already told Talcott enough to get his tentative approval). She began, "Ronan and Martha have spent some considerable time in the UK trying to line up some experts to counter the Selikoff group and the various US experts which they have spawned. He is willing to tell us a bit about those attempts as a preview to tomorrow's meeting. As you may remember, I asked the group at the last meeting to have Ronan and Martha be the lead counsel for our group on experts. A consensus here for tomorrow's meeting is the desired outcome. Questions?"

Fred Talcott stepped right up, "How can we agree when we do not have any idea of who or what we are dealing with?"

I started then, "That's why we asked for this meeting through Alicia. All Alicia knows is the experts do not include Sir Richard Doll."

"I would suppose not!" chimed Talcott.

I continued, "Although he has proven quite helpful. Would you agree, Martha?"

Smiling, "Oh my, yes! And I have never experienced any-thing quite like The Royal Physicians and Surgeons Club in Re-gent's Park where he took us for an incredible lunch. The food was wonderful. But Oh! The formal luncheon dress code was so exciting!"

Talcott sat back, his face mottled ever so slightly. Alicia and Sandra beamed. I continued, "Sir Richard was kind enough to arrange introductions to the McDonalds, Corbett and Alison, the most prolific of the British epidemiologists on the topic of as-bestos and its health effects, as well as to Julian Peto, co-author of Sir Richard's seminal asbestos study. We have met with all separately on several occasions and have their commitments to testify. But they do not wish their testimony to disrupt their work, so we shall have to arrange something appropriate. Also, each is clear that they will only work through us because of the background we explained to them.'

Talcott, "What is that?"

Martha stepped up as planned, "Ronan explained to them that we do not intend in defending these cases to make any at-tempt to defend on the issue of whether or not asbestos presents a health hazard. Rather, we are asking them to opine that in the absence of airborne fibers, the health hazards of exposure ap-proach nonexistent; and that abatement, in the absence of a real world need, endangers lives needlessly and is a waste of re-sources better used for those actually injured by exposure. That's the basic position to which they have signed on. Our client is willing to go along with it to secure the end of this type of liti-gation. Questions?"

Sandra, "And all three of them agree to that series of propo-sitions?"

Me, "Yes. Subject to those conditions."

Talcott, "I will speak to the client right now. Please excuse me."

I turned to Sandra, "What about Wallboard?"

"Trusting their sworn enemy from the coverage litigation would be a hard sell, but our work together on the *Mullen* case and others has convinced them to trust you on this issue, if we recommend it. I will call them after we hear from Fred," said Sandra.

He returned right after Alicia got menus to pass out, and asked, "The client is worried that this line will sound like an admission that airborne fibers are dangerous. But I told them we cannot win on that issue and this position with the absence of injury is far more compelling. I sent them your brief from *LAUSD*. They were on board with that position and this is a variant. Bottom line: USG is on board!"

Sandy was back in minutes, said a big YES, walked over to Adam and gave him a kiss, and she was the last to order a drink.

Alicia rose and said, "Remember, we are looking for consensus that Ronan and Martha can run these experts. If you speak against that now, you are buying your own dinner?"

No one spoke out. All six of us had a fine meal. Martha and I repaired to the Barclay. We had adjoining rooms, not connecting. Nothing went wrong, but I felt a pang that something just might as Martha left!

— — —

The next two nights at the Mayflower, we were in our usual rooms: no problem. My conclusion: more discretion was needed.

On Wednesday night, I called Mollie at the Waldorf in New York. Once again, I got the strange sound of what seemed to be a woman breathing irregularly. But when I called again, Mollie was there, answered and sounded fine. I was left to conclude that the Waldorf must have a real telephone system problem!

On Thursday when we got back from our meetings at Tinker's office, a fax was waiting for me. It was from Mary at Sir Richard's office. Could I make it next week to Paris for an initial meeting with Dr. Bignon? I felt I had to do it and asked Lily what she could do to arrange it. I thought an extra night in Paris would make sense after this trip to the East and back, to overcome all that jet lag. I was sure wrong on that point, but I loved my time in Paris.

31

Paris

France was a new experience. Because of basketball, sailing in the summers and being with the family, I never got to Europe while growing up. The United Kingdom as a starter was not so hard because of the language, a lifetime of interchange of movies and television, as well as the closeness of the cultures, especially in post-World War II England with the ongoing reign of Elizabeth II. But France, our country's once great, and first, ally at the time of shaping our independence, had become more distant following two world wars and the downfall of its empire. The De Gaulle years "estrangement" continued like a bit of a shadow over our two countries relationship, magnified by a certain casual rudeness from Parisians toward those who did not speak their language (Sir Richard's Mary told me to stick to English because the Parisians were even more dismissive of those who tortured their language. So, I did.) It worked in the hotels and some restaurants, but it helped to have friends. And I had Carolyn (AT THIS POINT, as it directly precedes that which is next, *you might wish to re-read the Prologue again here!*).

— — —

At the end of our first night's adventure, Carolyn offered to walk me back to *Le Meurice*. On the walk, she held onto my arm, and said nothing for the first few blocks, gently steering me over the damp cobblestones and across the bridge over the Seine toward the *Rue de Rivoli*. A block from the hotel, she stopped, turned to me at arms' length and said, "I offered to share you tonight. It had never occurred to me to do anything like that with you. That's why I've been so quiet. I am ashamed of myself! And I am mad at myself as well! I do not know what I was thinking. Can you forgive me?"

I looked at her, not quite straight in the eye, but close, gave her a wistful smile, and said, "I'm a big boy. If I had wanted to leave, I would have. I loved watching you, just you, and then you with her. Still, when invited to join, I said 'NO,' and I may come to wish I had not. Don't beat yourself up!" A pause: I thought she was going to tear up. So, I added, "Can just the two of us have dinner tonight?"

With that she nodded a yes, and leaned in to kiss me deeply. Turning ever so slowly then to go back the way she had come, Carolyn said, "Your door is a hundred feet ahead. Don't miss it! I will leave a message for you about where tonight. Or, cocktails at your bar at 7:00?"

"Cocktails!" I replied and I walked the other direction.

— — —

The next morning, I made some calls to California using the nine hour time difference. I had a fax from Jeremy Nobel saying he had to do dinner with some colleagues so could we have breakfast the next day?

When the valet brought my coffee and Croissant, there was a note for me. I opened it, reading:

Ronan,

I was so upset when walking back to your hotel and you made me feel so much better with those few words. I got a call at 5:30 this morning saying my shoot for today was cancelled and moved to 10:30 tomorrow when you have your appointments.

Is there any chance I could show you around Paris today and share an album of photos of Patrick?

I told Lisette that I wanted to spend some time with you and she's fine with that. She has lots of her own business. If you cannot make it, not to worry, we can still do cocktails and dinner tonight. Please call when you get this and decide.

With Love,
Carolyn

It took about thirty seconds thought to realize what a good idea this might be: a French-speaking guide, a chance to get ready for her visit to Sausalito with Patrick in a few months, and a beautiful companion for the day. I called and told her I was in the midst of a light breakfast, so we could have a lunch at somewhere important for me to go. Then we agreed Carolyn would stop for me at 11:00. Could she leave her clothes for dinner in my room? Do not overdress for the day, but dinner was a bit fancy and her treat. She would find me at my coffee in the restaurant.

At 11:05, Carolyn appeared in the doorway of the restaurant. She had a bellman in tow. I went to meet her, gave the bellman a tip and asked him to put her things in my room. We went back to my table ever so briefly for me to finish up and to sign my check (which turned out to be unnecessary as they routinely added a tip (10%)). As we went to leave, Louise from Colt Industries intercepted us at the door, saying, "Ronan, last night I thought the lady here with whom you departed was Carolyn Tyne. I hope you don't mind if I ask if you: are you really she?"

Carolyn, to whom that question was actually addressed, looked slightly nonplussed, but not annoyed at this interruption, and nodded yes. So, I introduced Louise to Carolyn and I thought Louise was going to feint. After a brief cordial exchange, we were on our way. I asked, "Does that kind of thing happen often?"

Carolyn, smiling ever so pleasantly as she set a nice pace walking, "Not in Paris, but largely because I do not appear all that often looking somewhat camera ready as I am doing for you today. It tends to happen more in the States where people are more aggressive, like Louise there was. Mostly I wear something over my hair like a ball cap, or have it up, little or no make-up and sunglasses. Also, I do not go out in public in big cities all that much. That's why I like our place in Sausalito, and my place in Connecticut."

Mostly, we chatted about her, her work life, Violet and Patrick, details about their place in Connecticut and her life in those splendid suburbs in that rolling countryside. She talked in vignettes, and would frequently interrupt herself to describe what we were seeing, both the sights themselves as well as her observations about so many of the people on the streets and in the shops. We walked away from the *Louvre* and *Notre Dame*, with Carolyn saying we would see more of that cathedral later and tonight. The arches of the *Rue de Rivoli* gave way to open air. We came to a huge plaza, the *Place de la Concorde*, site of so much in Dickens' *A Tale of Two Cities*, and turned right. Up the slight grade in front of us, towering across the wide boulevard on our left I could make out the *Arc de Triomphe*. Carolyn said only, "Welcome to the *Champs-Elysees*, the grandest boulevard in the world!"

And so our day began: palaces, grand restaurants, world famous shops, hotels and ever so much more. We walked half way up the hill toward Napoleon's arch before crossing the ultrawide boulevard and headed down the *Avenue George V* to the River Seine. World class clothiers had showrooms on that street, traffic was crazy as was the parking. We stopped in front of a magnificent edifice, "This is the *Hotel George Cinq*. It has one of the best dining rooms in Paris as does where we will eat tonight. You really must dine here if you have a chance! By the way, I do hope you like duck?"

Before long we were on the *Boulevard St. Germain* and she stopped at what she told me was a Parisian must for Americans, a sprawling sidewalk bistro called *Le Deux Maggot*. Carolyn got us a remote table inside as the weather was a bit brisk for dining outside and it gave less chance of her being recognized, or worse accosted. She asked to order for both of us, and I nodded agreement. Our menu was in French so I was at her discretion, as she said, "A *Croque Monsieur pour Mon Ami* and a *Croque Mademoiselle pour mois*." She added two glasses of wine and some water.

"Ronan, this is one of the most famous bistros in Paris, once a hangout for writers in the '20s, like Hemingway and FitzGerald. Now it's a tourist destination, but the food is said to be as good as when it got started and your dish was made famous by those two writers. Mine is a derivative of yours with quite a few less calories. Although I will not be watching my diet very carefully today."

"Intriguing! You have turned out to be a most incredible guide. Where to from here?" And we chatted over wine and sandwiches containing meat, melted cheese and a fried egg with a runny yolk on mine. No meat and a smaller egg on hers.

We walked only a few hundred yards, turned a corner and there was the *Eiffel* Tower. We gazed up in amazement and spent a few minutes discussing how that genius *Eiffel* had created this steel monument at a time when construction equipment and planning were primitive at best. Then we took two elevators and walked the rest of the way up to the highest tourist spot and spent an unseemly amount of time looking out over that great city. When we began to turn to go, we faced each other for a moment. Carolyn reached up, grabbed my chin, pulled me down to her and gave me one of the most amazing kisses of my entire life. When she had finished and I straightened up, I felt as if I could hardly breathe. She whispered, "I could really come to love you entirely, if I could somehow just make myself really try to do it."

The next thing I knew, we were in line for a tour boat ride on the Seine. The bulwarks lining the river with their expansive walkways were magnificent. The ancient bridges, the river boats and barges tied up singly or nesting abreast, the people, and (OH!) the buildings. What magnificent architecture! What a magnificent boat ride! Carolyn made sure we sat in the front row even though it meant waiting for "the next boat." We came around a bend, and there they were, the *Isle de la Cite*, *Notre Dame*, the *Isle de Saint Louis* and all those ancient bridges, that accessed those two islands sitting at the very heart of Paris. With the Left Bank on one shore and the *Louvre* on the other, we slowly circled those islands and started back. Right as he completed his looping turn, the tour guide said, "Look up there to the top floor of that building and he pointed, "That is *Tour d'Argent*, one of the most exclusive and perhaps the most expensive restaurant in the world!"

I smiled, and looked over at Carolyn, her head was nodding ever so imperceptibly in the affirmative.

— — —

Back at my hotel, we made love. Then, Carolyn pulled out a photo album and we spent an hour or so looking at pictures of her Patrick (dare I think *our Patrick*!). When we were done, she asked if I wanted it. I thought "yes," but said I had no way to manage it with all I had with me. Understanding when I explained, she said she would bring it with her in June. She also asked if I still had my key to our (now her) condo and when I said "yes," she said it could reside there for whenever I wanted to look and she would add to it. Then, it was time to get ready for dinner. She asked if she could come back afterward and, of course, I agreed, explaining that I would have to call Mollie and the office.

I only had two suits, so I wore the freshest one, navy blue

with a light chalk stripe, white shirt and red and blue regimental tie. Carolyn appeared re-born from my dressing area; she was breathtakingly beautiful with artful, but not overstated make-up, glamorous hair with just enough curl and a faintish lavender dress that showed off her still youthful and healthful figure. She had a darker lavender coat to match. I said, "I really have never seen any woman as beautiful as you are right now. I simply do not feel worthy to be going out with you."

Carolyn smiled a small smile with an almost Mona Lisa shape to her lips and said only, "Thank you, *Monsieur*. You are too kind; and, you are more than worthy to take me out and about!"

When we left the elevator and headed toward the bar on the *Le Meurice* Ground Floor, every head in the lobby turned, as did those in the bar when we entered. I had asked for a private table ahead of time and that was a good thing. One drink and then to the taxi, Carolyn entered first and said two words, "*Tour d'Argent*." The doorman smiled broadly as we pulled away.

That night, staring down at the incredibly well-lighted Cathedral of *Notre Dame* from our window seats was unforgettably memorable as was the duck and what happened afterward! Somehow, I wanted to tell Mollie about that dinner, but I just knew that would be a truly bad idea. The next morning, Carolyn had left a note. It said, "I know you will be in London for a few nights. I will be at the Sheraton Belgravia on Friday night after a meeting that afternoon in the West End. If you can get together, leave a message for me under my own name at the front desk. What a marvelous thirty-six hours! With Love, Carolyn."

— — —

When I told Dr. Arnaud about my time in Paris with Carolyn, she was more than a bit upset with me. She had always indulged me about Carolyn, but she said I was going too far and endangering my mar-

riage. Yet, I explained that Carolyn and I would never be a couple: once and again reiterating Carolyn's seemingly insatiable appetite for beautiful women. When I did that, immediately afterward, I thought about Carolyn's words at that top observation platform on the Eiffel Tower: could she really mean them?

Later, I would ask myself, why would she say them? After all, I had no intention whatsoever of leaving Mollie!

32

Jean Bignon, Then London

After talking with Jeremy and Dr. Bignon for 30 minutes, I began to sense that Sir Richard Doll had selected him as a younger surrogate for himself. His dark, going white hair and chiseled features were not unlike a youngish Maurice Chevalier. Throw in his French accent on top of his faultless English and I could see him on a witness stand in Philadelphia or Los Angeles charming a jury, especially the women. Moreover, his tone and delivery were elegant. Clearly, by virtue of his position at the top of the French scientific medical and public health communities, his reputation would put him beyond reproach and make him virtually impregnable to cross-examination.

When Dr. Bignon first addressed me, he said something like, "Sir Richard told me all about you and the beautiful young woman lawyer who was so incredibly smart. He explained that your position is a well thought out public health approach to dealing with in place asbestos. Which leaves me wondering: Do you have any idea why the United States Environmental Protection Agency passed the rules they did for dealing with those materials?"

— — —

After our meeting with Dr. Bignon, Jeremy and I shared a taxi to Charles de Gaulle Airport.

He said, "I cannot believe how convinced Dr. Bignon was before you got there. Even before I spoke to him. It must be Sir

Richard and perhaps others. Do you think it is timely to approach the USEPA now?"

My response was tempering, "I will speak to my old partner, Joel Tinker, who is with a good-sized firm in D.C. and they do lobbying work. Let's see what they say. The main obstacle would appear to be that there is nothing out there right now by way of a scientific study right on point. And, the one appellate decision that would have helped from California, a case called *Mullen*, was partially de-published by its very liberal Supreme Court. At this time, I think the reality is that we will have to wait until this position can become more evolved and gains some real scientific support, or something else happens to strengthen our position. Still, I will talk to Tinker about it."

— — —

In London, I checked into the Grosvenor House. Two notes were awaiting me: one from Wil, asking to beg off dinner that night, but to do it tomorrow; and the second from Carolyn, saying that she was free, at the Sheraton Belgravia and could we meet at its bar at seven for a cocktail before dinner at Sale et Pepe, an Italian bistro located just off Sloan Street behind Harrod's? That unexpected evening went swimmingly, the food was incredible and the atmosphere just this side of raucous, was loud, yet fun! Having walked back to Carolyn's hotel in Belgravia, we rode up twenty stories to Carolyn's floor. Her room was splendid.

I looked out one of the windows and was treated to a stunning view of moonlit rooftops with some very famous silhouettes sprinkled here and there, including the spire of the Victoria and Albert Museum, the dome of St. Paul's and the outlines of Westminster Abbey and the Parliament building, including Big Ben. Carolyn leaned in against me and said, "I do so love the view from these rooms. As soon as you are above six or seven stories, almost the whole of London begins to spread out before you. Isn't it just magnificent? I wish you could be here in the morning to see it. But, alas, I have to be at my shoot by 6:30!"

I turned, smiled, looked into those striking blue eyes, and said, "In that case, shall we make the best of the time we have?"

— — —

After those few days with Carolyn in Paris and Belgravia, I came to miss her greatly during my remaining brief time in London.

— — —

My meetings with Q and Wil showed promise. They seemed to feel that although Desert Mutual's London lead placing broker had gone out of business, one of his sons was still around, doing much the same thing, but not at his father's former firm. They were scheduled to meet with him in the next week to see what he could provide, if anything, of a roadmap to his father's London syndicate placement broker contacts, specifically for reinsurance placements, maybe even for DMIC.

Q thought this might be a very good lead. But what he really was hoping for was that the document search at DMIC HQ would turn up something about how Wellington Chase had placed the DMIC business and with which brokers. Shockingly, there appeared to be no HQ files at all! Who was it that ran this business at DMIC for the years in question? (I made a note to find out the history of who was in charge, but it did appear that Wellington Chase, utilizing its lead broker, had handled most of the day-to-day London work and had made all of the key contacts.) Still, it was hard to imagine that there were no reports or records of what was being done anywhere in the DMIC Scottsdale offices!

These thoughts carried over into cocktails and dinner. I mentioned my fondness for seafood and Wheeler's. Low and behold, it turned out there was one across the street from the entrance to the Temple. When I taxied back to Grosvenor House, I wondered what Carolyn was up to (then I caught myself and asked, "What are you doing?"). It all seemed to sort itself out with a long call to Mollie. I told her I was due back for a week or more of meetings in early May and maybe we should take the kids out of school so they could broaden their horizons. Mollie said she was more than ready!

— — —

I spent an afternoon with Julian Peto and dinner with the McDonalds, catching them up on what was going on in the U.S. asbestos litigation and asking them about how they thought we might approach the USEPA, with which all of them were quite familiar, but they had much the same thoughts as I had placed in front of Jeremy Nobel.

They all asked after Martha and I told them that she sent her best, but was otherwise occupied on Southern California property cases. I did, however, promise that when I returned in May, Martha would be along, and for some of the time, so would my wife and our four children. They all sounded enthusiastic about meeting my family, even Julian!

33

Time Starts To Shrink

When I got back from Paris and London, I went to the office, pulled out my calendar, and started to assess what was required of me in the weeks ahead, and to block out time for our family trip to London in early May and Carolyn's visit to SAUSALITO in late June and early July. Blocking out weekends for my Coast Guard Reserve duty made things even tighter. On the flight home from London, I began to think about bringing along the *au pair*, and even sneaking over to Paris at the end of the trip with Mollie for a quick two or three days, just the two of us.

A few days later, Mollie and I sat down and we talked about my, and our, plans for the upcoming months. Mollie, who was by then a Regional Vice President, was extremely busy at the moment with marketing and managing major client projects, including creative input on her part. Mollie's employer, the APP Store as it was then known, was going great guns with highly creative ideas and deft programming. (They were lowering their costs by outsourcing relatively routine coding to India and Liberia using U.S. intermediaries with family connections in those countries.) Mollie was actually enthusiastic about meeting Carolyn and her son as Carolyn was part of my past during those years when she rarely saw me. I explained that Carolyn was a war widow of sorts, not having had a chance to marry Patrick's father before he was killed in action in Viet Nam. (I felt somewhat guilty about that one, but thought better of it when I had the chance to lay some groundwork for that visit.) Finally, we were able to agree on everything except Paris. Mollie wanted to bring the children along. We decided to think about it for a day or so and revisit the issue. (I had also mentioned that Martha, who helped with all of the experts in the Asbestos cases, would be over there as well and would go to Paris with me at the end of the trip to meet Dr. Bignon, and that one or more clients might show up as well.) Finally, she acceded to sending the children home from London with the *au pair*, persuaded especially by Kate agreeing to be there to meet them on arrival and see them all safely home to Mill Valley.

Much of my ensuing time was spent on the phone with Desert Mutual people, Austin Smith, our CAL Board client contact, our various contacts in London (an 8 hour time difference!), and all of my team with input on *LAUSD*, the SCHOOLS Class in Philadelphia, and now the COLLEGES Class in South Carolina. Fortunately for me, all of the people working with me were first class, both as lawyers and also as human beings. I tried to have a lunch every week with one of our senior attorneys who did not spend much time with me. That worked well. The real problem was the Bodily Injury cases and the swelling volume in Southern California. As constituted, our firm, and especially my team, were stretched too thin. What to do about it was my next issue. I asked Phil, my recently promoted partner, for his thoughts at lunch.

The very next day, Phil told me that we needed to have some kind of "real presence" in SoCal! I talked it over with Reggie, Mary and Martha. They essentially agreed, but no one volunteered to go, except Phil. I went to my two founding partners and we talked low cost, short term facility rental, admin and hiring. But mostly, could we trust Phil, or were we setting up a new law firm. We agreed to have lunch with Phil the next day and just put the proposition to him. At the end of lunch, we elevated Phil to the same level of partner as Reggie and gave him a healthy raise (Mary got the same as Phil).

After a weekend of Coast Guard up in Rio Vista on the

Sacramento River, and then Coast Guard Air Station Sacramento, I took a 6:00 a.m. flight with Martha to D.C. for 3 full days in the East, including one in Philadelphia, then a Thursday flight to Phoenix and all day Friday at DMIC in Scottsdale – super busy week to be!

— — —

We checked into the Mayflower with only enough time to make a few quick calls and to freshen up for dinner. (It had been a while since Martha and I had been together and sitting next to her on the plane having cocktails wet my appetite for a get together on hotel arrival. Not to be! So, I put it down to "practice" for me for when Martha was in London and Paris and Mollie was with my family and me.)

Our diner at a Northern Indian restaurant was superb. The conversation focused on experts, the SCHOOLS Class in Philadelphia, but mostly on the Clemson COLLEGES Class venued in Charleston, South Carolina. We reached a decision that I would suggest to DMIC that we go ahead with filing a motion to dismiss on subject matter jurisdiction grounds since Josh's research of the public records of funding for Clemson tended to show support in that some, if not much, of its funding came from the State of South Carolina which should cause Clemson to be treated as a state operated institution. In turn, this should disqualify Clemson as an independent entity, either human or fictional (person, partnership or corporation) for purposes of diversity jurisdiction as required by the United States Code, federal law. Further, we were confident that a state court would never consider trying to assert jurisdiction over real property located outside its borders without regard to ownership. Certainly, not South Carolina, a bastion of state's rights!

At the end of the night, I asked Tinker to have Mace or Tod write something up that I could read on Wednesday when we were back in their office and which we could send ahead to Manny at DMIC and Austin at CAL Board to read before Martha and I arrived in Scottsdale on Thursday evening for dinner.

The next day's trip up to Philadelphia was uneventful. The meeting was at Abbott and Tweed, chaired by Alicia Gomes, as usual. Martha and I arrived almost an hour early and Alicia had left word at Reception for us to be ushered back to her office. Coffee awaited us. Alicia wanted to know the "news form Paris?" When I told her about Jean Bignon, she almost swooned. I still remember her saying, "His name reminds me of Jean Valjean in *Les Miserables*. What does he do?"

When we told her, she paused to think. "This is almost too good to be true," were her first words, then another pause, and, "Many today will be skeptical! Unlike us, your firm and mine, many of those at this meeting have only these BUILDINGS cases as their income stream. So, many, upon reflection, will at the least want to drag this out, and at the extreme, would prefer that you and your experts go away."

"The meeting should prove most interesting. Shall we see how this plays out?" from me.

Alicia, "Perhaps we should save this for the last item on the agenda. We would do well to be certain that you are secure as heading up the trial committee for SCHOOLS!

"Oh, and, by the way, I am not certain what firm will be representing which various clients in South Carolina. Some of these local South Carolina firms will not follow the chain of command, even if the client insists. They are very independent and many seem to have the ears of insurers!"

Me, "Forewarned is forearmed. We can only do the best we can."

There were no major issues at the meeting on *LAUSD*, SCHOOLS (I was reconfirmed as lead expert counsel), but things were a bit open-ended as to *Clemson* with a level of uncertainty prevailing (Martha and I did not discuss the motion to dismiss concept); and then, we came to the Experts portion of the meeting. I gave a description of my meeting with Dr. Bignon and his background, title and experience. Almost everyone's initial impression was exceedingly positive, but this was followed in a few silent beats by an almost restiveness.

Then, Phil Talcott, lead counsel of Bigstrom and Steel for USG offered a first salvo, "What will a Philadelphia jury think of a Frenchman coming over here and telling them that the cream of American medical science, not to mention the EPA, are wrong about asbestos? I am not at all certain that I see this playing out at that well for the defense. Ronan, we know you have worked hard on this and I am just thinking out loud at the moment."

I smiled, looked around, looked back at Fred, who wasted no time in back-sliding from his position at Alicia's dinner, and said, "I suggest we all reflect on this until we next meet again. Oh! And be sure to mention this to your clients. Do you think they should be here? (I would have liked to say, "Ours stand four-square behind these experts," but that needed to wait until after our client-types had met these putative experts witnesses and signed off.) After all, none of these experts will have anything good to say about airborne asbestos fibers. We already know that. Coming now or in the near future, many clients will accept that conceding those dangers, which realistically can no longer be refuted, is a necessary step to stopping this property litigation which can more quickly ruin insurers, not just the clients. Look at the chaos starting in the London syndicates markets, even now. Until our next meeting?" (I decided right there to omit any discussion of our plan for a motion to dismiss in *Clemson* as too controversial to bring on top of the Bignon discussion.)

Alicia adjourned the meeting and much buzzing amongst small groups followed. Sandra was suddenly next to me and asked me to lean down. She said, "Adam and I are no longer together. But what is most important is my father is ill. He thinks

I am too young to be in charge of this litigation. He will be in touch. He wants you to take over from him. Can we have a drink tonight in DC?'

"No, I have a dinner meeting. Breakfast tomorrow?" Sandra said yes and left.

Martha looked at me in a funny way. "Anything wrong?' she asked.

"I will tell you what I can on the train. Let's reconnoiter."

But Sandra was on the train and at the Mayflower. So, no stop at the bar, off to our rooms to make calls and we did some of that, but Martha and I did find a free hour or so to refresh, and to include my telling her about Sandra after the excitement subsided.

— — —

Dinner that night at Duke Ziebert's Steakhouse was crazy. No one could stop laughing. All Mace Snow could keep saying in a variety of tones and voices was different versions of, "I cannot help but want to watch all those folks realizing that their rice bowls were about to be smashed, or snatched, or stolen from them. My God, we might win a case and actually have a piece of major litigation come to an end!!" More laughter followed: a good thing we were closing that restaurant!

— — —

The next morning, I met Sandra in the dining room at 8:30. She looked glorious, unlike the previous afternoon. She was sitting, reading the Washington Post when I arrived. She started to get up, but I bent and kissed her cheek, so she returned to sitting. I pulled out a chair and she poured me a cup of black coffee. Then, she looked me straight in the eye and said, "I really blew it when I lost it with you because you decided you didn't want to work for the firm. There I've said it. I am truly sorry!" With that, she shuffled a bit in her chair, seemed to cross her ankles, and went on, "I spoke to my father at some length last night. He has testicular cancer, which has metastasized to his colon and intestines. He is resigned to the fact that he is dying. He wants to go on a cruise with my mother and come home and die. He says treatment will waste the time he has left and won't have much effect, if any. Do you have anything to say about that?"

I thought for a second to create a slight aura of gravitas, and said, "I think that's a very brave decision. I cannot say that I disagree, but then you know a lot more than I do. What does your mother think?"

"She's so fraught that she will do whatever he says. He's run their lives since before they were married. Hell, he'd run mine completely, if I let him. Still, after all of these years litigating these asbestos matters, it turns out to be you, the man who rejected him and his firm, it's you to whom he now wants to turn over the firm. What do you say to that?"

Looking her straight in the eye, I said, "I sure hope it's you who are buying breakfast. I don't think anything of it. I have clients that make my conflicts unwaivable. Surely you know that?" Her head bobbed affirmatively, "And I have no desire to take over a firm like yours, or to be a managing partner, for that matter."

Then matching her direct look in the eyes, I spoke slowly, in measured terms, "Did you order me scrambled eggs?" Sandra stared, paused, then laughed, nodding yes, so I went on, "I cannot do any of that. I will say this. I once loved you with most of my heart. I still have real feelings for you, maybe some residue of that love. And I like you. So, what I will do is talk to him and reassure him that you have what it takes to handle this litigation. Moreover, if you have issues and there is no clear conflict, I will be there for you as much as I can. Should the three of us have a drink, or just him and me. I'll make time next week." The eggs arrived.

— — —

The meetings at Tinker's office went well. We had our people from Philadelphia, New York and South Carolina. I let Martha do a good deal of catching them up. Then we worked on who would be doing what in each case. I told them about London and Paris in early May, with my family in town for the business in London and Mollie along for Paris, explaining that I might take a small amount of time for myself during these excursions. On my way out when it was just Tinker and me, I told him about Carolyn's upcoming visit at the end of June. He was surprised, saying, "I was never all that certain about how close you got with Carolyn. As I remember, she was more into girls than boys, but really, above all, about her career. I do know she was gone a great deal, even before you got there. Nice young woman though. Always had time to say a kind word. Was she successful?"

Me, "Incredibly successful! She has a son about 11 or 12 years old, and she is bringing him for his first trip to Sausalito. She still owns that same condo, uses it as her West Coast headquarters. I see her maybe once a year or so. She wants to meet Mollie and my family. So, I will be taking a few more days then, as well."

Tinker's parting was, "Give her my regards."

Mine, "I will. She's on the cover of this month's *Vogue* if you want to see her now."

— — —

Martha and I arrived at Phoenix Sky Harbor at 5:10 that afternoon. I got a rental car. She collected our suitcases and we were off to the Biltmore. (Club Fed had become the Phoenician, a high-end Westin property, and its room rate quickly became prohibitive. DMIC had a corporate rate at the Biltmore making it by far more affordable.) Dinner was set for 6:30 with only Charley Sewell, John O'Sullivan, Dudley and Manny in attendance. We had a private room off the main dining room. (By then, they had all agreed that trying to keep Martha out of this loop was a waste of time and resources, especially since her hourly rate was lower than mine and she could do some tasks faster than me, e.g., writing/typing reports.)

We ordered cocktails, but before they could arrive, Charley and John started in on the key issue of no records at DMIC Scottsdale. Dudley was beginning to appear defensive, saying that this was not really a claims function, but financial. John, former head of Finance was not happy saying it had been in the Claims province. Finally, Dudley said that he had been in the job only five years and only knew what Larry Decker told him as Larry had been there for more than twenty years. (Of course, Larry was not involved having been recused from all of the DMIC asbestos claims litigation because of his relationship with DMIC's taking on the Wallboard coverage, and his being a Name at Lloyds.) I tried breaking the tension by suggesting that perhaps Dudley could ask Larry tomorrow what, if anything, Larry might know about the placing of DMIC's reinsurance in London. Dudley agreed saying he would have it done before we showed up tomorrow.

The reason for this dinner was to talk about their reinsurance problem and what was happening in London, and had to be done now because Austin Smith would be in town tomorrow to talk about all of the cases as would Reggie from our office. So, between cocktails and courses, Martha, and mostly I, brought everyone up to speed.

I also told them all about London and Paris in early May and suggested now might be the right time for one or more of them to meet Q and Wil as well as some of the experts, especially Dr. Bignon. Charlie and John looked at Dudley. (I knew Manny really wanted to go.) Dudley said words to the effect: I guess since someone has to do it, it has to be me.

The rest of the night went fine. Martha was staying for the weekend. Her friend, our local counsel from Oregon was flying down for a day or so. We loaded my suitcase in the car and drove out to DMIC, getting there at 10:00. We spent three hours on the other litigation. Austin said he would go to London and Paris as well. (I made a note to schedule Q and Wil to meet Dudley before Austin arrived.)

After a nice lunch at a real Mexican restaurant in Old Scottsdale, we returned to DMIC briefly. Dudley had to duck into his office. He returned to the conference room in moments, his face was ashen. He could hardly speak. Finally, he got out, "Come with me," to Manny and me. We followed him. Inside Dudley's office, hanging from a light fixture was Larry Decker!

— — —

I missed my flight, but got home on the next one. Martha was shaken, but she never saw Larry. In fact, she never met him. Austin was aghast. Before I left, Dudley pulled me aside and said, "I spoke to Larry this morning before the meetings about the reinsurance placement and the total absence of any records. He said that seemed strange and he would see what he could find. We never spoke again. What do you think it means?"

I was fairly certain I knew what it meant and that Dudley and the others at DMIC would know in short order.

The weekend went poorly after that. I did hope Martha thought not to tell anyone until DMIC issued a statement.

34

Shifting Focus

Although I was spending seemingly almost all of my time on the handful of Mega-Cases about which I have written almost exclusively, I was, at the same time, involved in developing other business and supervising more than half of our firm's attorneys while acting as National Coordinating Counsel on the CAL Board asbestos cases of all varieties (I also had other insurance clients besides Desert Mutual and other corporate clients in addition to Cal Board, but I could foresee in the not distant future, an increasing need to groom junior partners on some of these other business sources.). So, when our trip to London with the children and onto Paris without them drew near, I had to scramble to see that my "state-side work" did not suffer while I was in Europe.

At the *LAUSD* hearing, plaintiff attorney Stoneman offered to dismiss CAL Board for a waiver of costs. (All of our counsel felt this was because of the aggressive nature of our defense tactics both at the Statute of Limitations trial, the subsequent writ petitions which could very possibly be upheld on appeal if there was no settlement, and the thorough and unexpected opposition which only CAL Board filed on the proof of product identification issue including the LAUSD proposal for resolving it by burden shifting on the content of each specific manufacturer's products.)

So, when LAUSD offered the exit, we recommended that CAL Board accept (of course, Desert Mutual was on board with the huge future fees savings). Stunningly, no sooner was that dismissal in place than another DMIC insured was added to the

LAUSD matter, and our firm was brought right back in (along with counsel for six other newly served defendants) to defend that Desert Mutual insured. Martha and I went to Los Angeles for the day to meet with the new client, a building materials distributor, called KK Small Enterprises. They were in Compton, an adventure getting there and then encountering heavy security, including ten foot high chain link fencing topped with barbed wire, electric gates, and armed guards. The first meeting was excellent. As DMIC had paved our way with glowing tributes about our CAL Board success.

Henry James was the President and Founder of this sizeable construction supplies wholesaler. His son, Harry Junior, was the Chief Operating Officer (COO). The two of them, a broker representative and one of their financial types sat in on the initial five hour meeting. Martha and I took turns addressing a wide variety of points coming from our backgound in the *LAUSD* litigation so far, the theories of recovery for that suit, *LAUSD's* lawyers and the overall pending status of the case. There were many issues that would be the same, but not all, for example, potential distribution liability for manufacturers that were no longer in business, or products with ACM which could not be attributed to a manufacturer but for which LAUSD might have a receipt of some type showing delivery by their company. (All during the meeting, I began to notice that Harry Junior could not keep his eyes off of Martha. When I mentioned it on our way to LAX, she laughed and said something like I wonder if he would feel like that if he had seen us an hour before we left Bunker Hill!)

At any rate, when I explained that I would be gone for the better part of a month coming right up and a few weeks more a month or so after I got back, and I was leaving Martha in charge of getting their defense up and running, Harry Junior jumped at the chance to say he would be pleased to work with Martha to make certain they got off on the right foot. (But, of course,

Martha would be in the UK and Paris for part of the time I was gone. We did not mention that.)

— — —

A few days before departing on our trip to London, I got a call from Dudley Chisholm at Desert Mutual. I thought he was probably calling to check about the details of his role on the upcoming trip. (The family would have almost two full weeks before Austin and Dudley arrived. A few days less for Martha as she was going to be with me for final preparation of the UK experts and a meeting with Quincy and Wilford on their progress with the placing UK broker (read "Syndicates' broker").) I was far wrong, yet pleasantly surprised.

Dudley related, in essence, that it appeared that Larry Decker, aware of the risks associated with his being a Name in the London market, had begun to carry home much of the paperwork related to DMIC's placement of its reinsurance through its London broker, with whom Larry had developed quite a relationship. His wife, Irene, in going through the many files which Dudley kept had come across any number of files relating to DMIC's business handlings. These confused her, and Larry had never mentioned their presence, not to mention his reason for their being in his home office file cabinets. She checked with the family accountant handling Larry's estate, and she suggested that Irene call someone at DMIC, who turned out to be Dudley.

Dudley's reason for calling was not just to relate what was going on, but to ask for advice on the next step. I thought for a few seconds and gave him a short list: ascertain the full scope of all DMIC documents found, preferably compiled by a third party like the family accountant. Using a chain of custody analogy, I suggested that "the originals" found in Larry's files be carefully copied by a third party, like a court reporting firm whose members were notaries public, and then undertake

Bates-stamped numbering to assure completeness. That third party, if willing, would retain the originals and the original Bates-stamped set. A copy service would come in and make sets for DMIC, our firm and the London barrister's chambers. Also, I would probably need additional sets in London. (Turned out to be two-plus file drawers; about three banker's boxes.)

Before departing the office that evening, I stuck my head into Martha's office. She was there. I told her about Dudley's call. I said I would really appreciate her taking a quick spin through all of the documents, and based on what she finds, give me a sample so I could read a few hundred pages on the flight to London or after I arrived. Also, I suggested she might need to come over a few days earlier. (She smiled at that, saying something like, "I think Mollie must be a darling!")

— — —

With Martha dealing with the new *LAUSD* client and the Science and Medicine issues (not to mention the DMIC placement documents), I felt Mary would be the right person to attend the next NCC meeting in Philadelphia, along with Tinker.

Manny at DMIC and Austin Smith at CAL Board were fine with this, especially as Dudley Chisholm of DMIC was going to be in London and Paris to meet experts, as was Austin. Martha would be overlapping by that time as well.

I had Martha over with five other senior members of my team for a cook-out a few weeks before our London departure, so Mollie and our children would have met Martha, who made a great impression, especially with our girls because she was a former athlete in college. (We had a pick-up basketball game in our driveway: four on four. My sons, Phil and me against my daughters, Reggie Fox, my partner who played in high school in Oakland, and Martha. We only played to 7 baskets, win by 2; but the game took at least a half hour as my side eked out a 13 –

11 basket victory. Serious players, especially my daughters!)

The family was delighted the day when I told them that Martha would be in London part of the time that we would be there. They were less pleased when I explained that I would need to work some of the time, and that Mom would have to go to some business meals, as would they. But I had a surprise for them: during the last week in London, Grand Mom Kate would be there and she would fly back with them and Ingrid while Mom and I would go on to Paris for my business and some sight-seeing.

— — —

Sandra had gotten back to me about her father; he was not doing well. Her mother was border-line hysterical half of the time. Adam Morris, her ex in Philadelphia, was trying to get back with her. Could I come over for a drink? I did, and barely kept it to that as Sandra was fairly volatile, with so many issues at once plus her practice and the onset of some massive office politics.

I got her attention when I asked a critical question; did her father's firm have any serious debt? She did not seem to know, but went and found some papers containing financial records from the end of the previous calendar/fiscal year. Without look-ing at the entirety of these papers, I went to the Liabilities section of the Balance Sheet, which showed short term debt (probably Line of Credit) of more than $600,000. When she told me the number of equity partners, the average debt/partner was high. Was she an equity? Yes. Did she participate in running the firm? No. Had all of the partners signed personal guaranties for this debt? She didn't know. Had she? Not sure!

I explained that what might happen is that one or more of the equity partners might leave and try to stick those left with the whole debt. If she wanted to hold things together, then she would need to move to take charge very soon with her father's blessing. If she failed or did not want to do that, would she leave and start her own firm or throw-in with another firm (conflicts of interest could be a deal breaker for that.)? Would her father's clients go with her? Did her father have life insurance at the firm to cover his equity and his share of the debt?

We had a second drink and talked some more. I told her I was leaving for almost a month in little more than a week, so she better get the needed information for me quickly if she wanted me to assist her in deciding what options she might want to pursue.

— — —

Carolyn called from Connecticut a few days before our departure for London. We talked about London and Paris. I told her I had not told Mollie anything about running into her. She would be in the East during most of our time in Europe. She seemed ever-more excited for me to meet Patrick after all of these years!

— — —

Sandra got back to me within a short day providing a good deal of information about her father and the firm. She was extremely nervous on the phone. I had only a few days left. Finally, I remember her saying, "Ronan, Dad has come to love you. I know you can not come into the firm now, and I'm sure you don't want to. But can you please see him before you go. He refuses to tell me what I should do, and I cannot figure it out. If you ask, maybe he'll tell you. He gets worse every day. I'm not sure that he will last until you get back. I'm desperate. PLEASE!"

Toward the end of visiting hours that night at California Pacific Medical Center, I went to see Sandra's father. He looked dreadful: gaunt, jaundiced and with too many tubes and wires. We spoke man-to-man for about thirty minutes. I was honest with him about why I was there. At some point, I think he just decided that he was really about to die. For a minute or two, I thought he might break down, but he held it all together. When we got to the firm and Sandra, he told me that some of the partners who had significant clients did not want Sandra (perhaps implicitly, any woman) running the firm or telling them what to do. So, then I asked what she should do in his opinion. He answered, "Leave the bastards! Tell my clients who are also hers that she thinks they will be better served when she is wherever she lands. Ask them to call me, if need be, but she should not wait at all long. As you can see, Ronan, my next trip will be in a wooden box. Thank you for coming to see me. Look after my Sandra, if you can. She told me about her blow-up. She regrets that more than any single thing in her life. Have a good life." With that, he rolled away. I never saw him again.

I called Sandra and told her what her father had told me about the firm, then wished her luck. I also told her where I would be staying in London if she really needed my help. She did not seem surprised!

— — —

With things becoming so busy before our departing for London, I was forced to call Dr. Arnaud rather than go into her office in North Sausalito. I described our family trip and explained about all of the business intervening in London and threatening to do so in Paris. I also mentioned that Martha would be part of the business in both cities. When I finished talking, the doctor was quiet for a long moment, then said words I shall not forget, "Ronan, you always tell me how you love Mollie with all of your heart and that she is the 'Love of Your Life.' Please be so very careful that you do absolutely nothing to hurt her during your time together, even when you two are separated. Show her your love and do not be afraid to do it in front of Martha, to show Mollie, Martha and yourself that you really do mean what you say. That's enough. Have a great trip! I'll see you in a month and before Carolyn arrives."

35

Our Family's First UK Trip

The day finally came. In fact, it was an afternoon, an evening and the next morning. (Although the flight time was only 10.5 hours, the eight hour time change made the transition from San Francisco to London a very challenging experience for the children. Maeve was 12, Robert was almost 11, and the Twins, Patrick and Meaghan, were almost 8. Ingrid was great.) The four children and Ingrid sat in the first row of Business Class while Mollie and I flew in First. The TWA Flight Crew, some of whom I had flown to London with before were fantastic! Shockingly, after finishing their dinners, all of the children got four or five hours sleep. (Not the excited Ingrid who could not believe her good fortune in getting a free trip to England.)

Mollie was so anxious, she just could not sleep. We talked for awhile, but I drifted off (certain that the two double vodkas, not to mention some wine and a glass of Port also helped). In what seemed like just an hour or two, our flight attendant asked if we wanted a full breakfast or just a continental. Mollie raised the shades on our two cabin windows and we could see first light over Ireland. The pilot promptly announced we would land at Heathrow in less than an hour. This great adventure was really beginning. With that, Mollie was up and about as was Ingrid. Children got their teeth brushed, faces cleaned and were generally freshened. The few seats in First allowed us (read: Me) to proceed at a somewhat leisurely pace relative to the rest of my family.

As the daylight increased, so did the children's excitement.

This was, after all, their first truly international travel. (Canada and Mexico were upcoming on the Society's meeting schedule.) With "wheels down!" things were close to a fever pitch. Ingrid was sounding excited as well, even though this was not her first trip to the United Kingdom, it was her first time headed to London's West End.

We disembarked the plane as a group and headed directly to Immigration and Customs. Having all of us flown upgraded, we seemed to have a bit of a head start on the throng and it not being Summer holiday, children were not greatly in evidence. The British Immigration Agent was a great friendly woman, making a fuss over our four children, especially with their brand new passports. She stamped everyone's booklet and we proceeded to Baggage Claim. While Mollie and I minded the foursome, Ingrid quickly rounded up two stewards with carts. Again, our bags seemed to arrive early on, so we loaded quickly. The stewards nodded to the Customs Agent, who looked at our crowd, smiled, and waived us into England. We had a van waiting to bring us to the Grosvenor House with all of our luggage. Not big enough for the seven passengers and all of their bags, Robert, Patrick and I took a black taxi as the van left and we went at our own pace to the hotel.

The redoubtable Mary of Sir Richard's staff had graciously made our arrangements at the Grosvenor House. As someone who was becoming a frequent guest and appearing to be well-connected, we were accorded a three bedroom suite with an adjoining room with connecting door to the girls' bedroom for Ingrid. The rooms were large, handsomely furnished and the street noise not at all bad as we were quite high above Park Lane. Everyone was excited! They had heard about the great park, now seeing it through the rooms' windows, they wanted to get right to exploring it. After a half-hour to unpack, and conferring with Mollie, we decided to do a light lunch in the park and an "early dinner" at Wheeler's!

We were off to Hyde Park, through a tunnel under Park Lane (they all loved that), across the bridle path (Can we ride horses?), through the great gardens, then down to the Serpentine Lake. Finally, they were ready to eat and put up little resistance to British food. Then onward we pushed around the Serpentine, and eventually, we came to the Kensington Palace area, which I had hitherto not explored. Of course, as a royal enclave, it was itself off-limits, but a great deal was surprisingly visible. Mollie and I tried to explain everything, but it was more than our four could absorb. Then, rather suddenly, the jet lag began to hit them. We all rallied enough to leave the park and find our way to the Hyde Park Hotel which allowed us to take two taxis back to the hotel. The children each had about a two hour nap, after which we woke them gently but firmly, to help fight the jet lag.

We were able to get Wheeler's to take us very early, at 6:15. Albert was there to Mollie's joy. The table arrangement, Albert's stories and jovial nature, created the atmosphere of another older world, all of which seemed to resuscitate everyone, and we again began having more fun. We shared four or five appetizers, and the four children split two Dover soles, while Mollie and I each had our own. Ingrid insisted on cod saying, "It's a Norwegian thing!"

On the way back to Grosvenor House, we all stopped at the Lord Cornwallis memorial plaque where I explained the British historians glaring omission of Cornwallis' surrender to George Washington at the Yorktown Battlefield in 1781, functionally marking the end of our Revolutionary War (I left out the Treaty of Paris and all of the history, and gossip, associated with our envoys to Paris in those days leading up to its signing in 1783. I also left out that Yorktown was my Coast Guard OCS training site. No one else knew to bring that up.).

The days were lengthening as we were far north of our home latitude, so the walk back to the hotel was enjoyable, yet suitably brief. Soon, everyone was in bed and the children asleep, their rooms across the living area spaces from our room. Although slightly tired, I thought of the advice of Dr. Arnaud and proceeded to give Mollie my undivided attention for almost the next hour! Afterward, we both slept soundly until Mollie awoke at about 3 a.m., and returned the favor!!

— — —

The children were at our door by 6:00 a.m. With a kiss, we rose and Mollie invited them in. I called down and was advised that breakfast commenced at 6:30. So, I asked for a suitable table for seven, mindful of four being children. Our accommodations included breakfast, typical of the British Isles.

Everyone was hungry: Ingrid persuaded Robert and Patrick to have the full English breakfast. Mollie and I ordered our favorites a la carte, and the girls had French toast with sides of berries and bacon. Our waiter was friendly, becoming more so after seeing how our children were quite well behaved. We asked to have the food brought as it was ready and almost all of it arrived invitingly warm, if not actually hot.

At breakfast, we decided to take a half-day bus tour to see more of London and to give the children more of an idea of the immensity of this ancient city. The weather was clear albeit a bit brisk. We were on our way by 9:45, sitting as a group in the first two rows on the weather deck. First we went through Westminster, then Chelsea, then back around the Thames. By then we had seen the Victoria and Albert Museum, the Museum of Natural History, Knightsbridge (with Harrod's, Harvey Nichols, and other famous shopping, including Sloane Street). By the Thames River, we passed Westminster Abbey, Parliament and Big Ben, some of the world famous bridges, the Egyptian Obelisk, some of the Inns of Court, then into the Old City itself with the Tower of London. Turning about into Fleet Street, we passed more famous spots than can be listed, including the famous clubs on the Pall Mall, and I focused them on the Reform Club, where *Around the World in 80 Days* begins and ends. Then into Trafalgar Square, past Nelson on his plinth, through Admiralty Arch, past St. James Palace and its park and straight up to the gates of Buckingham Palace. A more than satisfactory morning!

Upon our return to Grosvenor House, I asked the concierge about a place nearby where we night get a satisfactory lunch. He recommended a casual bakery/delicatessen in a mews (a gentrified alley way) across Audley Street from the Hotel's main entrance, called *Richoux*. First we found it, then we tried it, waiting about 15 minutes for their small staff to make up a table for six. (Ingrid had begged off from lunch to get 2 or 3 hours for shopping on her own on Oxford Street nearby.) I shall never forget that *Richoux's* menu included Welsh Rarebit. When Meaghan saw that, she gave a shocked sound! Robert and Patrick thought it sounded exciting. Maeve knew what it was, so remained aloof. When Maeve's turn came to order, she had "the Rabbit!" The boys started to have second thoughts, and Meaghan was visibly and verbally appalled. The waitress, no doubt a veteran of this "rabbit cruelty" behavior, Mollie, and I said nothing. The beverages and cold cut sandwiches arrived first. Then, Mollie and my grilled lunches and finally Maeve's grilled cheese with accoutrements were served! A good laugh was had by all, with perhaps Meaghan laughing the hardest!

In all of my trips to London over the years, every time I have stayed at the Grosvenor House, I have re-visited Richoux. Mildred, our waitress that first day, is there often and I share photos of the family and stories of our lives. As my latter years have passed, I. have come to miss London. However, old age robs many of us of so many choices. Still, I have all of my memories.

— — —

The time with my family in London remains a treasured memory as does that time with Mollie. We packed in the sightseeing and then created split-off options to do things in smaller groups, like shopping (the boys wanted to shop for different things than the women, and for less time). Not everyone wanted to see the Crown Jewels. But everyone, much to my surprise, wanted to take the river cruise down the Thames to Greenwich: another wonderful day, blessed with good weather and a marvelous tour guide; everyone loved the Royal Naval Museum and its explication of how time came to be determined and the role it plays in measurement, navigation and determining locations anywhere on our planet. We saved the museums (the British, Victoria and Albert, and the Natural History) for the days when rain was forecast and we walked not only in Hyde Park, but Regent's Park as well. Then Martha arrived and I had to start working a great deal more of my time.

One of the days, Corbett and Alison McDonald invited Martha and me to tea. I explained about my family, so they switched the day, made it for lunch and arranged a guided tour of the British World War II Museum across the street in what used to be Bedlam, the infamous mental hospital closed down by bombing in that war. They were beyond marvelous with the children, and they seemed all the more secure in their relationship with Martha and me having met my family (and Martha fit right in joining everyone for meals as well as Mollie and me for cocktails a few times).

— — —

Martha and I met with Corbett and Alison at their office twice, used the Chambers at 20 King's Bench Walk in the Temple (one of the four Inns of Court, historically housing all of the London area barristers stemming from centuries of distrust of England's lawyers by its aristocracy, as well as limiting their membership) for our own meetings as well as those with Quincy, a senior member of those chambers, and Wilford, the Chief Clerk of Chambers. We met with Julian once at the University (and he arranged a tour for Mollie and the children as well as Ingrid) and along with his significant other joined us all for a very festive gastropub dinner a short walk from the university in Chelsea.

In all, my meetings with Martha and all of our English associates went well, and we felt more than adequately prepared for the arrival of Dudley Chisholm and Austin Smith. Our progress with each had gone extremely well. If only we had more time to meet with Dr. Bignon, that would have saved travel, but he was too far behind the preparation curve to risk an introduction to the client-types quite yet.

— — —

So, at the beginning of my family's last five days in London, Dudley and Austin arrived. Plus, we were very pleased to welcome Grandmother Kate on the day before the clients arrived. Everyone was ecstatic. Kate allowed that she got to missing her grandchildren frightfully and began to feel that she needed to spend some time with her memories of travels with my father and their time together in SoHo. The number of attendees for the first client dinner climbed, but everyone enjoyed their evening at Wheeler's, regaled with cocktails, stories from the waiters and owner, many Dover Sole orders and wonderful wine. The clients loved meeting my family, and they found Kate interesting, and perhaps a bit exotic as did the owner and the waiters, especially when she told them about my Dad being stationed in London on Eisenhower's staff for almost two years and how she came to be a Congresswoman during the War when her boss, Congressman Burke, went into the U.S. Army. Ironically, both the congressman and my Dad, a Navy Commander, served on Ike's staff, where both acted as liaisons with the British and Canadian Army and Naval Staffs in preparation for D-Day and all that was to follow.

Surprisingly, at the end of dinner when I sked for the check, Arthur, the Head Waiter, told me that Mr. Smith was picking up the tab for dinner and that he had left an exceedingly generous tip as well. On the way walking back to the hotel, Austin leaned in and said, "Based on my chat with Dudley in the taxi coming from Heathrow, I am certain that Desert Mutual is coming under serious economic strain from our defense costs, and you should not have to pay for all of this yourself; so, tonight was a treat by Cal Board and a thank you to Desert Mutual, Martha, and especially you!"

— — —

The next day began with a family breakfast at the Grosvenor Dining Room, and the four children had so much fun explaining the menu and all of the English dining eccentricities to their grandmother. At another table, Martha had breakfast with the clients. according to our plan. Afterward, Ingrid and the boys went one direction while Mollie, Kate and the daughters took off for shopping on Beauchamp Lane and then onto Sloane Street and the King's Walk.

Meanwhile, the clients, Martha and I headed to the McDonalds' offices for an introductory meeting, briefing on their expert preparation, and a Pub lunch. As matters ensued, Dudley and Austin were impressed with the McDonalds themselves, their operation and facilities, and their intelligence tinged with humility. Both renowned epidemiologists shared auras of authority combined with gravitas. The day went by quickly, and fruitfully. At its end, the parting was one of perceived initiation of new relationships for Austin and Dudley with their kind praise of the McDonalds, their work, and their grasp and embrace of the CAL Board position on removal of undamaged asbestos containing materials.

In the black taxi on the return drive to the Grosvenor House while weaving through the convoluted streets of West London, Dudley gave a great sigh, and said, "After all of the time and expense in locating, recruiting and educating these witnesses, I was prepared to be disappointed, but the McDonalds so far exceeded my expectations that I am convinced you all have found the formula to end this litigation successfully. What do you think, Austin?"

Bringing himself to sit ever more slightly upright, Austin Smith echoed those thoughts, but from a different perspective, "The defense of these BUILDINGS cases has been masterful to date. I never cease to be amazed at the resourcefulness of our counsel. Ronan, Tinker. Reggie, and now Martha, are all extraordinary. This has been a harrowing confrontation for quite a few years; and I do not believe it will end soon. But I do believe it will end; and after today, that these cases, at least, will end successfully for our interests. The McDonalds are certainly inspiring potential witnesses with incredible credentials. Now, I cannot wait to meet Julian Peto on the day after tomorrow."

— — —

As I often mention, this book, like SAUSALITO, is largely reliant on Dr Arnaud's notes and audiotapes, which often decreased in number over time, when our sessions generated little of interest, only to increase in times of stress: with my memory superimposed thereon.

I especially remember the one day hiatus for Austin Smith that was occasioned by the unavailability of our experts on two consecutive days. In reality, it seemed Austin was very pleased to have the day off to renew several old acquaintances about whom he divulged very little.

That interim day began with a fine breakfast with the family, now eight of us with the addition of Kate. I listened as they discussed their plan for the day, which seemed to include an opportunity for Mollie to have much of the day to go about shopping for herself. (Of course, I thought, much as she might enjoy shopping in London, my informed guess was that she was very much looking forward to Paris even more for that purpose. Mollie had been in touch with some of the Parisian women residents who worked with her company, so I was not in the least concerned that she would be bored while Martha and I worked in Paris. Dudley alone would be along and just planning to meet Dr. Bignon for a brief lunch on this trip.) It seemed Kate, during a visit with my father years ago, had gone to the London Zoo in Regents Park, and thought the children would do well to see it. Ingrid enthusiastically agreed to join them.

After seeing my family off, we three, Dudley, Martha and I, took a black taxi to the Fleet Street entrance of the Temple and Inner Temple Inns of Court. Skirting the chapel and dining hall, we made our way through the maze of hundreds of years old brick and stone structures, most three or four stories tall (some rebuilt but looking undifferentiated from their mates following the German attacks of WW II). We emerged at the top of a wide esplanade surrounded on three sides by more buildings, while the fourth side was a northern view of the River Thames flowing to the East. Martha led the way down a stone path to the far end of the left row of buildings. We mounted four steps, and before we could knock, Wil opened the door. He stepped down to the level of the foyer, extended his hand, and said, "Good day, Mr. Chisholm. I am Wilfred Smythe, Clerk of these Chambers, commonly referred to as Twenty King's Bench Walk, located here in the Temple. Please step right this way."

With that, Wil briefly greeted Martha and me and led the three of us up a flight of stairs immediately in front of the entrance. After a turn of ninety degrees about halfway to the next floor, the stairs widened a bit and gave way to the entrance to a large room with multiple tables and chairs and a row of windows overlooking the river. At the table in front of those windows sat Quincy Franden-Jones. Upon seeing us, he rose, and ever so gracefully made his way around the table to Dudley Chisholm, extending his hand and saying, "My. Chisholm, I am most pleased to meet you. We are delighted that Mr. O'Neill and Ms. Walsh, who have proved so gracious to us, have seen fit to cause your coming to meet us. We are extremely grateful!"

(As I look at what I have written, it may seem Quincy was "sucking up to Dudley," but the effect was completely different. Just as an actor can give multiple meanings to the same words, those words uttered by Q conveyed humility, respect, even actually being honored, but more than anything else, they conveyed a sense of nascent power. Here was someone who had an exquisite command of the English language, far superior to that of the average lawyer.) I smiled inwardly at Q's performance. Martha's jaw seemed to drop just a mite as she fully recovered her composure. Q pleasantly directed Dudley to a chair having a commanding view of the river. I sat to Dudley's right and Martha sat next to me. Q sat across from me and Wil to his left. Just the five of us. None of the Chambers' young barristers were invited.

Quincey set to work directly, explaining that the papers recovered from Larry Decker's basement, while giving us some proof of coverage, did not go back far enough to resolve many of the proof of terms issues for most of the relevant years of reinsurance. On the other hand, there was, perhaps, enough to support our making sufficient enquiries and, in the end, to launch a physical search for missing documents. After discussion and explanations, Q got to his key point: London brokers could not destroy their documents over time as they were the functional keepers of the lead syndicate names and all of their evolving relationships as the syndicates added and subtracted named members and took on the same, different, or sometimes even inconsistent risks from year-to -year, all as they underwrote a wide variety of coverages, of which reinsurance was but one! YET, a very BIG ONE!

The one item of greatest import amongst Larry's recovered papers was the clear identification of the corresponding London Syndicate Placing Broker for the syndicates with whom Desert Mutual's London Broker had placed DMIC's business, and that was definitely Cheshire and Booth, over one hundred years old and still guided to a large degree by its founding families.

Without knowing it, we were more than 90 minutes into this meeting. Dudley had said hardly a word, one question to me for a clarification. He took the break well and allowed Wil to guide him to "the Gents." Martha departed briefly. Q asked me if we should finish the main points before lunch, especially to lighten the atmosphere of what was coming. I agreed. Wil had tea, coffee and water brought in along with biscuits (So-o-o dry!). I went to the loo very briefly and encountered Dudley on his way out. He looked at me, very directly, and asked, "Is there a solution here?"

I said, "Is this already a 'you bet your company matter'?"

Dudley's eyes met mine, and he said drily, "You know it is!"

The next hour, according to Dudley Chisholm eighteen months later, was the most chilling of his life. Quincy and I laid out the work needs, the potential staffing, the range of potential costs and the risks. The total bill might run upwards of ten million dollars, or more. Left to me was the recommendation, "Dudley, I remember what Charlie, John and you told me back in that conference room in Scottsdale. You all will need to appreciate the risks, but you cannot get to the rewards without them. Quincy's assessment and all that we have learned indicates Cheshire and Booth are essentially honest and that they have a reputation for protecting their documents, even throughout the Battle of Britain and the V-2's. That is the major factor that says go forward."

"The other factor is Thornton, Campbell and Thornton as your solicitors, led by Bradley Campbell. They will be expensive, but they are among the most respected firms in the City. We believe based on our research and preliminary meetings that, with the correct background work, we ultimately will get to Cheshire and Booth's 'Lloyds Filings documents' and prove up most, if not all, of your reinsurance. The last remaining risk, which we cannot assess at this point, is whether or not the syndicate names will be able to pay out all of the needed sums." (No one spoke in the silence that followed.)

"How about a pub lunch?" asked Quincy.

— — —

We had a round of cocktails and wine with lunch, but not anywhere near enough alcohol to cause any distress. Questions about some details were raised by Dudley, but all of us who were working on this solution were careful not to try to push him into a decision. Dudley, who had been to London before allowed that he would like to walk back to the hotel after our lunch.

Martha and I took a black taxi. When we had pulled away, she reached over and took my hand, holding it gingerly, and said, "Ronan, seeing you with your family is incredible. What a great father you are, and a caring husband. Despite what we have, Mollie is so very fortunate to have you. Please believe me this trip is doing nothing for me but reinforcing the conversations we had on our last trip here. I just wanted you to know that. I do not want to do anything that would upset the equanimity that is present among all of us. Love you!"

We made no effort to kiss. I gave Martha's hand a squeeze, and said, "Thank you."

— — —

I was in my room, changing for dinner. No one from the family was in their rooms (no cell phones yet). The phone rang and it was Dudley. He asked if I would meet him for a drink in the Red Bar downstairs right away and to come alone. Of course, I agreed.

Upon arriving, Dudley had a large clear adult beverage on ice in front of him. He waited for me to order, then started right in, "Ronan, Charlie is intensely upset at the costs that you suggested might ultimately be incurred. These are so much more than we have budgeted. I did not want to do this in front of anyone else. Why are they so high? We know it's not you driving up these potential expenses!"

I paused before responding, thinking how to make this seem more reasonable and potentially palatable for Dudley and his two superiors. "Dudley, I think you know, and I believe Charlie and John, upon reflection, would understand that we are undertaking this operation in one of the most expensive cities in the world. So, it's not unprecedented that their lawyers will be among the most expensive; and, solicitor firms, especially the more powerful ones, and we need one of those, will cost more than Q who is himself a senior barrister, albeit not a Queen's Counsel (QC). Someone like Bradley Campbell might run into 1,000 pounds/hour. That brings us to the exchange rate; and, right now, the pound costs $2.23. Finally, we cannot know with any real certainty what staffing needs we will actually have. So, we decided to be extremely conservative, on the high side, with all of our estimates in order to allow for a much lesser chance of defeated expectations."

Some time while I was talking, Dudley began making notes, then looked up and said, "So, what you're saying is you believe that these estimates represent what Quincy, Wilfred and you are hoping would be a probable maximum?"

"Something like that. I would love to give you a range of numbers, but we just do not know what we will be up against.," and I paused, "Maybe what needs to be done is either Charlie comes over here or we fly Quincy and Wilfred to Scottsdale. But I would point out that retaining that solicitor firm might help us with budgeting since Bradley Campbell might have a better handle on their staffing and the execution of the task which may come to hand. If we do that, then having Charlie fly here would make the most sense. What do you think?"

"I am not sure what to say. What if we start down the road and it turns out to be a dead end?" Dudley signaled for another drink.

"That's a reason to hire the solicitors. Go about this in phases. Please recall that in Scottsdale, you all were pretty clear that time was a factor. Let me ask this. You don't have to answer, but what do you all believe could be the total amount of reinsurance you might collect?" at which point I waited.

Dudley: "Understand that we believe some of our policies and some of the reinsurance coverages may have no stop loss provisions. The high end could reach into the nine figures. Right now, with BI payments and attorney fees, the total is closer to $30 million. But you are right, we need to think long term, not just our outstanding recoupment, but future payments as well."

"After we meet with Julian Peto tomorrow, I think I will skip Paris and fly home. Can you be available in Paris if we need to speak with you?"

I finished my drink, and said, "Please bear in mind in your next discussions with Charlie the two determinative factors I mentioned in our meeting. Then, add a third: Quincy Franden-Jones is a very fine lawyer, and from those here in London with whom I have discussed him, they say there are few barristers better 'on their feet' than Quincy. I would not make this recommendation if I did not believe at the core of my being that we will succeed."

Dudley rose, put out his hand for me to shake, and said only, "Thank you for coming straight downstairs."

— — —

The Julian Peto meeting went seamlessly. Dudley was enamored of Julian's quick wit and intelligence from the first minutes. I began to wonder, what with the rapport they quickly established, if Martha and I were even needed. (Martha doubtless was more needed as she contributed details and tid-bits along the way. I did little more than keep the discussions relatively on point and moving forward. Plus, I was conscious of Dudley's late afternoon direct flight to Phoenix.)

Austin Smith echoed his sentiments from the post-McDonald meeting after sitting through Julian's discoursive rendering on the wayward nature of how the United States EPA and its court systems were making a financial mess of the whole asbestos construction employment epidemic.

In the end, I taxied to Heathrow with Dudley. Austin walked back to Grosvenor House. We went over more details on the 'Quincy Plan," as we began to call it, during the ride. Martha had come along so we could do a debrief on Julian and plan for Dr. Bignon on the return ride to the hotel. As Dudley disappeared through the gates of British Airways, as B.O.A.C. had recently renamed itself, Martha squeezed my hand and pulled me ever so gently toward her, whispering, "I simply cannot wait until we can be together again. You have been magnificent throughout this trip. I do not know how you do it!"

But then, to work!

— — —

Back at the hotel, dinner with the family, while Martha and Austin excused themselves and went off to a pub for lighter fare and perhaps heavier cocktails!

The trip was ending the day after next for the children, Ingrid and Kate. Austin was returning home on the morrow (I would breakfast with Martha and him). Then, Mollie and I were to leave for Paris on a commuter flight later in the same day as our family's departure. Martha was going to remain in London for a few days on her own while Mollie and I enjoyed Paris.

The family, Ingrid and Kate had a last London dinner at Wheeler's. Albert came in just to wait on us with his son. The owner bought dessert and an after dinner round. It was all quite celebratory! One of the best trips Mollie and I ever took!

36

Mollie In Paris

The two full days that followed our late afternoon arrival in Paris are among the most memorable I ever spent with Mollie.

Dr. Doll's Mary had arranged for us to stay at the *Prince de Galles* on the *Avenue Georges V*, a few hundred yards from the *Champs Elysees* next to the palatial and overwhelmingly expensive *Hotel George V*, with a short, charming downhill walk to the Seine, the Left Bank and the Eiffel Tower. We could not have been better positioned to see and appreciate the cultural center of Paris.

Following check-in and being so pleased with our room (really a small suite and briefly viewing an erotic exhibition by a young couple across the street from our room making love with sound effects and no apparent inhibitions about whom might be watching), the concierge graciously directed us to a local bistro where we had a marvelous country-style French dinner and a bottle of excellent Bordeaux. We walked about the area after eating, ending up easily at our hotel. We fell into each other's arms as soon as our door closed: I was never more in love with "My Mollie."

With two days to sightsee, I wanted to retrace some of the sights which Carolyn had shown me, but I also wanted us to have some of our very own experiences, so I asked the concierge to arrange a tour for our second full day to see key important historical sights of the city, while explaining that, for our first day, I planned a morning cruise on the Seine, followed by a tour of the *Louvre* and the *Muse d'Orsay* (we both loved Impressionism and the *d'Orsay* is almost unanimously considered the leading center displaying exclusively that school of art).

The Seine cruise that day was a challenge for me as I wanted Mollie to think this was my first time, and I almost messed up on the *Tour d'Argent* when the opportunity presented itself. Mercifully, the tour guide did not pause after saying "the world's most expensive, if not exclusive, restaurant" as had occurred when I was with Carolyn and she had given the answer before the guide could say it. Instead, I asked Mollie, "Would you like to try it? I'll see if the concierge can get us in one of our free nights?"

We spent two hours in the *Louvre*, barely scratching the surface of all that was to be seen, but we did get Winged Victory, the Venus de Milo and the Mona Lisa. At the *Muse d'Orsay*, we saw room after room of Impressionists, all of the most famous, Manet (my favorite), Monet (whom we both loved), Mary Cassat (Mollie's most admired), and not enough of Van Gough (more would require a trip to Amsterdam!). So many others hung on those walls. Days were needed to appreciate fully the genius of those artists and how their school of painting had helped to reshape the entire world of art.

Back at the hotel, after conferring with the concierge, I explained to Mollie that the *Tour d'Argent* menu was comprised exclusively of duck dishes. She winced, paused, then shook her head "no."

So, instead, we went the next night, our last alone, to dine at the sumptuous Dining Salon at the *Hotel Georges V!* An INCREDIBLE meal, and a superb ending to our time alone, while together, in Paris.

— — —

The next day, Martha arrived in the morning. To allow the two of us to work in a quiet place, Mollie went back to the Louvre to explore as well as to spend time visiting Notre Dame and the two islands that had once formed the heart of the Holy Roman Empire.

At 2:30, Dr. Bignon met us at his office. He seemed immediately impressed with Martha, who looked almost glamorous in her suit with coordinated blouse and scarf. But he seemed even more impressed with how much she knew about him and his work. We had spent our time that morning preparing for this meeting and trying to come up with avenues to tie Bignon's work into what we hoped to accomplish from his testimony. (We made excuses for Dudley's being called back to Arizona, but Dr. Bignon seemed as if he could care less.) Mostly though, he seemed to direct his attention to interacting with Martha. I decided to let things play out by giving her more of the presentation than we had planned. Of course, having constructed much of it herself, she was the mistress of all she was saying.

At the end of our meeting, Dr. Bignon asked if we could join him for dinner at *La Caravelle*. I mentioned my wife. He did not even say if he had one. Instead, after asking where we were all staying, he said he would send a car for us at 7:00. In the taxi on the way back to the hotel, I asked Martha, "Did you have a sense that Dr. Bignon was more than occupationally interested in you and less so in what you were saying?"

Martha laughed, then said, "While you went to the Gents, he asked me if I would have dinner with him tonight. I told him that we were planning on eating together. Then you came back. My guess is that all of this might be part of an evolving plan to seduce me!"

"And what do you plan to do about that, may I ask?" was my response.

Martha said, "A lady never tells on her lover, any lover!" With that she took my hand and squeezed it.

— — —

The car, a large black Citroen, arrived at the *Hotel Prince de Galles* promptly at 7:00. Both ladies looked elegant, smartly attired in evening wear that seemed to me to be just short of formal gowns. I recognized Martha's ensemble from our luncheon with Sir Richard at the Royal College of Physicians and Surgeons. Mollie wore a lustrous purple, showing off her lush, and still quite youthful, figure despite four children. In heels, both women seemed to stand at six feet in height. Those occupying the hotel's lobby could not take their eyes off of them both, neither could the concierge who sprang from behind his counter to wish us all a successful evening! The doorman saw both ladies into the roomy rear seat, while I rode backward facing them both.

The driver took us down to the river, then past both royal palaces to the *Place de la Concorde*, then a few blocks up the *Champs Elysees* to a right turn into *La Caravelle*, almost hidden in its own little forest in the center of Paris.

This was a quintessentially exquisite evening: the company was spectacular, the conversation witty and interesting, the food sumptuous and the wine enchanting. Dr. Bignon had eyes mostly for Martha, but did strive to include Mollie and even me in his conversation. Mollie had a superb time and seemed to enjoy Martha's company very much.

Little of our discussions had much bearing on the litigation, until Mollie mentioned that she was from Philadelphia where the first of the giant class actions was pending. Then Martha asked Mollie how she thought a Philadelphia jury would accept Dr. Bignon. Mollie's answer was a surprise: she was uncertain. So much would depend on the jury selection. I pointed out that with a federal jury, the pool would be far broader than just the County of Philadelphia, and would include the entire region.

Mollie elaborated with an opinion that the natives of southeastern Pennsylvania could, despite being nominally liberal, often function as so home-bred in their thinking as to appear almost xenophobic. Then, she added, "However, in Dr.Bignon's case, he is so charming and handsome, that I very much doubt that any of the women jurors will be able to resist him. But I am more uncertain about the men: surely, the more educated, the better."

With those remarks, Dr. Bignon paid Mollie more attention, learning that she was a high ranking executive with a large American software company. I could see her stock going up in the Doctor's mind. (But not as high as Martha's!)

— — —

On finishing dinner, the Doctor asked Martha to join him for a nightcap. His car took Mollie and me back to the hotel. We went to our room. On the way, Mollie asked, "Is Dr. Bignon married?"

My response, "I don't know. But I imagine Martha knows as she has fully researched him. Even if so, I suggest that being French and a highly thought of man, the "Good Doctor" has probably had affairs in the past. Anyway, Martha is not a young woman just out of undergrad. My guess is she will be just fine."

An hour or so later, our hotel phone rang. It was Martha, who said, "Just got in. Hope I am not disturbing you. Doctor Bignon was a gentleman. He took us for a ride in his car and we had a nightcap at the Bar in the *Georges V*, next door."

I told Mollie what she said. Mollie smiled, and said, "Do you believe her?"

My reply, "I really do not care as long as he remains a highly useful expert witness." With that I reached over, turned off the light and began to cuddle with Mollie!

———

The next day, our last in Paris, we had a most productive meeting with Dr. Bignon. A very pleasant lunch, and the afternoon on the phones to the USA and packing. That night, the three of us had a nice quiet Bistro dinner a few blocks from the hotel, returning early to finish packing as we were to leave early the next day, which would involve gaining nine hours.

Mollie and I had a great night after the lights went out. I went to sleep with a feeling of renewal in our relationship.

37

Charleston To London

The second day after my return to Mill Valley, I was once again back in Scottsdale. We had the three Desert Mutual leaders and me at a conference table with Tinker and Quincy on the phone at 6:00 a.m. Mountain Standard Time. Dudley began by outlining the company's concerns with the budget for this work and the potential expectations, ending with their sense of lack of certainty in a positive outcome and potential excess funding layouts. He asked for other options, but no one could put forth any course of action more viable than the one before us on the table. Charles Sewell, the President, and John O'Sullivan, the VP/COO, both expressed their concerns that this plan was "essentially an uncapped expenditure" that could ruin the company. But in the next breath, they were acknowledging that to do nothing would bring the company to its financial knees within 24 months. (They could not raise their premium rates and remain competitive, and they could not increase their business book too fast without taking on "Bad Risks." Desert Mutual was, quite literally, between a rock and a hard place.)

Several concepts then came to the fore and coalesced to form the basis for DMIC's critical decision: first, I stepped up and asked, what other 'real plan' was available. (Certainly, no turning point on its face that anyone could articulate.) Then, Quincy in his inimitable style allowed, "My understanding is that in a few years the "Lloyds market, as we know it, will begin to fail. We hear rumors that documents that prove up coverage are disappearing. But that, ominous as it appears, is not the worst news. We are given to understand that Names are beginning to run, while others are defaulting. And perhaps, worst of all, that a great many American Names are simply refusing to pay. Much of this may be rectified in time, but surely not all. That seems to auger that you act now and secure a basis of payment which may well survive that forthcoming turmoil! Those that choose to wait, and hope, may get little or nothing. I suggest that this potentiality should be a serious part of your calculus in reaching your decision." *(While this is given as a quote, I am not certain that it is wholly correct. But I do have the substance and effect of what Quincy said, and some of his key words and phrases ring true. Alas, I wish he was around to verify what I have written, but he passed several years before I wrote this.)*

The silence that followed seemed to leave it to me to speak. I tried to sound objective and convey a sense of gravitas, "When you asked me to start down this road with Quincy, we had far less than we have now in terms of turning up the Lloyds stamped documents. First, Quincy was able to locate the son of your London placing broker; then, after Larry's death, his wife found some useful hidden documents, which together with the son gave us the name of the probable placing broker who inter- acted with your deceased London broker. Now, Quincy has made contact with a seemingly highly reputed Solicitor firm which may, by dint of their reputation and specifically that of Mr. Campbell, a son of a founder, gain us access to that placing broker. If Quincy is correct and that broker is ethically charged with maintaining all placement documents virtually in perpe- tuity by virtue of the long-tail exposure (in the BI cases, the plaintiff's exposures to asbestos products could go back 30, 40, even perhaps 50 years from the time of their lawsuit, this period all could trigger years of coverage: so, those very old coverages are called "long-tail") of these syndicates, then there is a very real chance of getting those documents. The big expenditure issue is the physical search for those documents. We can hope that the placing broker's document organization exists, and that it proves to be of some level of assistance to greatly reducing the search time and its expense.

"I believe you should authorize the retainer of Mr. Campbell. I will fly, if need be, from Charleston to London to meet with Quincy and this solicitor, and we will come up with a plan to get us in front of these brokers, Cheshire and Booth. Remember, we do not know the number of placements involved or what arrangement, if any, those brokers use to access these documents assuming they remain stored. That data alone would facilitate this discussion further. What say you, Quincy? Anything I missed?"

"Thornton Campbell will need a non-refundable retainer, probably ten thousand pounds (£10,000), but it will be chargeable against fees and their expenses," was his response.

John O'Sullivan asked Quincy and Tinker to sit on "hold" for a few minutes and for me to step outside. We did that literally, and I went to get fresh air. Quincy went out for a cigarette. (He was an inveterate smoker, claiming he knew better, and that it would not affect him.) Before Quincy finished, John O'Sullivan summoned us to return. Once in the conference room and on the line. John began, "The DMIC Board has asked me to take control of all of this related asbestos and coverage litigation as it threatens the very future of the company. Ronan, we have relied on you to date and you have not let us down. We have no plans to switch the lead lawyer horse now. Quincy, you came highly recommended, and you seem to know what you are doing. Certainly, your knowledge of the London and Lloyds insurance markets is most exceptional, and greater than anyone's here. Moreover, Ronan trusts you and that gives us the courage to move forward under the discretion the Board has vested in us and me.

"Ronan, please coordinate your schedule with Quincy and try to be present in London to meet with Bradley Campbell.

I shall make myself available whenever and wherever that meeting will take place. Ronan, I know you have people coming to San Francisco, and we will try to minimize our reliance on you during that time, but we do hope you can find time whenever urgencies require your input.

"Finally, I suggest that you all consult with whomsoever you find necessary so that we can establish retainers for all of you against which you will bill. This is a precautionary step to protect your firms and you. Any questions?"

After a few details were covered, I headed for Sky Harbor. I connected on Delta in Houston and was in the Mills House in Charleston, South Carolina, in time for dinner with Tinker and Josh Smoulders. I loved the she-crab soup and the crab-stuffed flounder!

— — —

The next day, we arrived about twenty-five minutes early in Judge Anderson's Court Room, part of a temporary facility in use while the federal courthouse on Meeting Street and Broad was being expanded to add courtrooms. The room seemed to have at least 100 seats and they looked to be filling rapidly, but we were able to get three seats together about ten rows behind the bar. Josh had checked the docket and the only other matter on calendar was already ordered continued.

At 10:00 a.m. promptly, a clerk appeared from a side door and announced that Judge Anderson would take the bench and that the United States District Court for the State of South Carolina would come to order. The judge, appearing to be mid-fifties, robes flowing, emerged first and went up two steps to his seat behind the elevated bench. Four other men followed. Tinker leaned over and said, "The last one is Arthur Miller. Not the writer, but a Civil Procedure professor at Harvard Law who co-publishes Wright and Miller on Civil Procedure. I have seen him speak."

The four all sat at the Plaintiff Attorneys' Table. The Defense Table was occupied by the self-appointed leaders of the Charleston Defense Bar. Everyone was standing. Before suggesting that all of the lawyers sit, Judge Anderson said, "I will only be hearing one motion on today's calendar. Would Counsel for CAL Board please move to the defense table."

The leaders, trying not to look too surprised, reluctantly assembled their materials and looked around for a close place to sit. As we began to move forward, Josh asked, "May I address this Court?" Identified himself, and continued, Mr. O'Neill is from California, and Mr. Tinker is admitted in California, Maryland and Washington, D.C. I would seek that they both be admitted to this Court's Bar *pro haec vice?* "

A lawyer in the third row rose and said, "Mr. O'Neill is a member of the Society of Civil Litigation Defense Lawyers, as am I. He is known to me, and I second that motion."

With no objections, I was admitted and so was Tinker. Still, Josh was prepared to argue CAL Board's Motion to Dismiss, and he so advised the Court, and the Judge somehow seemed slightly pleased. The lead Plaintiff Attorney, Ron Motley, rose and announced that Professor Miller, having been admitted *Pro Haec Vice,* would argue for Clemson University. The Judge announced that he had read our papers and felt he understood them. He then asked Josh if he had anything to add. Josh said about five sentences and sat down.

The Judge turned to the law professor from Boston (perhaps not a very welcome venue in South Carolina) saying, "I understand that you have an argument that is not necessarily well-developed, but at least presaged in your client's opposition papers. Please proceed."

Professor Miller stepped forward and began a discourse lasting more than a half hour, essentially pointing out that CAL Board's position on subject matter jurisdiction might be upheld on appeal as technically correct, but was not sufficient on its face and should be overruled if the Court did not consider the tendered outside evidence available for consideration at this Court's discretion utilizing Judicial Notice. Moreover, a vast array of other college and university candidates were available to represent this class so that this whole motion process was an exercise in futility.

Only at that moment did the Judge bestir himself, "Please tell me, if you know, Professor, if there were so many candidates, why did our eminent counsel chose Clemson?"

With a shrug of his shoulders and just a hint of frustration, the professor continued for many more minutes as the judge seemed to lose interest to such a degree that he might be napping!

Finally, Professor Miller thanked the Court and sat. The Judge looked around and asked if anyone else had anything to argue. Hearing nothing, He produced a sheet of paper and read, "This Court grants the Motions of CAL Board and those defendants joining them for Judicial Notice in its entirety and to Dismiss Without Leave to Amend. The Clerk of this Court will enter this Order today. If no objection is filed by noon one week from today, that Order will become a Judgment. Each side to bear its own costs, Any questions?"

Ron Motley walked over to me and said, "If I ever find your client's products in one of my states, you'll greatly regret the day you filed this motion!"

My flight to London connected from Dulles the next day at 10:30, so we went back to the Mills House and found a phone that allowed the three of us to call DMIC in Scottsdale together. We got Manny Garcia on the phone first. He put us on a speaker. Soon, Charlie, John and Dudley were on the phone with the Claims Staff. They were ecstatic. John said, "Have a great dinner on us, with a couple of good bottles of wine." Then, "Ronan, I'll see you in London day after tomorrow."

— — —

John and I met Quincy at 11:00 at Twenty King's Bench Walk for a fifteen minute final preparation. We then taxied into the City to the offices of Thornton, Campbell and Thornton, Solicitors, as displayed on a brass plaque next to an unusual double door giving entry to a very narrow, but quite tall building of uncertain stories a block or two from the Lloyds' Building itself. Ringing a bell was necessary to begin the process to gain entrance. (John and I looked at each other: more security than one would think necessary was my unspoken thought.) We were shown to a waiting room that seemed from a century earlier. The furniture was old, stained dark and marvelous in its condition, carvings, decoration and uses. The chairs were comfortable for a few minutes, but a bit overly upright to remain seated for a longer period.

Within minutes, an attractive, conservatively dressed and quaffed woman appeared. The lady's name was Madeline and she volunteered little while at the same time appearing pleasant in that she had the vestige of a smile on her face. We rode an elevator up to the top floor and upon exiting, walked left toward the rear of the building. The building made up for its narrowness with its depth. We entered a door at the end of this upper corridor into a room with windows at the far end, a good 18 -20 feet from that door, seeming to look down over much of the City.

With my penchant for rooftop views, I almost bumped into Madeline, who stopped halfway across the room to turn ninety degrees and face a dining table with chairs arrayed and places set. Rising from a chair at the far end was a gentleman of about my age who came forward, greeted Quincy by name and with a handshake, then turned to face us whilst Quincy made the introductions and we, too, shook hands.

Bradley Campbell was impressive in his custom clothing and aristocratic speech pattern, as were these facilities. He spoke while returning to his chair and reaching for what appeared to be a cocktail, "I trust you have met Madeline. Please tell her what you would have as a preference and we can get to know a bit of each other over drinks and our luncheon. Quincy here has apprised me of the purpose for your visit. So, please feel free to cut to the chase with questions and the like, or perhaps we should get to know each other a bit at first?"

In the days before the Internet, biographies were more difficult to acquire. So, in an informal manner, we exchanged background stories. With the exception of John, the two Brits were most surprised, I believe, by my telling them that I was nearing the end of my U.S. Coast Guard Reserve career, having spent much of my time involved in Judge Advocate reserve roles. Bradley allowed, "I was in the British Navy for six years as a Reserve, serving as a gunnery officer aboard cruisers. I got to Viet Nam for a three month stay. Were you there? I seem to recall that your Coast Guard had a very real presence. I remember they ran the ports and a great many patrol craft."

I responded only, "Yes, I was there as an Executive Officer on an eighty-two foot patrol boat. We were stationed fairly far up the north coast and had a mother cutter for resupply and support. Did you get into Cam Ranh Bay?"

"Yes. But we saw almost no action. A few bombardments and that was about it. Did you see any action?"

"Yes. Our main duty was the interdiction of arms, supplies and personnel coming from the North. As such, we saw more than our fair share of action," was my response.

There was a momentary pause, and before I could fill it, John O'Sullivan spoke, "I have never discussed it with Ronan, but one of the other attorneys who works with us on these matters was on active duty with Ronan and told me about him. Ronan is the recipient of the U.S. Navy's highest honor, the Silver Star. In a firefight with two North Viet Namese gunboats, his CO was killed as were several other crew. More were wounded, but Ronan, although wounded himself and two others saved their cutter, called in an air strike and damaged one of those gunboats. He is one of the Coast Guard's biggest heroes of that war, but he never talks about it."

A silence followed. Finally, Bradley Campbell spoke, "The O'Neills' reputation goes deep in Ulster history. You doubtless have that blood. You are to be congratulated for your valor and praised for your humility." He raised his glass as did the other two, pointed to Madeline to fill a glass, and then said, "Three cheers to a true hero!"

Following our main course, and before the salad, all presented by Madeline from what must have been a very near-by pantry/serving room, we spent an hour discussing how to go about approaching Cheshire and Booth. In the end, we settled on a letter emanating from Bradley and his firm laying out the facts of the various known brokerage firms and the potential whereabouts of the needed documents to prove up coverage for the many years of reinsurance placed through Lloyds' syndicates (and that some number of years were without any form of stop loss); and, asserting Cheshire's putative duty to Desert Mutual as the subagent of DMIC's London broker to assure those coverages could be proven up when the need arose, as it now did. (Both Quincy and Bradley went to some length to point out that some of these legal points were, just that, assertions and not necessarily statements of Common Law established under UK Insurance Coverage jurisprudence.) But both of them felt strongly that DMIC might prevail if this went to trial; and moreover, that Cheshire a and Booth might prove quite wary of this type of litigation in the current overall unhappy state of the London/Lloyds insurance market brought on mostly by U.S. environmental litigation, not limited solely to asbestos claims.

We mentioned, not in passing, the role several British and

French scientists were playing in the BUILDINGS cases. We pointed out that we were somewhat optimistic that this type of litigation might be halted in the years to come as "not ripe" since the claimants were not suffering any actual injury and their lawsuits might cause more harm than good if they proved successful and achieved the relief they sought.

John agreed that all four of us should approve the final draft of the letter and that Quincy and Bradley would formulate the first working draft, run it through me, and when the three of us agreed, I would run it past John.

Bradley asked Madeline to arrange for their firm's car to take us back to the hotel. After taking our leave of Bradley, Quincy and John went to the Gents. I stood outside with Madeline, who said, "You sound quite interesting, Ronan. I live a few blocks from your hotel. Could we have a drink later at a pub near my place?" With that, she pressed a paper into my hand. As the door opened to admit Quincy and John into the corridor, I nodded affirmatively at Madeline.

The three of us retired to the Red Room Bar at the Grosvenor House. After two drinks, John said he was going to make calls to Scottsdale and home, felt like skipping dinner or would have small room service. We could meet in the Lobby at 8:30 tomorrow morning, giving us almost four hours to make our flights home. Quincy allowed that he needed to spend an hour or two in Chambers. I wanted to make calls.

I looked at the paper Madeline had given me. I called her office number. She answered on the first ring. I told her that if I could do dinner and a pub meal after that big lunch, that would be perfect. We would meet at the King's Arms at 7:00. She gave me directions.

— — —

I arrived five minutes late. At first, I did not recognize Madeline. She stood to reveal a more form fitting dress of a soft lavender secured at the waist with a belt of slightly deeper version of the same color. Her hair was light brown with some blonde streaks, and she now wore it down in a casual style. In all, Madeline seemed to have dropped five to ten years in her transformation after work.

She held out her hand and we shook, and said, "I hope you do not think me overly bold? That is so very out of character for me. But after listening to you and about you, you are by far the most interesting American I have ever met. So, I acted!"

"Well. I could not feel luckier. Here I am alone in London for the night, and I have the good fortune to find a new friend and a new pub." With that, the waiter approached, and we ordered a small meal with a bottle of nice Bordeaux which arrived quickly!

We chatted amicably, ate our dinner and enjoyed the wine. I paid. It was not that late, only 8:30. Madeline asked if I would like to walk for a bit and I agreed. She led the way. In a few blocks, she stopped, saying, "This is where I live. As you can see, it's only a few turns and you're back at your hotel. We could go further or you could come up for a nightcap?"

There was nothing about Madeline up to that point which even hinted at her being up to anything, so I agreed to her offer of a drink. Fifteen minutes later, I was getting a great deal more than I had expected. WOW!

— — —

When I called Mollie I told her that I was exhausted, but I looked forward to seeing her the next day. Next, I spoke to three of the four children. Maeve was busy at an activity. They all wanted to know if I had been to Richoux. A white lie did wonders: a "yes" with a Welsh Rarebit made them happy, and left Meaghan giggling!

— — —

Not sure why I did it, as I do not tell her everything about my sex life, but I did tell Dr. Arnaud about Madeline. Of course, she was not pleased at my "lack of self-restraint" as she was wont to diagnose, but she found my explanation informative as well: her conclusion was that I was somehow susceptible to being seduced by beautiful, intelligent women. Further, that I rarely if ever showed any sexual interest in any others; moreover, that once I had unconsciously put a woman in my "Not of Sexual Interest" mental catalog, I never appeared to re-examine that decision.

38

Carolyn and Her Patrick

As the day for their arrival in Sausalito approached, I discussed some activities that we might undertake with Carolyn and her son. Mollie could not get over how Carolyn had lost her lover in the Viet Nam War yet kept his child. Over the days leading up to her arrival, Mollie had more questions. I deferred them for Carolyn (Of course, Carolyn and I had clarified that Patrick was named for his father, a U.S. Navy fighter pilot whose death Carolyn had researched after loss of contact with him following but a few letters.).

I recall one evening after dinner while the children were out in our neighborhood with their different friends, Mollie asked (again), "This is *the* Carolyn Tyne, the famous model?"

"Yes."

"And how again did you come to meet her?"

Me, "I am sure you have heard this before, but on my first day in the Bay Area, I was trying to find my way from one of the oil spill sites on the Marin Headlands to Tinker's place at the *Cote d'Azur*. Please recall your very first time down Alexander Avenue and the twisty turns, one yielding into another, each a rock wall, then suddenly the town appears and it's all you see! And within seconds, two or three at most, there on the right is the driveway onto the roof deck parking lot at the *Cote d'Azur*. *Voila!* I was going very slowly having been warned by Tinker. I pulled into a space and there was this wholesome looking young woman putting her bicycle in a bike rack nearby on that deck. When I got out of my Charger and she started walking over, I was surprised how tall she was. Two, maybe three, inches taller than you. Longish honey blonde hair, seemingly sun-streaked, not unlike yours when we were on our first trip and you had a lot of outdoor time. She was slender, but seemingly fit. She said something like, "Hi, I'm Carolyn. Are you new here?"

"I finished putting on my uniform coat and combination cap and told her that I was a friend of Joel Tinker. Then, she asked if I would like her to show me to his unit. I told her I would appreciate it and got my gear. She grabbed my briefcase, lead the way, and before I knocked told me if I wanted a drink later, she and some friends would be at the No Name Bar around 8:30 or 9:00. Later when Tinker had to prep for his classes the next day, I decided to go to that bar and see if she showed up. She did. We had a couple of drinks, and she drove us both back up the hill. That was it except that she left a note for me in Tinker's mailbox with her full name and mailing address. She had told me she was a model, a bathing suit model. Just getting started.

"I may have written her once. Not sure, but that was it. Never saw her again until I started in law school at Hastings and was dating Sandra seriously," and that was about it by way of our initial interaction.

"When Tinker and Elaine were about to marry, I was extremely reluctant to stay in their second bedroom. Right about then, I encountered Carolyn. She was looking for a new person to share her roommate's apartment as that model was older, her career was taking off, and she was moving to Paris. Plus, Carolyn was only nineteen and could not be on the lease, as you had to be twenty-one in California then. Please recall, that, by then, I knew Carolyn was a Lesbian. So, when she asked me to go on the lease and move in. that seemed to solve all of the problems I was facing. And, as an added bonus, Carolyn's career began to take off and she spent less and less time in Sausalito. Of course, one of those longer times during my third year at Hastings must have been when she was in the East with her Lesbian lover and gave birth to her Patrick."

Mollie, "What was she like when you did see her?"

"Mollie, surprisingly, since it was just about three years, I do not believe I saw Carolyn more than six or seven days a month at first and that diminished as time wore on. She had lots of friends, mostly in her field. She went out a lot and did not always come home, sometimes for days. Then again, when we did talk, she was like a travel reporter, constantly in awe about the places she got to visit in the course of her work. She was so young, but smart, and she worked very hard at staying fit!"

"Not much more to tell. After her long absences, I was with you. You had started working. I met with her briefly over in Sausalito. She told me about her Patrick and that most of her life was now in the East or Europe. Also, she had a fulltime lover. No idea of her name. I know she's mentioned it, but I don't remember. She's not much of a writer, and we talk pretty much whenever she gets around to it, and I happen to be available for a few minutes. Not often, until she decided she wanted to do this trip."

Mollie, "Even though she's gay, it sounds like you still really like her. Why is that?"

Looking Mollie straight in the eyes, while holding her hands in mine, I said, "You know I think she reminded me a little of you, and somehow over those intervening years, I was coming to realize how incredibly nice you were; and that you remained that way toward me despite how I had treated you. Look at how you dealt with Kate, then your mother's death, and your Dad. Carolyn was always unfailingly nice as well. I just liked her as a person. The fact that she was a Lesbian just always seemed irrelevant. Perhaps, I have come to think, over time, she may have helped me realize that all along, it should have been you, not Sandra."

Mollie, "Oh!"

— — —

*I like to believe that conversation made Mollie more comfortable
with this imminent visit by Carolyn and her son, Patrick. Mollie began
to come up with ideas for spending time herself, and with our daughters, with Carolyn. I could take the boys and Patrick and do "guy
things" (an always unspecified category that was meant to include all
forms of sport and, perhaps as the boys were getting older, how to deal
with girls.) Mollie knew they would be going on side trips, and even
suggested they do one or two with us.*

*Finally, two days before Carolyn and Patrick were to arrive, Mollie
asked if we, or just me, should pick them up at SFO. I thought about
it, called Carolyn, and let Mollie know they would be delighted to see
us both (a plus was that Patrick could meet new people more slowly,
thus lowering any level of intensity).*

*On the way to SFO, Mollie asked me where they would be staying.
I responded by saying the Cote d'Azur, and explained that Carolyn
had taken over the whole lease shortly after turning twenty-one. I told
Mollie that Carolyn referred to it as her West Coast base, but I thought
it was also because it was her first real home.*

— — —

In the days before 9/11, you could meet in-coming passengers
at the baggage claim. Carolyn and Patrick were flying in from
JFK, First Class. Indeed, I saw Carolyn first, as she was taller
than almost all of the passengers, wore little make-up, sunglasses, and was dressed in nice casual clothes with no bright
colors. One of the few passengers taller than Carolyn was a
young man, who must have been six feet, four inches tall, with
a lean, perhaps powerful build, a pleasant Irish looking face and
a mop of black hair. He trailed Carolyn by a step, or two. Carolyn saw me at that point and waved. Mollie gulped and said,

"my God, she is tall, and beautiful!"

Mollie saw the wave and nudged me forward. I looked again for Patrick, but then saw Carolyn reach out for the hand of the very tall young man, and knew at that moment, that this was my son, Patrick!

Carolyn moved more quickly, and I pushed Mollie in front of me, but she became rigid. So, I reached out to Carolyn, took her by the hand a bent to give her a kiss on each cheek and one on the lips. Carolyn immediately pushed Patrick forward, and he extended his hand. I took it and we shook hands, as we did, he said, "Uncle Ronan, at last seeing you, I can put a face with your name. Mom wants me to give you a hug. May I?"

I thought both women were going to cry. As Patrick hugged me, Carolyn said to Mollie, "Of course, you are Mollie, the Love of Ronan's Life, as he describes you. I have heard much about you over the years, nothing but good things, great things. You are so generous to do so much planning for our stay. I simply cannot thank you enough and want to tell you how much I look forward to getting to know you."

All of Carolyn's little speech was delivered as she was holding Mollie's hand in a hand shake-like grip. When Carolyn stopped, Mollie gently seemed to pull Carolyn forward and move forward herself, so that the two were having a woman-to-woman greeting hug. Carolyn seemed to respond by hugging a little more strongly. And in a moment, that spell was broken, tears that perhaps had begun to well up were suppressed, and our attention turned to their luggage. As Carolyn indicated might be the case, her luggage was first off the flight and our skycap, whom I had secured, began to load bags. They had six, all matching and looking very expensive.

Carolyn told the skycap when he had them all, then glanced at me. I told them that we had brought our Suburban which we used for family trips of short duration with six or even people and limited luggage, usually Lake Tahoe or Carmel. I had gotten a special permit and we were parked at the end of the tunnel next to the garage. In a matter of minutes, we were all loaded. Patrick went to get in the second row when Mollie said, "Patrick, this is your first time to the San Francisco Bay Area, please sit up front. I insist."

Carolyn said, "Mollie, so generous." Patrick offered thanks and got in. Those of us in front made sure the tall ladies in the next row of seats had adequate room.

I started the car, and paid the toll after a short drive. No fog that day, so I headed to the coast rather than take US 101 straight through the City, explaining as I shifted routes, "Patrick, as your mother has doubtless told you, Summer is the fog season here. When we get a beautiful clear day like today, it should not be wasted. So, we are going straight out to the coastal route, then to the Golden Gate Bridge. Hopefully, you will find the views exciting, if not spectacular!?"

Carolyn chimed in, "Your Uncle Ronan is right. And you know what: I cannot remember the last time I came this way."

At the top of southbound Route 1, we merged on to the northbound Pacifica Freeway just a few miles south of the Great Highway. The day was unusually clear: crystalline! I slowed on the merging ramp as much as safety would allow while all of us looked to the north, panning from West to East, pointing out the very distant Point Reyes Peninsula (almost never visible in the usually dense marine air), to the nearer Marin Headlands, forming the north shore of the Golden Gate, with Mount Tamalpais in the background, then to the westernmost hills of the City covered with homes, and finally to the tips of the towers of the Golden Gate Bridge. As I was driving, Mollie told them, especially Patrick, what they were seeing, ending with, "what a spectacular view and unfortunately nowhere to pull off to celebrate it for a few minutes."

I added, "If they put a view pull-off up there, no one would get on with their business. It is such a special spectacle. By the

way, we just passed the Olympic Club, where the U.S. Open
Golf Tournament is played some years." We continued this tour
with Ocean Beach and its great sand dunes, then the Cliff House,
and into the Presidio with its winding, undulating tree covered
road, finally emerging on the steep climbing cliff road, around
an easterly bend, and there before us in all its majesty, glistening
in sunlight was the Golden Gate itself with its magnificent burnt
orange bridge.

Patrick was in awe of the Bridge. I opened the sun roof and
he stuck his head out and swiveled for every view he could collect. As we passed the north tower, I suggested that he pull back
in. I closed the roof and signaled to exit at Alexander. As I proceeded carefully, I looked in the mirror at Carolyn. For a few
seconds, her eyes met mine and the tiniest hint of a smile began
to form.

Then she spoke, "Patrick, in a matter of seconds, you will go
back into my life as a girl. As I told you, I left home at sixteen."
The Suburban turned right onto the roof deck parking of the *Cote
d'Azur*. I pulled into an available space with plenty of room
around it. Carolyn continued, "this is where I first met your
Uncle Ronan. I was putting my bike away when this very tall
man exited a sporty car and looked at me. He was in uniform,
but seemed friendly, by then I had lived here for almost six
months and knew just about everyone because of the odd hours
of my jobs. Not recognizing him, I asked if he needed help finding an apartment. He kept adding uniform and answered that
he was looking for where Joel Tinker lived. I knew Tinker, nice
guy, going to law school in the City. Had a nice girlfriend. I told
Ronan my name and asked him if he wanted me to show him
the way. Then he said yes, got his things and I took him to Tinker's place. It was a week night, and I figured Tinker might need
to prep for classes the next day, so I told your Uncle Ronan I
would be at the No Name Bar if he wanted to have a drink later
that evening. We had that drink, two in fact, and I left him a note

in Tinker's mailbox the next morning. But I never wrote back to his first letter. So, imagine my surprise when he showed up many months later! But that's another story, and we need to get our bags and let these wonderful people get on with their lives."

We had been parked for a minute or two while Carolyn finished her story of our first meeting. As everyone went to open their doors, Mollie said, "Carolyn, didn't Ronan tell you, we are having a bar-b-que for you all tonight. Our children are dying to meet you and so is Ronan's mother, my step-mother, Kate. Please don't say 'no'?"

They came to our house. Mollie rode over in Carolyn's Porsche to show her the way through the back streets of Mill Valley. Patrick rode with me. That was the beginning of a fantastic few weeks: a large stitch in time that all of us would relish in our own ways, forever.

— — —

The days went by quickly. Mollie took Carolyn and all of the children to our place near Carmel for a few days. Carolyn took just Patrick for a two night trip to the Napa Wine Country, then out to the Sonoma Coast and down through western Marin County and over Mount Tamalpais, another spectacular ride, especially in her Porsche. Then, Mollie asked if Kate and she could spend a few days showing the children the wonders of Lake Tahoe (implicitly giving Carolyn and me some time together).

Carolyn and I shared some of that time together in her place at the *Cote d'Azur*. She was so nervous at first. And paused at the outset to say, "Suddenly, I feel more than a little like a home wrecker being here with you."

I took her hands and held them, and in a quiet, serious voice, said, "Carolyn, I have told you so many times how much I love you. But I have also told you that my lifetime devotion is to Mollie. That will never change. None of it will! Now just lay back and relax. I have you, and for a few days, we have each other. Let us appreciate all that we can have."

Carolyn did relax, lay back, and we did enjoy our three days and two nights together. Also, the traveling group returned exhausted late on a Saturday afternoon. They went to drop off Patrick at Carolyn's place, but we surprised them there with pizza and salad. When we got to our place, Mollie walked into a kitchen that was stocked for both a brunch and a cook-out later on the next day. Only one week remained and we were going to make certain that this trip was memorable for Carolyn and her Patrick. (Both of our daughters were quite taken with Patrick, his shyness at first was charming, but he seemed to flourish around our foursome, even becoming at ease around the girls). Our Patrick, and especially Robert who was closer in age, got on famously with Carolyn's Patrick from the get go. They even agreed to have a bed in their room so Patrick could be their overnight guest on a couple of occasions (Carolyn slept in Kate's bed).

Carolyn still had a few business friends in the area and she was careful to visit all of them. Her Patrick preferred being with Mollie (or Kate or Ingrid) and our children when Carolyn was seeing her friends. (Mollie still had an important job and got in her hours almost every day.She seemed to grow ever more fond of Carolyn and they spent more time together each day as the visit was coming to an end.) This relationship led to Carolyn pushing their departure back a day when TWA called and asked them to do so. Carolyn came to me and asked, "Ronan, would you mind a night with all of the children and Ingrid or Kate. I would love to thank Mollie for all of her gracious hospitality. I remember her saying how much she missed driving on the PCH in west Marin and Sonoma. I was thinking of taking her in my Porsche up to the Inn at Bodega Bay for a nice dinner and back the next morning in time for a long afternoon and early evening with all of you?"

Funny thing, as the weeks flew by, I never had a thought about Carolyn's being a Lesbian. But in that moment, I had a flash to those strangely answered phone calls to Mollie's New York room in the Waldorf over those last years. Could it have been? Not Mollie? How silly of me!! Coming quickly to my senses, I looked at Carolyn who affected a wisp of a smile, and said, "Of course, you can. I imagine she will love it. But do not scare her with that Porsche on those roads and do be especially careful if they are at all wet."

— — —

We had movie night while the ladies were away: pizza first, then popcorn, candy and a general good time. First there were separate theaters, one for the boys and one for the girls, but that gave way to a comedy, *Ghostbusters*, for which everyone joined in with lots of screaming and fake fear with hidden eyes. Then, off to bed for the big last day tomorrow.

Mollie called just as I said my last good night to Carolyn's Patrick (tears were starting to form in my eyes). She wanted to say a good night and check up on the children (Carolyn had called Patrick a while ago). I told her they were all in bed and we would be in readiness for their return tomorrow, but no need to hurry.

When they drove in the next day, we were playing basketball in the driveway, something we had done on several occasions during the visit. Patrick Tyne was a very good ball handler who told us he was small when he started to play and had only started to really grow in the last eighteen months. Mollie and Carolyn exited the Porsche, took their bags inside and returned in a few minutes with their basketball shoes on and ready to play.

We broke up the game around 4:00, had beverages and Kate, Ingrid and Mollie put out two salads (one seafood), corn on the

cob, fried chicken, a half of a baked ham, and all the other nec-
essaries.

Carolyn and Mollie told us about their drive, the hotel (later
Mollie allowed that the two of us needed to get away there for a
night) and dinner at the Bodega Bay Restaurant, grown many
times over since being featured in Hitchcock's original *The Birds*
movie. They described a dinner of oysters, clam chowder and a
shared salmon –sounded perfect to me. Then it was time for
them to leave. I was to take them to SFO the next morning. Mollie would get all of the children to church, so their good-bye was
a long, briefly tearful affair, but with many promises of future
visits, which I believed just might happen.

— — —

The next morning's drive to the airport was foggy most of
the way, but it cleared as we pulled into the Departure Lane. We
pulled up to a TWA First Class Skycap who checked their bags
and gave them boarding passes. Patrick started by shaking my
hand, but quickly transitioned to a firm, long hug. When he finished, he turned away immediately and told his mother that he
would meet her inside by the entrance to the gates.

I took both of Carolyn's hands. We stood, with our toes almost touching. We looked into each other's eyes. Carolyn said,
"I love you. You are the only man I will ever love. He loves you.
We will be back. The two of us really do need to visit more
often."

Then we kissed, not like friends. When I went to breathe, I
asked, "Do you think he suspects?"

Carolyn whispered, "I think he knows, but will never say.
It's our fiction. I do believe he is wise beyond his years. If there
are changes, I'll let you know.

"Oh, by the way, Mollie said we should write. Time changes
things. She's simply marvelous and I want to be her friend. So,

don't be surprised when I write to her." Then she pulled me closer for one last kiss, turned and was gone through the door without a glance back.

39

Mollie On My Mind

After so much time off, and despite my efforts to stay current on everything, the rest of the Summer was a nightmare of travel, meetings and court appearances.

The asbestos plaintiffs' bar was launching a new enterprise in Alameda County Superior Court under Judge Woo who appeared set on testing the limits of a new California Complex Litigation statute. (Perhaps more on that at a later time.)

LAUSD was moving forward. Martha had been doing her best with the new client by keeping the Court and Plaintiff Counsel fit to be tied by our leading the newest defendants to be added after the Statute of Limitations Phase I trial with a motion for their day in court on that very issue. The other briefing sidetrack involving *LAUSD* trying to find a means to shift the burden of product identification remained unresolved and was looking ever more dubious.

The SCHOOLS Class in Philadelphia continued to drag along with a variety of briefing matters. CAL Board's second round of Motions to Dismiss were again denied as premature because Plaintiffs had not yet completed their discovery (now involving multiple years and their own lawyers' failures to bring motions, or even make demands, for whatever it was they deemed was being withheld). Nonetheless, there was a rumor that depositions would soon start, with an expert phase beginning sometime in the next year or so.

South Carolina and the putative COLLEGES Class was silent, presumably while those counsel sought one or more qualified class representatives. (They also faced the very real problem that many of the largest institutions were either on their face state schools, or like Clemson got serious state funding rendering them an adjunct arm of the state, either of which would destroy subject matter jurisdiction.)

In London, Bradley and Quincy had put together what we deemed was a satisfactory draft letter to Cheshire and Booth. It awaited the approval of Charlie Sewell and John O'Sullivan with whom I was to meet the next day in Scottsdale.

Reggie was steering a tight ship in the Bay Area BI cases and my other junior partners and Martha were doing tremendous jobs on the other BUILDINGS Cases. Phil was becoming successful with the SoCal BI cases. Still, all of the non-California BI cases and all of the BUILDINGS cases were my ultimate responsibility and although I did have Tinker, all of this was proving to be a major burden!

Mollie too had been busy: the APP Company was going great guns, making huge strides into the computer game market, and others. Plus, its products were developing international demand. She seemed to be constantly on planes, in meetings, and putting in long hours.

We were both home that night and both had to fly the next day. Ingrid toured about the house doing homework/bedtime duty while Mollie and I snuck off to our room using the pretext of needing to pack. We did, but we spent time caressing each other in what had become our prelude to making love. Suddenly, Mollie sat up very straight. I asked if she was OK. To which she responded only about a sharp lower stomach pain, probably a reaction to all of the stress of her job. She said she would go to see her OB/GYN when she finished her trip, if it persisted. (Mollie liked him better than her Primary Care Physician). When we made love, I was careful to monitor Mollie's position so as not to put any stress on the area where she showed me it hurt.

The next morning was a flurry of activity at the very earliest hours: final packing, a quick nibble of something to tide us to the first airplane meal, good-byes to waking children, and then off in separate cars with separate return dates and schedules.

— — —

We had an early working lunch at DMIC HQ in Scottsdale. Charlie Sewell was not in a good mood, no doubt precipitated by the efforts of all involved to come up with some methodology to cap the potential open-ended expense of a document search of Cheshire and Booth. That singular failing caused DMIC's CEO's unwillingness to sign off on the carefully worded letter which as recently crafted did not offer anything remotely proposing open-ended spending.

Half-way through my roast beef sandwich, I began to think out loud about how this process might play forward with Charlie and John (Dudley, by then, understood that inaction was the one option that DMIC could not afford): What if we added a request for a meeting forthwith at the end of the letter, perhaps indicating that it could be used to facilitate joint planning for the resolution of any critical issues?

Before I could finish writing a sentence, Charlie said, "I would go to a meeting like that. John, what do you think?"

"Let's see what our Brits say," was O'Sullivan's response.

So, I finished a draft of two sentences. We made a couple of minor edits, passed it around, and when no one objected, we faxed it to Bradley and Quincy. In less than fifteen minutes, the phone rang and our UK colleagues were on the line. We all agreed on the concept, but they felt a more careful rewrite was necessary to preserve the over-all context of no overtly demonstrable aggression. As I was headed over to London to meet with our experts, we agreed that I would go forward on this task forthwith and do so by having Martha begin to run interference with the experts for a few hours, as need be.

We adjourned at three, with plans to dine at a local authentic Mexican restaurant at 5:30. Martha would join us as we had planned to work the next day on the flight to Heathrow. When I got to the hotel, Martha had left a message that she was at the pool right outside our rooms. I put on my swimsuit and joined her. She had ordered me a smoothie and I told her what had transpired. She stretched when I paused, looking glamorous in her light blue bikini with a light tan and oil all over. She saw where I was looking, smiled, and asked if I would like to go to her room, saying, "It's been a very long time since we've been together. I don't want to wait until tonight either."

We went directly to Martha's room. We were a few minutes late for dinner, but no one seemed to notice or care.

— — —

At the Grosvenor House, we had adjoining rooms, checking in at Noon. We were prepared to meet at Quincy's chambers, finish the draft to Cheshire and Booth, and then have dinner at the gastropub outside the Temple's Riverside Gate. Martha and I were doing our fair share of making up for lost time. She was all smiles as we headed out to taxi to Thornton, Campbell and Thornton in the City.

Bradley had not met Martha. At first glance, he was instantly taken with her, and it showed on his face. He could not take his eyes off her! Our work got off to a quick start as Quincy and Bradley had a new draft prepared, but only three copies. As Quincy went to see about a fourth copy and while Martha and I were trying to read the latest draft, Bradley was peppering Martha with questions. I could sense that Bradley was making Martha nervous (after all, she had not been in Scottsdale, but I had briefed her). She was giving clipped answers to Bradley's incessant inquiries (some being almost trivial, and perhaps he thought not openly flirtatious).

After the fifth or sixth one, Martha looked up at Bradley, and just as Quincy was walking back into the room, Martha said rather quietly, "Bradley, I think at the outset of our working relationship, you should know that I am an avowed Lesbian."

Bradley simply froze. For more than a few seconds, he showed nothing. Then he began to laugh, at first lightly to himself, but when I joined in, he became more robust. Then, when Martha chimed in, Bradley's laugh became absolutely hearty! Quincy, meanwhile, knew he had missed the point of some serious humor.

In a little more than two more hours, we had a draft about which we felt strongly enough to recommend approval, so that we could start to act on it forthwith. We faxed it to Scottsdale and went to dinner at the gastropub. To get to Fleet Street and a taxi stand, we had to cut back through the Temple. Quincy said he would run into their Chambers and check the fax machine. When he came back out, he was all smiles, saying "They said 'Send it as is, first thing tomorrow'!"

With that Bradley said, "Have you been to the American Bar at the Savoy Hotel as yet?"

When Martha and I answered in the negative Bradley said, "Then, it will be my pleasure to buy you both your first double, double there!"

— — —

The American Bar at the Savoy was singularly impressive, looking every inch a wealthy British designer's interpretation of what an American bar might look like, with dark colors, heavy wood and lots of leather. The double-doubles, all scotch whiskey, mine Mac Callan's 24, appeared to be about the same size as a generous double from the Grosvenor House Red Room, but nowhere near as generous as the Bull and Bear in the Waldorf-Astoria. The Room's host greeted Bradley by name, "Good evening, Mr. Booth. We have your requested table. How is Mrs. Booth?"

When we got to our table and started to sit, Martha looked at me and gave the hint of a wry smile. The rest of the evening was spent in polite conversation with some mild banter about British football between Quincy and Bradley.

— — —

The next day, we went to Chambers and met there with Julian Peto. Wil stopped in on a few occasions as did Quincy. The second time, he asked the three of us if we should care to join him for cocktails and dinner at his club. Julian, an avowed Socialist asked, "What club might that be, if I may inquire?"

Quincy turned to face him and said, "Why the Reform Club."

This brought a smile to Julian's face. "I should, for myself, be delighted to see that very famous club from whence Mr. Verne's erstwhile hero, Phineas Fogg, began his journey to circumnavigate the globe in 80 Days," was his response. Quincy invited Bradley to join us.

That night turned out to be memorable: Starting with drinks mixed on trestle tables set up in the lobby of the Club with its vaulted ceilings, then dinner in an antiquated (but charming) dining room, and most fun of all, followed by snooker in a private room with a private bar pouring too much cognac for way too long. Bradley took Martha as his partner, I got Wil, and Quincy got Julian who was a maestro with the cue stick (losing but once all night to Bradley and Martha, of course).

Once again, Julian would not accept a taxi to take him home. He reported the next day that he got home uneventfully!

— — —

That following day, Martha and I spent with the McDonalds.

We made great progress on the issues accompanying potential avenues of cross-examination, which was not a foreign concept to these British experts. But none of them were avid watchers of any legal shows on television and had no structured prior experience with the concept. Being very smart, however, both came to the basic concepts quickly, but the tailoring of testimony proved far more difficult (and sometimes seemed to border on becoming contentious—needless to say "hard feelings" had to be avoided at all costs as these scientists were, after all, volunteers).

Having done a pub lunch with the McDonalds, we returned to the hotel by 5:00. After stopping off at the Red Room for some "hair of the dog," we went to our rooms and made calls to the West Coast. I also called Tinker in D.C. and got Mollie on the second try in New York before she left the Waldorf for meetings. She said, "Ronan, that pain in my abdomen I had on our last night is just persisting. I am going to try to cut my trip short and be home on Sunday. Do you think you could ask Kate, Ingrid or even Lily to try to get ahold of my OB/Gyn today and get me an appointment for Monday?"

Knowing Mollie was all-business on her trips, I quickly came to realize that this was not a "Mollie-like" request. I hung up and called my mother. She was quickly on board and said she would get the contact for the OB/Gyn from Ingrid and get right to that appointment today. I mentioned that Lily could help if needed. Then, I called Lily and told her about Mollie. She said she would help Kate, if needed. Finally, I called Martha and told her what was happening.

We went to Wheeler's, close-by and had a tasty dinner. On the walk back to Grosvenor House, Martha took my hand, saying, "Ronan, I'm sure it will be nothing serious. But if it is, I will be right there for Mollie and you. Please do not hesitate to ask." Then, after squeezing my hand, she continued, "I know you are very concerned. So, if you are at all uncomfortable under these circumstances, we do not need to be together tonight, that will not hurt my feelings. I will, and do, understand your concern."

I squeezed her hand back, saying only, "Thank you." Then, we walked on in silence. On the elevator going up, I said, "Martha, I know you remember what I've told you about you, me, Mollie and 'love.' For that reason, I do want to make love with you tonight because, if this is serious, I am not at all certain when that will ever happen again."

— — —

On arriving at SFO on Saturday afternoon, I called Mollie at the Waldorf. She picked up on the first ring. I told her that Dr Eisenberg would see her Sunday night at the hospital, if she wanted. She paused, "What about Monday?"

I told her that his first appointment was at 9:00, but he would be ready for her at 8:15. Mollie said, "Let's do Monday."

"Mollie, do you want me to meet you at SFO and bring you home? Ingrid or Kate can come with me and bring your car home," I asked.

Without hesitation, Mollie said, "Yes, please. That would be great."

Martha, when I hung up, said, "If I were ever to marry, I would want your clone for my husband. Don't worry. Reggie, Phil, Mary, Lily and I will take care of everything at the office. Tinker is always there, if we need him. You take care of your Mollie. After all, she is 'The Love of Your Life.'"

— — —

I saw Mollie approaching the baggage claim area before she saw me. Her face had a drawn, exhausted look, but also she held her chin as if she was dealing with something on the verge of overwhelming pain. I moved toward her, and her face broke into a big smile as she saw me. (I had thought about bringing the two older children, but the way she last sounded made me decide against that.) She moved more quickly, came up to me, pushed herself against me (gave a very small, almost inaudible gasp) and turned her face up to be kissed. I was more than happy to oblige. We stood there in our close embrace for what suddenly seemed a very long time for a public display of affection. When we broke apart, Mollie asked, "Did you have to wait long?"

To which I replied, "No. But how are you? I have been very worried about you. Is it that same pain you were experiencing the night before we both left?"

Her eyes quickly averted from mine, and she said in pretext, "I have to spot my bags. I have two extra ones as I brought home the ones I store at the Waldorf for use when I am in New York. But to answer your question: yes, it is the same pain, only it has gotten worse and is covering a bigger area. As you could tell from my call a day or so ago, I have had bouts where the pain becomes incredibly severe,"

I checked for bags and seeing none as yet, gently pulled Mollie around to face me, saying, "Mollie, you know Dr. Eisenberg will meet us at Marin General. Why don't you let me take you straight there?"

I looked into her eyes and I saw tears begin to form, "Please just take me home. I want to see my children. I want to sleep with you tonight. And, I want to call Carolyn. We'll talk more in the car. Where's my driver?"

"Kate's at my car waiting for us. Here come your bags." So, I grabbed four bags and stacked them on the trolley and put Mollie's pull bag on top of those. In less than five minutes we were at my car, a Mercedes SEL with plenty of trunk space. Mollie embraced Kate and gave her a kiss on each cheek as was their custom, then handed her the parking ticket and keys indicating that her car, a Volvo station wagon was only a few rows away from where I was parked on the first level of the garage.

We watched Kate locate Mollie's Volvo. I helped Mollie into the front seat, and saw her wince visibly as she swiveled to get her legs inside.

Once on the US 101 Freeway, I started to ask Mollie a question, but she cut me short saying, "Ronan, I am afraid. Very afraid! I've never experienced anything like this. I am hoping it's menopause, but I am awfully young for it to be that. It may be muscular, but it feels more internal and I didn't do anything to hurt any muscle group. All I can think of is my parents and the cancers that took them. But that was gradual and this seems so sudden. Oh My God, how I have wanted to talk to you!" with that, she began to weep quietly. I stayed silent.

After a few minutes when the sounds of her crying seemed to abate, using a low, controlled voice, I said, "Mollie, you know you are the Love of My Life. We'll see the doctor together tomorrow morning. I will take you. I will stay with you as much or as little as you wish during the appointment. I would like to be there for any diagnosis or treatment discussions. If this is serious, we'll be in it together. I promise to stay by your side as much as you want or need. Why don't you try to relax a bit so that you will be able to put on your best brave face that I know you will want to show to our children."

Mollie did put on her best brave face, and we had a lovely, loving family evening. I had mentioned before leaving for the airport that Mom might not be quite well and asked that they all be on their best behavior toward her. (They were.!!)

In our bedroom, I put an extra blanket on the bed. After our toilet, we looked at each other and I took off my pajama top. Mollie pulled at the spaghetti straps on her night gown and it fell to the floor. I dropped my pants. Mollie sat on her side of the bed, but did not move for several seconds. With that, I came around to her side, put my hands under her legs, lifted them gently and turned her lengthwise in our bed. I pulled her covers up, went to my side, climbed in, and rolled toward Mollie.

She tried to roll over toward me, but I sensed that her efforts were causing increasing pain. I gently moved her onto her side, facing me, using her hip and shoulder for purchase, while trying to be deft so as to minimize her pain. We shared a long, slow, intense kiss. I could feel her tears on my face. I hugged her ever so gently. Mollie moved ever so slightly. Then, she whispered lowly, "Ronan, my love, hold me like this, all night if you can. I do so want to awake in your arms.

— — —

To this day, I remember that night as if it was last night, and my last night. I barely slept. I listened for the sound of Mollie's breathing. I was consciously thinking that she might die.

But instead, Mollie awoke in my arms. I was not the least bit tired, and mightily relieved!

40

Oh, Mollie!

After our visit with Dr. Eisenberg, our lives changed radically. Mollie told me how impressed she was with Carolyn during her visit with Patrick and that they were in touch. In fact, while she was in New York, she had called Carolyn to ask her to stop by and talk at dinner one night. They had a bite in the Dining Room of the Bull and Bear, on the Lexington Avenue side of that grand hotel. (It is one of the few hotel restaurants frequented by New Yorkers as it was renowned for its American cuisine, large drinks, generous portions and a diverse wine list.)

Mollie gave Carolyn her family health history at their meeting. Carolyn confided in Mollie that she had a troubled upbringing in rural Oregon, which included more than one family molestation event. Enough so that she left at sixteen and never returned, changed her name, got a social security card and became Carolyn Tyne. She was working in a restaurant on Fisherman's Wharf when she was seventeen and a woman approached her and asked if they could talk when Carolyn finished working that night. (The woman, named Lisa, got her into modeling and became her best friend and lover. They moved in together in Sausalito where Carolyn and Patrick had stayed during their visit and where I lived during my three years in law school until Mollie appeared out of nowhere!)

Mollie asked Carolyn after the evening had worn on, "Carolyn, do you love Ronan?"

Carolyn, knowing Mollie was unwell, realized that her question was not a ploy to find out if I was Patrick's father, but seemed to have a broader meaning. Still, rather than answer directly, she offered, "Why do you ask?"

"I'm afraid!" was Mollie's answer.

"Yes,' was Carolyn's response, "But not like I would want to take him away from you, or anything like that. After all these years, I am nothing if not a confirmed Lesbian. I still think of Ronan as the first real heterosexual man with whom I found any very real relationship, an adult friendship. He was there for me when I needed someone and has always been in the backgound of my life where I could talk with him. I quickly came to feel that way about you too, you know. That was why I wanted to get away with you to Bodega Bay, even if for only one night, to be sure that I could count on you as a friend. AND you must know right now, you can count on me!"

"Carolyn, if anything really bad were to happen to me, Ronan would be devastated. I am certain, and I fear him becoming lost and making a bad decision as to which woman to whom he should turn next. I do not know if he ever told you about Sandra, his fiancé, and what happened when they broke up?"

She responded, "Mollie, of course I knew about Sandra, but really not much. Even though I spent less and less time over those years in Sausalito and we didn't write. But when I was in Sausalito, Ronan and I would talk. He may have mentioned you once or twice when talking about going home to Philadelphia or D.C. for the Christmas Holidays, or other visits. I did come to know that he remained close to his mother as her only son. But as to Sandra, Ronan was never very forthcoming, nor would I have expected him to be so. But, to me, there was always a sense that something was going terribly awry in that relationship, but actually I saw him so rarely after Patrick was born, and it seemed too difficult to try to explain that feeling, or any intuitive feeling, to a man. But to answer your question, No. We never talked in any detail about them as a couple.

Suddenly, Sandra was gone and you were there: Only you,

the Love of His Life!"

"Oh My!" was Mollie's response. "Ronan has forgiven her. Enough on that point. But her father recently died and Ronan helped her leave her father's firm and to start her own firm in San Francisco with a couple of people who are Ronan's friends from law school and another from his work. Essentially, they are competitors, but that is the kind of man Ronan is. All that is fine, but if anything happens to me, please do not let it be Sandra who comes to his rescue! She'll hurt him again, I know it. Will you please, please be there for me, please?" And Mollie's voice broke on those last words.

— — —

Mollie told me part of this conversation and Carolyn told it to me as well. I repeated it to Dr. Arnaud, I do not know how many times. I do not know what possessed Mollie to become so taken with Carolyn. Or for that matter, for Carolyn, after so little time with Mollie, to reciprocate so fully.

— — —

After more tests and more examinations, Mollie and I sat together in Dr. Eisenberg's office. He opened a file, but did not seem to actually look at it. He looked straight at Mollie and said, in an even voice, "Mollie, you have cancer. The cancer appears to have started in either your cervix or your large intestine. At any rate, the metastasis involves both of those organs. I am afraid that we will need to have two specialists undertake any exploratory analysis, including some limited surgery, to try to determine the precise scope of involvement so far and to help us plan a course of treatment. Both of you should know that this is critically serious and that time is of the utmost essence in reaching a plan on what can be done to try to save your life, Mollie."

Mollie could not speak. I filled the vacuum, "Doctor, how soon could this begin, the surgery?"

Mollie looked at me as the doctor spoke, "I can try to get it scheduled in the next day or two. This is very serious!"

Neither Mollie nor I spoke. The doctor continued, "Do either of you have questions?" PAUSE. Mollie and I look at each other. She moved her head ever so slightly in a negative fashion. He continued, "You must have some questions?"

Mollie's eyes are fixed on mine. Her pupils are wide open. I sense she is in deep emotional shock. I reached over to take her hand and she looked down at mine. I took her hand. It was limp. Finally, I said to the doctor, "I'm afraid this has come as a terrible shock to Mollie. Even with her family history, Mollie is not prepared for something this potentially serious. Are there other options?"

His eyes left Mollie and fixed on mine. Then, "I am afraid if we do not move quickly Mollie's chances for survival will be gone. As things stand, I cannot tell you what those chances are. That's why this surgery to gain a more meaningful assessment cannot wait." His eyes went back to Mollie, "Time may be our biggest enemy, but above all, you must not lose hope. Please, Mollie, whatever you do, do not give up."

Mollie began to squeeze my hand ever so softly. Her eyes came up from our hands up to my eyes. In a low voice, she almost whispered, "Oh, Ronan. I had a premonition when this pain started, a week or two after Carolyn and Patrick left. It was intermittent, and not at all intense at first. I deferred for all the other things in my life, our lives, the children and their lives, my work. Now, we are left with no choices, and perhaps no time."

Mollie pivoted just enough to fix on the doctor, "Dr. Eisenberg, you've been my OB/GYN for as long as I have lived here in Marin County. Of all my doctors, I trust you the most. If I have this surgery, will I survive it? What are my chances of just that? And, before you answer, will I be bed-ridden and die? Will I ever have sex with Ronan again? How long do I have if we do nothing?"

The three of us talked for another twenty minutes or so. I took Mollie home. We called all the children together, and Ingrid. We asked Kate to hurry over. While we got this meeting together, I ordered some pizza and salad to be delivered. Mollie went to our room and began to pack. She returned with a very little suitcase and a small carry bag. We gathered in the living room. Dead silence followed as we assembled. All four children sat on the couch with the older two flanking the twins. Ingrid stood behind them. Looking at Mollie, she began to cry silently. Mollie and I were on the settee, and Kate sat a chair not far from Mollie.

Mollie said first, "I am very sick. I have cancer. I have to have an operation tomorrow. We do not know just how bad it is. But we do know it's bad, very bad. Your father and I will be spending quite a bit of time at Marin General Hospital and with the doctors for the next few days. Your Dad will need to do a little work. I have called my company and told them. We have their full support."

Mollie was tiring visibly, I wondered how long she could continue, "The four of you are so much at the center of our lives. I do not want to leave you. I do not want to leave your father. I have asked Carolyn to fly out to help with you all. I really like her and trust her immensely. Please listen to your grandmother, Ingrid, and Carolyn when she gets here. I will be home as soon as I can be. I love you all. Now, I want to spend a few minutes with each of you. But first, Ingrid."

— — —

By the time Mollie was prepped for her surgery, Carolyn was at her side holding her right hand while I held her left. As she rolled toward the Operating Room door, Mollie slid her wedding band off her hand, passing it to me. She whispered, "I left you a note on my writing desk in our bedroom. If I don't make it, read it. Otherwise, please do not open it. Remember, I will love you with my whole heart for all Eternity."

EPILOGUE

TWA Lounge Charles de Gaulle

*M*ore than a year has gone by—

Our family had just settled into a cozy corner of the glamorous TWA Ambassador Lounge at *Charles de Gaulle*, France's finest airport. It was late June and the days were long and often sunny in France that time of year. The 6:00 a.m. flight from Dulles had arrived timely and we needed to wait more than two hours to begin to head for the plane taking us on to Geneva. Having supplied ourselves with snacks and beverage from that lounge's ample buffet, we seated ourselves in a semi-private area with a pleasant view. As we began to talk among ourselves, the tall gentleman, whom I recognized from Seat 1F on our flight, approached us. He stopped and said, primarily addressing me, but at the same time taking in our whole family with a subtle sweep of his head, "Hello, my name is Bill,....Bill Rehnquist. I could not help but notice you were doing some legal work on our flight over."

With that pause, I stood, put out my right hand to shake his and said, "It is an honor to meet you, Mr. Chief Justice." Then turning to my family, I introduced each one of them by name (so that later in life, each could say that he or she had met the Chief Justice of the United States Supreme Court).

He then turned and addressed them saying, "My travelling friend and I have about 90 minutes until we have to leave for our next flight. So, I was hoping to ask Mr. O'Neill to join us for a few minutes to talk about his law practice, if you would not mind terribly? I rarely get to have conversations with practicing lawyers who are not appearing before us, and I am conscious of trying to remain interested in the very real practice of law."

A few moments ensued with chatting about destinations and itineraries, then I departed with him to a small isolated, windowless area and he introduced me to his friend, McGeorge Bundy, a name and reputation with which I was vaguely familiar, something to do with the Kennedy era, but remaining associated with the D.C. power structure. Then, he said, "You must call me, Bill. The reason I wanted to talk to you was that I could see you were analyzing a deposition with exhibits on the plane which led me to believe that you are a litigator. Am I correct?"

When I answered affirmatively, he asked what type of law did I primarily practice, and I answered as generally as I could, "Environmental, mostly concerning exposures to asbestos and ground water contamination. I represent product manufacturers, usually retained by their insurance companies, whom I sometimes represent as well."

"Excellent. Please let me ask you, with what legal concepts or issues do you struggle in your current practice?" A question which he seemed to have posed to others before.

After a few moments thought, which focused on my search for experts yielding my many trips to the UK and France, I formulated, "Junk Science."

McGeorge Bundy sat up straight, and said, "Excuse me. Did you just say, 'Junk Science'?"

And when I nodded, he next ventured, "What is that?"

And the Chief Justice kicked in, "Yes, would you please explain?"

So, I spent a few minutes explaining my practice, my clients and my role relative to Science and Medicine, as so many of us had come to call it. Then, I explained about the law review type article I had written very recently with my senior associate, Martha Walsh, for publication in my Society 's quarterly current legal issues publication. It analyzed the split among the federal court circuits on what kind of novel medical or scientific causation testimony by putative expert witnesses should be allowed to go before the jury for its consideration.

For the next roughly forty-five minutes, we discussed a series of the concepts which I espoused favorably in my article, including:

Many proffered experts tended to rely on their personal experience in advancing theories for novel scientific causation for which plaintiffs sought admission into evidence as "the bridge" to connect cause and effect in order to prove liability. Often, this opinion was a series of recitals of anecdotal events, sometimes more than one, but not based on a statistically reliable data set, nor a learned publication, especially one which was peer reviewed.

Most of these judicial decisions which proved critical often hinged on the proffered expert saying words to the effect, "Based on my experience I know this to be true." While in response to cross-examination seeking the basis of this opinion, the response was often, "Based on my forty years of observations in the course of my years of treatment and study." I allowed that this personal history of reiterative clinical experience was little more than the proffered expert saying, "It is because I say it is," or in Latin, an *ipse dixit.*

To bolster what I was trying to say about actual Science, I advanced the Scientific Method, first taught to me in high school General Science: essentially to prove a hypothesis, an experiment was needed with its results determining the outcome. But to be able to have your fellow scientists agree on the proof of your hypothesis, the reviewing scientists needed to be able to repeat your process and get the same result each time. That term was "replicability."

As a final persuasive tool, I used the example of a computer. Data would go into a "black box" and a report would come out.

In Junk Science, the putative expert was the "black box," but no one else could attest to the conclusions in "the report," because no one else had what was uniquely that proffered expert's experience. Whereas in "Real Science," as in a computer, the experiment is documented just like a computer program. So, when the same data is fed into a known program in the computer's black box, you get the same result every time, and it gives you the same answer every time, "Replicability," the earmark of Real Science!

The Chief Justice and McGeorge Bundy were very gracious in their praise of what I had said. They allowed they would have liked to talk more, but they had to hurry to catch their plane.

Less than two years later, I saw Bill Rehnquist in his robes, asking an Appellant's lawyer, "Can the process of analysis of your client's expert be replicated by other similarly skilled scientists?" and "How do we get to know that?"

In three years, the U.S. Supreme Court rendered three decisions that changed the course for the admissions standard for novel scientific evidence in federal courts. The central controlling factor was that the *ipse dixit* was specifically banned by its very name.

MILL VALLEY CHARACTERS

These pages explain the main, recurring characters from SAUSALITO and this novel. The organization is by relationship to Ronan, then by place or event.

THE O'NEILL'S

Robert Emmett O'Neill, Ronan's father, who dies in SAUSALITO

Mary Katherine (Kate) Garrity O'Neill, Ronan's Mother, Twice Widowed

Rose Mary (1940), Meaghan and Mary Clare (Twins, 1948), Ronan's siblings

Ronan Joseph O'Neill (1943), Autobiographer

Mollie Phelan (1945), Ronan's Wife and Mother to their four children;
Her brother, Chad (1943) was a teammate of Ronan at Georgetown;
Her father, a widower, marries Kate later in life

Ronan and Mollie's Children: Maeve (1977), Robert (1979), Patrick and Meaghan (Twins, 1982)
Au Pairs: Yolanda (their first) and Ingrid (through MILL VALLEY)

— — —

Carolyn Tyne (1954), a model and the first person with whom Ronan becomes friendly; Unknown to Ronan for some time, she has his son, Patrick (1975)

Sandra Allen (1949), UC Hastings law student, becomes engaged to Ronan; her father, Ken, is senior partner in large San Francisco law firm

Margot Arnaud, M.D., Ronan's psychiatrist for forty years; on her death, she sends Ronan all of her notes and tapes on his treatment. That material forms much of the basis for these novels.

Joel Tinker (1942) marries Elaine, Sandra's law school roommate, both UC Hastings grads. Ronan's best friend and classmate in the USCG. Lived is Sausalito. Assisted Ronan in getting his first law job at Klein Kelly in Oakland. Moves to D.C. to practice law to accommodate his wife and maintains long relationship with Ronan and Klein Kelly.

Jerry Klein and Sean Kelly, founding partners in Ronan's firm in Oakland.

Ronan's Team at Klein Kelly: Reggie Fox, Partner; Mary Smith, Partner; Phil Hassard, Partner;
Martha Walsh, Senior Associate (Ronan's sometimes mistress); Deirdre, Senior Paralegal; Lily, Team Administrative Assistant

Tinker's Team in D.C.: Mace Snow, older litigator; Tod Clifford, younger litigator; both partners

— — —

DESERT MUTUAL INSURANCE COMPANY (DMIC) – Scottsdale, Arizona

Charles Ezra Sewell, President (CEO)
John O'Sullivan, Senior Vice President and Chief Actuary (COO)
Dudley Chisholm, Vice President, Chief of Claims
Larry Decker, Assistant Vice President – Claims
Emmanuel (Manny) Garcia (Esmeralda), Senior Manager, Major Claims
Geraldine (Gerry) Dwyer, Chief, Casualty Claims (leaves for The Hartford)
Angela Lenovo, replaces Gerry Dwyer
Richard (Richie) Goldberg, Claims Coverage

CAL Board Products, Inc. (CAL Board) – Sacramento, California:
Austin Smith, JD, Vice President and General Counsel

— — —

WALLBOARD Corp. – San Francisco; Millard Granger, former Risk Manager

SF CASUALTY, immediately prior primary insurer of WALLBOARD before DMIC

Hon. Isadore Greenberg, Judge, San Francisco Superior Court jurist on the WALLBOARD and other Coordinated Coverage Litigation for California
Ken Allen, National Coordinating Counsel and Lead Trial Attorney for WALLBOARD

Sandra Allen, Ken's Partner and Co-Lead Attorney for Wallboard

Ronan O'Neill. Lead Trial Attorney for Defendant, DESERT
MUTAL INSURANCE COMPANY

— — —

Other NATIONAL COORDINATIONG COUNSEL (NCC)

NATIONAL GYPSUM – Abbott and Tweed, PHILADELPHIA
Alicia Goines, Lead NCC Coordinator
Leonard Tweed, Co-Lead NCC

UNITED STATES GYPSUM – Bigstrom and Steel, PHILADEL-
PHIA
Fred Talcott, Lead NCC
Melinda Sykes and Adam Morris, Co-Lead Counsel

W.R. GRACE – Black, Weiss and Marsh, NEW YORK CITY
Alan Maycroft, Lead NCC
Dexter Wells, Co-Lead Counsel

— — —

MULLEN CLASS ACTION, Martinez, California Superior Court

Judge: Hon. John Kendall
Marvin Jones, Plaintiff Lead Attorney
Ronan O'Neill for CAL Board, Co-Lead Defense Attorney
Ken Allen for Wallboard, Co-Lead Defense Attorney

— — —

LOS ANGELES UNIFIED SCHOOL DISTRICT ACTION (*LAUSD*), Los Angeles, California Court

Judge: Hon. Bernard Weitzman
Charlie O'Reilly, Plaintiff Lead Attorney
Abel Stoneman, Co-Lead Attorney
Avery Schein, Glass, Schein and Shea for National Gypsum, Lead Defense Coordinating Attorney
Rod Gorman, Glass Schein, Co-Lead Defense Trial Attorney
Ronan O'Neill for CAL Board, Co-Lead Defense Attorney

— — —

CONSOLIDATED SCHOOLS CLASS ACTION (SCHOOLS), U.S. District Court, Philadelphia, PA.

Judge: Hon. James McGirr Kelly
David Berger, Lead Attorney for Plaintiff Lancaster School District
Ron Motley, Lead Attorney for Plaintiff Spartanburg School District
Scott Kelly, Lead Local CAL Board Attorney
Ted Darrow, Co-Lead Local CAL Board Attorney
OTHER NCCs, above, plus Ronan O'Neill as NCC for CAL Board and
Ken Allen and Sandra Allen as NCC for Wallboard

— — —

CLEMSON UNIVERSITY CLASS ACTION (COLLEGES), U.S. District Court, Charleston, SC.

Judge: Hon. John Anderson
Ron Motley, Lead Plaintiff Attorney
Arthur Miller, Harvard Law Professor, appearing specially for Plaintiff
Josh Smoulders, Lead Local CAL Board Attorney

— — —

OTHER LOCAL CAL BOARD ATTORNEYS

WA: Tom Felix
OR: Lucy Baines.
AZ: Bob Hoover
TX: David Simms.
NV: Joyce James

NYC: Reggie Black
NJ: Barry Brown
MA: Ramona Kingsley
MD: Alan Kinnard

— — —

EXPERT WITNESSES

FOR THE PLAINTIFFS; Irving Selikoff, M.D., Epidemiologist, Mt. Sinai, NYC
And OTHER Medical Scientists from Mt. Sinai

Consulting for CAL Board:
Jeremy Nobel, M.D., Harvard School of Public Health
Sir Richard Doll, M.D., Epidemiologist, OXFORD
Mary, his Executive Assistant, Ratcliffe Infirmary, OXFORD
Julian Peto, Ph.D., Mathematics, OXFORD
Alison McDonald, M.D., Epidemiologist, U. Of London
Jean Bignon, M.D., Chief (CEO), INSERM, Paris
FOR CAL Board: J. Corbett McDonald, M.D., Epidemiologist, McGill University, Montreal and University of London Medical School

— — —

LONDON/LLOYDS INSURANCE MARKET

WELLINGTON CHASE Brokers for U.S. Clients/Lloyds Placements, London (Defunct),
(Undertook DESERT MUTUAL Reinsurance placements to Lloyds Placing Brokers)

TWENTY KING'S BENCH WALK CHAMBERS
Quincy Franden-Jones (Q), Senior Barrister FOR DESERT MUTUAL
Wilfred Smythe, Chief Clerk of Chambers

THORNTON, CAMPBELL and THORNTON, Solicitors, The City, London
Bradley Campbell, Senior Partner/Founder's Son, FOR DESERT MUTUAL
Madeline, Bradley Campbell's Executive Assistant

CHEHIRE and BOOTH, LLOYDS Placing Broker
Stanley Booth IV, Chairman of the Firm

PIERCE FIELDS, Solicitors, The City, London
Frederick Perce, Jr., Senior Partner/Grandson of Founder, FOR CHESHIRE and BOOTH

ABOOKS

ALIVE Book Publishing and ALIVE Publishing Group
are imprints of Advanced Publishing LLC,
3200 A Danville Blvd., Suite 204, Alamo, California 94507

Telephone: 925.837.7303
alivebookpublishing.com